Whisper Goodbye

Other books by Myra Johnson

One Imperfect Christmas

Till We Meet Again Series
When the Clouds Roll By
Whisper Goodbye
Every Tear a Memory

Autumn Rains
Romance by the Book
Where the Dogwoods Bloom
Gateway Weddings (anthology of above 3)
A Horseman's Heart
A Horseman's Gift
A Horseman's Hope

Whisper Goodbye

Myra Johnson

a novel approach to faith

Whisper Goodbye

Copyright © 2014 by Myra Johnson

ISBN: 978-14267-5366-4

Published by Abingdon Press, P.O. Box 801, Nashville, TN 37202

www.abingdonpress.com

All rights reserved.

Published in association of the Natasha Kern Literary Agency, Inc.

Scripture quotation marked ASV taken from the American Standard
Version of the Bible.

Scripture quotations from The Authorized (King James) Version.
Rights in the Authorized Version in the United Kingdom are vested
in the Crown. Reproduced by permission of the Crown's patentee,
Cambridge University Press.

Library of Congress Cataloging-in-Publication Data

Johnson, Myra, 1951-
  Whisper goodbye / Myra Johnson.
    pages cm. — (Till we meet again)
  Includes bibliographical references and index.
  ISBN 978-1-4267-5366-4 (pbk.)
1. Disabled veterans—Fiction. 2. World War, 1914-1918—Veterans—United States—Fiction. 3. Veterans' hospitals—Fiction. 4. Nurses—Fiction. 5. Women immigrants—Fiction. 6. Irish Americans—Fiction. I. Title.
  PS3610.O3666W48 2014
  813'.6—dc23

2013033585

Printed in the United States of America

1 2 3 4 5 6 7 8 9 10 / 19 18 17 16 15 14

In honor of my brother-in-law and Vietnam War veteran,
James Stanley Johnson,
for his service as Hospital Corpsman
2nd Class–Combat Medic

In memory of my grandfather
Joseph King,
a second lieutenant in France during the Great War

With deepest gratitude to all who have served so valiantly in
the United States Armed Forces,
and with appreciation for doctors, nurses, and corpsmen for
the selfless care they provide

Acknowledgments

Once again, my heartfelt gratitude to Liz Robbins and the staff and volunteers of the Garland County Historical Society for their research assistance. The deeper I delve into the history of Hot Springs, the more fascinating stories I uncover! Mr. Goodine really did serve beer to elephants the last day before Prohibition went into effect, and Thomas Cockburn really owned a prize ostrich named Black Diamond. The Hot Springs Army and Navy Hospital, the Arlington and Eastman Hotels, Fordyce Bathhouse, Happy Hollow, Gulpha Gorge— these places all actually existed at the time my story takes place. Even so, this is a work of fiction, and I ask the indulgence of true historians for any errors made or liberties taken.

I'm grateful to my acquisitions editor, Ramona Richards, and my macro editor, Teri Wilhelms, for their attention to detail and commitment to bringing out the best in my writing, and to the Abingdon Press art department for the amazingly gorgeous covers they consistently produce. Thanks also to Cat Hoort, Marketing Manager at Abingdon Press, for her expertise in promoting Abingdon's outstanding fiction line. I'm proud and honored to publish under the Abingdon Fiction imprint.

As always, a huge thank-you to my beloved agent, Natasha Kern. I wouldn't be where I am today without you. Your guidance is invaluable, and your friendship is irreplaceable. I pray we enjoy many more years of working together.

No writing day is complete without regular email chats with my "Seeker Sisters," Audra, Cara, Debby, Glynna, Janet, Julie, Mary, Missy, Pam, Ruthy, Sandra, and Tina—award-winning Christian authors and the greatest friends ever! You can meet us all at www.seekerville.net.

Thank you to my husband, Jack, and to our beautiful daughters, Johanna and Julena. During the twenty-five long years before God's perfect timing made my publishing dream a reality, you never wavered in your belief in me (or if you did, you kept it to yourself!). Since then, you've become my most ardent cheerleaders and "PR reps." I wish every writer could enjoy such devoted family support.

For my readers, you complete the picture. A story isn't a story until it's shared. Thank you for accompanying Mary and Gilbert on their journey in *Whisper Goodbye*.

Finally, brethren, whatsoever things are true, whatsoever things are honorable, whatsoever things are just, whatsoever things are pure, whatsoever things are lovely, whatsoever things are of good report; if there be any virtue, and if there be any praise, think on these things.—Philippians 4:8 (ASV)

Till We Meet Again

There's a song in the land of the lily,
Each sweetheart has heard with a sigh.
Over high garden walls this sweet echo falls
As a soldier boy whispers goodbye:

Smile the while you kiss me sad adieu
When the clouds roll by I'll come to you.
Then the skies will seem more blue,
Down in Lover's Lane, my dearie.

Wedding bells will ring so merrily
Ev'ry tear will be a memory.
So wait and pray each night for me
Till we meet again.

Tho' goodbye means the birth of a tear drop,
Hello means the birth of a smile.
And the smile will erase the tear blighting trace,
When we meet in the after awhile.

Smile the while you kiss me sad adieu
When the clouds roll by I'll come to you
Then the skies will seem more blue
Down in Lover's Lane, my dearie,

Wedding bells will ring so merrily
Ev'ry tear will be a memory
So wait and pray each night for me
Till we meet again.

Music by Richard A. Whiting,
lyrics by Raymond B. Egan

1

Hot Springs, Arkansas
Saturday, June 14, 1919

*S*earing sunlight assaulted Gilbert Ballard's burning eyes. He rubbed them furiously, cursing both the brightness and his battered heart for the wetness sliding down his face. Stupid to have stayed this long. Stupid to have come at all.

But no. He *had* to see for himself, had to be convinced beyond question that the girl he'd once pledged his heart to—the girl whose heart he'd broken—was utterly beyond reach.

Annemarie Kendall. Now Mrs. Samuel Vickary. And all because of Gilbert's own pride. His foolishness. His arrogant, self-serving, pain-induced idiocy.

Groaning, he drew his gaze away from the happy couple beaming from the steps of Ouachita Fellowship Church and concealed himself behind the glossy leaves of a magnolia tree. A physical craving rolled through him, every nerve screaming for the deliverance one morphine tablet could bring. Not an option, though. He'd sworn off the stuff after promising Mary he'd kick the vile addiction.

He'd gladly settle for a stiff drink instead. Although how much longer he could count on alcohol's availability remained uncertain. With hard liquor already in short supply thanks to wartime bans on production and sales, on July 1 the Wartime Prohibition Act would shut down all bars and saloons, denying him even the solace of a frothy mug of beer.

"Drinking yourself into oblivion's no less a sin than losing your soul to drugs, Gilbert Ballard." Sweet Mary McClarney's chiding tone sang through his brain like the voice of reason it was.

And he would listen. With God's help, at least this once, he would listen.

He climbed into his blue Cole Eight Roadster and drove away before anyone at the church across the street could notice him. Somehow, some way, he had to purge Annemarie Kendall—Annemarie *Vickary*—from his heart once and for all.

He sped through town, dust flying as he left the paved streets for rougher roads. If he could drive far enough, fast enough, he might outpace the unrelenting emptiness that had haunted him since the war. Those weeks lying in a French field hospital, then the voyage home on the *U.S.S. Comfort*, had given him plenty of time to think. Plenty of time to conclude he'd never be the husband Annemarie deserved, to vow he would not consign the woman he loved to marriage to a cripple.

As if to spite him, the stump of his left leg began to throb. Slowing the car, he reached down to massage his thigh. The fit of his newest prosthesis had eliminated the worst of the discomfort, but it didn't stop the recurring phantom leg pain. Sometimes invisible flames tortured his nonexistent foot. Other times he imagined a thousand needles stabbing his calf. Today, it felt as though giant pincers squeezed the entire length of his leg.

He swung the steering wheel hard to the right and jammed his foot on the brake pedal. The roadster lurched to a stop at the side of the road, while the grit raised by his skidding tires swirled through the open windows, nearly choking him. Stifling a spate of coughs, he patted his shirtfront, fumbled through his trouser pockets, felt along the underside of the automobile seat. *Just one pill . . . one pill . . .*

Sweat broke out on his forehead. He lifted trembling fists to his temples. How many weeks now had he been off the morphine, and yet his body *still* betrayed him!

Mary. He needed Mary.

By force of will, he steadied himself enough to get the automobile turned around and aimed back toward Hot Springs. Mary would be at the hospital now. He pictured his dimpled Irish lass's flame-red riot of curls spilling from her nurse's cap as she made her rounds. If he could wheedle a few minutes alone with her, lose himself to her tender touch, she'd drive the demons away.

She was the only one who could.

"Time for your medication, Corporal Donovan." Mary McClarney filled a water glass and handed it to the frail young soldier in the bed. As he swallowed the pills, she frowned to herself at his sallow complexion. Possible liver involvement? Something the doctor should follow up on.

With a thankful nod, the corporal handed her the empty glass. "You're an angel of mercy, Nurse McClarney."

"Aye, and don't be forgettin' it." Mary winked as she made a notation on the corporal's chart.

"Will Dr. Russ be making rounds soon?" The soldier shifted, one hand pressed to his abdomen. "I wanted to ask him why I've still got this pain in my side."

"Postsurgical soreness is to be expected." She lifted his pajama top and gently peeled back the dressing where the surgeon had repaired a bowel obstruction earlier in the week. "Your incision looks good, though—healing nicely."

"Yeah, but . . . I don't feel so well. Kinda nauseous, you know?"

"I'll see what we can find to calm your stomach." With a sympathetic smile, Mary glanced at the watch pinned to her smock. "However, I fear the good doctor may be a tad late this afternoon."

"Nearly forgot—Chaplain Vickary's wedding." Corporal Donovan gave a weak chuckle. "The padre's sure been floating on air lately."

"Indeed. Everyone on staff is happy for him." Perhaps Mary most of all—if only she dared hope the chaplain's marriage to Annemarie Kendall meant the end of Gilbert's obsession with his former fiancée.

Mary sent an orderly to fetch warm tea and soda crackers for the corporal, then gave him a reassuring pat on the arm before continuing her rounds. Best to keep busy. Best not to think about Gilbert or wonder how this day affected him.

As if she could keep from wondering! Even as she went about her nursing duties with all the necessary attention to detail, an invisible force tugged at her spirit, dividing her will, drawing away pieces of her heart in an unrelenting search for Gilbert, always Gilbert.

"Miss McClarney." The snapping tone of Mrs. Daley, chief nurse at the Hot Springs Army and Navy Hospital, glued Mary's shoes to the floor.

"Yes, ma'am?" Gripping the medicine tray she carried, Mary inhaled slowly between pursed lips and turned to face the gray-haired tyrant. What now? Had Mary failed to properly dispose of a soiled bandage? Left a syringe uncapped? Overlooked a vital notation on a patient's chart?

Mrs. Daley dropped a folded sheet of paper on Mary's tray. "A message for you from Reception. Please don't make me remind you to keep your personal affairs separate from hospital work."

"Yes, ma'am." Mary curtsied before she could stop herself, although it seemed only fitting, considering Mrs. Daley's imperious nature.

The woman gave Mary an odd look before pivoting on her heel and marching away.

Anxious to learn who'd sent the message, Mary hurried into the work area behind the nurses' station and deposited her tray. *Please, Lord, don't let it be about Mum.* Mary's mother's chronic bronchitis often left her weak and short of breath. If she'd taken a turn for the worse . . .

Fingers trembling, Mary unfolded the slip of paper.

Meet me at the oak tree. Please.

No signature. Not so much as the sender's initials. Only seven simple words rendered in the manly scrawl that never failed to set her insides aquiver.

Her nerves hummed with the compulsion to rush from the hospital and straight to Gilbert's side. In every stroke of the pen, she sensed his need, his longing, his pain. She should have expected that today, of all days, he'd need her most of all. She should be glad of anything that drove him into her arms.

If only it were anything but his despair over losing Annemarie.

Well. With more than an hour left on her shift, she couldn't exactly march out of the ward and hope to escape the wrath of Mrs. Daley. She certainly wasn't of a mind to risk her career—her livelihood—at the whim of a hazel-eyed rogue who'd drop her in a moment if there were a ghost of a chance he could reclaim his lost love. Let Gilbert Ballard stew in his own juices awhile longer, and maybe one of these days he'd realize Mary McClarney was not a woman to be trifled with.

She'd just convinced herself to ignore Gilbert's pull on her heart and go on about her work when footsteps sounded behind her. Certain it was Mrs. Daley come to chide her for shirking her duties, she tried to look busy sorting medicine vials and hypodermics.

"Ah, Miss McClarney. Just the person I was looking for."

She recognized the familiar baritone of the kindly Dr. Russ, and relief swept through her. Turning, she stifled a surprised gasp to see the doctor was now beardless—and, dare she say, even more handsome than before. She offered the tall man a shy smile. "Back from the wedding festivities already, sir?"

"Duty calls. I stayed long enough to see the happy couple off in style." The doctor laid a chart on the counter between them and ran his finger down the page. His breath smelled faintly of strawberries. "You were the last to check on Corporal Donovan, I see."

"Yes, I gave him his three o'clock pills on schedule." Mary bit her lip. "Is there a problem, Doctor?"

"I hope not." Dr. Russ stroked his chin, looking almost surprised to find no facial hair beneath his fingers. He must have shaved only this morning, no doubt a concession to his best man duties. "You noted he's still having abdominal pain. Did you check his surgical incision?"

"Perfectly fine and healing nicely."

The doctor glanced again at the chart. "Your notes also say he looks jaundiced. When did you first make that observation?"

Mary flicked her gaze sideways as she weighed her answer. "I'd have to say it's been a gradual thing, sir. Yesterday I thought it might only be the light, but this afternoon the yellow tinge to his skin and eyes seemed more pronounced. I knew you'd want to be informed."

"Good work, Miss McClarney." Dr. Russ's eyes twinkled with an approving smile. "Your sharp eye might well have saved Corporal Donovan's life."

"Really, sir?" Mary's face warmed. She stood a little taller. "What do you suspect?"

"Not sure yet, but if his liver is failing, the sooner we start appropriate treatment, the better his chances." The doctor's jaw flexed as he perused the chart. He glanced at Mary. "Are you in the middle of anything pressing?"

"Well, I . . ." Mary looked away, guilt tightening her chest as she crumpled Gilbert's note and stuffed it into her pocket. Hadn't she already made up her mind on that score? She cleared her throat. "Sir, if you'd give me five minutes to finish putting away these supplies—"

"Perfect. While you do that, I'll make a list of medical conditions I'd like you to research for me."

"Research? You want *me* to . . ."

The doctor was already scribbling on the back of a wrinkled envelope—by the looks of it, from a wedding invitation. "Go to my office and look through my medical reference books. You'll find pen and paper in the desk."

A thrill of anticipation sped Mary's movements as she emptied her supply tray. Taking Dr. Russ's list, she marched past the nurses' station, barely acknowledging her friend Lois's confused stare.

But she couldn't ignore Mrs. Daley's stern glare when the wiry chief nurse blocked her path. "Exactly where are you off to in such a hurry, Miss McClarney? I certainly hope that cryptic message you received wasn't your lover summoning you to another tryst."

She should have known Mrs. Daley couldn't resist peeking at Gilbert's note. Still, the woman's accusation cut deep—and far too close to the truth. Mary squeezed her eyes shut briefly while she formed a careful reply. "Lieutenant Ballard is *not* my lover." And certainly not in the tawdry sense Mrs. Daley's tone implied. "I assure you, ma'am, I've the utmost respect for hospital policy and would never jeopardize my position in the Army Nurse Corps."

"I sincerely hope that is true, young lady." The woman hiked her chin. "Now, hadn't you best get back to work? I'm sure you have plenty to do right here on the ward."

Mary couldn't resist a haughty look of her own. "As a matter of fact, I'm off on an urgent errand for Dr. Russ. A patient's life could be at stake."

That silenced the old biddy. Lightness returning to her step, Mary brushed past Mrs. Daley and strode to the exit. She marched along the connecting breezeway and into the elegant, Swiss chalet–style administration building, where she finally reached Dr. Russ's office on an upper floor.

Sometime later she was grateful to realize that during the time she spent researching diseases of the liver, thoughts of Gilbert hadn't interrupted even once.

✍

Traffic sounds and exhaust fumes wafted up the hill between the bathhouses lining Central Avenue. Propped against a spreading oak tree within sight of the Army and Navy Hospital wing where Mary worked, Gilbert mopped his brow with a handkerchief already damp enough to wring out. He checked his watch. Again. Five minutes more, and he'd have waited a full hour. Did Mary purposely keep him cooling his heels, or couldn't she escape the old hag of a chief nurse?

Obviously, Mary wasn't coming. If he had a lick of sense, he'd march—make that *limp*—to his car and go home.

Someone called his name just as he reached the long flight of steps leading to where he'd parked his roadster on Reserve Avenue. Leaning on his cane, he turned.

A young, dark-haired nurse waved from the path as she hurried toward him. "Wait, Lieutenant, please!"

She looked familiar . . . a colleague of Mary's, perhaps? He racked his brain for a name but came up empty. Which wouldn't surprise him, even if he'd known her for ages. Ever since a whizzbang—a shell from a German 77mm field gun—found him at the Marne, he did well to remember his own name.

White smock billowing, the nurse nearly mowed him down in her rush to catch up. She caught his wrist and clambered for breath. "I'm . . . sorry. . . . Didn't want you to . . . get away."

"Not likely, considering the death grip you have on my arm." He stared pointedly at her white-knuckled hand.

With an embarrassed gasp, she released him. "You must think I'm crazy." Tucking strands of nut-brown hair into her bun, she gave a nervous chuckle. "See, I was just getting off work when I noticed you under the tree. I figured you must be waiting for Mary."

Gilbert hesitated, his jaw shifting to one side. This woman could very well be one of Mrs. Daley's spies.

"You don't remember me, do you?" The young nurse smiled coyly. "I'm Lois Underwood. Mary's friend."

"Lois. Of course." He only wished he could honestly say he remembered her.

"Anyway, when I saw you out here, waiting just forever on this hot summer day, I felt awful for you." Lois dropped her voice. "I guess Mary didn't tell you she's doing special research work for Dr. Russ."

Gilbert bristled at the name. Army surgeon Donald Russ had been Gilbert's physician aboard the *Comfort*, then later transferred to the Hot Springs Army and Navy Hospital. Rather too conveniently for Gilbert's taste, considering the role the man had played in keeping Gilbert and Annemarie apart.

With a muted groan, he edged sideways, forehead pressed into his palm. When would he get it through his thick skull?

The *only* person responsible for losing Annemarie to Samuel was Gilbert himself.

"Are you all right, Lieutenant?"

He lowered his hand to see Lois Underwood staring up at him with a worried frown. "I'm fine. And you can drop the 'Lieutenant.' The Army mustered me out months ago."

"Honorable discharge. I know. You're a hero, Lieuten—"

"Stop, will you?" With an apologetic sigh, he added, "Just call me Gilbert. Please."

"Really? Well, thanks!" Lois beamed as if he'd just presented her with the Medal of Honor. "I guess that means we're friends, right?"

"Certainly. Any friend of Mary's . . ." An automobile horn tootled at the intersection below, reminding Gilbert he just wanted to go home. Except now, he had this image in his head of Mary and Dr. Russ, the two of them ensconced in his cozy little office—doing *research*.

He hammered down the surge of jealousy threatening to blow the top of his head off. The green-eyed monster had destroyed his life once before. He wouldn't let it win twice. "Look, Miss . . ." Blanking again. Not good.

"Lois. Lois Underwood. Like the typewriter. No relation, of course." Her laugh jangled like a tin can filled with marbles.

"Lois. Yes. Thanks for your concern. I'm just on my way home, if you don't mind." Once again, he started for the steps.

And once again, Lois Underwood's strident call drew him up short. "Hey, you wouldn't want to give a girl a ride, would you? I need to pick up some things downtown, and it's an awful hot day for walking."

Gilbert drove the tip of his cane into the top step. Shooting her a rakish grin that belied his annoyance, he motioned for Lois to join him. "Where can I drop you, Miss Underwood?"

"Oh, thanks! Thanks loads!" She scurried to his side and linked her arm through his as they proceeded down the steps. "And you can call me Lois. I mean, since we're friends now."

Reaching the street, he held the passenger door of his roadster while she climbed in, tucking the skirt of her nurse's uniform around her legs. "What a fancy automobile! Must have cost you an arm and a le—" She clamped a hand to her mouth. "I'm sorry. I didn't mean—"

"What's an arm and a leg between friends?" Gilbert winked and clinked the end of his cane against his prosthesis before circling around to the driver's side.

Truth be told, if Mary wouldn't deign to interrupt her *research* to respond to his urgent plea, then delivering the vivacious, if rather cloying, Miss Underwood to her destination might distract him just as effectively from the day's events.

As long as the route didn't take them past Ouachita Fellowship Church.

2

$\mathscr{S}$houlders stiff and aching, Donald Russ trudged to his office. He'd been up since before six that morning, with two surgeries and several patients to see before taking most of the afternoon off for Samuel and Annemarie's wedding. Picturing their happy faces brought a smile to his lips. They'd endured so much since the war ended, what with Samuel's battle with the Spanish influenza and the debilitating flashbacks from his year at the front.

And then there was Gilbert Ballard.

Donald couldn't deny a certain amount of sympathy for the young lieutenant, forever scarred and crippled from his own battle wounds. But what gave Ballard the right to destroy two other lives? There'd been plenty of hurt to go around already.

With a sad shake of his head, he pushed through the door to his office.

Mary McClarney looked up with a start. "Oh, Doctor, you nearly frightened ten years off my life!"

Startled himself, Donald whistled out a breath. "Didn't think you'd still be here. Your shift ended at six, didn't it?"

"Is it past six already?" Mary shuffled medical books and pages of notes. "The research was so interesting I completely lost track of time."

Forgetting his fatigue, Donald tossed his lab coat onto a hook and came around the desk to look over Mary's shoulder. "Let's see what you found."

"Jaundice could indicate any number of conditions. Hepatitis, cirrhosis, malaria. Corporal Donovan's symptoms are nonspecific at this stage, so I haven't been able to narrow it down much." One by one, Mary showed him the pages she'd marked in the medical books, pointing out any details matching what she'd observed in their patient. "I truly don't know, sir. At worst, it could be liver cancer."

Donald ground his teeth. "It's the cancer thing that worries me. So little to be done." He straightened. "I'll order some tests first thing in the morning."

"Tomorrow's my day off, but I'd be glad to come in if you need me." She looked so sweetly earnest, green eyes gazing up at him, lips parted hopefully.

Something twisted in Donald's gut. He fumbled with the books, stuffing markers into the pages and stacking the tomes in a rude pile at the edge of his desk. "Now what kind of tyrant would have you give up your day off? Besides, tomorrow's the Lord's Day. You'll be wanting to take your mother to church."

Mary chuckled softly as she arranged the pages of her notes into a neat pile and then topped them with a marble paperweight. "I can name one tyrant who'd have not a single qualm about denying me a day off."

"Then all the more reason you must take it when you can." With a gentle hand at Mary's back, Donald ushered her toward the door. When she turned at the threshold, an unspoken question on her lips, he shook his head firmly. "I mean it, Mary.

Go home. Enjoy your Sunday, and don't worry about Corporal Donovan. You've already helped more than you know."

When the door closed behind her, the emptiness left in her wake hit Donald like a medicine ball to the solar plexus. Some days the loneliness was worse than others, and today was one of those days. The life of an army surgeon left little time or energy for romantic pursuits. Past forty now, he considered himself a confirmed bachelor. Not to mention his service in the Great War had aged him even more. The horrors he'd seen, the broken bodies, shattered lives . . . that one human being could inflict such savage brutality on another continually haunted him. Probably would until the day he died.

Sinking into the chair behind his desk, he settled back with a groan. His gaze slid to the paperweight Mary had so recently touched. He pictured her soft but capable hands, the curve of her hips beneath her starched white uniform—and then shoved the images from his mind with the force of a shell fired from a howitzer. She was a child, a mere child, young enough to be his daughter.

Besides, misguided as she might be, the girl had eyes for only one man: Gilbert Ballard.

Mary's stomach pinched. He hadn't waited for her.

She stood in the shade of the old oak tree, the one she could see from the ward as she went about her duties. The tree where Gilbert would sometimes while away the time before Mary's shift ended so he could drive her home.

When she'd allow him to, that is. When he wasn't glassy-eyed from too much liquor or surly and rude from abstaining. Considering how he'd treated her the past few months, *used* her more often than not, why she continued to pine for him made no sense at all.

Except for the fact she loved him beyond all measure of sensibility. And he loved her, if only he had the courage to admit it instead of bemoaning the loss of the woman he'd intentionally driven away, straight into his best friend's arms. He had no one to blame but himself for his troubles.

And Mary had no one to blame but herself for the pain Gilbert Ballard continually inflicted upon her poor heart.

So, then, what was she doing pacing beneath the oak tree while silently cursing Gilbert for not waiting? Hadn't she deliberately stayed beyond the end of her shift, knowing how her delay would torture him?

You can't have it both ways, Mary McClarney.

With a shudder and a sigh, she marched along the hospital drive toward the main gate, then turned up Reserve Avenue. Perspiration trickled along her ribs and down her spine in the warmth of the June evening. Her feet already ached from a full day's work, and now they screamed for mercy as she tromped uphill and down toward the cozy cottage she shared with her mother—a luxury, really, since most of the nurses resided in dormitory-like quarters on the hospital grounds. Soon she'd enjoy a cup of tea, a foot soak, and then—

At the sight of the shiny blue roadster parked in front of her house, Mary snapped her head up. So, Gilbert had come looking for her after all. She quickened her pace, scurrying around to the passenger side to peer in the window.

Empty!

Saints above, did the man put no value upon his own life? Mary could only imagine the tongue-lashing her mother would waste no time delivering to the cad she believed was destined to break her only daughter's heart.

All thoughts of aching feet forgotten, Mary dashed up the front steps and burst through the door. "Mum?" Her voice creaked like an old shoe. With a hand to her throat, she edged toward the parlor. "Mum? Are you here?"

"Come in, lass," came her mother's raspy reply. "About time you got yourself home. We've a guest."

As Mary forced unwilling feet to carry her into the parlor, Gilbert pushed up from the settee. Leaning on his cane, he locked his artificial knee before straightening. With a nod and a hesitant smile, he whispered her name, and her own knees went weak at the sound.

Only the hand braced upon the back of her mother's chair kept her upright. She wedged as much resolve into her tone as she could muster. "What are you doing here, Gilbert?"

"Now, Mary," her mother chided. She reached up to pat Mary's hand. "He's only come to chat. About time we got better acquainted, don't you agree?" The tiniest touch of sarcasm tinged her mother's tone. "Since he's set his heart on courtin' you and all."

Mary shot Gilbert an icy glare. "Has he, now? Well, that's news to me."

Gilbert's right fist tightened around the handle of his cane. "If I could just talk to you, Mary. Please."

With a wheezing breath, Mary's mother rose from her chair. "I'll just be seeing to supper. You two talk as long as you like."

"Mum—" Panic laced Mary's tone. With her mother present, she might find the strength to resist Gilbert's charm. Alone, she had no hope.

"It's all right, luv." Her mother smiled encouragement. "I've had my say with the lad, and he knows where I stand. He'll not be hurting you unless he wants to answer to me." She winked. "And I've assured him your dear departed father's old shotgun still works fine."

Flames raced up Mary's neck and singed her cheeks. She wasn't sure which was worse: her mother's longstanding disapproval of her relationship with Gilbert . . . or her mother's blessing.

The moment they were alone, Gilbert closed the space between them and reached for Mary's hand. "I waited for you, Mary. For over an hour." The tormented look had returned to his hooded, gray-green eyes. "I thought you'd realize, hoped you'd understand—"

She jerked free of his grip. "Understand how you suffered knowing your precious Annemarie wed the chaplain today? How you always only seem to need me when you're aching to be with *her?*"

"It isn't like that. I promise—"

"I've heard enough of your promises to last a lifetime. And every one of them broken in the blink of an eye." Locking her arms across her abdomen, she stepped around him. The setting sun cast a golden beam through the front window, a fragile assault on the chill cloaking Mary's heart.

Gilbert's long, rasping breath tore through the air behind her. "All right, if you want me to admit it, I will. Seeing Sam and Annemarie get married today—"

Mary whirled around. "You attended the wedding?"

"No. No!" Gilbert tunneled stiff fingers through his mass of ebony curls. Another pained exhalation, then a grimace. "I watched from across the street. No one saw me."

Hands clenched at her sides, Mary heaved a sigh. "Oh, Gilbert."

"I had to see for myself, all right? It's the only way I could close the book forever on that chapter of my life."

Mary clamped her teeth together to keep from blurting out he'd authored his own tragic ending to that story. Less than a week after his return from the war, as Annemarie had sat at his hospital bedside, ever the faithful fiancée, he'd told her it was over. A selfless gesture, some might say, but Mary knew better. It was nothing less than self-pity, along with a hefty dose of misguided male pride. Believing he'd never be whole again after an artillery shell took his leg and mangled his left arm, he'd refused to burden Annemarie with his disabilities.

But when his strength and confidence began to return, along with his renewed vigor came regret. Only by then it was too late. Chaplain Vickary, who for a time had been Gilbert's closest friend, had himself fallen in love with Annemarie, and she with him. No one could deny they were meant to be together.

No one except Gilbert, anyway. His cruel attempts to keep them apart made Mary cringe with shame.

And yet, she loved him still.

"Say something, Mary." Gilbert's murmured plea drew her to the present.

Fatigue weighed her shoulders. "What would you have me say?"

"Say you understand. Say you forgive me." He stepped in front of her, his cane falling against a chair as he clasped both her hands against his chest. "Say you still have hope for us."

"Hope?" She swallowed—or tried to. Her throat swelled and ached with a confusing knot of emotions. Saints in heaven, she was falling for his charms again, and after she'd vowed to resist. With a tiny cry, she freed her hands and sank upon the settee.

"Mary . . . don't." Gilbert sat down hard beside her, his stiff artificial leg braced upon the frayed oriental carpet. Drawing her beneath his arm, he pressed his lips against her temple, eliciting a shiver. "I need you, Mary, and for reasons that have nothing to do with losing Annemarie. I don't know where I'd be without you. At the lowest point in my life, you gave me a reason to live again."

Trembling, Mary brushed the flood of salty tears from her cheeks. She shifted so that she could look straight into Gilbert's eyes, because she had to be certain, had to see for herself—just as Gilbert had had to see it was truly over with Annemarie. Had to read in every plane of his face that he spoke sincerely.

Heaving a tired sigh, she gave a single nod. "Very well, Gilbert Ballard. Today we start fresh. We put the past behind us, with no more guilt, no more regrets. Do I have your word?"

"You have my word. I'll prove myself worthy of you, Mary. I promise."

✐❤

Adjusting the silk sofa cushion at her back, Gilbert's mother nodded to Marguerite, the Ballard family's slender, dark-skinned servant. "Just a tad more sherry, please. It's the only thing that quiets my heart palpitations."

Marguerite fetched a crystal carafe from the sideboard and decanted a meager teaspoon or two into Evelyn Ballard's glass. "We only got two more bottles, Miz Ballard. You might oughta go easy."

Gilbert's mother screwed her mouth into an exaggerated frown. "I do declare, what is our government thinking, prohibiting honest, upstanding citizens from purchasing alcohol for medicinal purposes?"

"Medicinal purposes. Right." Gilbert slid lower in his chair and studied the play of light through the minuscule serving of scotch he'd allowed himself following Sunday dinner. Mary wouldn't approve, of course. Only a day after he'd vowed to make a fresh start with her and already he'd failed to meet her impossible standards. Was he utterly hopeless?

At least he'd had the good sense not to mention driving Lois around town yesterday. Mary would surely get the wrong idea about *that*. Nothing had happened, of course. Lois was a flirt, no denying it. But Gilbert saw nothing in the woman that appealed . . . beyond her availability, anyway.

And she'd made it plenty clear she was available.

Speared with guilt, Gilbert set his scotch glass down with a thunk and sat up straighter. He pictured Mary's innocent face last evening, her hopeful gaze when he'd promised to try again. How many chances did one man get in this life? How many did Gilbert deserve?

"Two British flyers are attempting a trans-world flight. What do you think of that?" Newspaper pages rattled as Thomas, Gilbert's younger brother, crossed his legs. "Train travel's unnerving enough, the speeds today's locomotives go. Not sure I'd want to be airborne over the Atlantic."

Gilbert stared at his left thigh and felt all over again the force of the artillery explosion, the shock of coming to at the bottom of a crater . . . the finality of returning home a broken man. "There are worse things than plummeting from the sky into a cold, dark ocean."

"Boys, boys." Gilbert's mother fanned herself with a *Harper's Monthly Magazine*. "Enough of such talk. Is there no good news in the paper, Thomas?"

"I would have thought advances in transportation to be quite fascinating news, actually." Exhaling between his teeth, Thomas laid the newspaper aside. "But far be it from me to add fuel to my dear brother's chronic melancholia."

"Don't put this on me." Gilbert gripped the arms of his chair. His head had resumed its relentless throbbing, another aftereffect of the artillery blast.

"Perhaps if you'd attended church with your brother and me this morning . . ." Gilbert's mother thrust out her chin. "How do you expect to conquer depression if you continually dwell on your infirmities? As Paul wrote to the Colossians, 'Set your mind on the things that are above, not on the things that are upon the earth.'" Her words slurred the tiniest bit. "And again in Philippians, '. . . whatsoever things are true, whatsoever things are lovely, whatsoever things are of good report . . . think on these things.'"

Leave it to his mother to close her eyes to the ugly side of war. Evelyn Ballard surrounded herself with only the best life had to offer. If it were possible to buy happiness—her own or her sons'—she'd have the check written and delivered before the ink dried.

Slumping forward, Gilbert rested his aching head in his hands. "I'm sorry, Mother. I must be a miserable disappointment to you."

"Not at all, son." Rising, his mother stood over him and massaged his shoulders. "You've had a bad time of it, poor dear. Your recovery hasn't been the easiest. And, of course, there was the unfortunate business with Annemarie." She sighed audibly, her warm, sherry-scented breath ruffling his hair. "But we must look on the bright side. The war is over, you're home, and you're getting stronger and healthier every day. You can begin again, meet someone new, start fresh."

Start fresh. Mary's exact words.

Whatsoever things are pure, whatsoever things are lovely . . .

Gilbert straightened, his mouth firm. "You're right, Mother. I'm more than ready for a fresh start. But it won't be with someone new."

His mother looked aghast, one hand flying to her throat. "Certainly you can't mean with Annemarie! No matter how vehemently we may disapprove, she has made her choice."

Closing his eyes briefly, Gilbert shook his head. "Give me some credit. I knew the battle was lost months ago."

"Then who?" Eyes twinkling with curiosity, Gilbert's mother sank onto the footstool in front of him. "Someone from church?

Patrice Yarborough, perhaps? The pastor's daughter is a bit past her prime, but she's poised, well-educated. She would make you an excellent wife."

Gilbert rolled his eyes at the mention of the uppity Miss Yarborough. "Absolutely not."

Thomas strode over, hands in his pockets and a sly grin lifting one corner of his mouth. "No, Mother, Patrice is definitely not Gil's cup of tea. In fact, I have a feeling his choice in women isn't going to meet with your approval at all."

Glaring his brother into silence, Gilbert returned his gaze to his mother's dubious frown. Gently he clasped her hands. "You said you wanted me to be happy, Mother. Well, there's one woman who makes me happier than I've been since before the war. She's good and kind and understands me like no one else."

"That's . . . that's wonderful, son. But who is she? If she's so dear to you, why haven't you brought her to meet me?"

There were a thousand reasons why, beginning with the fact that Evelyn Ballard, the cream of Hot Springs society, would never deign to associate with a working-class girl like Mary McClarney. Mustard gas, machine guns, and Big Berthas couldn't care less about social standing. But here on the home front, the lines of demarcation were clearly drawn.

Steeling himself for his mother's umbrage, Gilbert tightened his grip on her hands. "Her name is Mary McClarney. You've already met her. She's a nurse at the Army and Navy Hospital."

Confusion etched deep lines across his mother's forehead. Her glance flickered as if she searched her memory, and then her mouth hardened into a grim line. "Not that slip of a girl with the fiery red hair—the nurse responsible for having you put in restraints?"

Thomas gave a low chuckle. "He slugged her, Mother. Nearly knocked her out cold. What'd you expect?"

Gilbert would just as soon forget that day and wished everyone else would, too. He'd been home only a few days, continuing his recovery in the Hot Springs Army and Navy Hospital and still having horrendous nightmares about the war. Mary had tried to settle him during an especially brutal hallucination, only to have him flail at her and send her careening to the floor. She'd borne an ugly bruise on her jaw for a full week afterward.

And Gilbert had borne the shame.

Feeling the shame all over again, along with regret over every vile thing he'd done these past few months, Gilbert lowered his head. "Mary's my fresh start, Mother. I need her. All I'm asking is for you to give her a chance."

3

*M*ary didn't particularly favor doing household chores on a Sunday, but she wouldn't have another day off until Thursday, so she did what she must and prayed the Lord's forgiveness. After all, Jesus permitted his hungry disciples to pick grain on the Sabbath, proving God was more concerned with His children's well-being than with the letter of the law.

And Mary must see to the well-being of her mother. Dear Mum tended their home as much as she was able, but her chronic cough and weak lungs meant Mary carried most of the load.

"I'm going out back to hang the laundry," Mary called from the kitchen. She hefted the wicker basket and propped it against her hip, then nudged open the back door. "There's a nice breeze in the shade. You should come out for a bit. The fresh air'll do you good."

"Perhaps later," came her mother's frail reply from the parlor. "After Mass and your lovely lunch, I'm in need of a nap."

Just as well. Mary wouldn't complain about a quiet hour to herself. She had little enough time to call her own, what with her work at the hospital, attending to her mother, and taking care of household chores. And she certainly had a bit of thinking to do after Gilbert's visit last evening. Though she'd continued to see him after the ghastly plot he'd hatched against Chaplain Vickary—and though he'd rightly and thoroughly repented—as long as he put his enjoyment of drinking and gambling ahead of Mary's wishes, how could she fully trust him as she should?

She plopped the laundry basket down beneath the clothesline and took a moment to relish the warm June sunshine on her upturned face. No doubt she was inviting a few more freckles across her cheeks, the price she paid for red hair and fair skin, but nothing cheered her like a summer day.

She'd just shaken out a heavy, wet muslin sheet and clipped one corner to the clothesline when the rumble of an automobile drew her attention. Her heart danced beneath her breastbone—*Gilbert!* Hurriedly, she finished hanging the sheet, then smoothed the tangles from her hair as she darted to the side gate. No need for Gilbert to disturb her mother's nap.

By the time Mary skirted the cottage, the car had halted at the front walk. Not Gilbert's Cole Eight, though. This car was smaller, sportier, not one she recognized. Curiosity battled disappointment. Gilbert knew she'd be at home today. She thought surely his promise of a new beginning meant he would come to call.

A tall, reed-thin man climbed from the driver's seat. When he closed the door and turned, Mary saw it was Dr. Russ. Shaking off thoughts of Gilbert, she strode across the lawn. "Dr. Russ, what brings you by on a Sunday afternoon? It isn't Corporal Donovan, I hope?"

His lazy grin eased her worries. "No change. I just . . . well, I thought you might be missing this." He slid his hand into his vest pocket and withdrew something small and shiny.

Mary's fingers flew to the empty spot beneath her collar where she usually pinned her watch. "Goodness me, I wondered where I'd mislaid it. Where did you find it?"

"On my desk. It must have fallen off while you were straining your eyes reading all those medical books." Dr. Russ laid the delicate pink-gold watch pin upon her open palm. "I've noticed you wearing this before. It's an interesting design."

"It's a Celtic trinity knot. The watch belonged to my mother's mother, Irish through and through." Lovingly, Mary fingered the outline of the pin. "Some say the interlocking ovals remind them of Saint Patrick's three-leaf shamrock. Others see the Christian symbol of the fish. All I know is it keeps me in mind of the faith handed down to me from generation to generation."

"Your faith is important to you. I could tell from the first time we met." Dr. Russ's blue-gray eyes glimmered in the afternoon sunshine. "You're a joy to work with, Mary. I hope you know it."

A strangely pleasant prickle edged up Mary's nape. She flicked her gaze downward, settling it upon the white fluff of a dandelion growing near the curb. "You'd have some argument from Mrs. Daley, I'm sure."

"Aw, she's more bark than bite. And take it from me, of all the nurses on the ward, you're her favorite."

"And now it's more than clear you've been kissin' the Blarney Stone." Before her face grew any hotter, Mary turned away and attempted to pin the watch to her blouse. If only her nervous fingers would cooperate! She drew a quick breath as the watch slipped from her grasp—and then gasped again when Dr. Russ swooped in to rescue the watch before it landed in the grass.

"Allow me." Dr. Russ loomed over her, and she stood frozen while he attached the pin to her bodice with surgical precision.

"I couldn't help noticing the clasp is a little weak. You should have a jeweler take a look."

"I . . . I will. Thank you." Mary raised her glance to the doctor's pensive smile.

Then the sound of an engine and a blur of motion behind him drew her attention to the street. This time there was no mistaking Gilbert's blue roadster. The car skidded to a stop inches behind Dr. Russ's, and Mary waited, nerves a-tingle, as Gilbert clambered from the vehicle and marched stiff-legged around the car. Reaching the lawn, he crushed the lone dandelion beneath the heel of his shoe, and Mary's heart twisted, for no matter how many promises Gilbert made, he owned the power to crush her heart just as easily.

Judging by the scowl he wore, he was inches from doing so.

Dr. Russ turned, barely concealing a scowl of his own beneath a genial smile. "Lieutenant Ballard. You're looking fit."

Gilbert's gaze shifted between Mary and the doctor. "Is this a social call? Or aren't you feeling well, Mary?"

Mary hiked her chin. "I don't care for your tone one bit. The kind doctor was merely returning my watch. I lost it at the hospital yesterday."

At least Gilbert had the decency to look sheepish. For a moment, anyway. Then his smoky eyes grew even darker. "And I suppose the *kind doctor* was also helping you pin it on."

"Look here, Gil." Dr. Russ kept his expression friendly, but his tone spoke a warning. "I'm well aware you and Mary have an understanding. I assure you, nothing else was going on here."

Leaning on his cane, Gilbert massaged his temple. He inhaled deeply through his nose as if striving for a measure of sanity—which Mary prayed he found quickly. A jealous snit was *not* an auspicious start to their new beginning. "Sorry," he mumbled. His eyes implored Mary's forgiveness. "It's just I wasn't expecting to find you had . . . company."

"Not to worry. I was just leaving." Dr. Russ pivoted to offer Mary a parting smile. "Remember what I said about the watch clasp, or next time you might not be so lucky."

"Indeed, and thank you." Mary waved as the doctor climbed in his roadster and drove away. Then, facing Gilbert with a disappointed frown, she said, "How could you even suspect me of carrying on with Dr. Russ? You know there's no one else I care for more than you."

He shrugged, glancing away. "What can I say, Mary? I'm a first-class fool."

"No argument there." In spite of her frustration, soft laughter bubbled from her throat. "I suppose I should be flattered you cared enough to be jealous—though the good doctor's nigh old enough to be my father, in case you hadn't noticed."

"He is indeed." Mischief in his eyes, Gilbert seized her wrist and drew her against him, silencing her startled cry with his lips. After he'd kissed her so soundly her legs grew limp as overcooked noodles, he tilted his head with a little-boy grin. "How many kisses will it take to earn your forgiveness?"

Though everything in her longed to melt deeper into Gilbert's embrace, Mary pressed her palms hard against his chest and pushed away. Sweet as his kisses were, the taste of alcohol lingered, and it brought an anxious quiver to her belly. With stuttering breaths, she clamped her arms across her abdomen, struggling to control the roaring freight train of her emotions. "When I asked you for a fresh start, Gilbert Ballard, I meant in every way. If you really lo—"

She bit her tongue, unwilling to speak the word *love* aloud until she felt certain Gilbert could say it in return. Instead, she licked her lips and tried again. "If you really cared for me, you'd understand there's more I need from you—and you from me—than kissing each other senseless."

"I know, Mary, and I want the same." Gilbert's mouth twitched. He lowered his head and closed his eyes. "I'm sorry I'm so bad at this courting thing. Guess I'm out of practice."

The sincerity in his tone, the acquiescence in his stance, tugged at Mary's heart. She crept toward him, catching his hand in hers but keeping a respectable distance between them. After all, the neighbors might be watching—though Gilbert's kiss had surely given them quite a show already. "Well," she began shyly, "they do say practice makes perfect. And I have the perfect exercise in mind for you."

He looked at her askance. "What would it be, exactly?"

With a saucy smile, she hooked her arm through his and ushered him toward the gate to the backyard. "I've a whole basket of wet laundry to hang, and you're just the man to help me do it."

The next morning, nose buried in a chart, Donald marched out of his office, intent on chastising the incompetent orderly who'd overlooked the orders for a patient's hydrotherapy session. As he rounded the corner heading for the staircase, he barely avoided colliding with a civilian visitor.

"Pardon me—" Donald snapped his head up. "Sam! What are you doing here? Aren't you supposed to be on your honeymoon?"

Chaplain Samuel Vickary, very much out of uniform in gray slacks and an open-collar shirt, cast his friend an embarrassed grin. "Pretend you never saw me. I slipped in to pick up the train tickets I left in my desk drawer."

Chuckling, Donald arched a brow. "Been a bit preoccupied lately, eh?"

"Just a bit." Sam glanced away, his face turning a glorious shade of pink.

It did Donald's heart good to see Sam so happy, considering everything the man had been through during the war. Not to mention how Gilbert Ballard had nearly destroyed him. Sam may have forgiven Gilbert, but Donald would never forget the night Gilbert's scheming had driven Sam to the brink of madness.

Shaking off the memories, Donald slapped an arm around Sam's shoulder. "As long as you're here, how about joining me for a cup of coffee? Can your bride bear to have you out of her sight awhile longer?"

"Annemarie's over at her parents' house gathering up a few more things for the trip. Once she and her mother get chatting, I doubt she'll even miss me."

"I find it hard to believe." Donald steered his friend toward the doctors' lounge. They filled mugs with steaming coffee and then carried them to Donald's office, where they could talk in private.

Seated across his desk from Samuel, Donald sat back and steepled his fingers. "So, are you going to tell me where you and Annemarie are headed, or are you keeping your honeymoon destination a secret?"

"We're taking a leisurely sightseeing trip out east, eventually arriving at Niagara Falls. On the way home we'll spend a few days at my mother's in Fort Wayne." Samuel smirked. "With Mother planning to relocate to Hot Springs in a few months, she has insisted I help her clean out my boyhood room."

"Ah. A task every grown man must face eventually." Donald reached for his mug, his glance falling on the stack of medical books Mary had left on the corner of the desk. Random slips of paper marked the pages she'd been studying. For a moment, he thought he could smell her fresh rosewater scent. He'd certainly been close enough to catch it yesterday as he'd helped her with the dainty watch pin.

Abruptly he straightened, nearly spilling his coffee. No sense even allowing such thoughts to enter his mind. The poor girl was smitten with Lieutenant Ballard, misguided as her affections might be.

Samuel set his mug on the desk, concern narrowing his gaze. "Something wrong, Donald?"

He tried to laugh off his . . . whatever this was. It certainly was *not* attraction. Though no denying he found Mary McClarney attractive. "Let's just say this old confirmed bachelor is feeling slightly envious of his happily married young friend."

His expression relaxing, Samuel crossed one leg over the other. "For one thing, you're not old. And for another, there's nothing preventing you from falling in love except your own stubbornness. I noticed you chatting with Patrice Yarborough at the reception. You two would make a handsome couple."

"Patrice is a fine woman, true." Donald's mouth twisted as he pictured the prim, Wellesley-educated daughter of Ouachita Fellowship's pastor. She was certainly of a more appropriate age for Donald. And he did appreciate the woman's progressive social and political leanings.

"But . . . ?" Samuel tapped his index fingers together.

"But with Patrice I'm never sure where I stand." With Mary, on the other hand, he never failed to sense her respect, her admiration, her genuine interest in his views, whether on medical topics or life in general.

He only wished he could influence her away from this dangerous infatuation with Gilbert Ballard.

Glancing at his watch, Samuel sucked air between his teeth. "If I stay much longer, I'll be late for my own honeymoon." He reached for his coffee mug and downed the rest in one gulp, then stood to go. "Well, I have no doubt you'll find the right woman soon. If not Patrice, then someone who suits you even better—though I really think you should give Patrice a chance."

"We'll see." Donald rose to see his friend out. "Got your tickets?"

"Right here." Samuel patted the envelope protruding from his shirt pocket. At the door, he paused to pump Donald's hand in farewell, but the handshake quickly became a brotherly hug. "Thank you, friend. For everything."

"See you in a couple of weeks, Padre. Have a wonderful trip with your beautiful bride." Thumping him on the back, Donald sent Samuel on his way.

He returned to his desk chair and sank into it with a groan. Time to get his brain back on track. He had plenty of patients to worry about, after all, starting with Corporal Donovan and the man's still undiagnosed liver problems. Reaching for a medical book, Donald pulled it onto his lap and let it fall open to the page Mary had marked.

And found himself thinking not about diseases of the liver but about a redheaded Irish lass with the greenest eyes he'd ever seen.

*

Ensconced in his tiny office deep in the bowels of the Arlington Hotel, Gilbert propped his good leg on the corner of the desk, leaned back, and rested his head in his folded hands. Hotel housekeeping schedules might well make him cross-eyed. Reporting to his younger brother might slowly nibble away at whatever pride he had left. But nothing could dim the glow of yesterday afternoon and helping Mary with the laundry. Who knew hanging sheets could be so delightful?

Or was it because—for once in his sorry life—Gilbert had dropped all pretense and merely savored the moment, a beautifully simple activity shared with a simply beautiful woman?

The office door creaked open, and Thomas stepped into the cramped space. "How are you coming on next week's schedule?"

Gilbert lowered his foot to the floor and scooted up to the desk. Too late to even pretend he hadn't been sitting there daydreaming. "Almost done. I'm waiting to hear if Minnie Parker's ready for work again after having her baby."

"I just talked to her husband down in Maintenance. You'd better give her another week. Pull Freda off kitchen duty if you need to."

"Fine." Gilbert penciled Freda's name into his chart then handed the page to Thomas. "That should do it."

Taking the schedule, Thomas drew an empty chair closer to the desk and sat down, looking as if he might stay awhile.

Gilbert flicked his pencil. "Is there . . . something else?"

Lips pursed, Thomas rolled the schedule into a tube and tapped it against his knee. "How long have you been working here, Gil? Three months?"

"Sounds about right." A nervous twitch tickled Gilbert's gut. "So which is it? Are you firing me or kicking me upstairs?"

"Neither, actually." Thomas hauled in a deep breath and sat forward. "Truth is I'd like nothing better than to promote you. The past few weeks you've really buckled down and given a tedious job your best effort."

"But . . . ?"

"But, like I told you when I hired you, management-level openings at the Arlington are few and far between. Besides, aren't you ready for something a bit more challenging? Or at least something that suits you better than hotel work?"

Swallowing, Gilbert glanced away. He couldn't deny he found the work less than fulfilling. After four years at West

Point, then leading an infantry platoon on the battlefield, sorting out housekeeping staff schedules wasn't exactly the post-military career he'd envisioned.

Of course, neither had he envisioned coming home from the Great War half a man. What options were there for a one-legged former soldier with chronic headaches and a mangled left arm that would never regain full strength?

Still, if he had any hopes of making things work with Mary, any hopes of living out the rest of his life with some semblance of dignity, Thomas was right—there *had* to be something better for Gilbert than this.

The pencil snapped between his fingers, and he stared at the broken ends as if somehow he could will them back together, like the pieces of his broken life. Lifting his gaze, he cast his brother a feeble smile. "Any suggestions?"

Thomas shook his head. "I only know if you work here much longer, you'll come to resent me." He released a humorless chuckle. "Worse than you already do."

"I don't resent you, Tom." Gilbert pushed to his feet, almost forgetting to lock his knee in his rush to circle the desk. He had to make sure his brother knew how much he appreciated this job—how much he appreciated Thomas for sticking by him during the bleak days since he'd returned from the war. "Letting me come to work for you—it was exactly what I needed to get through these past few months. I haven't thanked you nearly often enough."

Rising, Thomas waved a hand. "The job's lousy, low-paying, not to mention you've got the shoddiest office in the entire building. I should be thanking *you*."

"Just stop, will you?" Gilbert clapped Thomas's shoulder. "You know good and well I've been a royal pain in the—"

"Okay, okay. Let's both quit while we're ahead." Shrugging off Gilbert's hand, Thomas grinned and turned to go. "Since you're so crazy grateful for this job, I'll let you get back to it."

"Tommy, wait." Gilbert edged into the narrow space between his brother and the door. "I need to say something."

Thomas closed his eyes while he drew a long, quiet breath. Then, meeting Gilbert's gaze, he said, "You don't have to say anything, Gil. Really."

"No, I do. So let me say it before I lose my nerve." Bracing himself against the doorframe, Gilbert struggled for the right words. "What I did after the war, the way I acted, the way I treated people . . . I know I lost your respect. I have a lot to make up for. I just hope you'll give me the chance."

Glancing into the corridor, Thomas shoved one hand into his pants pocket. "I don't blame *you*, Gilbert. I blame the war. The lousy, stinking, stupid war."

"The war took my leg, but it was my choice to let it ruin my life. I have to take responsibility for that. For . . . everything I've done since then."

"You're right, you do." Thomas's dark-eyed stare pinned Gilbert to the wall as fiercely as his jabbing finger poked at Gilbert's chest. "But don't let guilt and remorse blind you to who you were *before* the shell took your leg. You're a hero, Gil. You saved lives over there. Be proud of that man. Be that man again."

Throat constricted, Gilbert watched silently as his brother disappeared around the corner at the end of the hall. A *hero*? Certainly not in his own eyes. Anything but!

Against his will, his thoughts carried him back to France, to the rat-infested trenches, miles of barbed wire, fields and forests blackened by artillery fire. He could almost smell the cordite, taste the smoke and ash in the air.

And the carnage—soldiers lying dead or nearly so, as far as the eye could see. And so young! Boys forced to become men under the worst possible conditions, and far too many would never see home again. They were the real heroes.

Gilbert's stomach clenched. Eyes squeezed shut, head pounding, he suddenly couldn't bear another moment in this cramped, dismal space of an office. It reminded him too much of the underground bunkers where he'd served on the front. He reached across the desk and snatched his cane, then slammed the door behind him in a dash toward the rear exit.

Minutes later, he made his way to Fountain Street and paused to gaze up at the verdant mountainside behind the hotel. A bracing breath of warm summer air edged aside the battlefield stench he could never quite forget.

"You're a hero, Gil."

Thomas's words jolted him again. Nothing would do more to assuage his battered conscience than reclaiming his little brother's regard.

And Thomas had hit the nail on the head. It was high time Gilbert took a hard look at his life, made some decisions, mapped out his future. If he couldn't pursue the military career he'd always planned on, surely he could find some other avenue for utilizing the skills he possessed.

A bounce in his step—or as much of a bounce as he could manage with an artificial leg—he started down Fountain Street toward Central Avenue, his only thought to trek over to the Army and Navy Hospital, where he'd search out his best friend and—

His best friend had just left on his honeymoon.

Besides, Gilbert had barely spoken to Samuel since *that night*, not to mention Gilbert himself had broken off the friendship weeks prior. He halted in the middle of the sidewalk, sweat trickling down his spine and remorse chewing a hole in his gut.

Did everything have to remind him what a wretched fool he'd been?

A beer. He'd gladly drown his sorrows in a tall, frothy, ice-cold beer.

Setting his sights on the gaudy front doors of a Central Avenue saloon, Gilbert stepped into the street.

The next sound he heard was the screech of an automobile horn and someone yelling, "Get out of the way!"

4

*N*ot cancer, praise God! Mary smiled as she perused Corporal Donovan's chart. The unfortunate soul had apparently contracted serum hepatitis while serving in France, the symptoms only now presenting. His condition should improve with bed rest, but the remainder of his life he must take care to neither spread the disease nor inflict more damage on his liver.

Prohibition couldn't have come at a better time for the corporal.

Mary only hoped the unavailability of alcoholic beverages would bring about a positive change in Gilbert as well. She thanked God every day Gilbert had overcome his morphine addiction—another consequence of his battlefield injuries. Unfortunately, he'd come to rely too heavily on strong drink instead. Mary had privately celebrated when Prohibition was announced, for she couldn't help worrying Gilbert's taste for liquor might someday come between them.

Ah, but yesterday had been sweet indeed. She'd never seen Gilbert so relaxed, never heard him laugh so freely and so much. To think a simple chore like hanging laundry could awaken even deeper feelings for this man with the irresistible claim on her heart.

A secret smile curling her lips, she jotted a note on Corporal Donovan's chart before moving to the next patient.

"Why, Mary McClarney." Lois came alongside and nudged her elbow. "Aren't you just the picture of sweetness and light. I'll wager you've been making time with your handsome lieutenant."

Heat rose in Mary's cheeks. She hurried Lois to the other side of the ward. "I'll thank you not to embarrass me in front of the patients. Worse, what if Mrs. Daley had overheard?"

"Oh, the old bat." Lois flicked a hand. "If she had her way, we'd be spinsters the rest of our lives—which is definitely not in *my* plans." She leaned closer, a conspiratorial gleam in her eye. "Listen, honey, if you ever grow tired of your beau, make sure I'm the first to know, okay?" With that, she marched away.

And what, exactly, did Lois mean by *that* remark? Refusing to give it a second thought, Mary hiked her chin and strode in the opposite direction, only to run headlong into Mrs. Daley.

"Watch where you're going, young lady!" The hoary-haired chief nurse seized Mary by both wrists to keep her from toppling over. Then, with a caustic look beyond Mary's shoulder, she added, "And I'd watch my step with Miss Underwood as well. You could do much better in your choice of friends."

Mary released a nervous chuckle as she found her footing. "I'm sure Lois means no harm."

"Humph. I'd be happy if she had even half your skills and work ethic."

Mary felt another blush coming on. A compliment from Mrs. Daley? Would wonders never cease! "I—well—thank you."

"Now, now, don't look at me as though I've never once said a kind word to you." With a flinty glare, the woman set her arms akimbo. "I'm not the ogre you and half the other nurses on this floor make me out to be."

"No, ma'am, of course not." Mary crossed her fingers behind her back and adopted her most placating smile. She sent subtle glances to either side in search of some urgent task to remove her from Mrs. Daley's scrutiny. "If you'll pardon me, I should really—"

"Not so fast, Miss McClarney."

Mary couldn't refrain from flinching at the chief nurse's crisp command. "Yes, ma'am?" Her voice was little more than a squeak.

"I've been meaning to speak with you about this research assignment you did for Dr. Russ. Did you find it enlightening?"

"Quite, ma'am." Mary relaxed slightly, recalling how she'd relished the thrill of discovery while paging through Dr. Russ's medical books. "The study of pathology is fascinating. That—and, of course, using the knowledge to help others—is why I chose to become a nurse."

Mrs. Daley half-closed her eyes as she nodded thoughtfully. Then, hooking her arm through Mary's, she ushered her toward the exit. "Come to my office, dear. There's a matter I'd like to discuss with you."

Almost before she could catch her breath, Mary found herself seated across the desk from Mrs. Daley. Perched on the edge of the chair, she clenched her hands and tried to still the nervous jumping of her right foot. She thought she'd lose her mind while waiting for Mrs. Daley to adjust her glasses just so, then page through a sheaf of papers with excruciating slowness.

Finally, the woman looked up, a benevolent smile carving deep parentheses around her mouth. "You may not be aware I've had my eye on you for quite some time, Miss McClarney."

Oh, Mary had been aware, all right. But she had the eerie sense, at least today, Mrs. Daley's attention was for reasons other than Mary's relationship with Gilbert Ballard. Uncertain about the direction of this conversation, she simply nodded.

Lacing her fingers atop the desk, Mrs. Daley tilted her chin. "I have concluded you are ready for increased responsibilities. You may have heard Mrs. Hatcher is retiring at the end of the month, which leaves me with a position to fill."

Mary gulped. Surely, she wasn't being considered for Mrs. Hatcher's job. It would mean . . .

"I'm contemplating promoting you to the third-floor charge nurse position for ward two. It would entail changing permanently to the day shift, plus you would have weekends off." Mrs. Daley arched a brow and cast Mary a questioning look across the top of her glasses.

Surely, she must be dreaming! Mary chewed her lip. "This is completely unexpected, ma'am. I . . . I hardly know what to say."

"You'll want to think it over, naturally. Give me your answer by Friday, or I shall have to offer the promotion to someone else." Retrieving a folder from the corner of her desk, Mrs. Daley dismissed Mary with a nod toward the door.

Stunned and disoriented, Mary paused in the corridor and propped herself against the wall. A promotion would mean a small raise, and with her mother's chronic health concerns, the extra income could make a huge difference. And no more worries about working swing shifts or leaving her mother home alone at night, not to mention every weekend off—what more could she ask?

Yes, indeed, Mrs. Daley's offer seemed like the answer to a prayer Mary hadn't even thought to pray!

"Miss McClarney? Are you all right?"

At Dr. Russ's softly spoken query, she gasped and pushed away from the wall. "Oh, fine, sir. Just a wee bit flabbergasted."

"You're sure? You looked rather pale there for a moment." The kind-faced doctor tilted his head with a probing gaze. "Perhaps you should sit down."

"Perhaps I should." Spying a bench on the opposite wall, Mary crossed the corridor and sank down with a thud, handfuls of her white apron bunched in her fists.

Dr. Russ plopped down beside her. "Dare I ask what has you so . . . I believe *flabbergasted* was the word you used?"

"Mrs. Daley just offered me a promotion." Mary turned a wide-eyed gaze upon the doctor, her mouth stretching into an amazed grin as she explained about Mrs. Hatcher's retirement and the change this new position would mean for Mary.

"Terrific! Mrs. Daley made an excellent choice." Dr. Russ extended his hand in congratulations. "You're going to accept, aren't you?"

"I suppose I am." Mary nodded thoughtfully as she shook the doctor's hand. "I truly didn't believe you yesterday when you spoke of Mrs. Daley's regard for me. Especially after . . ." She glanced away as she recalled stolen kisses with Gilbert, romantic trysts in hospital storage closets—and Mrs. Daley's stern rebukes for Mary's allowing herself to become romantically involved with a patient.

No matter by then Gilbert had been an *out*patient. Nonetheless, though Mary had tried earnestly to keep their relationship from interfering with work, she couldn't deny Gilbert's relentless attention had distracted her to no end—until she'd forcefully put a stop to it, insisting he must no longer call on her during work hours.

"Mary?" Dr. Russ's gentle tone returned her thoughts to the present. He pressed her hand firmly between his own. "Don't for a second question your worthiness for this promotion. You've earned it. You're a good nurse. A good *woman*. I consider it a privilege to work with you."

Mary smiled her gratitude. If only all the doctors on staff were as cordial. Or, more to the point, more appreciative of the nurses who worked so tirelessly on their patients' behalf. Certain doctors—Mary could name more than a few—treated the nursing staff as little more than housekeepers in white uniforms. Such old-school physicians considered a nurse's "excess" medical knowledge a detriment to patient care. And they wouldn't want a nurse to actually *think*, now, would they?

Thank heaven for physicians like Dr. Russ.

With a self-conscious sigh, Mary rose. "I should get back to the ward. I've dallied long enough." She bade the doctor farewell then checked the time as she hurried along the breezeway. Less than an hour left on her shift. She could hardly wait to get home and share her good news with Mum!

But before then she'd see Gilbert. He'd promised to be waiting for her at the oak tree when she got off work. He'd drive her home, and she'd tell him all about Mrs. Daley's offer. This highly respected hospital position would surely garner a measure of approval from Gilbert's family—approval Mary desperately desired if she and Gilbert were ever to have a future together.

An hour later, when she rushed down the path and across the lawn to "their" tree, she found Gilbert conspicuously absent. Standing beneath the spreading branches, she strained her eyes in all directions, hoping for a glimpse of Gilbert's glossy, dark curls. Was he perhaps repaying her for working late on Saturday and keeping him waiting? Reprisal certainly wasn't outside Gilbert's nature . . . but she dared to believe he'd changed.

After giving him the benefit of the doubt *and* another twenty minutes' grace period, Mary gave up and started home. She'd walked only half a block when an automobile horn sounded behind her.

The driver pulled up alongside her and leaned out the window. "Miss McClarney, wait."

The man looked familiar, and he obviously knew Mary by name. She hugged her handbag at her waist. "Yes? Do I know you?"

"Sorry, I'm Thomas Ballard. Gil's brother. Guess we haven't officially been introduced."

Mary relaxed slightly. "Of course. I remember when you visited Gilbert at the hospital." Except why would he stop her on the street, unless . . . "Oh, my, something's happened, hasn't it?" She stepped to the curb, her imagination going wild with the possibilities.

"Nothing to panic about." Waving his hand, Thomas offered a crooked grin. "Gil's had a little accident. He's home resting, but—"

Mary's brain had shut down after the words *little accident*. "He's hurt? How bad?"

"Just a little bumped and bruised after a near-miss on Central Avenue earlier today."

"*Near-miss?*" Mary gulped air as she pictured Gilbert's broken and bleeding body sprawled on the pavement. "Is he—"

"I assure you, he's fine. He knew you'd be worried when he wasn't waiting for you after work, so he asked me to meet you at the hospital gate. Unfortunately, I didn't get there in time."

A bitter taste clung to the back of Mary's throat. She rubbed her forehead. "He's seen a doctor, of course?"

"Dr. Lessman checked him over thoroughly. Our housekeeper's making sure he takes it easy for the rest of the day."

"Your housekeeper. You left your *housekeeper* in charge of an injured man?" Indignant, Mary started around to the passenger door. "Be so kind as to take me to see Gilbert immediately."

"Now hold on here." Thomas grabbed the door handle before she could pull it open. "I'm not so sure it's a good idea." Glancing away, he muttered something under his breath, something about *mother*.

It was enough to snap Mary out of her headlong rush to reach Gilbert. Giving the door a yank, she wrenched it free of Thomas's grip and climbed inside. "My mother will worry if I'm late getting home. Drive me there first, and then to see Gilbert. I won't take no for an answer."

⌇❧

"Here's a fresh cold compress, Mister Gilbert." Marguerite lifted the dripping cloth from Gilbert's head and dropped it into an enameled bowl before replacing the cloth with another.

"Thank you." Gilbert groaned as he pressed the cool, wet towel against the goose egg on the back of his head. He supposed he should be thankful he'd had sense enough to leap aside before the delivery truck plowed into him. However, the lump on his head and the bruises on his backside would remind him of his carelessness for days to come.

"You sure you don't want me sendin' for your mama? She'll be fit to be tied when she gets home to find you laid up like this."

"I wouldn't have you interrupt Mother's spa appointment for anything. A mineral bath and massage at the Fordyce will leave her in a much better mood." Gilbert shifted in the cushioned chair to ease the pressure on his left hip. At least he'd had the presence of mind—or perhaps the good fortune—to fall toward his bad side. No sense damaging his remaining good limbs.

Marguerite stood over him, arms crossed and a petulant frown twisting her mouth. "I swan, Mister Gilbert. How you can survive gettin' all shot up in the war and then come home and near get yourself killed crossing the street—why, you must certainly have a guardian angel sitting on your shoulder. Looks to me like a message from the Almighty. He expects you to do somethin' worthwhile with the life He keeps saving."

Gilbert shot the family housekeeper a doubtful glare. "Or maybe He just wants to punish me for all my many sins."

With a *tsk-tsk*, Marguerite rolled her eyes and marched out of the parlor, leaving Gilbert to mull over the sorry state of his battered body . . . and his battered life. Only hours ago, Thomas had tried to tell him he needed to find an occupation more worthy of the man he was.

Was being the operative word. Gilbert still hadn't figured out who he was *now*.

And his latest stupidity had resulted in yet another failure. Realizing how disappointed Mary would be when she didn't find him at the oak tree, he'd sent Thomas rushing over to the hospital. By now Thomas would have relayed the news of Gilbert's accident, so at least Mary would know he hadn't intentionally stood her up.

His insides curled in upon themselves with the sudden need to be near her. She would know what to do to soothe his throbbing head. She could make him feel like a man—a *whole* man—while the rest of the world seemed intent on reducing him to a crippled has-been.

The rest of the world . . . or had Gilbert alone declared himself worthless?

Sounds from the rear of the house announced Thomas's return home. Then Gilbert detected a second set of footsteps pounding down the hall, and a split-second later Mary rushed through the parlor door. Red curls spiraled around her anxious face as she jerked to a halt mere feet from Gilbert's chair. Her hand flew to her mouth. "Oh, Gilbert, Gilbert!"

"Now, Mary, it's not as bad as it looks." Lowering the compress, he motioned her to come closer. When he could reach her hand, he pulled her onto the arm of his chair and buried his aching head in the folds of her sleeve. She smelled of starch and hospital antiseptic, commingling with the faintest scent of rosewater.

Heaven. Pure heaven.

He could tell the moment she shifted from anxious concern to clinical detachment. With practiced fingers, she probed the knot behind his left ear, eliciting a gasp through clenched teeth. "Sorry," she murmured, gentling her touch. "Feels like a typical scalp hematoma—a good deal of swelling, but the skin isn't broken. Where else are you hurt?"

"Not worth mentioning." He'd just as soon avoid a discussion of his nether injuries. Capturing Mary's wrist, Gilbert drew her hand to his mouth and pressed a kiss into the soft center of her palm. "Doc Lessman already examined me thoroughly. I'm roughed up a bit, that's all. By tomorrow I'll be good as new." In a manner of speaking.

Gilbert glanced up to see his brother standing in the doorway. Head cocked, Thomas set his hands on his hips. He spoke with quiet concern. "Not sure it's such a good idea having her here. Mother will be home any minute now."

Tensing, Gilbert sat straighter, punishing himself with the pressure on his sore left hip and shoulder. In his relief to see Mary, he'd conveniently pushed aside any concerns about his mother's opinion. Another world war might break out if Mother found Mary making herself at home in the Ballards' parlor—and practically seated on Gilbert's lap!

Giving her hand another kiss, Gilbert looked up with pleading eyes. "You should go, Mary. I'll see you tomorrow at the oak tree, and—"

Too late. Both their heads snapped up as Evelyn Ballard swept into the parlor. "Thomas! Someone heard a rumor—" Then her glance fell upon Gilbert, and her mouth dropped open, first in shock and then in confusion. "It's true—you *were* in an accident."

Gilbert lowered his head. "It was nothing. I'm fine."

"Yes, so I see." Arching a brow, Gilbert's mother pinned Mary with a dagger-like stare. "I'm so utterly *relieved* to see you're in the care of your *private nurse.*"

As if only now realizing her peril, Mary popped off the chair arm and stood primly at Gilbert's side. "Mrs. Ballard, ma'am."

Gritting his teeth against the pain and a brief wave of dizziness, Gilbert found his cane and eased himself to his feet. "This appears to be as good a time as any for formal introductions. Mother, may I present Miss Mary McClarney. She's very dear to me, so I beg you to welcome her with utmost cordiality."

For several long seconds, Gilbert wondered if his mother had lost her tongue. Her chin quivered with barely controlled annoyance . . . or was it disgust? Either way, a lowly nurse would never best Gilbert's mother. Pride alone would prevent Evelyn Ballard from lashing out with the venom of self-righteous vanity that ruled her every thought.

Thomas edged forward. "You've had a long day, Mother. Perhaps you'd like to lie down before dinner is served?"

"I feel quite rested, thank you." A semblance of a smile found its way to her lips. Not a particularly welcoming smile, but a smile nonetheless. "In fact, I have decided we should invite Miss McClarney to stay for dinner. We should get to know one another better, don't you agree?"

Gilbert recognized the smile for what it was: treachery incarnate. "Mary was just leaving. Thomas, you'll drive her home, won't you?"

"Of course, if—"

"Tut-tut!" Gilbert's mother moved to the entrance hall. "Marguerite! Set another place in the dining room, if you please."

"No, Mrs. Ballard, I can't stay, really." Mary kneaded her hands. "My own dear mum will be holding supper for me. I told her I'd be home as soon as I made sure Gilbert was all right."

"Well, for heaven's sake, dear child. Let's send for your mother and you can *both* join us for dinner. Thomas, have Zachary take the Peerless and fetch Mrs. McClarney at once."

Thomas looked askance at Gilbert as if pleading for his intervention, but Gilbert had already determined this was one skirmish he'd never win. As his mother ushered Thomas from the room and then hurried off as well, no doubt to issue more kitchen orders, Gilbert enfolded Mary beneath his arm and rested his chin against her silky red hair. "It'll be fine, Mary. Your mother will be treated like visiting royalty."

Leaning away, Mary craned her neck to give Gilbert a worried frown. "Ah, but don't you know the Irish have little regard for royals. I fear you'd best be more concerned for your own mum than for mine."

✍

Nell McClarney may be frail of body, but she'd proved again tonight she could match wits with the best of them. Mary could do little but smile and nod as her mother faced off with Evelyn Ballard over a sumptuous dinner of broiled pork tenderloin, asparagus tips in a buttery sauce, and potatoes au gratin. Both Mary and her mother declined the offered wine. Gilbert acknowledged Mary's raised eyebrow by stopping at one glass, but Mrs. Ballard didn't exhibit the same restraint.

"They served wine at the wedding in Cana, you know." Mrs. Ballard used a cream-colored linen napkin to dab a spilled droplet from the matching tablecloth, and Mary could only surmise the ever-present Marguerite knew the best way to remove such stains.

Mary's mother gave a polite cough. "True enough, but I don't think our Lord Jesus was much impressed with intemperance."

"Mum . . ." Mary found her mother's foot under the table and gave a warning tap with the toe of her shoe. "Perhaps we should be getting you home. You've had a long day."

"Not to worry, lass. I had a good long nap after lunch." Mary's mother beamed her most charming smile in Mrs. Ballard's direction, but the tone of her voice held an edge. "Besides, I'm just gettin' to know our lovely hostess."

The regal nod Gilbert's mother offered in return set Mary's insides aquiver. "Yes, do stay awhile longer, Mrs. McClarney. You and I have *much* we should talk about."

"Ah, but only if you'll call me Nell. After all, we're nigh on family already, seeing as how our children have set themselves on the path to matrimony."

"Mum!" Mary shoved her chair away from the table. "We're no such thing, and you've no cause to assume so—much less be discussing my future with Mrs. Ballard."

"Mary's right, Mrs. McClarney." Gilbert, seated at Mary's left, set one hand on the back of her chair. "She and I are . . . well, we're still exploring our feelings for each other."

Across the table, Thomas cleared his throat noisily. "I just remembered some business I need to attend to." Crumpling his napkin next to his plate, he stood. "You'll excuse me, won't you, Mother?"

"No need to rush off." Mrs. Ballard motioned Marguerite over with the wine carafe. "We're all *family* here, as Mrs. McClarney—pardon me, *Nell*—has so kindly pointed out."

"You've had quite enough, Mother." Gilbert's pointed stare halted Marguerite before she could decant the wine. "I think it's time we bade our guests good evening. If no one else is tired, I certainly am."

Mary's concern immediately shifted to Gilbert. Distracted by their mothers' duel of words over dinner, she'd almost forgotten about his accident. Swiveling, she studied his face in search of any telltale signs of a concussion she might have missed earlier. But his eyes were clear, if dark and brooding, and the only outward evidence of his mishap was a grimace of pain as he shifted his weight.

She turned to Mrs. Ballard, gathering what little confidence remained after the subtle condescending glances she'd endured all evening. "My mother and I are indeed grateful for your hospitality, but it's time we take our leave. We'd be most appreciative if you could spare your driver to see us home."

"Most certainly." With one snap of her fingers, the woman sent Marguerite to fetch the chauffeur. Then, directing her cool-eyed smile toward Mary's mother, she said, "Nell, dear, we *must* get together again soon and continue this conversation. Are you a Country Club member? Their weekly ladies' luncheon is delightful."

The dig was not lost upon Mary—or her mother. "I'm afraid not, Evelyn. However, you're most welcome to come to my home for tea some afternoon."

Mrs. Ballard replied with a sniff. "I suppose I can't entreat you to stay a little longer and have dessert. Marguerite has prepared a lovely Dutch apple pie."

"You're most kind," Mary's mother said with a dip of her chin, "but we've clearly stayed too long as it is."

Far, far too long, in Mary's opinion. What little dinner she'd managed to swallow now sat like a cold, hard rock in the pit of her stomach. She should have realized Mrs. Ballard would never accept her, never approve of her seeing—or being seen with—Gilbert. And tonight had been all about showing her exactly that.

5

$\mathcal{D}$espite the warm summer morning, Nell McClarney huddled on the settee beneath a thick afghan. Her ribs ached from all the coughing she'd done since Monday night, and she suspected a fever had taken hold. She dare not let on to Mary, though, or she'd never hear the end of her daughter's lectures.

Poor lass, giving her heart to a man like Gilbert. Could Mary not have fallen for someone with whom she had more in common? Rich beyond imagining, his family was, not to mention both he and his mother certainly had a taste for wine! Disaster loomed, Nell felt certain. An iceberg more fearsome than the one that sank the *Titanic* would scuttle this relationship before sweet Mary could find rescue.

Another coughing spasm rattled Nell's chest. She reached for her teacup and found it empty. Without the energy to make her way to the stove to heat more water, she moaned and burrowed deeper into the cushions.

She dozed off only to awaken when someone touched her shoulder.

"Nell? Are you all right?" Genevieve Lawson, her silverhaired next-door neighbor, hovered over her.

"Oh, Ginny, I didn't hear you come in." Nell pushed up on one elbow, then had to stifle a cough.

Genevieve gently pressed her against the pillows and adjusted the afghan, then laid the back of her hand against Nell's forehead. "You're burning up. I'm going to call Mary and have her come home."

"No, please, I don't want her to fret. I'll be fine." Again, Nell tried to sit up, but the effort caused spots to dance before her eyes. "Perhaps you'd brew me another cup of tea . . ."

"Glad to. However, I'm *still* calling Mary." Genevieve set her hands on her hips, eyeing Nell with a schoolteacher frown. Recently retired after thirty years of teaching, the woman had plenty of experience staring down wayward students.

"I wish you wouldn't," Nell wheezed, but her protest went unheard—or perhaps Genevieve simply ignored it, turning abruptly and marching to the kitchen.

A few minutes later, the teakettle whistled, and shortly Genevieve returned with a steaming cup of tea. She set it on a side table, then helped Nell to a sitting position. "I'm going to run home now and call the hospital, and I'll hear no arguments about it. Don't you dare move from this spot until I return." On her way out the door, she grumbled something about the foolishness of Nell's not having a telephone of her own.

Aye, and see how far your money goes when you've no other income and must rely solely on your daughter to provide.

However, Mary did say she'd be earning a bit more after her promotion. Nell was so proud of her girl, such a hard worker and smart as a whip. *If only you could see our daughter now, Charles. Why did you have to be so thoughtlessly careless that day?*

Ah, if only it had been the one day. But no, Charles McClarney was dead before his time and all on account of his own folly. Nell had loved him, always would, but she prayed every day that when Mary fell in love, it would be with a man truly worthy of her affection.

Unfortunately, as far as Nell was concerned, Gilbert Ballard had much to prove.

The hot tea soothed her raspy throat and helped to loosen the phlegm. She felt measurably stronger by the time Genevieve returned. "I hope you didn't alarm Mary. I'm just having a bad day, that's all."

"Bad day, indeed." Genevieve plopped into a chair and smoothed the skirt of her deep green shirtwaist. "What am I going to do with you, Nell McClarney? One of these days I'll drop in only to find you stone-cold dead, all because you're too miserly to have a telephone so you can call someone when you need help."

Nell sniffed. "There's a big difference between miserly and frugal."

"Not when your health is at stake." Arms crossed, Genevieve arched a brow.

Neither spoke for several minutes as Nell sipped her tea and tried not to resent her friend's interference. Ginny was only being kind, and heaven knew Nell appreciated her concern. With Mary working long hours at the hospital, it comforted Nell to know Ginny was right next door. Nell's chronic bronchitis was chronically unpredictable. Fatigue, stress, excitement, a weather change—she never knew what might precipitate a worsening of symptoms.

And she'd certainly experienced an untimely amount of stress at the Ballard home two evenings ago. Never had she encountered a woman as haughty and vain as Evelyn Ballard. Only the most ignorant of simpletons would have failed to notice how the woman strove at every turn to intimidate Mary, to subtly drive home her conviction that Mary would never be good enough for her son.

Well. Nell McClarney would just see about that. Clearly, the young lieutenant's mother hadn't an inkling of what passed for quality. If ever there were a true Proverbs 31 "worthy woman," it was Nell's daughter, Mary.

☙

"And here's where I note any changes in medication dosage." The petite Mrs. Hatcher tilted her head upward to catch Mary's eye. Her pixie-like smile beamed warmth and encouragement, reminding Mary how much she'd miss seeing the sweet woman around the hospital after her retirement.

Mrs. Hatcher might be small in stature, but she'd certainly leave behind some big shoes to fill. Mary could only pray she'd live up to the challenge.

She bent over the counter for a closer look at the pages spread out there. "Your system makes good sense. Can you tell me—"

"Mary! There you are!" Out of breath, Lois Underwood barged up to the third-floor nurses' station. "Excuse me for interrupting, Mrs. Hatcher, but I've chased all over the hospital looking for Mary."

"Is there a problem, dear?" Mrs. Hatcher's expression remained unperturbed, but Mary caught a slight edge to her voice. Rumor had it the usually even-tempered charge nurse tolerated no rudeness or insubordination. However, she was much more likely to kill one with kindness than berate with a tongue-lashing in the style of Mrs. Daley.

In this respect, Mary decided she'd try to emulate Mrs. Hatcher.

In the meantime, she drew back her shoulders with a sniff and turned her attention to Lois. "Anyone on the ward could have told you I was up here with Mrs. Hatcher going over my new job responsibilities."

"Excuse me for not taking time to check your social calendar." Lois blew out an exasperated breath.

Mrs. Hatcher stiffened, the toe of one shoe tapping out a rhythm on the tile floor. "That'll do, Miss Underwood. Pray tell, what is so urgent?"

"Reception got a call from Mary's neighbor." Lois's tone turned contrite. Her gaze softened as she turned toward Mary. "Your mother isn't well and needs you to come home."

The starch went out of Mary's limbs. "Saints above, I should have known! She was looking a bit peaked this morning when I left for work." Apologizing both to Mrs. Hatcher and to Lois, she raced downstairs and over to the administration building, praying all the way Mrs. Daley would give her permission to leave early. If necessary, and Mum's health permitting, she could give up her day off and make up the lost hours tomorrow.

Near tears by the time she'd spoken with Mrs. Daley and then clocked out, Mary stumbled down the corridor, bypassing the painfully slow elevator and heading for the main staircase. *Dear Jesus, watch over my mother, I beg you! She's all I have, and I need her—*

"Mary! Have a care!" Dr. Russ grabbed her by the shoulders just as she tripped on the landing. Guiding her out of the way of the other two doctors taking the stairs with him, he tucked a steadying arm around her waist. "You're crying. Did something happen?"

With a sniffle, she explained about her mother. "I've no idea how serious it is, but if Mrs. Lawson thought it worth calling the hospital, it can't be good."

Dr. Russ chewed his lip. "Wait here. I'll be right back."

Before she could insist she must be on her way, he caught up with the doctors he'd been in conversation with and murmured a few words Mary couldn't hear. One doctor nodded brusquely, the other shook Dr. Russ's hand, and then they bustled off.

"All right, let's go." Dr. Russ tucked her hand beneath his elbow and started for the staircase.

Mary held back. "I beg your pardon?"

He gave a sympathetic chuckle. "I'm driving you, Mary. My colleagues will cover for me while we go check on your mother."

Both relieved and stunned, Mary released a soft cry. "Oh, thank you. Thank you!"

After a quick detour to his office to grab his medical bag, Dr. Russ escorted Mary out to his car. Within minutes, they left the hospital grounds and drove up Reserve toward Mary's neighborhood. The instant Dr. Russ parked his roadster at the curb, Mary threw open the passenger door and charged up the front walk.

When she skidded to a halt in the parlor to find Mum and Mrs. Lawson sipping tea and chatting like two busybodies, all the breath whooshed out of her lungs. One hand to her bosom, she waited for her thudding heart to work itself loose from her throat and settle back down where it belonged.

"Don't look at me that way," her mother scolded as she set her cup and saucer aside. "'Twasn't my idea for Ginny to call the hospital."

Genevieve Lawson *tsk-tsk*ed and shook her head. "She's acting better than she feels, mark my word. She's feverish, and she's been coughing up a storm. I knew you'd want to know."

"Indeed I would, and thank you, Mrs. Lawson." Finally able to catch a full breath, Mary perched on the settee next to her mother and felt her head. Definitely warm, and Mum's chest rattled with every inhalation.

Just then, Dr. Russ appeared in the doorway. Still wearing the white lab coat he hadn't taken time to remove, he looked decidedly out of place in their tiny parlor. His glance bounced between Mrs. Lawson and Mary's mother as if determining who the patient was.

Mary stood. "Mum, this is Dr. Donald Russ. He was kind enough to drive me from the hospital. Doctor, my mother, Nell McClarney." She tilted her head in her mother's direction. "The very *obstinate* Mrs. McClarney, I should add."

Mary's mother quirked her lips. "Now look who's calling the kettle black." She coughed softly into a handkerchief before smiling sweetly at Dr. Russ. "My apology for my daughter dragging you away from your duties on a fool's errand, Doctor. As you can see, I'm none the worse for wear."

"Would you let me be the judge?" With a chiding smile, he crossed the room and took Mary's place on the settee. Reaching into his medical bag, he brought out a thermometer. "Open, please."

The moment Mary's mother parted her lips to protest, Dr. Russ slid the thermometer bulb beneath her tongue. She tried to mumble something, but he shook his finger at her, then calmly withdrew a stethoscope from his bag. "Sit forward, please. I'd like to listen to your lungs."

Casting Mary a poison-dart stare, her mother resigned herself to Dr. Russ's examination. As Mary watched and waited, her heart swelled with gratitude toward the doctor. Knowing Mum received his expert attention went miles toward relieving Mary's worries. Her mother was always so reluctant to spend money seeing their regular physician.

"Mary, dear . . ." Mrs. Lawson rose and motioned Mary toward the kitchen. When they were alone, she continued, "I hoped calling you at the hospital wouldn't cause problems, but I truly felt you were needed."

"It'll be fine. I explained to my supervisor." Mary glanced toward the parlor, her lips clamped together. "She hasn't seemed well since I heard her coughing in her sleep Monday night. I should have known dinner with the Ballards would be too strenuous for her."

"She told me about the evening. She has . . . concerns."

"I'm sure she does." Mary certainly had a few of her own.

"If I may be so bold," Mrs. Lawson began, resting a hand on Mary's arm, "the Ballards are . . . well, let's just say they think more highly of themselves than they ought."

Mary squared her shoulders. "Mrs. Ballard, perhaps. But it's unfair to lump them all together. Gilbert is nothing like his mother, nor is Thomas, if I'm any judge of character."

"I hate to speak in clichés, but as the saying goes, the apple doesn't fall far from the tree." Folding her arms, Mrs. Lawson crossed to the window over the sink, staring out as if remembering. "I taught both boys in school, you know. Gilbert was definitely the more industrious, but he could be adamant about wanting his own way."

Mary could vouch for that aspect of his personality. She firmed her mouth and remained silent.

"Thomas, while a clever lad, was too intent on escaping his older brother's shadow," the older woman continued. "And their mother—oh my! She simply would not hear either of her sons required correction."

"If you're trying to convince me I should stop seeing Gilbert, it's no use." With an apologetic shrug, Mary strode to the pantry. "I should see what we have on hand for supper."

Mrs. Lawson caught her arm. "Please don't trouble yourself. I have a chicken stewing at home, and I was going to make a batch of dumplings. Plenty for all of us."

The weight of her worries, the strain of the afternoon, and now more dire warnings about Gilbert and his family—it all began to close in on Mary. Shutting the pantry door, she turned with a tired sigh. "It's very kind of you. I'll just go check on Mum."

She found her mother reclining on the settee, eyes closed, a damp cloth on her forehead. She looked to Dr. Russ.

He glanced up from rearranging things in his medical bag. "She'll be fine, Mary. Not to worry. I think it's just a bad cold."

"But her lungs—she sounds so congested."

"Unfortunately, with weak lungs, an infection often settles there." He snapped his bag shut and straightened, then handed Mary a small square of paper. "I've written a prescription for a different cough medicine. When she told me what she's been taking, well . . . let's just say it's a rather outdated formulation."

Mary exhaled noisily. "I've suspected for a while Dr. Quatman hasn't kept up with modern medicine."

Dr. Russ's grimace spoke more than words. "New discoveries are being made every day. A doctor who doesn't stay abreast of developments is doing a disservice to his patients."

"He's been our family physician since I was a girl. I can't get Mum to consider seeing anyone else."

One of her mother's eyes cracked open. "Now, lass, Dr. Quatman's a good man. Don't be speaking ill of him."

"A good man who's ancient as Methuselah. It's the twentieth century, Mum, and if you continue letting him treat you with nineteenth-century medicine, he'll be the death of you yet."

Dr. Russ started for the door. "An argument best settled another day. Your mother needs rest, and I must get back to the hospital."

Following him out, Mary touched his coat sleeve. "How can I ever thank you?"

He patted her hand, a strange smile lifting one side of his mouth. "Get the prescription filled and see to it your mother takes it faithfully for the next several days. You should see significant improvement by the weekend."

A fierce headache had driven Gilbert out of the office early in the afternoon. No doubt, he'd returned to work too soon after Monday's encounter with the pavement. But one more day stuck at home with only his mother and the house help for company, and he'd gladly have dived headfirst off the observation tower atop Hot Springs Mountain.

Aspirin. He needed aspirin. Pulling his roadster to the curb in front of Sorrell's Drug Company, two blocks south of the Arlington, he cut the engine and then waited for a horse and dray to pass before stepping from the car. Plenty of horse-drawn conveyances still traversed Hot Springs streets but seemed more and more like oddities as the number of automobiles increased. Standing on the sidewalk, Gilbert stared after the horse as it rounded the corner onto Bath Street.

Memories assailed him. The plodding horse, though straining against its heavy burden, still held its head high and proud, so like Rusty, the chestnut gelding Gilbert had ridden in France. Recalling the horse's tragic end evoked a pained moan from Gilbert's throat. Ambushed, his company had taken many casualties. Weakened by meager rations, bleeding profusely from a bayonet wound, the poor animal had bravely stumbled onward as Gilbert rallied his platoon and shouted orders. Only when the battle had ended and the survivors had straggled back to camp did the valiant horse succumb to his injuries. With a final shudder, Rusty dropped to his knees, breathed his last, and fell over dead.

Rusty . . . and so many like him. Horses and mules driven past the point of exhaustion then left to die where they fell. Gilbert could still smell the stench of rotting carcasses, and it tortured him to this day that while human soldiers were afforded at least a semblance of a proper burial, these animals, as crucial to the war effort as any doughboy, were treated as so much refuse.

Nausea curdled his stomach. Leaning hard upon his cane, Gilbert tipped his head forward and squeezed his eyes shut. The war would always be with him . . . always.

Gathering himself, he turned to enter the drugstore, only to see Mary march out the door, a small brown pharmacy bag clutched in her hand. Instead of the nurse's uniform he'd grown so accustomed to, she wore a plain white blouse over a pale blue pleated skirt. Except for a section of hair tied back from her face with a thin black ribbon, the rest of those thick, curling tresses hung loose about her shoulders, exactly the way Gilbert liked it.

He grinned in spite of himself, memories of war fading like mist beneath a searing summer sun. "Mary!"

She looked up with a start. Eyes the color of emeralds shimmered in recognition as a smile lit her features. She touched a hand to her temple as if to smooth her hair into place. "What are you doing out and about this time of day? Shouldn't you be at the Arlington?"

"I left early." He glanced at his watch—only half past four. "And shouldn't *you* be at the hospital? I thought your day off was tomorrow."

A worried look stole the smile from her lips as she explained about her mother. "Dr. Russ thinks this medicine will be better for her than what she's been taking."

"Dr. Russ thinks so, eh?" Gilbert instantly regretted his sarcastic tone. With an inward sigh, he ushered Mary beneath the building's awning and out of the line of foot traffic. "I mean, he's an army doctor. Are you sure he's the right one to be treating your mother's illness?"

"Not long-term, of course." Mary gave her head a tiny shake. "I'm just hoping I can finally convince Mum to leave Dr. Quatman's care and—"

"Quatman? *Quackman* is more like it! The old fuddy-duddy wouldn't know measles from malaria. I can't believe he's still allowed to practice medicine."

Mary harrumphed. "He may be behind the times and getting on in years, but his heart's in the right place."

"Ah, Mary, such an innocent." Gilbert tweaked one of her curls, the feel of it like satin sliding through his fingertips. If he thought she'd let him, he'd kiss her right here in front of Sorrell's and let every man traveling Central Avenue look on in envy.

"Don't patronize me, Gilbert Ballard." Her lower lip pushed out in a pout, an invitation for a kiss if Gilbert ever saw one. His stomach clenched. With effort, he raised his glance to her eyes as she continued. "I know it's high time we changed physicians, but with Mum's poor health and us not bein' rich like your family, Dr. Quatman's always let us pay what we could. I don't know who else would be so generous."

"Let me take your mother to see Dr. Lessman. He's the best civilian doctor in town."

"The best doctor money can buy, you mean." Lowering her gaze, Mary fingered the little brown bag. "We couldn't afford him, I'm certain."

Gilbert lowered his voice to a pleading whisper. "Then let me help."

She looked at him as if he could never understand—and maybe he couldn't. He'd never known anything but wealth. Even while he squandered his army pay on morphine, booze, and gambling debts, he'd always had family money to fall back on.

Suddenly, as he looked down at Mary in all her guileless-ness, his money seemed tarnished, even repulsive. He hadn't earned a cent of it. His wealth was merely a lucky accident of birth. All his life, the Ballard name had effortlessly opened doors for him when others of lesser means fought to beat down those doors with bloody fists.

His gaze fell to Mary's work-worn hands, and every broken fingernail, every tiny callus, every rough, red rash accused him. More than ever before, he grew determined to make his own way in the world, to be worthy of a woman like Mary. The Army may be through with him, but he still had a brain, and at least half a working set of limbs. There had to be something of value he could contribute to society.

Something besides his mother's money.

And he'd find it. Then he'd make Mary his wife, and they'd raise their children to know what truly mattered in life.

6

$\mathcal{D}$onald nudged his chair away from the table and patted his full belly. "Please, Mrs. Kendall, your pie is delicious beyond words, but I can't force down one more bite."

When Samuel's new in-laws had invited Donald to dinner after church, he'd hesitated at first. He hadn't had many opportunities to get acquainted with Annemarie's parents, and he suspected this might only be a "sympathy invitation" for a lonely bachelor with no family in town.

Then he'd spotted Pastor Yarborough headed his way with the austere but brilliant Patrice in tow, and he decided he'd take sympathy over matchmaking.

"In which case, I'll just have to send some pie home with you." Mrs. Kendall turned toward the kitchen with the pie dish. "I'll bring more coffee shortly, gentlemen."

Rising, Joseph Kendall crumpled his napkin beside his berry-smeared pie plate. "Why don't we have our coffee in the parlor, where the chairs are more comfortable?"

"I should go, really." Donald followed the burly man out of the dining room. "I'm sure you have better things to do with your Sunday afternoon than entertain a boring old army doctor."

"Nonsense. Ever since Samuel first introduced us, Ida and I have been looking forward to getting to know you better." Steering Donald across the foyer, Mr. Kendall ushered him to a plush sofa and then folded himself into an easy chair. "Ah, much better," he said, extending his legs across an ottoman.

Mrs. Kendall appeared in the doorway, coffeepot in one hand and the other propped against her hip. "Should have known I'd find you two sprawled out like a couple of idlers."

Her husband wagged a finger but didn't lift his head from the chair cushion. "It is the Sabbath, after all, my dear."

"What was I thinking? I should never have cooked dinner but simply let us all go hungry." She plopped the coffeepot onto a side table before flouncing off to the dining room. Moments later the clatter of cups and saucers echoed through the house.

If not for the twinkle he'd seen in her eye, Donald would have tried once again to politely take his leave and avoid a major marital showdown. Instead, he cast Mr. Kendall a wry grin. "It might be a good idea for us to give your wife a hand. Otherwise, we might find ourselves *wearing* our coffee."

"Perceptive young man, aren't you?" With a grumble, Mr. Kendall heaved himself out of the chair. "My poor dear Ida, do let us help you. We are absolute cads for not fetching our own cups."

When at last they'd all settled in the parlor and were sipping Mrs. Kendall's perfectly brewed coffee, Donald asked if they'd heard from the newlyweds.

"Not a word," Mrs. Kendall replied with a titter, "which doesn't surprise me in the least. I'm sure they're having a wonderful trip."

Donald set his cup on the lamp table at the end of the sofa. "I was walking downtown the other day and noticed Annemarie's shop is open. I take it she found someone to clerk for her while she's away?"

"Her good friend Dorothy Webb is helping out."

"Oh, yes, Annemarie's maid of honor." An attractive, if overly flirtatious young lady, and outspoken as well. Donald had no doubt she'd be a persuasive saleswoman.

Mrs. Kendall hiked a brow as she peered at Donald over the rim of her cup. "You should get to know Dorothy better. Perhaps next Sunday we can have you both over for dinner."

Great, more matchmaking. Everyone in town seemed intent on putting an end to his bachelorhood. "Very kind of you, but my rotation has me on duty at the hospital next weekend." Or at least he'd make certain such was the case. He glanced at his watch. "Speaking of the hospital, I really must be going. There's a patient I've been concerned about."

He failed to mention the patient was neither at the hospital nor serving in the military. But Nell McClarney had been on his mind since he'd accompanied Mary home the day her mother had taken ill. Yesterday, Mary had told him her mother was much improved, and thanked him again for the medication he'd prescribed. He had no real reason to return—Mrs. McClarney wasn't actually his patient, after all. Even so, he felt the need to see her again, just to set his mind at ease.

Yes, that was all. To set his mind at ease.

"Hello, Mrs. Lawson, it's Mary." One hand on the telephone earpiece, she used the other to dab a droplet of perspiration from her forehead. Even with all the windows wide open and electric fans circulating the air, the ward felt as toasty as a kitchen on Thanksgiving day.

Mrs. Lawson greeted her with a cheery hello. "Are you calling from the hospital, dear?"

"Yes, and we're shorthanded today, so I've been asked to work a second shift." Mary perused a patient's chart as she spoke. "Would you let Mum know, please? And remind her there's leftover pot roast in the icebox. All she has to do is heat it up."

A soft chuckle hummed through the telephone line. "I doubt pot roast is on the menu tonight."

"What?"

"Honey, your mother's had a gentleman caller all afternoon. Before they left in his fancy roadster awhile ago, she asked me to—"

"A gentleman caller?" Mary's pitch rose several notches. She ignored an orderly's wide-eyed glance as he fetched a stack of linens from a shelf beneath the counter. "They left in his *roadster?*"

"I was supposed to give you the message after you got home from work. They've gone out for a Sunday drive and then dinner."

"My sainted mother is out with a man." Swiveling, Mary collapsed against the counter. "I don't suppose you know the gentleman's name?"

"Well, of course. It's the tall, good-looking fellow you brought over from the hospital the other day. Dr. Russ." Mrs. Lawson tee-heed. "Oh, Mary, I've never seen your mother looking so radiant. Like a starry-eyed schoolgirl, she was!"

"Was she, now?"

"Don't sound so shocked, Mary. Your mother's still young and pretty, and she's been a widow long enough now to respectably take herself off the shelf."

"I suppose." Swallowing with difficulty, Mary explained she needed to return to her duties and ended the call.

Then, breathing hard, she pressed a hand to her mouth. In all the years since Da's death, Mum had never once voiced a desire to meet someone new. She was Mrs. Charles McClarney and always would be, at least in Mary's mind.

But to be fair, Mrs. Lawson was right. Mum had only turned forty-two last month. She boasted far more auburn in her hair than gray, and she bore scarcely a line or wrinkle upon her clear, ivory complexion. Only the ravages of bronchitis and a touch of arthritis in her hands made Mum seem older at times. Certainly not her looks nor her spunk.

And Dr. Russ? Mary hadn't thought about it before, but he must be close in age to Mum. He'd certainly seemed quite attentive the day he'd come to the house, and how many times since then had he pulled Mary aside at the hospital to inquire about her mother's health? Mary had thought it merely professional concern, but . . . could there be more to his interest?

For the rest of the afternoon, Mary pondered these thoughts while striving to make sure her preoccupation didn't interfere with the task at hand. She realized she'd failed miserably when a patient informed her she'd delivered him to the chiropody department, not his scheduled hydrotherapy session.

"Saints have mercy, I'm so sorry, Petty Officer Joelson." She bustled him back into the elevator and pressed the down button.

The wizened sailor reached up to pat her hand. "Not to worry, Nurse McClarney. I'm enjoying the ride."

"That may be, but if Mrs. Daley gets wind of how my head's been in the clouds today, she's likely to change her mind about my promotion."

"I heard you're moving up to the third floor at the end of the month. We'll sure miss your cheery face on the ward."

"Not to worry. I'll pop in to say hello as often as I can." They arrived at the lower level, and Mary aimed the wheelchair out of the building and along a covered gallery toward the hospital's expansive bathhouse. Handing her patient off to one of the attendants, Mary shot the petty officer a teasing grin. "Now, just you be behavin' yourself, or you'll find no dessert on your supper tray when you return."

Petty Officer Joelson responded with a crisp salute and a crooked smile. Mary waved as she turned to leave, but the moment she was alone in the walkway between buildings, fatigue washed over her. The new position as third-floor charge nurse sounded better all the time. Regular hours and higher pay—not to mention she'd have both more energy and more time to spend with Gilbert.

Oh, no—Gilbert! Mary checked the time on her watch pin, glad she'd taken it to a jeweler last week to have the clasp repaired. Half past six already, and Gilbert had expected her to finish work at four. He'd promised to have a picnic supper waiting for her at the bandstand just outside the hospital's upper gates on Carriage Road. The elegant marble structure and cascading stairways leading down to the Fordyce and Maurice bathhouses gave one the sense of treading the streets of ancient Rome.

How could she have neglected to telephone Gilbert with word she'd be working a double shift! True, she'd thought about calling . . . once or twice . . . only to talk herself into putting it off awhile longer. She hadn't been able to stomach the thought of Mrs. Ballard answering the call. If anyone could intimidate Mary more than Mrs. Daley, it was Gilbert's mother.

And then, of course, her remaining good intentions had been subverted by Mrs. Lawson's news. Mum and Dr. Russ—oh, my!

Well, like it or not, she must telephone the Ballard house at once. If Gilbert hadn't returned home yet, perhaps the kind servant Marguerite would answer. *Please, Lord, Mrs. Ballard thinks little enough of me as it is. Don't force me to make my apologies to her.*

"You owe me an apology."

Gilbert's brusque tone spun Mary around. She thrust a hand to her chest and peered up into hooded hazel eyes. "Gilbert! I'm sorry, truly I am."

"Do you have any idea what time it is?" He strode toward her, his shirt collar open and a stray lock of raven hair curling against his damp forehead. A small hamper swung from his left hand.

"I meant to let you know I'd be working late, but I got distracted and—" Just then the aromas of smoked ham and fresh-baked bread reached her nostrils. Her stomach growled loud enough to be heard on the other side of the mountain.

"Aw, Mary." Gilbert's resentful glare softened into compassion. He set down the hamper and laid his cane across it, then extended his hands to her. "You've been working all this time? You must be starved."

His sweet show of concern surprised her—and proved Mrs. Lawson wrong. Gilbert did care about others. He cared about Mary. She edged forward and took his hands. "Then you're not angry?"

He tucked in his chin, eyes closed for a moment as he squeezed her fingertips. When he glanced at her again, his brows slanted downward in chagrin. "You always think the worst of me, don't you? What will it take for me to win your trust?"

Looking away, Mary wondered as much herself. She knew in her heart Gilbert had changed. He was no longer the wounded soldier lashing out at everyone around him, depressed and angry and devoid of all hope of living a full life again. Nor was he the same vindictive man who'd intentionally set out to destroy his best friend. Gilbert's remorse was real; of that, Mary had no doubt.

But trust took time, and the love between them remained untested. And what of Annemarie Kendall Vickary? How long before Mary could be certain Gilbert had truly and fully put aside his feelings for his former fiancée? How long before Mary could trust he loved her and her alone?

She chewed her lip. "They'll be wondering what happened to me back on the ward. I should go."

"But you still haven't eaten." Releasing her hands, he gathered up the hamper and his cane. "I'll walk back with you. We'll have our picnic in the hospital corridor if we must. I'll toss bites of your sandwich to you as you flit between patients."

A thrill swelled beneath Mary's breastbone, a pleasant warmth completely unrelated to the heat of the summer evening. "Now, that wouldn't make a very pretty picture. I'd feel more like a trained seal at the circus than the girl who—" Her throat closed over the words she couldn't speak aloud: *the girl who loves you to distraction.*

Gilbert held her with his gaze, his eyes smoldering with unspoken affection. With the crook of his cane hooked over his wrist, he raised his hand to her temple and brushed aside a stray curl. "If you weren't on duty, I'd tear this silly cap from your head, lose myself in the scent of your hair, and kiss those luscious lips of yours until your knees went weak."

"My knees are weak just standin' here with you looking at me that way." Mouth dry as dust, still tingling from his touch, Mary sucked in a shivery breath. "And all the more reason you must let me return to work—*alone.*"

"But what about our picnic? Can't we—"

"No, we can't." Pleading with her eyes, Mary edged backward. "Things'll be different after my promotion. We'll have more time together, I promise."

"But it's still over a week away." Petulance had returned to Gilbert's tone. He planted the tip of his cane on the walkway then thrust the picnic hamper into her hands. "At least take this. You have to eat sometime."

"Gilbert—"

Ignoring her, he swung around and marched back the way he'd come, along the path toward Carriage Road and the bandstand.

What Mary wouldn't give to leave the cares of work behind and follow him! He could be so charming one moment, so possessive and needy the next. His neediness had drawn her to him in the first place; his charm held her.

But what attracted Gilbert to Mary besides his need? From those first stolen kisses in hospital storage closets, he hadn't concealed his physical desire for her—a desire she'd treasured but had never fulfilled, and wouldn't until the day he made her an honest woman.

Or, more correctly, made an honest man of himself by admitting he loved Mary for who she was and not simply as a substitute for the woman he'd given up, and then proving it by pledging his troth to her before family, friends, and God.

With an ache in her heart, she glanced down at the red gingham napkin covering the picnic hamper. The starched creases where the napkin had been folded were crisp and straight, no doubt Marguerite's handiwork. Sadly, more evidence of the great gulf separating Mary's family from Gilbert's. The Ballards had servants to iron Gilbert's shirts and press perfect creases into table linens. Twice weekly, Mary toiled over an ironing board to press the wrinkles out of her freshly laundered nurse's uniforms. The cloying smells of soap and starch would cling for hours afterward to the insides of her nostrils, while she often nursed burnt fingers and an aching back.

And just supposing Gilbert did marry her someday, Mary pondered as she strode back to the ward. Would she then have servants to clean and cook and wash and iron? Would she have to work at all, or would she spend her days in idle luxury?

A shudder raced along her limbs. She couldn't think of anything less satisfying.

7

*J*uggling housekeeping staff schedules—the least satisfying job Gilbert could imagine. Shoving away from his desk, he massaged his throbbing temple. His fingers grazed the jagged scar above his left ear, yet another reminder a whizzbang had shattered his arm and blew his leg to kingdom come. Being stuck in this foxhole of an office didn't do much to allay his war memories, either. One of these days—soon—he'd find another line of work. Preferably something to get him out into the fresh air.

No sir, no more office jobs. He'd rather drive a milk truck or walk a mail route. He could even raise ostriches like that crazy Thomas Cockburn. Yes, indeed, old Cockburn became the talk of Hot Springs when stunned visitors first saw him racing along Central Avenue in a cart pulled by Black Diamond, his prize ostrich.

At the sound of footsteps in the corridor, Gilbert shook off his daydreams and tried to look busy. He wasn't in the mood for another dressing-down from his nagging younger brother.

"Hello, Gilbert." Mary peeked through the open door. "Am I interrupting?"

Gilbert shot to his feet, bracing himself against the desk until he could lock his artificial knee. His eyes went immediately to the cloth-covered picnic hamper she carried. With a hesitant smile, he asked, "Is it *my* turn to forget some plans we'd made?"

"Not at all. I meant to surprise you." Looking fresh and lovely in a summery lavender-print frock, her thick, red hair curling about her shoulders, Mary sidled into the room and set the hamper on the desk. "After standing you up the other evening, I thought the least I could do was bring you lunch."

"Then you've forgiven me for walking away in such a snit?" He leaned forward, palms pressed into the desktop, hoping his eyes conveyed the depth of his regret. "I can only blame it on my disappointment that we couldn't spend the evening together."

"No more disappointed than I." Her lowered lashes, a mesmerizing shade of auburn, feathered against her cheek. With a sigh, she began spreading the contents of the basket across the desk. "I hope you like cold roast beef. I've also brought bread and cheese and apples."

"Wait." Gilbert thrust out a hand, and she looked up with a start. "I mean, not here. Let's go someplace where it doesn't smell like mildew and kitchen grease. Somewhere with grass and sunshine and wide-open spaces."

A smile turned up her pretty pink lips. "I'd love to, but can you get away?"

"Sure. Thomas won't mind." If he did, it was just too bad. Gilbert helped Mary repack the lunch items. "Let's go. My car's parked out back."

A few minutes later, Gilbert steered his roadster north along Park Avenue. Soon the pavement ended and the tires bounced across rough gravel. At the edge of town, he turned onto a rutted lane winding through the encroaching forest of pines and hardwoods.

"I've never been out this way before." Mary peered through the windscreen. "Do you fancy yourself another Meriwether Lewis, or do you have a clue where we're going?"

"It's a place where Thomas and I often played when we were boys." Gilbert's spirits lifted in anticipation. He hadn't expected to feel so excited about introducing Mary to this scene from his childhood. "There's a pond where we used to swim, and a big meadow where we'd fly kites."

"Sounds lovely. Your parents brought you?"

"We came out with . . . church friends." Why spoil the moment by mentioning names? "By then, my father had already been killed in the Spanish-American War."

Mary slid him a sideways glance tinged with sympathy. "I'd forgotten you were so young when he died. It's good you had family friends to step in."

"Yes, we were fortunate." Drifting into silence for a moment, Gilbert concentrated on the road ahead and tried not to think about those lazy Sunday afternoons he and Thomas used to spend with Annemarie and her parents.

"I must say, though, I'm having a wee bit of trouble picturing your mother going for a jaunt in the countryside."

Gilbert barked a laugh. "She did come out with us. Once. But you're right—this place is a tad too rustic for her tastes."

"Rustic, you say?" Hugging her knees, Mary sucked air between her teeth. "I hope there are no snakes."

"I'm sure there are, and plenty of them." Sensing Mary's genuine fear, Gilbert reached over to squeeze her hand. "Don't worry. We'll make enough noise to scare away any lingering reptiles."

"I promise you, Gilbert Ballard, if one tiny snake so much as flicks its forked tongue in my direction, I'll flee straight back to Ireland, sure enough."

"Ah, yes, I forgot dear old Saint Patrick banished all snakes from the Emerald Isle."

"So the story goes, but I've read scientists have other notions. Either way," Mary added with a shiver, "I may just have my lunch right here in the car with the doors closed tight."

Up ahead, Gilbert spied the beginnings of the split-rail fence at the edge of the property he searched for. Vines and scrub brush wove through the rotting timbers in a tangle, evidence of age and neglect. Had it been that long since he'd been here? He slowed the car and tried to remember how far it was to the gate.

"Are we almost there?" Mary asked.

"Close. I just didn't expect . . ." He gnawed his lip, his stomach tensing when he spotted the wide iron gate—or what was left of it. Rusted and crumbling, it twisted from one hinge and blocked the entrance to the property. Gilbert nosed the car into the space in front of the gate and breathed out a labored sigh.

"It doesn't look as if anyone's been this way in a while." Mary smoothed the cloth covering their lunch. "Maybe we should go back."

"Not until I find out what's happened." Shoving his door open, Gilbert grabbed his cane and climbed out of the car. He tried his weight against the gate and managed to nudge it a few inches, but not enough for the automobile to fit through.

Mary appeared beside him. "Let me help."

"Careful, you'll hurt yourself."

"I'm stronger than I look," she said with a laugh. Using a handkerchief to protect her palm, she grabbed hold of one of the iron crosspieces. "Let's each take one end and push together."

Their combined effort moved the gate far enough that when Gilbert inspected the opening, he decided the car had room to pass. They dusted off their hands, got in the car, and continued onto the property. Acres of overgrown pastures and weed-infested farmland stretched in both directions. Cleared areas amidst the pine forest now teemed with saplings, vines, and wild shrubs.

Mary pointed up ahead. "Is that a house?"

"Should be the barn. The house is farther back."

"It looks ready to collapse in a stiff breeze. Does someone still live here?"

"I don't know anymore." Gilbert tightened his grip on the steering wheel. He craned his eyes in search of the two-story farmhouse he remembered from his youth. "The Frederick family used to own the farm. I went to grammar school with their son, Hans. He dropped out in ninth grade to help his parents work the farm."

Mary exhaled softly. "It doesn't look like anyone's farmed this land in many a year."

The lane angled to the left, and they bounced past the remains of a silo covered in honeysuckle vines and swarming with bees. Just beyond, a figure beneath a dense veil of netting moved between two rows of hives.

Gilbert stopped the car and swung open his door. "Mrs. Frederick? Is that you?"

The woman looked up, paused for a moment, then sidled toward him. She brandished a stick, her posture not the least bit welcoming. "Who is it?" she barked, faint traces of a German accent still evident. "What do you want?"

Standing beside the roadster, Gilbert extended his hand. "It's Gil Ballard, ma'am. Remember? My brother, Tommy, and I used to ride out with the Kendalls after church and play with Hans and Emma."

"Gil. Gil Ballard!" The woman's shoulders sagged, and with a stifled cry she rushed forward, throwing off the netting. "Oh, son, I wondered if you'd made it back alive. How long have you been home?"

"Since December."

Her gaze fell to his cane. "You were wounded?"

"Lost a leg, that's all." Gilbert's dry laugh belied his sudden self-consciousness.

"Oh, you poor boy. If I had known . . . but I . . . I don't get to town so much." Her glance skittered sideways. She wavered, her free hand darting to her forehead. Distractedly she murmured, "It has all become so . . . hard."

The passenger door snapped shut, and Mary came around the front of the car. She took one look at Mrs. Frederick and then gently grasped her arm. "You should sit down, ma'am. Gilbert, there's a bottle of spring water in the hamper. Fetch it, please."

Confused and with growing concern, Gilbert obeyed. By the time he'd found the water and unscrewed the cap, Mary had guided Mrs. Frederick to a tree stump. He strode over and handed Mary the bottle. "Is she all right?"

"Exhausted and dehydrated." Mary helped Mrs. Frederick take several sips of water. Turning to Gilbert, she whispered, "Is she all alone here?"

He palmed the back of his head. "I don't—"

"They're gone. All gone." Mrs. Frederick released a shuddering moan as she gazed up at Gilbert. "Hans died of the influenza before he ever left Camp Pike. A month later his father died of grief."

Gilbert's heart clenched. "I'm so sorry. I didn't know." He stood at the woman's side, his hand resting on her shoulder. "But Emma—where is she?"

"Married and living in St. Louis." Bitterness laced Mrs. Frederick's tone. "She never cared a whit for the farm."

Gilbert remembered her well enough. While he and Thomas romped with Hans through the fields or took their fishing poles down to the pond, Emma would insist Annemarie come inside and play. Annemarie had often described how they'd cut paper dolls from the Sears, Roebuck & Co. catalogue, then furnish their dolls' make-believe houses with the latest kitchen appliances and home decor. Emma made no secret of her plans to have a fine house in a big city someday.

"How have you been getting by?" Gilbert's gaze swept the barren fields, the rundown house with its sagging front porch, the ancient tractor rusting away amidst a clump of weeds. "Have you had no help at all?"

Mrs. Frederick's eyes darkened in a scowl. "The folks in town, they don't like us Germans." An angry sob choked her. "I gave America my only son, but still I am an outcast."

Gilbert clenched his jaw. The Fredericks were good, upstanding, hardworking people. They'd emigrated nearly thirty years ago, and both their children were natural-born American citizens. "I can't believe this. Tell me who's treated you badly and I'll personally straighten them out."

At this, the woman looked away, rubbing her hands along her thighs. Her mouth moved silently, and she looked deathly pale.

"We must get her into the house," Mary said, touching Gilbert's arm. "She's not well." Lowering her voice, she added, "I'm not even certain she's in her right mind."

Mary hadn't pieced together exactly how Gilbert knew the old farm woman, but clearly he was concerned. Together they helped Mrs. Frederick up the path to her house and settled her on a faded brown settee in a sparsely furnished parlor. While Gilbert offered the woman sips of water, Mary found the kitchen and scoured the cupboards and pantry to see what was edible. The poor Mrs. Frederick was mere skin and bones, and Mary couldn't imagine she'd eaten a decent meal in days, if not weeks.

Finding nothing more substantial than a dry biscuit and some soured milk, Mary marched back to the parlor. "Go and fetch the picnic hamper. This woman needs food."

Looking helpless but determined, Gilbert strode out the front door. Mary returned to the kitchen and wet an old dishtowel, then had Mrs. Frederick lie back while she bathed the woman's face, neck, and arms with the cool cloth. "Just rest. We'll take good care of you, ma'am."

The tension lines in the woman's face began to ease. She lifted a hand to Mary's cheek. "Emma?"

"No, ma'am. I'm a friend of Gilbert's. My name is—"

"Annemarie." The momentary smile of recognition faded. "But no. Annemarie has dark hair."

Mary stifled the jealous twinge in her belly. She should have made the connection when she'd heard Gilbert explain to Mrs. Frederick about coming out to the farm with the Kendalls. How typical he'd choose to bring Mary to a place with so many memories of the girl he'd almost wed.

Hearing the front door open, Mary stood and turned as Gilbert walked into the parlor.

He met her gaze and froze. "Is she—is everything all right?"

Refusing to give in to her tangled emotions, Mary reached for the hamper and unpacked the contents onto a side table. She arranged thin slices of roast beef, a square of white cheese, and a slab of soft, doughy bread on one of the small china plates she'd brought. "Help her sit up, please."

Again, Gilbert did as he was told.

Sitting next to Mrs. Frederick, Mary placed the plate on the woman's lap. "Here, ma'am, eat something. It'll help you get your strength back."

Eyes wide, Mrs. Frederick looked down at the food as if it were manna from heaven. Tentatively she tasted first the bread, then the meat, and finally the cheese. Then, with a grateful sigh, she ate heartily, nodding and moaning as she chewed.

Gilbert's mouth firmed. He released an indignant snort. "Poor woman. She was starving."

Mary rose and stood beside him. "She can't stay here alone. There's not a thing worth eating in her pantry, the house is in dire need of repair, and she has no means of support."

"I have my bees." Mrs. Frederick's quiet declaration snapped Mary's head around. "A jar of honey for a few eggs and a loaf of bread is a good trade."

Gilbert cast Mary a doubtful frown. "Who trades with you, Mrs. Frederick?"

"I . . . well . . . a neighbor sometimes." She nibbled on a bread crust, her glance darting sideways. Then, lower lip trembling, she looked up as a tear slid down her cheek. In a small, frightened voice she said, "It's been so long, I can't remember."

"That settles it, Gilbert." Mary speared him with an insistent stare. "Surely there's someone in town who'll take her in. I'd offer myself, but Mum and I have barely enough room for the two of us."

Gilbert began to pace, his cane thumping against the creaky floorboards. "She'll come home with me, and—"

The china plate crashed to the floor. Mrs. Frederick stumbled to her feet so violently Mary rushed to her side before she collapsed. "*This* is my home. I will not leave!"

"There, now, no one's trying to take your home away." Mary wrapped one arm around the slight woman's waist and gently patted her knotted fists with the other. "But what will it hurt to let someone take care of you for a while? Just till you're stronger. Your farm will be right here waiting for you."

Mrs. Frederick swallowed and sniffed. Relaxing slightly, she looked from Mary to Gilbert. "To rest for a while would be a good thing, yes. I'm tired . . . so tired."

The woman's full weight, insubstantial as she was, pressed against Mary. She helped Mrs. Frederick back to the settee, gathered up the broken plate and scraps of food, and repacked the picnic hamper. Nudging Gilbert into the front hall, she whispered, "Are you sure about taking her home with you? What will your mother say?"

"She'll call me a bleeding-heart fool, naturally." With a quick glance into the parlor, Gilbert shook his head. "Why in God's name has no one else bothered to check on her?"

Mary wondered the same thing. Where was the church at times like this? Where were the neighbors? She pictured Annemarie Kendall in her fancy pottery shop, dressed in the latest fashion, hair done up in swirls and poufs like the Grand Duchess of Luxembourg. If the Kendalls had known the Fredericks well enough their children played together, how could they now have turned their backs on the family?

Perhaps Annemarie Kendall Vickary wasn't the paragon of virtue Gilbert and the rest of Hot Springs imagined her to be.

Thomas Ballard had more sense than to stick his nose into an argument between his mother and Gilbert. Still, he couldn't resist eavesdropping from the upstairs landing. He'd wondered all afternoon where his brother had disappeared. Someone from the hotel kitchen mentioned seeing Gilbert leave around noon with a redhead carrying a picnic basket.

Mary, obviously.

Thomas had nothing against Mary, but he certainly had a bone to pick with Gilbert about taking off work without notice.

Except now, Gilbert was downstairs insisting Mother put Mrs. Frederick up in the guest room. The hapless woman looked emaciated, not to mention much older and grayer than Thomas remembered. She must have fallen on hard times. What had happened to her husband, her children? And what in the world had led Gilbert to find her and then bring her here?

It had been a good ten years since Thomas could recall being at the old Frederick place. His friendship with Hans had faltered when Mr. Frederick insisted Hans drop out of school to help his father on the farm. A waste of a smart kid, in Thomas's opinion. Hans outscored Thomas on every exam.

Then there was Emma. Pretty Emma with flaxen curls and eyes the color of blue Delft china. She'd captured Thomas's heart when he was barely a lad of twelve, and he'd entertained visions of marrying her someday.

There was one small problem, however. From the time she first became aware of her own beauty and learned how to flirt, it was obvious Emma had a mountain-size crush on Gilbert.

First Emma, then Annemarie, and now Mary. Gilbert always got the girls.

Yes, apparently, Thomas was doomed to remain in his older brother's shadow. It wasn't a position he much cared for.

8

*M*rs. Daley had graciously given Mary the last two days of June off, which allowed her time to catch up on errands and household chores before beginning her new position on Tuesday. She hadn't had much time to miss Gilbert while on duty at the hospital, but now Sunday had arrived, and with a whole afternoon stretching before her with only Mum and the laundry to keep her company, she wished he'd drop by.

She'd tried the past few days not to let disappointment get the best of her, but she couldn't help feeling sorry for herself. Gilbert seemed too busy seeing to Mrs. Frederick's concerns even to meet Mary after work to see her home.

Resentful of an impoverished widow? How could Mary be so callous? Truly, she did have sympathy for the woman. *Forgive me, Jesus. I'm just missing Gilbert.*

Balancing a wicker laundry basket on her hip, Mary edged down the narrow hallway to her mother's bedroom. She found Mum sitting at her dressing table fiddling with a pot of rouge.

"What do you think of this color, luv? Too rosy for my complexion?"

Mary's eyebrows shot up. "And when, pray tell, did my dear old mum start coloring her cheeks?"

"I hate looking so pale and sickly all the time. Ginny picked this up at Schneck's for me."

"Oh, did she, now?" Mary lifted her nose in the air as she set the laundry basket on her mother's bed. "And I suppose you're expecting your gentleman caller again this afternoon?"

Her mother had the decency to blush—all the color Mary cared to see on Nell McClarney's face. "Donald said he might come by after he makes his rounds."

Donald. Mary had been hearing about Mum's outing with the good doctor all week. And trying not to think about it. She was still sorting out her feelings about the possibility of her mother's falling in love again at this stage in life—concerns she'd dearly hoped to share with Gilbert while on their picnic last Tuesday, until her plans fell to nothing when they'd come upon Mrs. Frederick's sad state of affairs.

Mary's mother came up beside her as she folded a nightgown. "Dearest, what's the matter? You've not been yourself since we returned from Mass. And Ginny noticed you seemed a bit sad during Father Francis's message this morning."

Mary winced to realize she'd done such a poor job of hiding her feelings. Not that Genevieve Lawson wasn't almost like a second mother to her—or a beloved, if sometimes a bit too nosy, aunt. "It was just the text had me teary-eyed. 'Jehovah preserveth the sojourners; He upholdeth the fatherless and widow; But the way of the wicked he turneth upside down.'"

"Psalm 146, verse nine." Mum pressed her cheek against Mary's. "I've dwelt upon that Scripture many a time since your father went to be with the Lord." She lifted an embroidered cotton pillowcase from the basket and laid it in Mary's growing stack of ironing to be done. "I'm praying it daily for the poor woman you brought to the Ballards' house last week. Have you any news about what's to become of her?"

"I've heard nothing from Gilbert since he delivered me home afterward." Useless to even attempt to disguise the petulance in her tone. Again, she silently pled the Lord's forgiveness. With a sigh, she gathered up the linen and clothing destined for the ironing board. "I'd best get started, or I'll never finish by suppertime."

Later, with an electric fan circulating sultry air through the kitchen, Mary sweltered over steamy sheets and pillowcases and wondered how people like Mrs. Ballard passed a Sunday afternoon on a hot June day. Sipping iced beverages on a breezy front porch, no doubt.

She'd just pressed and folded an embroidered pillowcase when a distant knock sounded from the front of the house. For a happy moment her heart skittered in hopes it might be Gilbert. Self-consciously she buttoned the collar of her housedress and tucked damp strands of hair into her bun.

Then, before she could make her way to the door, her mother's voice echoed in the foyer. "Why, Donald, what a delightful surprise!"

The bubble inside Mary's breast turned to stone. Bad enough Gilbert seemed to have forgotten she existed. Now she must don a cheerful attitude and pretend it didn't scare her half to death her dear mum could well be falling in love with the handsome and brooding Dr. Russ.

Gilbert sat in the study behind his late father's massive desk, a warm breeze lifting the gauze window curtains. Across from him, Mrs. Frederick twisted a handkerchief in her lap. For the past few days Gilbert had been examining the woman's financial options—or lack thereof—so thoroughly preoccupied he'd hardly taken note of the celebrations in town during the weekend. News had come yesterday that Germany had at long last signed the Treaty of Versailles.

Peace may have been finally and officially declared in Europe, but there would be no peace for Mrs. Frederick unless Gilbert found a way for her to keep her farm. Apparently, no amount of argument or common sense would compel her to sell.

Her health, at least, wasn't of so much concern since she'd been eating three hearty and nutritious meals every day. Dr. Lessman had come over Tuesday evening to examine her and found nothing to add to Mary's diagnosis of exhaustion and dehydration.

Gilbert could have gladly strangled Pastor Yarborough for failing so miserably in seeing to the needs of his flock, until Mrs. Frederick reluctantly confessed she'd run the pastor and "all those pious hypocrites" off her property immediately after her husband's burial. Seemed the pastor and his cronies had wasted no time in badgering the recent widow to divest herself of the farm—at a price well below its worth, so she insisted— and "live a life of ease" in town. Well intentioned, true, but clearly they'd disregarded the woman's pride.

Pinching the bridge of his nose to stave off the beginnings of another headache, Gilbert eased his chair away from the desk. With a quiet groan, he lowered his hand and cast Mrs. Frederick a regretful glance. "I know it isn't what you want to hear, but maybe the church folk were right. Your life at the farm has become unsustainable. If you go back to the way things were, you'll work yourself to death out there and no one will know."

The woman stiffened. "I would rather work hard and die alone on my own land—the land my family sacrificed their very lives for—than to idle my days away in a rocking chair like a rich, pampered dowager."

Cringing, Gilbert peered toward the door, thankful he'd had the good sense to leave it closed so Mother couldn't eavesdrop. She was peeved enough Gilbert had allowed Mrs. Frederick to stay so long already.

He stared again at the list of Mrs. Frederick's assets he'd compiled, which didn't amount to much more than eight beehives, a wagon (but not the mule to pull it; she'd traded old Buster last year for enough smoked pork to see her through the winter), a cow who hadn't given milk in months, plus the house and outbuildings—or what remained of them—and the land itself.

He shook his head. "I'm sorry, Mrs. Frederick. I don't—"

The idea hit him so hard he nearly tipped his chair backward. One hand slammed against the desktop. He swiveled sideways, his brain spinning faster than an airplane propeller.

"I have made you angry." Mrs. Frederick stood, her spine straight as a fencepost. "You will let me go home now, please. I will not trouble you further."

"I'm not angry—far from it!" Gilbert couldn't suppress the smile spreading across his lips as he turned to face the wiry little woman. "In fact, I may have the solution to both our problems."

Confusion contorted Mrs. Frederick's weathered face. "I don't understand."

"Sit down and I'll explain." Except he couldn't, really. No easy way to put into words his discontent after the Army discharged him, the private humiliation of working for his brother, his need to make his own way apart from his family's money. No way to describe the futility and frustration of searching for something to do with his life to provide the personal satisfaction he craved.

Finally, he stated simply, "I want to buy your farm."

Once again, she shot up from the chair. "Have I not made myself abundantly clear? The farm is *not* for sale!"

"Hear me out. Please." Gilbert waited until she lowered herself to the edge of the seat cushion, still poised for flight. "I propose to purchase your farm and then commence repairs immediately on the house and barn. While the work is underway, you may continue to live here. Once the house has been refurbished, I'll take up residence and—"

"I beg your pardon!"

"I'm not finished yet." He inhaled long and slow as he framed his next words. "Mrs. Frederick, I fully intend you should live and work at the farm as long as you desire and are able. In exchange, I'm asking you to allow me to assume ownership and management. I would also be most grateful if you would serve as my . . . my helper and advisor."

She scooted deeper into the chair, her teeth working her lower lip. The handkerchief had become a wrinkled lump between her hands. As if speaking to herself, she murmured, "I know the seasons of planting and reaping, yes. And I am strong. I can cook and clean and tend the hives." With a tentative glance at Gilbert, she asked, "You would do this for me?"

"I would. I want to. Desperately." Rising, he edged around to her side of the desk and reached for her hand. "Please consider my offer, Mrs. Frederick. If you agree, you would be doing me an immeasurable kindness."

Silence stretched endlessly between them, the woman's tight-lipped frown and darting glance the only signs of her inner struggle. Finally, she lifted her gaze to Gilbert's. "I could keep my bees?"

"I wouldn't have it any other way."

"In that case, yes, I will consider your offer." Mrs. Frederick rose. Chin in the air, she added, "But I will see it in writing, please. What you will pay, when you will begin work, what my status will be. Everything legal and official."

Relief swept through Gilbert, along with an urge to wrap the woman in a bear hug. Instead, he solemnly took her hand and gave it a single, firm shake. "I shall present a formal offer to you as soon as my attorney can draw up the papers."

✐

Nell suppressed a giggle as Donald set the bell of his stethoscope against her back. The cool metal chilled her all the way through her dress and chemise.

"Deep breath, please. . . . Very good." Donald moved the stethoscope to the other side. "Again."

Exhaling, Nell glanced over her shoulder at the wavy-haired doctor. "Forgive me for askin', but is this a social call, or only another medical examination?"

Donald's eyes twinkled. "Will you send me on my way if I answer 'both'?"

"It depends on what brought you here in the first place."

"Hmm, then let me be careful how I answer." A mischievous smile curled his lips as he folded his stethoscope and packed it away in his medical bag. "I'd have to say . . . definitely a social call. But, of course, it's essential the lady of the house is feeling well enough to socialize."

Nell's heart fluttered and not because of any health problems. Truth be told, she hadn't felt this well in years. "I've been faithfully taking the medicine you prescribed, and it's worked wonders." Or was it merely the attentions of the good doctor himself?

"I'm glad. Your lungs sound even clearer than when I visited last Sunday." Donald nudged his medical bag aside and stretched one arm along the back of the settee.

Nell shivered when his fingers grazed her shoulder. She tucked her hands into her lap and released a shaky sigh.

"Nell? What's wrong?"

"It's just . . . I don't quite know what to make of your visits." She trembled again. "Or the way they make me feel."

He withdrew his arm and sat forward. "If I've made you uncomfortable in any way—"

"It isn't that," she hurried to say. "But I'm not a girl anymore, not young and pretty like my sweet child, Mary. Are you sure you wouldn't rather—I mean—"

Donald edged closer and wrapped his hands around hers. "In case you haven't noticed, I'm a bit worse for wear, myself." His tone mellowed to a throaty murmur. "I won't deny Mary caught my eye more than once as we've worked together at the hospital. But after meeting you, I could see how Mary came by her beauty, kindness, and charm. Age brings its own beauty, and along with it, maturity and grace. These are the qualities I see in you, Nell, and why I want very much to spend more time with you."

She studied the hands holding hers and admired the neatly manicured nails, the manly tufts of dark hair along each finger, the ropy veins traversing the backs of his hands. So unlike Charles's, palms callused from hard work, nail beds permanently darkened with grime. She tried to imagine waking up every morning to find those soft but firm doctor's hands caressing her face.

After all these years, was it truly possible she could fall in love again? Possible someone as charming and considerate as Dr. Donald Russ might cast his affections upon her? Oh, she wanted to believe so!

With a timid smile, she glanced up. "If you're asking permission to court me, Dr. Russ, I'm agreeing."

Pressed against the kitchen door, Mary spread her fingers across her cheeks. There could be no doubts now; Mum was falling for Dr. Russ, and he for her. Mary shouldn't have listened in, but how could she help herself? They sat right there in the parlor with her just around the corner finishing up the ironing.

When Dr. Russ had arrived earlier, she'd swallowed her disappointment it wasn't Gilbert, then dabbed the perspiration from her face and marched to the parlor to offer a polite greeting. The doctor fooled no one with his pretense of stopping by to confirm her mother's good health. Anyone could see by the adoring look in his eyes, he'd come a-courting.

Mum was certainly beyond the age of needing a chaperone. Even so, after returning to her chores, Mary made sure to slam the iron down once or twice and give the linens a good snap now and then so Dr. Russ would have no doubt he and Mum weren't alone in the house.

More than anything, she wanted her mother's happiness, and seeing Mum so vibrant and healthy these past several days was a blessing indeed, but . . .

Oh, Da, how I wish you were here! Dr. Russ is a good man, but he's not you, and no one will ever take your place in my heart.

She set the iron aside and slipped out the back door, letting the afternoon breeze waft across her perspiring face. Memories of her father crept in—his booming laugh, the shock of red hair cresting his forehead, the smells of sweat and grime permanently embedded in his clothes. He'd trudge home exhausted from a hard day's labor but still find the strength to sweep Mary into his arms and tell her she was his precious Irish lass.

"Now be an angel and help your ol' da off with his boots," he'd say, the pungent scent of peppermint lacing his breath.

Then he'd plop into a kitchen chair while Mary's mother brought supper to the table.

"Did you bring a peppermint for me, Da?" Mary would ask as she worked to loosen the stiff laces of his dirt-encrusted boots.

He'd mutter and grumble while fishing through his pockets, and Mary would fear this time he'd forgotten. But then his eyes would twinkle and he'd produce a wrapped candy, always from a different pocket just so Mary would never guess which one.

She'd been so young then, so innocent, never suspecting those happy days would be cut short.

Her stomach clenched. She gripped the porch rail and squeezed her eyes shut as an image of a rearing horse flashed through her mind, then her father bleeding and unconscious in the middle of Central Avenue.

Then the long years of Da's recovery . . . only he never *really* recovered. His body healed, but the headaches, memory lapses, and uncontrolled rages only worsened with the passage of time. The playful, tenderhearted father Mary remembered had vanished.

"Mary, there you are."

Drawing a quick breath, Mary spun around to find her mother framed in the back door. "Just catching a breath of air." She pasted on a quick smile and shoved aside the sad memories. "High time I finished the ironing, isn't it?"

9

On Monday morning, as Marguerite dished scrambled eggs onto Gilbert's plate, he glanced at his brother across the table. "Can you do without me at the hotel this morning? I have some business I need to attend to."

Thomas smirked. "*Asking* for time off? Generally you just take it whenever the mood strikes."

"Admit it. My job is basically a charity position anyway." Gilbert stabbed a sausage. "When I don't show up, I'm saving the hotel money they could better spend on lobby accoutrements or new china and silverware."

Gilbert's mother sashayed into the dining room. "Boys, are you bickering again?"

"Absolutely not, Mother." Thomas stirred cream into his coffee. "Bickering is for sissy schoolgirls. Gil and I prefer fisticuffs."

Gilbert narrowed one eye. "And I could still give you a good thrashing even missing a leg and with my good arm tied behind my back." He shoved a forkful of eggs into his mouth and washed them down with a gulp of coffee. "So, may I take the morning off or not?"

"Never let it be said I was uncharitable toward my elder brother." Shifting sideways, Thomas reached for the folded newspaper next to his plate. He spread it open and disappeared behind the pages.

Draping a napkin across her lap, Gilbert's mother nodded for Marguerite to serve her breakfast. She raised a brow in Gilbert's direction. "I do hope your reason for taking the morning off involves returning our . . . houseguest . . . to her own abode."

"I'm afraid not, Mother. Mrs. Frederick will be staying on awhile longer. A *good* while longer, most likely, seeing how her *abode* is virtually unlivable." Fortunately for Mrs. Frederick, the woman preferred taking her meals in the kitchen with Marguerite and thus avoided the worst of Evelyn Ballard's not-so-subtle disparagement.

"I daresay," Gilbert's mother said with a sniff, "you have developed quite an unpleasant habit lately of involving yourself with people beneath your class."

She referred to Mary, of course. Clamping his teeth together, Gilbert refused to acknowledge such prejudice.

A dramatic sigh filled the air. "I shall forever regret I shan't have Annemarie Kendall as my daughter-in-law. How you could let that lovely girl get away—"

"Mother!" Gilbert shoved away from the table. "First of all, I didn't *let* her get away. I *pushed* her away. And yes, I was a blasted fool for doing so. But it's done. She's married to Samuel now, and I've had to accept he's more the man for her than I could ever be. It's time you accepted it as well."

Leaving his breakfast unfinished, Gilbert grabbed his cane and strode from the room. With a folder of notes on the Frederick farm in hand, he found Zachary and asked him to bring the roadster around. Within minutes, he parked the automobile on Central Avenue in front of his attorney's office.

While he described his intentions to Martin Greenslade, the bushy-browed lawyer puffed on a smelly pipe and muttered, "Hmmm . . . hmmm."

"Well? Is it feasible or not?"

"Certainly feasible. Advisable? That's another question entirely." Greenslade set his pipe in a large marble ashtray. "I don't see the wisdom in pouring money into a hopeless enterprise. You're not a farmer, Gil. What can you honestly expect to do with the place?"

Get out from under my mother's roof and my brother's employment, for starters. "Mrs. Frederick has enough experience for us both. I'll depend upon her for anything I need to know about farming."

Greenslade hemmed and hawed some more while perusing Gilbert's financial calculations. "Even if I agree the Frederick farm is a worthwhile investment—which I don't by any means—what makes you think your mother will advance you the funds from your trust account? I feel quite certain she will not approve of this purchase."

"I feel quite certain you're correct." Gilbert massaged his left thigh. It was aching again. "But let me worry about Mother. With a little persuasion, she'll come around."

"Very well, then. I'll draw up the necessary documents. Provided you can work out the monetary details with your mother, you may bring Mrs. Frederick in . . ." The attorney consulted his calendar. "Let's say Thursday morning at nine."

Gilbert left the attorney's office with more hope in his breast than he'd felt in months. It felt good—so very good—to move forward again with a clear goal. Not since his acceptance to West Point had he sensed anything so close to resembling a true calling, a purpose, a reason to exist.

It may not be the U.S. Army career he'd planned, but he hoped his father would look down from heaven and be proud of him all the same.

He halted on the sidewalk next to his roadster, a pang of regret twisting his heart. *I wish you were here, Dad.* Since the war, he needed his father more than ever. What he wouldn't give for a hefty dose of fatherly advice and affirmation. But Captain Noah Ballard would remain little more than a vague childhood memory for Gilbert, even more so for Thomas, barely a toddler when enemy fire felled their father at the Battle of San Juan Hill.

Nostalgia crowding out his earlier enthusiasm, Gilbert felt a familiar craving deep in his gut. Old habits took hold, and he rummaged through his pockets in search of a nonexistent vial of morphine tablets. *Just one . . . just—*

Cursing his weakness, he carved trenches through his hair with leaden fingers. What would Mary say to such idiocy? Probably chastise him with Scripture. She seemed particularly fond of the verse that stated, "for of whom a man is overcome, of the same is he also brought into bondage."

Yes, he'd been a slave to morphine for far too long. Not to mention self-pity, despair, and misdirected rage. Reminding himself he'd just set in motion a plan to propel him toward a much more satisfying future, he drew his shoulders back and inhaled a brisk, bracing breath of Ouachita Mountain air.

Then, as he started around to the driver's side of his roadster, someone called his name.

"I say, it *is* you, Gil Ballard!" A gentleman in an expensive-looking gray suit and bowler hat strode up the sidewalk, a grin splitting his face. "Why, I'd know you anywhere, you old reprobate!"

It took only a moment for Gilbert to recognize his former school chum. "Watch who you're calling names, Arthur Spence. I know where your secrets are buried."

Arthur guffawed. "Don't I know it!" He extended his arm for a handshake only to draw up short. "A cane? Not the bloody war, I hope?"

Gilbert deftly switched the cane to his left hand and seized Arthur's with his right. "Just a scratch, hardly worth mentioning."

"Glad to hear it. Lost too many of our boys over there." Arthur clapped Gilbert on the shoulder. "Bet you gave your sweetheart a real scare, though. I suppose you and the fair Annemarie have tied the knot by now?"

Hiding his wince with a nonchalant laugh, Gilbert glanced away. "Afraid not."

Arthur shook his head in disbelief. "Don't tell me she didn't wait for you? I thought more of her."

"And you still should." Gilbert shrugged. "It just wasn't meant to be. She's happily married now, and I wish her only the best."

"Aren't you the noble fellow? Better man than I, for sure."

Time to change the subject. "What are you doing back in town? I thought you'd gone to Boston to join your uncle's manufacturing firm."

"Indeed. And we were doing quite a lucrative business supplying the war effort with textiles for uniforms, blankets, tents, and such. However, the factory is in a retooling mode, so my uncle sent me home for a few weeks." Arthur glanced toward the ground with a dejected sigh. "Unfortunately, demand dried up considerably after the Armistice."

Gilbert couldn't see anything *unfortunate* about the end of the Great War. He was also beginning to remember why he and Arthur hadn't remained particularly close after graduation.

The man had always been an opportunist, perfectly willing to succeed at someone else's expense.

Having enough of this unexpected reunion, Gilbert switched his cane over to his right hand again and angled one foot toward the street. "It's good to see you again, Art. We'll have to—"

"Not rushing off, are you? Look, it's the last day before Prohibition shuts down all our favorite haunts. Have a drink with me for old time's sake. Goodine's is just down the street."

"Well, I . . ." Gilbert swallowed, imagining the yeasty taste of a cold beer, the foam tickling his upper lip and the amber liquid sliding down his suddenly parched throat. One drink— what could it hurt? "Sure, why not?"

✑

"Gilbert's a busy man about town, lass. Stop your frettin' and help me figure out this knitting pattern before I go cross-eyed."

Mary turned from the parlor window with a frown. "I'm *not* fretting. I'm only watching for . . . the postman."

"Yes, and Father Francis will be waiting for you in the confessional as usual next Sunday." Mary's mother squinted at the detailed instructions for a man's cardigan sweater. "Do you suppose I should make this a wee bit smaller through the chest for Donald? He's tall, but not nearly so brawny as your da was."

"Yes—no. I mean—" If Mary were not a mature adult, she'd give her foot a good, hard stomp. "And what are you doing starting on a woolen sweater in the middle of summer anyway? That's work for a cold winter's day."

"Not if I want it finished before winter comes. Besides, these old fingers don't work as well when the cold sets in."

Mary plopped onto the settee. "All right, then, if you're bound and determined to roast like a Christmas goose. Let me see those instructions."

Mum handed her the paper with a glare. "And you'll curb your snappish tone with me, young lady."

"Sorry, Mum." Meekly, Mary perused the directions, but once she read past how many stitches to cast on, she was as lost as her mother. "This is beyond my meager knitting skills. You'd best ask Mrs. Lawson for help."

"Oh, dear, I was afraid when I ordered this pattern it might be more of a challenge than I expected." Mum patted Mary's arm. "Be a lamb and run next door to ask if Ginny can pop over."

Mary groaned inwardly. "Now?"

"Yes, *now.*" Her mother quirked her lips. "If I once get started, I'll have something to keep me busy when you're back at the hospital tomorrow." She shooed Mary toward the door. "Off with you, child. And don't dawdle."

While Mary couldn't be gladder to see her mother in such good spirits, she wasn't sure she cared for *all* the changes she'd observed since Dr. Russ came into Mum's life. Why, this morning Mum had even suggested perhaps it was time they installed a telephone—a suggestion less to do with calling Mary at the hospital in case of emergency and more with receiving calls from a certain doctor on staff.

Although, if Mary had a telephone right now, she'd be sorely tempted to ring up Gilbert and insist he tell her exactly where their relationship stood. Where had he been keeping himself all week? Surely, Mrs. Frederick didn't require *that* much attention?

Grumbling all the while, Mary stepped into the afternoon sun and traipsed across the lawn to Genevieve Lawson's front door. She pressed the buzzer then crossed her arms and glared toward the street while she waited. Through Mrs. Lawson's open parlor windows came the tinny sounds of a phonograph recording:

> *There's a song in the land of the lily,*
> *Each sweetheart has heard with a sigh.*
> *Over high garden walls this sweet echo falls*
> *As a soldier boy whispers goodbye:*
> *Smile the while you kiss me sad adieu*
> *When the clouds roll by I'll come to you.*

A tender melody Mary had heard often over the past year, in recordings, radio broadcasts, or from the lips of melancholy soldiers and sailors as they stared out the window in the hospital day room.

Then another memory assailed her—the night last winter when Gilbert had taken her to dinner at the Emerald Club. Mary had felt like a princess as she followed Gilbert in his wheelchair to their table. From the attentive waiters to entertainment by the lovely songstress Carla Steiner, the evening couldn't have been more delightful.

At least until Gilbert had noticed Annemarie seated at a table across the room. Then he couldn't seem to leave the restaurant quickly enough.

And the song Carla Steiner sang as they stopped in the lobby to retrieve Mary's wrap from the coat check was "Till We Meet Again."

. . . a soldier boy whispers goodbye . . .

Mary shivered despite the harsh glare of sunshine. *How long before you tell me goodbye, Gilbert? How long till it's over between us before it's barely begun?*

With a sigh, she thumbed the doorbell again, then rapped her knuckles hard against the door. Surely Mrs. Lawson was home, or she wouldn't—

The door swung open. "Hello, Mary. Sorry, I had the Victrola playing too loudly to hear the bell. Come in, dear."

"No, thanks. I'm just on an errand for Mum. She'd like your help with a knitting pattern, if you've the time."

"Of course. Tell her I'll be there shortly."

Mary nodded and started down the porch steps. Chiding herself for the self-pity she couldn't seem to shake, she stared at her toes as she shuffled through the grass and paid little notice when an automobile careened around the corner. Only when the brakes squealed and the car halted at the end of her front walk did she look up.

When she recognized Gilbert's blue Cole Eight Roadster, her belly slammed into her backbone. With one hand smoothing imagined wrinkles from her skirt and the other tucking a stray curl behind her ear, she strove for composure that simply wouldn't come. How could she ever hope to stay peeved with Gilbert if her knees turned to jelly every time she saw him?

"Mary, I'm glad you're home!" A crooked grin dimpling his cheeks, Gilbert latched the car door and marched around to the sidewalk.

She tried to wedge some starch into her tone. "It's my day off. Where else would I be?" What she wanted to ask was, *Where have you been?*

Then he came near enough for her to notice his breath, and she knew *exactly* where he'd been. She thrust both hands to her hips, this time having no trouble at all pouring the full force of her disappointment into her words. "Gilbert Ballard, you've been drinking."

He had the decency to look sheepish, but the smile never left his face. "Just a couple of beers is all." Then he laughed out loud. "Oh, Mary, I wish you could have seen it! Ol' Goodine was serving beer to elephants!"

Mary snapped her head back. "Elephants? Now I'm certain you've had too much to drink."

"No, I'm serious. With Prohibition closing the saloons tomorrow, Goodine's been pouring beer like crazy all day. Then this man comes in with two elephants—right up to the bar! Apparently, the pachyderms love beer, so Goodine fills a tub and carries it out to the sidewalk, where three more elephants are waiting, and now there are *five* elephants slurping up the suds like nobody's business!"

"Is that so? Are you sure it wasn't a bunch of inebriated sots who were *drinking* like elephants?" Mary spun on her heel and marched up the porch steps. The man was hopeless, and so were their chances of ever making this relationship work.

"Mary. Stop." The timbre of his voice had mellowed. "I know you're mad, and I'm sorry. But I'm not drunk, and I'm not making this up, I promise." He caught up to her on the porch, blocking her from escaping inside. "Look, none of it matters anyway. I came over because I've got something to tell you. Something important." He lifted his hand to her cheek, his touch gentle yet pleading. "Something to change everything."

She trembled, her gaze searching his for any clue to his meaning. Once again, he'd taken her through the full gamut of emotions in a matter of moments—from hope to despair to anger and back to hope again. Twisting away from him, she clung to the porch rail as if it could save her from drowning in this torrent of confusing feelings. "All right, then, say what you've come to say, and be quick about it. I've still some chores to do before—"

His grip on her upper arm startled her into silence. He loomed over her, his eyes darkening, his breath hot upon her face. His voice grew deep and quietly commanding. "Mary. Listen to me for once, will you?"

Her tone in response seemed feeble in comparison. "And why should I, when you've ignored me for almost a week now? Nary a word—"

His exasperated sigh ended with his lips smothering hers. Heat suffused her limbs, driving every rational thought from her brain. The heavy sweetness of a malty ale clung to his mouth, a reminder of where he'd spent the last few hours, and though the taste of his lips evoked a haunting sense of unease, Mary couldn't bring herself to pull away. She wanted more . . . desperately. She wanted to believe this kiss embodied the love he had yet to speak aloud to her.

His mouth softened into a lazy grin as their lips parted. "Does this tell you how much I've missed you?"

After that kiss she wouldn't even feign annoyance. She only nodded, her breathing shallow, her lips ablaze.

"Now, then, if you've forgiven me for enjoying a beer or two with an old friend, I'd like to tell you my news. Do you want to hear it here, or shall we go inside?"

Mary glanced toward the open parlor window, where surely her mother had heard every word they'd spoken. Then, at the sound of Mrs. Lawson's front door closing, she caught Gilbert's wrist and tugged him down the steps. "Let's talk out back, where it's more private."

Once they were side by side on the backyard glider, Mary folded her hands in her lap, spine stiff as a primly laced-up spinster. Which she might well remain unless Gilbert changed his ways. "I'm ready. You may tell me now."

Giving his head a small shake, Gilbert chuckled softly. "Don't make it sound as if I'm signing your death warrant. It's *good* news, Mary. Good for both of us." When she slid her gaze toward him, he leaned closer. "I've spent the past week figuring out how best to help Katrina Frederick stay on her farm, and I've come up with the perfect solution." Sitting taller, he stated,

"I've decided to purchase the farm. With my money and Mrs. Frederick's experience, we're going to make it profitable again."

His words left Mary momentarily speechless. She could see how this plan might benefit Mrs. Frederick, and possibly why Gilbert saw restoring the farm as a far more compelling challenge than juggling Arlington Hotel staff schedules. But as for what it meant for Mary, she hardly dared imagine.

Setting the glider in motion, Mary stared out across the lawn and chose her words with care. "It's no wonder you've been so preoccupied. I'm glad for Mrs. Frederick, but especially glad for you. Managing a farm will at last bring you the satisfaction you've been lacking."

"You don't understand, Mary. I'm not doing this only for myself, or even to rescue Mrs. Frederick from her dire circumstances." Gilbert reached across the space between them and found her hand. "I'm doing it because I need to see your eyes light up with admiration and respect." His voice grew husky. "I'm doing it because I need your love."

10

Thomas drew a clammy hand across his mouth as he perused the Fourth of July holiday staff schedule—one he'd had to draw up himself, thanks to Gilbert's untimely absences the past few days. Too many employees wanted Friday off to celebrate with their families. But the hotel still had its guests to consider, and this being the first Independence Day since the end of the war, nearly every hotel in town was booked solid for a weekend filled with festivities.

Must be nice to have a reason to celebrate. Not to mention having someone to celebrate with. Gilbert had Mary, Annemarie had Samuel. Even the stuffy and boringly erudite Patrice Yarborough had appeared in church last Sunday with a gentleman in tow. True, the man looked old enough and bald enough to be twice Patrice's age, but he'd had the look of a lovesick puppy about him, and Patrice seemed equally smitten. Thomas had never seen the pastor's daughter so simperingly sweet.

He tapped today's date on his desk calendar. Given it was already Thursday the third, he felt quite sure he'd be attending the festivities unescorted.

Well, there was always Mother.

Thoughts of his mother reminded Thomas of the scene at dinner Monday night. When Gilbert announced his intention to purchase the Frederick farm and asked for a portion of his trust fund account, Thomas feared their livid mother would expire face down in her cucumber soup.

"Have you lost your mind?" she'd shrieked. "The Ballards are not *farmers*"—this last word having been uttered with the utmost contempt and enough spittle to douse a house fire.

Of course, ladies didn't spit, so Mother then conveniently toppled her water glass to camouflage the evidence.

In the end, though, Gilbert got his way. As usual. Though Mother might rant and rave, she was also quite practical. Gilbert's expansive vision of the farm's future grandeur soon convinced her of the potential for breaking new ground— both literally and figuratively—among Hot Springs elite, and Mother had agreed to transfer the necessary funds into Gilbert's account first thing Tuesday morning.

Yes, good old Gilbert. First-born son, war hero, man about town, soon-to-be gentleman farmer. Thomas shouldn't be resentful—he'd looked up to his older brother all his life, even hoped to follow in the footsteps of both Gilbert and their father and join the Army someday until rheumatic fever nipped that plan in the bud. God's providence, no doubt, since time and experience had proven Thomas much more suited to hotel management than bravery on the battlefield. Better to utilize his skills on the home front and admire his brother from afar.

Then Gilbert came home from the war a changed man in both body and spirit, and there were days—too many of them during those first few months—when Thomas hardly recognized his own brother. The bitterness, depression, unprovoked rages, and one irrational decision after another made Thomas wonder if the old Gilbert was lost to them forever.

Only in the last few weeks—since Annemarie married Samuel, in fact—had Gilbert seemed to come out of his fog and start living again. Maybe the farm really would be a good investment for Gilbert, not merely financially but also spiritually and emotionally. Thomas hadn't seen his brother this enthusiastic about life since he'd received his acceptance to West Point.

Now, if the old boy would just propose to Miss Mary McClarney, settle down in the country, and start raising a brood of children, maybe Thomas could finally step out of his brother's shadow and truly become his own man.

_

"Just sign here, Mrs. Frederick, and that's the last of the documents." Martin Greenslade leaned across his desk to tap the signature line.

When she finished, Gilbert took the pen and scrawled his name in the space beneath hers. Nerves jumping, he could barely contain his anticipation. "That's it, then? The farm is legally mine?"

"For all intents and purposes." Greenslade gathered up the myriad documents they'd just waded through. "I'll have my secretary file the papers with the county clerk immediately."

Mrs. Frederick clutched her handbag. Her lower lip trembled. "This feels . . . so final."

Sensing her remorse, Gilbert sat forward and touched her arm. "Remember, you're not losing the farm. You'll always have a place there as long as you want it. It's in the contract. Besides," he added with a gentle laugh, "I'll need your help and advice for a long time to come."

"I know, but . . ." The woman released a shaky breath. "I cannot help worrying I have betrayed John's memory, his dream."

"The betrayal would be to let the dream die. Instead, you're giving it new life. Your husband would be proud and grateful for the decision you've made today."

She raised hopeful eyes to Gilbert's. A tear slid down her cheek, and she nodded. "I always knew you were a good boy. So kind, so thoughtful. And you have grown into a good man."

Escorting Mrs. Frederick out of the attorney's office, Gilbert hoped she was right. He wanted desperately to be a good man, someone worthy of respect, someone who chose right over wrong, love over hate. He was tired of holding on to pain and anger and regret.

He had so much to do, so many plans to make! Plenty to fill his head with exciting possibilities for the future and drive out the demons of the past. And no time like the present to begin. After returning Mrs. Frederick to the Ballard house, Gilbert set about arranging for repairs to the Frederick farmhouse and outbuildings. A contractor followed Gilbert out to inspect the property and offer an estimate, and once they'd agreed upon the work to be done, promised to send crews out immediately after the holiday weekend.

It was late afternoon by the time Gilbert returned to the city. The heat had drained him, leaving his shirt drenched in sweat and clumps of hair clinging to his forehead. An ice-cold beer would certainly hit the spot—out of the question, of course, with Prohibition in full effect. He should go home to shower and change, but despite his fatigue, he felt too exhilarated to end the day quite yet.

He'd stop in to see Mary, that's what he'd do. She should be getting home from work about now, and he was bursting to tell her all about his latest plans for the farm.

Bringing the car to a stop in front of her house, he shut off the motor then combed his fingers through his hair and straightened his collar. As he strode around to the sidewalk, he realized he'd grown so accustomed to the artificial leg, he hardly needed to use his cane. One more reason to celebrate. Each day brought him closer to becoming the man he strove to be.

Mary's mother answered the door, her smile welcoming but reserved. "Hello, Gilbert. Is Mary expecting you?"

"No, ma'am. I was just on my way home and thought . . ." Why did he suddenly feel as tongue-tied as a schoolboy called to the headmaster's office?

"Who is it, Mum?" came Mary's voice from another part of the house.

"It's your young man, dear." Mrs. McClarney called over her shoulder. "Best set another place at the table. Looks like we'll be a foursome tonight."

Gilbert retreated a step. "I'm interrupting. I should—"

"Gilbert?" Mary entered the foyer. She'd brushed out her thick, red hair, and the way it curled about her shoulders brought an ache to his belly. "My goodness, you look parched! Come in and let me get you a glass of water."

"Water . . . thank you." His throat did indeed feel dry as the Sahara, but whether from the heat or Mary's nearness, he couldn't say. Following her inside, he wished he could grab her hand and whisk her away where they could be alone. All the plans he'd made this week, all his newly defined dreams for the future, were coming together in his mind with one purpose: to take Mary as his bride and make a home with her. He'd propose right this very minute if—

Stepping into the kitchen, he drew up short. Across the room, seated at the small dining table, was Dr. Donald Russ.

"Lieutenant Ballard," the doctor said, rising. "Nice to see you again." His tone suggested otherwise, not to mention the wary look in his eyes.

Gilbert glanced from Dr. Russ to Mary and forced a weak laugh. "Really bad timing on my part. I should have called first." He edged toward the foyer. "Except—how silly of me—you don't have a telephone and—"

Blathering like an idiot! Now he just wanted to escape. He spun around so fast he lost his balance.

Instantly, both Mary and her mother grabbed his arms, which only served to heighten his embarrassment. Gathering his dignity, he shook them off. "I'm fine. Really, I've got to go."

Mary caught up with him as he reached the front door. "You don't look at all fine. Won't you tell me what's wrong?"

He jerked the door open, then sighed and braced one hand on the doorframe. Without looking at her, he muttered, "*Nothing* was wrong until I saw Dr. Russ at your table."

Swinging around in a small circle, Mary jammed her hands on her hips. When she stopped and faced him again, her gaze shot daggers. "Is this still about your irrational and utterly groundless jealousy?"

"I'm not—" He clamped his mouth shut. Then, seizing Mary's wrist, he tugged her onto the porch and yanked the door closed behind them. Letting his cane fall to the floor, he clutched Mary by the shoulders and forced her to look at him. "Don't you get it, Mary? Even thinking about you with someone else makes me crazy. I can't help it. I—I need you. I—"

He gulped, easing his grip. This wasn't going the way he'd planned.

"Why can't you say it, Gilbert?" Mary's jaw firmed. Her tone became an accusing whisper. "Is it because you're still in love with *her*?"

"No. No!" He pulled Mary against him, crushing her to his chest. "It's you, Mary. Only you."

Her hands crept up between them. She tilted her head to search his face, and the tortured look in her eyes undid him. If he couldn't say the words she longed to hear, at least he could show her how he felt. With one hand cradling her nape, the other arm grasping her waist, he lowered his mouth upon hers and kissed her hard and hungrily until he sensed her knees go weak.

He felt more than heard the deep-throated growl rising up from her abdomen the instant before she shoved him away. "Stop. Now!" Chest heaving, Mary stumbled backward. "You'll never kiss me like that again, Gilbert Ballard, until you convince me I'm more to you than—" She stooped to retrieve his cane and thrust it into his hand. "More than a crutch to use while you heal from the loss of Annemarie."

Seconds later, the front door slammed in his face.

Breathless, shaken, Mary leaned against the closed door and waited until she heard Gilbert drive away. It galled her he could still reduce her to such insensibility. It galled her even more she craved his kisses and his touch like nothing else on earth.

Her mother appeared in the kitchen doorway. A questioning smile creased her cheeks. "Gilbert didn't stay?"

Mary's lips still pulsed with the intensity of Gilbert's kiss. She straightened and smoothed perspiring palms along her skirt. "He . . . had other plans."

"I'm sorry, lass. I know how you've missed him of late."

"Yes, well . . . we've both been busy." Ushering her mother back to the table, Mary wedged a bit of cheer into her tone. "I hope you and Dr. Russ started without me. Cold mashed potatoes aren't worth the bowl they're served in."

Mary tried to enjoy the rest of the evening. The dinner was in her honor, after all, celebrating her hospital promotion. Mum had invited Dr. Russ to join them, then planned and prepared the meal herself—no small accomplishment since not so long ago bronchitis had left Mary's mother too weak to even consider cooking a full meal.

Mainly, though, Mary simply sat quietly and feigned interest while Mum and Dr. Russ chatted. After dinner they moved into the parlor, the doctor showing no signs of leaving anytime soon. Tomorrow being the Fourth, he'd arranged for a full three days off from the hospital and had already planned special outings with Mary's mother.

Listening to them laugh together over all Dr. Russ had lined up for the weekend only increased Mary's frustration, both with Gilbert and herself. After she'd sent him away so abruptly, could she hope to see Gilbert at all this weekend?

Her glance drifted to the small, square table in the foyer and the new black instrument sitting there. If Gilbert's sudden mood shift hadn't flummoxed her so, she might have had the presence of mind to tell him as of today they did indeed own a telephone.

At the first possible moment, Mary excused herself, claiming exhaustion from the mental strain of adapting to her new hospital duties. Besides, unlike Dr. Russ, Mary did have to work on the Fourth. Nurses, even in supervisory positions, didn't receive nearly the same privileges as doctors.

On Friday morning, Mary found the hospital abuzz with patriotic fervor. Nurses and orderlies busily hung red, white, and blue bunting from window ledges and doorposts. Wheelchairs sported miniature flags and streamers, and every ambulatory patient had donned his uniform. By mid-morning patients and staff had organized a parade through the hospital buildings and along connecting breezeways, their off-key renditions of "The Star-Spangled Banner," "America the Beautiful," and "Battle Hymn of the Republic" echoing down every corridor.

As Mary watched the revelry from a stairwell, a familiar masculine voice caught her by surprise. "Quite a spectacular production, isn't it?"

She turned, a thrill of recognition warming her face. "Chaplain Vickary, you're back!"

"How are you, Miss McClarney?" The chaplain's easy smile showed no hint of the demons she'd once seen behind haunted eyes. "I heard about your promotion. Congratulations."

"Thank you. And congratulations to you as well. I wish you and Mrs. Vickary every happiness."

A flicker of motion in his right eyebrow gave the only outward sign he grasped the deeper emotions behind her good wishes. His voice softened. "Annemarie and I are happy beyond measure. I wish the same for you, Mary. If you ever need a friend to talk with . . ."

"You're very kind. Especially after everything—" She bit down on her lower lip, still mortified to recall what Gilbert had done to the chaplain.

"It's all in the past now." Chaplain Vickary released a quiet sigh. When a patient recognized him and called out his name, he smiled and waved. The smile remained in place, but his eyes darkened in concern as he asked, "How is Gilbert? Do you see him often?"

"He's . . . better." It was true—Gilbert *did* seem better in many ways. "I don't think the headaches are as troublesome."

"That's good. I've been praying for him."

"As have I."

"Would you tell him something for me?" The chaplain fingered the cross pinned to his lapel. "Would you make sure he knows I forgive him?"

Mary tilted her head. "Isn't that something you should tell him yourself?"

"I would, and gladly, if only he'd—"

"Sam, there you are!" A swirl of navy and white announced Annemarie Kendall Vickary's appearance. Her happy smile faltered as she recognized Mary. "Oh . . . hello, Miss McClarney."

Mary nodded, her stomach tensing. "Ma'am."

Sliding his arm around his bride's waist, Chaplain Vickary truly had the look of a man in love. Mary wished with all her being that someday Gilbert would look at her that way, would gaze at her with eyes that saw only her.

Edging away, Mary tucked a strand of hair beneath her cap. "I must get back to my floor. It was lovely seeing you, Chaplain. . . . Mrs. Vickary. All the best, really."

Once safely behind her desk, Mary dared to release her pent-up breath. The encounter with the Vickarys only reminded her all over again she'd never be first in Gilbert's heart. As long as he lived, that place would be held by Annemarie.

The captivating, poised, and polished Annemarie.

Everything Mary was not.

Cursing herself for such flagrant self-pity, she seized a pen and set to work reviewing the stack of patient charts awaiting her attention. Then, glimpsing her stubby fingernails and cracked cuticles, she tossed the pen aside in disgust. In the desk drawer she found a bottle of hand lotion, shook a hefty dollop into her palm, and massaged vigorously.

For all the good it would do. When next she made her rounds through the ward, she'd be soaping and scrubbing her poor hands raw again.

You're a nurse, Mary McClarney, and a good one. Stop this futile grumbling and be about the work God's given you to do.

The afternoon brought an influx of paperwork, along with a new civilian orderly the hospital had hired. Mary had to set the man straight more than once, not only concerning standard procedure at a military facility but about her rules for the floor.

"You'll do your smoking out of doors, mister," she snapped, whipping the cigarette from his mouth and crushing it beneath her heel. "We've patients here with lung problems who don't need to be breathing your foul tobacco fumes."

During a break, she telephoned her house just because she could. "It's me, Mum. Everything all right there?"

"Oh, Mary, I never imagined I'd love having a telephone so much. Why, Ginny and I have been calling each other all day about one thing or another." A delighted laugh bubbled from her throat. "I feel so silly, when I could just as easily walk next door and talk to her in person."

Mary smiled to herself. No doubt a few of those calls had to do with Mum's dilemma about what to wear when Dr. Russ called for her later. She'd gushed over breakfast about his plans to take her up the mountain for a picnic, after which they'd join the throng for a Fourth of July concert at the bandstand. "So, did you decide on the red gingham or the white cotton voile?"

"The white, I think. When I tried on the red, it seemed a wee bit tight."

"Did it, now?" Mum's wardrobe choices might be more limited, but Mary wasn't at all sorry to know her mother's improving health had added a pound or two to her delicate frame.

"I'm so sorry you have to work today, darlin'," Mum said. "But you'll have a lovely time with Gilbert tonight, I'm sure."

Mary swiveled away from the prying gaze of that annoying smokestack of an orderly. "I'm not expecting to see Gilbert tonight. He's been so busy with Mrs. Frederick and all."

"He hasn't reached you at the hospital? Why, it's been a good two hours since he called here asking for you."

"He stopped by?"

"Yes, and all in a dither he was, apologizing for leaving in such a rush last night and saying he'd make it up to you today."

Mary squeezed her eyes shut as a tiny bubble of hope pressed against her heart. *Dear Jesus, all I need to hear from him are just three little words.*

I. Love. You.

But somehow, even after the ultimatum she'd leveled at Gilbert yesterday, Mary doubted tonight would be the night. No, the man was still far too driven by need and guilt. There wasn't yet room in his heart for the true love Mary longed for.

Remembering her mother, she cleared her throat. "I must get back to work, Mum. If I'm not home before you leave with Dr. Russ, have a lovely evening."

"Mary—"

"Good-bye, Mum. Love you!" She replaced the earpiece and reached for the chart she'd been working on, only to stifle a groan when a shadow fell across her desk. At this rate, she'd never finish by the end of the day. "Yes, may I—"

Instead of the nurse or orderly she expected to see, her gaze fell upon a massive bouquet of red and white roses. A pair of brooding, but hopeful, hazel eyes peered between the blossoms.

Gilbert.

11

*D*onald grinned across the top of a bouquet of daisies as he stood on Nell's front porch. Her girlish smile when she whisked open the door brought a quiver to his belly and a knot to his throat. "You look stunning."

A lovely blush deepening her color, she raised a hand to her cheek. "Are these for me?"

He wiggled his brows. "Actually, I thought your neighbor would enjoy them. Give me a moment and—"

A dainty hand clamped down upon his wrist. Next thing he knew, Nell had wrested the bouquet from his grip and marched to the kitchen, her gauzy white skirt swirling about shapely calves. "I've a vase here somewhere . . ."

With a rumbling laugh, Donald followed the sounds of slamming cupboard doors and rattling dishes. He reached Nell's side in time to catch a tall crystal vase before it toppled off a high shelf. "Careful there, Mrs. McClarney. I left my medical bag in the car, and I'm not in the mood to stitch up a head wound this evening."

Gently she relieved him of the vase and carried it to the sink. As the vase filled with water, she winked at Donald over her shoulder. "It's sure nice to know I've my very own personal physician lookin' out for me."

Before he did something crazy, like sweep her into his arms and plant a kiss on those inviting lips, Donald shoved his hands into his pockets. He'd thought himself far too old to fall this hard for a woman, not to mention so quickly. Romantic love was for young folks like Samuel and Annemarie. Mary and—

Blast it all, why did he have to ruin a perfectly wonderful moment with thoughts of that irascible lout. Mary was too good for Gilbert. She deserved better. Donald had seen the hurt in her eyes last night after Gilbert left. Something had happened out there on the porch, no doubt about it. Too much to hope Mary had sent the bum packing. No, she was too patient and forgiving.

And too much in love.

"A penny for your thoughts." Nell glanced up with a coy smile as she arranged the daisies in the vase.

"Don't waste your money." Plucking a flower from the bouquet, Donald broke off the stem and tucked the blossom behind Nell's ear. "There, pretty as a picture. Ready to go?"

"Just let me grab a shawl. Up on the mountain it can get a tad chilly as the sun goes down." She plucked at his sleeve. "And don't think you'll get off so easy. I've learned to tell when something's weighing on your mind."

"Perhaps later. For now, let's just enjoy the evening." Still, he liked knowing she noticed, knowing she cared. He liked it very much.

"Is there somewhere we could . . . talk?"

The plaintive tone in Gilbert's voice clawed at Mary's heart. If she wasn't careful, all her best intentions about keeping him at arm's length would come to naught.

Stiffening her shoulders, she pushed away from her desk and stood, trying to ignore the heavenly fragrance of roses filling the room. "I'm afraid I'm on duty. Is it something that can't wait?"

Stupid, stupid question! As if she *wanted* to wait! Memories of stolen kisses in hospital storage closets threatened to tear away the last vestiges of her resolve.

"Mary, about last night . . ." Edging closer, Gilbert darted a glance over his shoulder then lowered his voice. "Give me another chance. Please."

Mary crossed her arms. If the scent of roses grew any stronger, she'd swoon. "And how many chances, precisely, do you think you deserve?"

"Deserve? Not even one. I've hurt you too many times already. It's why I'm throwing myself on your mercy. I'm not above begging, Mary. I'll do whatever it takes."

"Even bring me expensive roses, apparently." Oh, they did smell divine!

He released a deep, sighing breath as he fingered a rose petal. "The white ones, they're for new beginnings. At least, so the florist told me."

"New beginnings." Mary drifted nearer, inhaling ever so gently. "And the red ones?"

"Beauty and perfection. Everything you are to me. Mary, I—"

"Aren't those something!" That wretched orderly! The miasma of stale tobacco hovered around him like a flock of carrion birds. He paused for a moment, casting Gilbert a sidelong glance. "Sorry if I'm interrupting, Nurse McClarney, but you did say to fetch you when Corporal Eddleman returned from hydrotherapy."

"Indeed I did." Nervously fingering her collar, Mary slid her gaze toward Gilbert. From somewhere deep inside she dredged up her most matronly tone. "As you can see, Lieutenant Ballard, this is a working hospital. If you want to pay a social call, you'll do so at my home, if you please, or not at all."

Then, remembering something vitally important, she seized a pen, jotted a quick note, and thrust it into Gilbert's hand before rushing out of her office.

A shame those roses wouldn't be there waiting for her when she returned. But at least Gilbert would leave knowing he could now telephone her after hours at home.

☙

Alone in Mary's small office, Gilbert wrestled with the dichotomy between the haughty tone of her rejection and the curious note she'd just slipped him: *"I've a telephone now. You may reach me at home."*

So . . . was she giving him another chance, or not?

So much for letting the roses speak the words he carried in his heart. With a frustrated groan, he slid one red rose from the bouquet and laid it across Mary's desk. "I'll be telephoning you, Miss McClarney. Count on it."

Somehow, despite his bumbling ineptitude, his fits of jealousy and angry outbursts, he had to convince her how much he cared. Life without Mary simply wouldn't be worth living.

True, he'd thought the same about Annemarie not so long ago. And learned the hard way life indeed went on, even with a shattered body and a broken heart.

Leaving the ward, he saw a crowd already forming outside the hospital gates on Carriage Road near the bandstand. He'd hoped to escort Mary to the concert tonight. There'd be fireworks afterward, the grandest Independence Day celebration since before America entered the war. Firecrackers already echoed in the streets below, and with each *snap* and *pop* and flash of light, Gilbert flinched.

With or without Mary, maybe it was best he didn't attend the festivities. Another infernal headache had begun to throb as his mind filled with memories of machine-gun fire, mortar explosions, flamethrowers, and anti-tank guns. His right hand gripping the hilt of his cane, he felt instead the cold steel of his Colt .45 automatic. If he hadn't lost his pistol somewhere in the mud the day the whizzbang took his leg, if he'd been able to lay hold of a handgun in the grueling days following . . . well, he'd have saved Annemarie, Samuel, and everyone else he cared about—not to mention himself—a shipload of pain and misery.

Sure, they'd have grieved for a while. But they'd have remembered him as a brave war hero, not the despicable scoundrel who cast aside the woman he loved and then set out to destroy his best friend.

I'm not the same man anymore. God help me, I'm not!

Maybe that was the problem. He'd ceased believing God even cared.

And thanks to his own despicableness, the one man who could always be counted on to speak God's truth and hold Gilbert accountable was lost to him.

He missed Sam. Missed him something awful.

The concussive burst of another firecracker, this one near enough to make Gilbert's ears ring, sent him careening across the hospital grounds to where he'd parked his roadster on Reserve Avenue. He needed to get out of town before the racket drove him mad.

With no thought for his destination, he headed south on Central, hoping the route marked his best means of escape. Mouth dry as ash, he longed for a drink, but of course every bar and saloon was locked up tight.

Soon the sounds from downtown faded, until all Gilbert heard was the roadster's rumbling motor and the pounding of his own heart. Up ahead, the empty Oaklawn Park grandstands loomed. Horse racing—yet another casualty of Arkansas politics.

Curious, Gilbert slowed and turned into the parking area. He noted little sign of activity around the track and stables, but as he nosed the car up behind one of the long barns, he glimpsed a dark-skinned man leading a horse in from an exercise paddock. The horse walked with a decided limp, head hung low and eyes heavy-lidded.

Shutting off the motor, Gilbert climbed out of the car and made his way along the building until he found an entrance. He spotted the man closing the door on a horse stall. "Hey, there," he called.

"Yessuh?" The lanky groom ambled over. "If you's lookin' for somebody, ain't nobody else around."

"No, just passing by." Gilbert nodded toward the stall. "Didn't know they were still stabling horses here."

"Jes' this one. They done forgot about him 'cause he's lame."

Aware of his own lameness, Gilbert shifted his weight. "Who's the owner?"

"That'd be a widow woman over to Tennessee. She done sold off all her healthy stock." The groom tugged off a dusty tweed cap, revealing close-cropped salt-and-pepper hair. He ran the back of his wrist across his damp forehead. "I's s'posed to take this boy out an' shoot him, but I ain't got the heart."

Gilbert sidled up to the stall door, his gaze sliding over the animal's sleek coat. Judging from the horse's well-kept appearance, if Gilbert hadn't already observed the limp, he'd never suspect anything was wrong. "What's his name?"

"Registered name's Bonnie Angus MacTavish, but I calls him Mac." The groom reached across the stall door to massage the horse's rump. Mac responded with a contented snort and leaned into the pressure.

Something niggled at Gilbert's brain. "I think I've seen this horse race."

"You'd'a remembered, that's for sure. Till he got kicked comin' off the straightaway in his last race, he was headin' for a big win." The old groom chuckled softly. "Lots o' folks lost their shirts on that race."

Ah, yes, memory returned. Gilbert hadn't lost his shirt, but he'd certainly unraveled a few threads. Descended from the famed Bonnie Scotland of Belle Meade Plantation, Bonnie Angus MacTavish had all the makings of a winner, until fate intervened.

Not unlike Gilbert himself.

The horse nickered and came closer. Gilbert patted the well-muscled neck. "I can't believe the owner doesn't even want him for stud service. She could make a fortune."

"They done lost ever'thing on that race. Ol' man died of a heart attack three days later. His widow don't want nothin' to do with racehorses no more."

"What happens to him now? Surely you aren't still getting paid to take care of him?"

"Like I said, I's s'posed to put him down. I ain't gettin' nothing 'cept the deep-in-the-soul satisfaction of makin' his last days good as I can." The man sighed and folded his arms along the stall door. "Least I can do for one o' God's creatures. Hope someday somebody'll do the same for me."

Backing off a step, Gilbert turned and rubbed his chin. He knew only slightly more about horses than he did about farming, but this was an opportunity he couldn't pass up. Besides, he somehow felt a special kinship with the animal. Both of them maimed, both desperate for elusive second chances. And how could he forget Rusty, his faithful war horse? Maybe saving

Mac could atone in some small way for all those animals sacrificed on the fields of battle.

He kicked at a piece of straw. "Can you put me in touch with the owner?"

"Reckon I could, but . . ." The groom shot Gilbert a dubious frown. "You ain't about to get me in no trouble, are you?"

"Remains to be seen. But if I do, I'll make it right." Shifting his cane to the other side, Gilbert thrust out his right hand. "What's your name, sir?"

"Obadiah Squires." Hesitantly, the man accepted Gilbert's handshake.

"Pleased to make your acquaintance, Mr. Squires. I'm Gil Ballard, and if you'll assist me in gaining ownership of this fine animal, I'll hire you myself to take charge of his care."

Obadiah's mouth spread into a gap-toothed smile. He pumped Gilbert's hand more firmly. "Now that's an offer I'd be most obliged to accept."

Mary may have had to work on Independence Day, but she counted it pure blessed relief to have an entire weekend to call her own. She awoke Saturday morning not to the clamor of her despised alarm clock but to the dulcet tones of her mother humming "Blessed Assurance."

Slipping on a robe, Mary trod barefoot down the narrow staircase from her tiny bedroom loft. She found her mother in the kitchen stirring up a batch of pancakes. "My, but you're sounding cheerful this morning."

"Up at last, I see." Mum paused to drop a kiss on Mary's cheek. "I was beginning to wonder if you planned to sleep the whole day away."

Mary hiked a brow as she went to the stove to see if the coffee was ready. Piping hot, just what she needed. "I thought you'd be the one sleeping the day away, seeing as how it was well past midnight before the doctor saw you home."

"Watching the clock, were you?" Mum chuckled. "And here I thought it would be me waiting up for you and your beau. You two must have ended the evening early."

"I'm afraid my evening never began."

Her mother turned with a gasp. "What? Gilbert didn't take you to the concert and fireworks?"

"He came by the hospital, but I didn't have time to talk." Mary stirred milk into her coffee and carried it to the table.

"You didn't have time to talk." Mary's mother set her hands on her hips, pancake batter dribbling from the spoon she clutched. "Not even two minutes to accept his apology and tell him what time to call for you?"

"You're making a mess." Mary hurried to the sink for a dish cloth, then bent at her mother's feet to mop up the spilled batter.

"*I'm* making a mess? Indeed!" Mum spun around and scooped up the mixing bowl. At the stove, she ladled batter onto a sizzling griddle, muttering under her breath all the while.

Choosing to ignore her mother's snit, Mary went to the cupboard for plates. After setting the table, she fetched butter from the icebox and a jug of maple syrup from the pantry. "Coffee, Mum?"

"Yes, please. And you'd best go about mending some fences today, lassie. Be angry but sin not, the Good Book says. Gilbert may have his faults, but it's clear he loves you. I'm startin' to believe his heart's in the right place."

So now it was Mary's fault she'd spent last evening alone? After returning home from work, she'd changed into her prettiest summer frock, a dark blue dress with a pristine white sailor collar, then planted herself in a parlor chair where she could see the telephone in the foyer. She'd waited for hours hoping it would ring, but the black sentinel mocked her with its silence.

"You don't understand, Mum." Mary plopped her mother's coffee mug on the table. "He doesn't come calling for days at a time, then flies off in a jealous rage at the least provocation. He says he cares for me, but he's always holding a part of himself back. I can't wait forever for a man who isn't completely committed to me, who can't—or won't—say the words I long to hear."

"Ah, child." Mary's mother set a platter of pancakes on the table and then wrapped her daughter in her arms. "Don't think I can't see how lovin' this man rips your poor heart to shreds. But you know as well as anyone what he's suffered, all he's had to overcome." She sniffed, and a hint of steel crept into her tone. "You went through it with your da, don't forget."

"I do know, Mum, and I'm sorry for him." Mary rested her chin on her mother's shoulder. "But it isn't my pity he needs, and what I have to offer, he resists at every turn."

"I know, lass. I know." With a final squeeze, Mary's mother nudged her into a chair, but before she could take her own seat, a raucous clang startled them both. Mum gasped a laugh and covered her mouth. "Oh, dear, I doubt I'll ever get used to the sound of the telephone!"

12

$\mathcal{T}$he telephone jangled twice, three times, and neither Mary nor her mother rose to answer.

Mary scooted up to the table and tried to look busy slathering butter across her pancakes. "You should get it, Mum. It's probably Mrs. Lawson asking about your evening with Dr. Russ."

"Nonsense. I've already had a lovely chat with Ginny this morning, long before you roused your lazy self from bed." Mum drizzled syrup across her plate while the telephone rang twice more.

"Mum!" Mary shot her mother a desperate look. "You can't just let it go on ringing!"

"Then *you* answer it, darlin'. It might be Gilbert, you know."

Exactly what concerned Mary most. Drawing a bolstering breath, she pushed up from the table with both hands and glared at her mother then stormed out of the kitchen.

In the foyer she paused to smooth a lock of hair and tighten the sash of her robe before reaching for the earpiece. "H-hello?"

"Mary?" Gilbert's resonant bass. "I almost gave up hope you'd answer."

"We were just having breakfast and—"

"I've called at a bad time." Disappointment brought an edge to his tone.

"It's fine. Really." Mary didn't mind cold pancakes in the least. Not when the mere sound of Gilbert's voice could warm her through and through. Oh, she was a terrible lost cause! "I should apologize—"

"I was wrong to—" Gilbert said at the same time.

Mary released a nervous laugh. "No, truly, I'm sorry. I shouldn't have been so abrupt with you at the hospital yesterday. The roses were . . . lovely." The single red rose he'd left on her desk now stood in a bud vase on her nightstand, the sweet fragrance wafting in and out of her dreams all night.

"I'd still like to give you the roses, if you'll let me. May I come over?"

Glimpsing her reflection in the oval mirror over the hall table, Mary shuddered. Her hair looked like a rat's nest, and— oh, my—a coffee stain on her bodice? She cleared her throat. "You may, but not for at least an hour. I—I've a few things to do before you arrive."

The instant they said goodbye, Mary dashed upstairs. The navy sailor dress she'd worn last night lay crumpled in the chair where she'd discarded it in a teary-eyed fit of pique. While tearing a brush through her hair, she stood in front of the wardrobe and studied her remaining options. The gray gingham? Too mousy. The brown velveteen? Too hot!

She finally settled on a coral print housedress. Certainly nothing she'd wear into town, but it was clean and pressed and the color flattered her complexion. Besides, she didn't want to give Gilbert the impression she'd belabored her appearance *too* long just for him.

After securing her hair with two tortoise-shell combs above her ears, she returned downstairs, where she found her mother washing up the breakfast dishes. "Oh, Mum, I could have done that."

Her mother smiled over her shoulder. "My, and don't you look lovely for a Saturday morning! So your sweetheart's coming by, is he?"

"He is." Heat raced up Mary's cheeks as she reached for a dishtowel. Then her stomach growled, reminding her she'd never finished breakfast.

Mum nodded toward the oven. "I kept your pancakes warm. Best eat up while you can."

She forced down less than half the meal before her nerves told her to stop. As she stood at the bathroom sink scrubbing her teeth, she chided herself for being so jumpy. True love should feel more comfortable, shouldn't it? Less anxious. Less awkward. Less uncertain.

When Gilbert rapped on her door twenty minutes later, Mary felt as if a hundred centipedes were doing the fox trot up and down her spine. He looked so dashingly handsome standing there on the porch, one wayward curl drifting across his forehead. He wore no coat on this hot July morning, and his shirt collar lay open to reveal the pulse throbbing at the base of his throat.

His Adam's apple bobbed with an anxious swallow. He offered a hesitant smile. "Are you going to leave me baking in the sun, or may I come in?"

"Yes, yes, come in!" Mary held the door wide, making room for the massive bouquet of roses cradled in Gilbert's left arm. The scent was even more pervasive than yesterday, and Mary suddenly longed to bury her face in the blossoms and breathe in their beauty until she fainted dead away.

Shaking off such folly, she murmured a thank-you as she took the roses and carried them to the kitchen.

Her mother, turning from the sink, let out a gasp. "Saints above, but those are lovely! Go on about your visit. I'll put them in a vase for you."

With nothing further to delay this encounter, Mary squared her shoulders and marched to the parlor. When Gilbert swiveled from the window, Mary motioned toward the settee and joined him there. Leaving several inches between them, she smoothed her skirt, unable to look at him. "I hope you had a pleasant Fourth."

"It wasn't what I'd planned." He tapped his index fingers against his thighs in an agitated rhythm. "And your evening? Did you attend the concert?"

"I stayed home alone, actually. It was a very quiet evening, though I could hear the fireworks in the distance. I'm sure they were spectacular."

"I'm sure."

Silence cloaked the room. Finding it hard to breathe, Mary rose and switched on the electric fan. When she returned to her seat, Gilbert reached out and caught her hand. Her stomach clutched, and she resisted the compulsion to snatch her hand back.

He must have felt her apprehension. His grip tightened yet remained gentle. "I'm trying, Mary. Truly I am. Please don't push me away. I n—"

"Don't you dare say you *need* me, Gilbert Ballard." Her throat closed, and she crushed his fingers with urgency. "I don't want to be needed. I *need* to be *loved.*"

"I love you, Mary. I do." The intensity behind Gilbert's words made his chest ache. "I want us to be together, always."

She peered up at him with eyes the color of a stormy sea. Eyes filled with questions. "You're not just saying so because you know it's what I want to hear?"

"I may be a lot of things, but one thing I'm not is a liar." Spreading her palm, he centered it over his throbbing heart. "See what you do to me, Mary? When I'm with you, nothing else matters."

When a tear slid down her cheek, he brushed it away with his thumb and then pulled her into his arms. His fingers caught in her curls as he angled his mouth over hers. She grew limp in his embrace, her eyelids falling shut, breath quickening.

His own breath set his lungs on fire. She smelled so fresh and clean, her skin like the petals of those roses. Her softly rounded curves nestled against him, and he groaned with barely controlled passion. He wanted her . . . needed her . . .

No! He would no longer dishonor Mary by reducing what he felt for her to the level of physical desire.

He gentled the kiss until it was no more than the touch of butterfly wings, a sensation so delightful in itself, Gilbert was loath to end it. Mary's mouth followed his as they drifted apart, and she whispered out a reluctant sigh before sinking against the cushions.

Gilbert shifted, pressing his eyes shut, hands clasped between his knees. "I want to do this right, Mary. I don't want to give you any more reasons to distrust my feelings for you."

"I've always believed you loved me—or could, if you'd only let yourself forget . . ."

He looked up to see her gnawing her lower lip. Still her eyes held questions, doubts. And he knew the source.

"Annemarie is out of my life. Out of my heart. She won't come between us again." He slid to the edge of the settee and swiveled to face Mary. His gaze imploring, he clutched both her hands and drew them to his lips. "I'll say it again, Mary: I love you. I love you, and I'll spend the rest of my life making you believe it."

She collapsed into his arms then, weeping wet, noisy tears into his shirt collar. She sobbed so loudly, Gilbert feared he'd said the wrong thing again. He stroked her back, kissed her hair. "Mary . . . Mary, please don't cry. What's wrong?"

Her only response was a strangled breath as she shook her head against his neck. Her arms tightened around him, and the harder she leaned into him, the more precarious his balance became. "Careful, Mary, or—"

Too late. They tumbled to the braided rug, both of them gasping in surprise.

Footsteps sounded in the foyer. Gilbert glanced up to see Mary's mother staring at them, eyes wide with shock. He raised himself on one elbow while helping Mary to sit up. "It isn't what you think, Mrs. McClarney."

Mary brushed wetness from her face with the backs of her hands. "It's true, Mum. We just . . . fell."

"I'm hoping you *just fell*, because otherwise I'd be going for your da's shotgun." Mrs. McClarney stepped into the room and helped Mary to her feet, and none too gently. "Now, would you care to explain what all the commotion is about? I could hear you wailing like a banshee even with the kitchen door closed."

Another sob burst from Mary's throat, but all she managed was, "Oh, Mum. Oh, Mum!"

Mrs. McClarney wrapped Mary in a protective embrace, while her dagger-like glare homed in on Gilbert. "I warned you, young man. Hurt my daughter, and you'll answer to me."

"I didn't, I assure you." Fighting against his confounded prosthesis, Gilbert used the arm of the settee to lever himself to a standing position. By the time he found his cane, his stump throbbed from the contortions. He limped across the room, reaching out to touch Mary's shoulder, but Mrs. McClarney spun her aside.

Impaled by her piercing glare, he decided he'd better keep his distance. "Please, if you'll only let me explain."

With a final sniffle, Mary slipped from her mother's arms. "It's all right, Mum. I'm—I'm crying from happiness."

This is what a happy woman in love looked like? Red-eyed, blotchy-faced, quivering lips twisted into more of a grimace than a smile? Hair in a tangle, collar askew, nose dripping like a leaky faucet . . .

He'd never seen any woman look so beautiful.

He fished a handkerchief from his pocket. Taking a tentative step closer, he held it out to Mary.

She accepted it gratefully, her eyes shining. Blowing her nose, she uttered a nervous laugh. "I must look a fright! I'll just go wash my face."

When Mary had scurried from the room, Mrs. McClarney folded her arms and raised her chin. "So you've made my daughter happy, have you? I take it you've confessed your feelings for her?"

"Yes, ma'am."

"Then I'll repeat my warning yet again. Trifle with my Mary, besmirch her character in any way, or dare to break her fragile young heart, and you'll be prayin' for God's deliverance from my wrath."

Gilbert nodded respectfully, no doubt in his mind Nell McClarney meant every word.

"Thomas. Thomas!" Evelyn Ballard's strident voice and the *rat-a-tat* of designer Italian pumps reverberated along the hotel corridor.

What now? Steeling himself, Thomas neatened a stack of paperwork while he waited for his mother's inevitable explosion through his office door.

Seconds later, his mother flounced into the room, tossing a parasol onto one side chair and her handbag onto another. She sank with a flourish into the center chair across the desk from Thomas and released a noisy huff. "Why haven't you returned my telephone calls?"

"In case you forgot, I have a job to do. I can't always drop what I'm doing just because you want something." He perused a business letter his secretary had just typed, although he scarcely saw the words. "What's got your dander up today, Mother dear?"

"Don't use that disrespectful tone with me, young man, or you'll find yourself booted from my home *and* my good graces."

Not exactly the worst thing to happen. Thomas wondered often why he didn't simply pack up and move out. A grown man had to be insane to reside with his overbearing mother indefinitely. Especially if he had any hopes of finding the right girl and someday starting a family of his own.

Although he couldn't complain about having servants at his beck and call, and no need to cook his own meals, iron his own shirts, make his own bed. Spoiled rotten is what he was. And not the least bit proud of it.

Laying the letter aside, he crossed his legs and leaned back. "I'm sorry, Mother. Please, tell me what's on your mind."

"Your brother, of course."

Of course. "What's Gil done now? Bought another farm? Rescued another widow in distress?"

Her stern glare warned him to watch his words. "It's perfectly ridiculous, this attraction he has for that shabby Irish nurse. We *must* put a stop to it before Gilbert does irreparable damage to his reputation."

Dipping his chin, Thomas rose slowly and came around to his mother's side of the desk. He propped one hip on the corner and folded his arms. "Gilbert's in love, Mother. If you try to keep him and Mary apart, you'll only drive him away."

"Love, pshaw!" She flicked her fingers dismissively. "He's still on the rebound from Annemarie. He'll come to his senses eventually—sooner than later, if I have anything to say about it."

"That's the problem. You *don't* have a say in this." At his mother's haughty frown, Thomas marched around to her other side, giving her his back as his gaze fixed on the plaque for distinguished hotel service he'd earned last year. The staff had feted him with an after-hours reception, which his mother had found herself too busy to attend. Yet, the same evening she'd chosen to host a sewing bee to stitch together pajamas for the doughboys.

Thomas did not begrudge a thing to the soldiers who'd sacrificed life and limb to beat back the Germans and restore peace to the world. But somehow everything always came back to Gilbert. Mother's firstborn. Mother's favorite.

With a sigh, he turned to face her. When he glimpsed her troubled expression, genuine concern etching her face, sympathy bloomed. He laid his hand on her shoulder. "I know you're worried about Gil, but he's an adult now. An intelligent, ambitious man with a good head for business. I'm actually quite proud of him for how he's taking charge of his life. You should be, too."

"I *am* proud of him" She sniffed. "All the more reason I want him to fall in love with the *right* woman, someone deserving of the man he's become."

"I daresay Mary's the woman. She's good for Gilbert, brings out the best in him. She may not travel in your social circles, but she's kind, caring, hardworking, and true." Thomas kissed his mother's cheek. "Give her a chance. You might actually end up liking her."

"Humph. We'll see." Thomas's mother stood and collected her things. Heaving a resigned breath, she paused at the door. "Very well, for Gilbert's sake I shall patiently endure this dalliance while praying he will eventually see the light."

Then, muttering something about "Annemarie" and "quality" and "wasn't it a crying shame she'd wed the insipid chaplain," Thomas's mother marched out of the hotel.

He should move out, he really should. His mother was a hopeless snob. Too bad Thomas couldn't come up with his own widow to snatch from the jaws of destitution. Not that he particularly wanted to live on a farm. No, city life suited him just fine. Neither did he have any complaints about working at the Arlington.

But oh, wouldn't it be nice to be a hero in some woman's eyes. To make a difference.

To fall in love.

☙

Mary scanned the note one of the nurses had just delivered. *Ten o'clock, my office*, the summons read. Mrs. Daley's looping signature graced the bottom of the page.

She'd known to expect regular reviews during the first few months in her new position, but apprehension curdled her stomach nonetheless. Had she performed her duties satisfactorily? Had she neglected anything important? In her own mind, she'd done a quite respectable job, relishing the challenge of supervising the nursing staff on her floor. True, she didn't have as many opportunities for the hands-on patient care she enjoyed so much, but she found it immensely fulfilling to help the younger nurses grow in skills and confidence.

Younger nurses, indeed. Mary wasn't exactly *old*, now, was she?

Truth be told, she'd been feeling younger than springtime and lighter than air since last Saturday. Tomorrow made one week since Gilbert had finally professed his love, and there were days she still pinched herself.

Everything could change tonight, though. Earlier in the week, Gilbert had telephoned to say his mother would like to host a small dinner party in Mary's honor. "Let's take this as a good sign," he'd pleaded. "If Mother's ready to introduce you to her friends, I'm hopeful it means she's finally accepted we're together."

If anything could make Mary more nervous than a meeting with Mrs. Daley, this dinner party did the trick.

She checked the time on her watch pin. Half past nine already. She just had time to check her appearance in the ladies' room before hurrying over to the administration building. She'd rather pace the corridor outside Mrs. Daley's office for fifteen minutes than risk being late for the appointment.

After neatening her bun and straightening her cap, Mary made her way across the hospital grounds. Mrs. Daley's door stood open, so she tapped lightly on the jamb to make her presence known.

The gray-haired woman looked up with a thin smile. "You're early, Miss McClarney. But come in and we'll get started." She nodded toward the straight-backed metal chair across from her. "And close the door, please."

Closed doors meant serious talk—or was she reading more into Mrs. Daley's summons than necessary? Cold seeped through her skirts as she took her seat on the hard chair. She tucked her hands into her lap and waited.

Mrs. Daley reached for a file folder on the corner of her desk and spread it open before her. Shifting pages, she examined each one through wire-rimmed glasses perched on the end of her nose.

At last, she removed her glasses and laced her fingers atop the folder. "It appears you're settling in quite nicely in your new position. Would you agree?"

"Yes, ma'am. I'm enjoying the work very much."

"Getting along well with your staff?"

"Yes, ma'am."

"You feel you have their respect?"

Mary hesitated. How did one gauge respect from those who reported to you? By the absence of apparent conflict? By how competently they performed their duties with minimal supervision? By whether or not they greeted you with a smile when you passed them in the corridor?

"Miss McClarney." The head nurse tapped one finger on the desk. "Do you believe your staff is respectful of your authority?"

"Well, ma'am . . ." Mary pulled her lower lip between her teeth. If she reported the orderly she'd been having difficulty with, would Mrs. Daley judge her incapable of effectively managing the people under her?

"Clearly this question is causing you concern." Replacing her glasses, Mrs. Daley lifted one of the pages from the folder. "I have here a memo from one of your orderlies, a Mr. Ernest Deeds. He claims you have been unfairly harsh in your treatment of him."

The smokestack, who else? Mary stiffened. No choice now but to lay the problem before Mrs. Daley. "I've warned Mr. Deeds time and again about the danger of smoking around oxygen tanks, but he continually disregards my reminders."

"I see." Mrs. Daley closed her eyes briefly. "Well, he is new here, and a civilian. I suggest you give him additional time to acclimate himself to the rules. Perhaps if you were less caustic with your admonitions, he would be more receptive to correction."

"I hardly consider it *caustic* when I must continually repeat myself about a simple rule everyone else on staff is well aware of."

Mrs. Daley chuckled. "Now there's the spunk I want to see in my charge nurses." She leaned forward, her expression warming. "I know you have a spine, Mary, because since you came to work here, I've seen evidence of it all too often—and not always under the most auspicious circumstances," she added with an arched brow. "So don't let Mr. Deeds or me or anyone else shake your confidence. That'll be all. You'd best get back to the floor."

The head nurse's words of encouragement stayed with Mary through the rest of the day, even when the incorrigible Mr. Deeds flicked cigarette ashes in her direction when she shooed him off the ward.

Then, once she'd returned from a short mid-afternoon break, she began counting the minutes until quitting time—and growing more uneasy with each tick of the clock. Mrs. Daley was wrong. The prospect of dinner with Evelyn Ballard shook Mary's confidence like nothing else.

13

*G*ilbert surveyed the progress as the work crew stowed their tools after another hot but productive day at the farm. The house was coming along nicely, the roof shored up and reshingled, the siding freshly painted a gleaming white. Gilbert had selected brick red to set off the front door and shutters, with the porch a soothing shade of slate gray.

Inside, crews worked to refinish the floors, paint or paper the walls, and scrub and repaint the woodwork. New kitchen appliances were on order, the most up-to-date available and with every modern convenience. With the exception of the gas range, of course, those appliances would remain utterly useless until the utility company brought electricity to the farm. Fortunately, a rural power line already extended as far as a neighboring farm, and since Ballard money spoke loudly, engineers were already working on continuing the line out his way.

"Hey, Mistah Ballard." Obadiah Squires ambled around from the back of the house. "You fixin' to call it a day?"

"Big doings at home tonight. Can't be late." Gilbert furled his sheaf of plans and stuffed them in a leather tube. "How's Mac? Does he like his new paddock?"

The silver-haired groom chewed on a piece of straw as he gazed toward the meadow behind the house. "Seems right content out here. Quiet, peaceful. 'Course he'd like it even better with a mare or two."

Gilbert laughed. "In time, in time." He waved to a truckload of workmen heading down the lane. "You have everything you need for the weekend, Obadiah? I may not make it out again before Monday."

"You done set me up real fine in the lean-to out back. Me an' Mac will be happy as clams." Obadiah tipped his ever-present tweed cap. "Meantime, you tell Miz Frederick her bees is in good hands. My grandpappy was a beekeeper, so's I knows what needs doin'."

"That'll ease her mind, I'm sure." Gilbert clapped the man on the shoulder. "See you in a couple of days."

Tossing his cane and the tube of plans into the car, Gilbert climbed in behind the wheel. Before long, the roadster bounced along the rutted road toward town, and Gilbert nodded in satisfaction to see several more power poles had been erected since early morning.

Progress. Definitely progress. Wouldn't be much longer until he could take up residence at the farm and *really* get started on his new life.

At home, he went straight upstairs and drew a bath. While the tub filled, he laid out a starched white shirt along with his favorite gray slacks and matching vest. He'd forgo the tie, however. He'd urged Mother to keep this evening somewhat casual, hoping a relaxing of formality would put Mary more at ease.

Even so, Gilbert couldn't stem his concern that, one way or another, his mother would do everything in her power to make Mary as uncomfortable as possible.

After bathing, ridding himself of his five-o'clock shadow, and donning the fresh set of clothes, he used the upstairs hall telephone to ring Mary. "Ready for me to pick you up?"

"Well, I'm dressed, and Mum's done up my hair. But I wouldn't go so far as to say I'm *ready* for this little soirée." A nervous breath shivered through the telephone line. "What if I say the wrong thing? Pick up the wrong fork? Spill gravy all over your mum's fine linen tablecloth?"

He laughed softly. "Mother's friends will be too enraptured by your beauty and charm to notice."

"Oh, so now you're saying I'm sure to commit some horrible faux pas to embarrass your mother to kingdom come."

"I didn't mean—" He pinched the bridge of his nose. "Isn't it enough I'm crazy about you? Stop worrying, Mary. I'll be there in twenty minutes."

But when he arrived at her door, she seemed no less inclined to worry than when they'd spoken on the telephone. On the other hand, she looked positively stunning in a pale yellow drop-waist dress and white shoes with dainty pointed heels. She wore her hair pinned up in a pompadour and adorned with a bejeweled comb.

He gave a long, low whistle. "Mary McClarney, one look at you, and Mother's guests will be fawning at your feet. You look amazing."

He leaned in for a kiss, but she shoved him away. "You'll not be spoiling my hair and lipstick. Nor what's left of my composure, for that matter. I'll just fetch my purse so we can get this dinner party over with."

After she bade her mother good night, Gilbert escorted her to his car. She said little on the short drive to his house, but her noisy sighs filled the automobile. More than once, he reached across the seat to give her arm a reassuring pat.

By the time he parked in his driveway, he could use some reassurance of his own. Three autos lined the curb in front of the house, and another arrived as Gilbert led Mary up the porch steps. He took one look at the couple making their way along the front walk and clenched his jaw. So much for a casual evening. The O'Neals appeared to have dressed for a night at the theater.

Forcing a smile, Gilbert paused at the door as the middle-aged couple approached. "So glad you could make it. Quincy and Rose O'Neal, may I introduce Miss Mary McClarney."

"A fine Irish name, to be sure." Quincy O'Neal pinched the brim of his fedora and swept it across his body in a gentlemanly bow. "Delighted to make your acquaintance, Miss McClarney."

"My pleasure," Mary answered. "How do you do, Mrs. O'Neal?"

"Call me Rose, dear." The fair-haired matron offered Mary her hand. "I've heard so much about you already. Gilbert, darling, she's as pretty as your mother described."

The front door swung open, and Gilbert's mother, dressed in a lavish violet gown, filled the entrance. "I thought I heard voices out here. For heaven's sake, Gilbert, be a gentleman and invite our guests inside. Marguerite is serving hors d'oeuvres in the parlor."

Apparently she'd decided on theater attire as well. Did no one understand the meaning of *casual*?

While Gilbert's mother scooped up Rose's arm and led her through the foyer, Quincy O'Neal tugged on Gilbert's sleeve. "Going coatless, I see? Good idea." He shrugged out of his suit coat and loosened his tie. "Ah, much better. I tried to tell Rose it was too hot a night for formalwear, but you know how these ladies are, any excuse to dress up."

Mary tucked her hand beneath Gilbert's elbow. Brows arching, she said in a frantic whisper, "I've nothing so fancy as these ladies are wearing. Why didn't you say something?"

Motioning Quincy to enter ahead of them, Gilbert drew Mary aside. He cupped her face and gazed into her eyes. "How many times do I have to say it, Mary? You look beautiful just the way you are. You make these fussy old women look like simpering peahens."

"And all the while I'm feeling like the ugly duckling."

Her worried pout brought an ache to Gilbert's chest, but he'd probably earn a slap on the arm if he followed his instincts and kissed those pouty lips. He settled for dropping a kiss upon her forehead while drawing her beneath his arm and gently nudging her through the door. "Hold your head high, Mary McClarney, and remember, you're my girl."

Seated on an ivory brocade chair that appeared to have come straight from a French palace, Mary couldn't have felt more out of place. All around her, Hot Springs's elite clustered in pairs, threesomes, and foursomes, the men talking finance or golf games or baseball, while the women compared fashion notes and social calendars.

And the man who'd so reassuringly told her she was *his girl* was nowhere to be found. After bringing her a cup of cider and a plate of finger foods, he said he'd spotted an acquaintance he really must speak with and would be back shortly.

Shortly had stretched to nearly half an hour. If Mary had to sit here much longer looking prim and proper while hoping someone—anyone—would deign to engage her in conversation, she might just decide to slip out the front door and walk home. No one would notice her absence, she felt certain.

A shadow fell across her chair, and she glanced up to see Rose O'Neal's chiding smile. "What are you doing over here in the corner where no one can find you? Come, Mary, let me introduce you around."

True enough, a part of her *did* secretly hope she wouldn't be noticed in this out-of-the-way corner of the room. Much easier to feel sorry for herself at being ignored than to actually converse with these society folk.

Which now she must do, for Mrs. O'Neal had seized her hand and was already drawing her across the room toward two ladies admiring a figurine on Mrs. Ballard's mantel. "Judith, Helena, have you met Miss Mary McClarney?"

Hands clenched at her waist, she inclined her head to each of the ladies in turn. "So pleased to make your acquaintance."

Judith, the taller of the two women, peered at Mary through silver-framed glasses. "McClarney . . . McClarney. My husband has done business with a St. Louis furniture magnate by that name. Might you be related?"

"Not that I'm aware, ma'am. My family came over from Ireland when I was just a wee girl."

"What does your father do?" the other woman asked.

"He passed away several years ago, but he was . . ." Mary bit her lip. She could only imagine the disdainful looks she'd receive if she told how her father had come to Hot Springs as a laborer. He'd worked on a construction crew to build the Majestic Hotel on Park Avenue, then later the observation tower atop Hot Springs Mountain. The last job he held before his accident was building stone retaining walls along Hot Springs Mountain roads.

Remembering the accident never failed to bring a lump to Mary's throat. Da had been a good man and a diligent worker, and no condescending society lady would shame her into forgetting it. She stood taller and straightened her shoulders. "My father was a construction worker, one of the best. Take a walk with me around Hot Springs any day, and I'll point out to you the many projects that turned out all the better for having him on the crew."

Helena's eyebrows arched. "I'm sure." She released a nasal-sounding titter. "Judith, my glass is empty. Do excuse us, Miss McClarney."

As the two women departed, Rose O'Neal touched Mary's arm. "Don't mind those snobs. Helena grew up milking cows on a dairy farm. Judith's family was so poor she and her mother both had to take jobs in a garment factory. They're only where they are today because they had the good fortune to marry well. As did most of the overdressed biddies you see here this evening."

Mary glanced around the room, seeing the guests with new eyes. Then a disconcerting thought jolted her. If she married Gilbert, would affluence eventually mold her into yet another boring, snobbish society matron who took twisted pleasure in lording her status over those less privileged?

A Scripture verse flashed through her mind—Jesus's words to the rich young ruler concerning how hard it was for the rich to enter the kingdom of God.

"There you are, Mary!" Gilbert's arm slipped around her shoulders, and she gladly released the troubling thoughts. "Thanks for looking after my girl, Rose."

"My pleasure." The friendly blonde woman shared a smile with Gilbert, then winked at Mary. "She's a quiet one, but one hundred percent class."

A flush raced up Mary's cheeks. She dipped her chin. "I don't know about that."

"Oh, I do." Gilbert's arm tightened, and the pride in his eyes restored a measure of her confidence. "Come along, Mary," he urged with a quick kiss to her temple, "we're summoned to the dining room."

Relief poured through her to find herself seated between Gilbert and Rose. At least she could count on one or both of them to discreetly educate her on proper table manners should the need arise. Even with the confusing array of dishes, glasses, and silverware, she succeeded in maintaining her composure and selecting the correct utensil right through the main course.

Then, as servants whisked away dinner plates, Mrs. Ballard tapped her water goblet with the side of her spoon. "While we await the delicious dessert Marguerite has prepared, let's hear from our charming guest of honor, with whom I'm sure we'd all like to become better acquainted."

Mary glanced around the table to see which distinguished dinner guest Gilbert's mother referred to—only to realize all eyes were on her! She attempted to swallow, but the sides of her throat felt thick as cold molasses. Her gaze slid longingly to her water glass, too far away to reach without exposing the tremors rushing down her arms.

Gilbert found her hand beneath the table and drew it upon his lap, giving a reassuring squeeze. "Now, Mother, you mustn't put Mary on the spot."

"Do forgive me, darling." Mrs. Ballard snorted a dismissive laugh. "The *last* thing I'd want to do is cause Mary the *least* embarrassment."

Perhaps no one else caught the gleam of triumph in the woman's eyes, but Mary certainly took note. Saints help her, she'd *not* be intimidated by the likes of Evelyn Ballard. Steely determination spread through her veins as she withdrew her hand from Gilbert's and stiffened her spine. "I assure you, Mrs. Ballard, it isn't embarrassment I'm feeling, but rather . . . awe-struck gratitude."

Glimpsing Mrs. Ballard's subtle lift of her brow, Mary knew she'd chosen exactly the right words. "For truly," she continued solemnly, "how can I help but stand in awe of all these good folk who have so generously welcomed me, a stranger in their midst, and made me feel so perfectly at home among you?"

Across the table, lips thinned and glances drifted. All except Gilbert's brother, Thomas, who crossed his arms with an appreciative smirk.

Encouraged, Mary sat forward, beaming her most disarming smile toward Gilbert's mother. "And you, dear lady, your kindness goes without saying. I'm so looking forward to spending more time with you, which is why I'm thrilled you've agreed to accompany Gilbert to dinner at my home this Sunday after church."

Gilbert shot Mary a surprised grin. "Yes . . . won't it be . . . fun?"

Mrs. Ballard covered her sudden pained grimace with a napkin. A tiny choking sound emanated from behind the cloth. "Well." She cleared her throat and lowered the napkin to reveal a slightly more composed expression. "Turnabout is fair play, I suppose."

Seconds later, Marguerite and her helpers appeared carrying silver trays laden with dessert plates, and it seemed as if everyone present breathed a collective sigh of relief—Mary most of all.

Gilbert leaned close to whisper, "That was brilliant! Mother would die before controverting your announcement in front of all her guests."

"It was all I could think of." Mary waited until Marguerite had set a plate of raspberry cheesecake at her place before continuing. "And now I must find a way to tell Mum we're having unexpected company."

Then another thought assailed Mary. She cast Gilbert a worried frown. "Mum will want to include Dr. Russ, you know. I can't ask her not to invite him."

He toyed with his dessert fork, pushing a raspberry through the chocolate sauce drizzled across the plate. "Looks like Donald and your mother are getting serious, doesn't it?"

"Seems so." Mary lifted a forkful of cheesecake to her mouth and savored the creamy texture, almost as sweet as the fact Gilbert's attentiveness toward her appeared to have deepened. "I'm glad for Mum, though it was quite disconcerting at first."

"I can imagine. Although I have to say I'm relieved it's your mother he has eyes for and not you."

Mary's throat tightened. "You're not still jealous, are you?"

"Of course not." Gilbert laughed unconvincingly and stabbed another raspberry.

"Because you've no reason to be and never had."

"I know."

"Do you, now?" Mary harrumphed and took another bite of her dessert.

"I'm no more jealous of Donald Russ than you are of—" Gilbert clamped his teeth together, drawing a sharp breath through his nose.

Annemarie. He was about to say Annemarie.

Mary laid her fork aside. With studied movements she lifted her napkin to her lips and then quietly scooted back her chair. "Forgive me, Mrs. Ballard," she said, rising. "It's been a lovely evening, but I fear a headache has deprived me of further enjoyment. With your permission, I'll take my leave . . . if Gilbert will be so kind as to see me home."

"Why, certainly, dear," Mrs. Ballard replied, perhaps a little too quickly. "We wouldn't want you to stay if you're unwell."

Gilbert now stood at Mary's side, one hand resting gently at her waist as he escorted her from the dining room. She retrieved her handbag from the foyer table while Gilbert called for Zachary to bring the roadster around.

As they stepped onto the front porch, a balmy summer breeze ruffling Mary's hair, Gilbert strode to the rail and gazed into the night sky. "I'm always putting my foot in my mouth. You know I didn't mean it, Mary."

"You're always saying you didn't mean it. But she's there between us just the same." Mary edged up beside him, close enough to feel the brush of his shirtsleeve against her bare arm. "We need to make peace with this, Gilbert. *You* need to make peace with Annemarie. And with Chaplain Vickary."

He sighed, deep and long. "I know. I just . . . don't know how."

Mary slipped her hand into his. "Perhaps the place to start is prayer."

14

*M*ary was right. Gilbert should be praying more. Because he certainly didn't have the strength within himself to do what he needed to do. The bodily wounds he'd suffered during the war may have healed—as much as they were going to, anyway. But his spirit still chafed with anger. Remorse. Shame.

He gazed out his bedroom window in the predawn hours of Sunday morning after another sleepless night of wrestling with his conscience. Wrestling with the Lord. *Why, God? Why did You let this happen to me?*

All the loss, all the pain. All the selfish, foolish mistakes he'd made. What would it take to get past it all and live fully again? He'd hoped his growing affection for Mary would eventually eclipse any lingering feelings for Annemarie. He'd believed purchasing and renovating the Frederick farm would restore his sense of purpose.

But maybe his attempts to mend his broken life were misdirected.

Maybe he needed to quit striving on his own and start listening to the people he cared about.

The people who cared about him.

An hour later, showered, shaved, and dressed, Gilbert made his way downstairs. His sudden appearance in the kitchen took Marguerite by surprise.

She turned from kneading biscuit dough, flour coating her hands. "What you doin' in here, Mister Gilbert? It's a mite early for breakfast."

"I'll just make myself some toast, if you don't mind. I have some things I need to do this morning." He opened the pantry door, only then realizing he had no idea where to find the bread.

"Over here on the counter. In the breadbox." Marguerite nodded to a metal container with a rolltop lid. "And don't tell me you got business to attend to on the Sabbath, young man. You need to be heading to church with your family."

"Probably so, but not today." He sawed off two slices of bread from the loaf and set them on the toaster. While the toast browned, he poured himself a mug of coffee and leaned against the counter to watch Marguerite work.

She cast him a slant-eyed glance as she pounded the dough into a ball. "Ain't used to havin' an audience for my biscuit makin'."

Gilbert flexed his fingers. "Think you could teach me how to do that?"

"Ain't hard," she said, reaching for the rolling pin. "Just takes some flour, baking powder, shortenin', and buttermilk. Mix it all together, roll it out, cut your biscuits, and stick 'em in the oven."

"Anything's hard if you don't know what you're doing." Biscuit making. Farming.

Apologizing.

A toasty aroma reminded Gilbert what he'd come to the kitchen for. He unplugged the toaster and flicked the slices onto the counter, wincing as the hot crust stung his fingertips.

"Knives and plates are right handy for servin' up toast," Marguerite chided, handing him both. A fine dusting of flour coated the knife handle. "Jam's in the pantry, in case you was wonderin'."

Sheepishly, Gilbert eased the toast onto the plate then retrieved a jar of plum jam from a pantry shelf. Cursing his weaker left hand, he struggled to unscrew the lid, and Marguerite came to his aid. He mumbled his thanks.

She propped a floury fist against her hip as she watched him spread jam across his toast, and he caught her grinning at him. "You come a mighty long way," she said, a hint of pride in her tone. "Yes, indeed, I was a-feared we'd lost our old Gilbert after you come home from the war all shot up. I'm mighty glad to see you gettin' back on your feet—in more ways than one."

With a wink, she returned to her biscuit making. Seconds later, she was humming an old familiar hymn. Gilbert listened to a few bars before he recalled the title, but as the lyrics rose up in his memory, bittersweet longing filled him.

> . . . *Whatever my lot, Thou hast taught me to say,*
> *It is well, it is well with my soul.*

He turned away, toast and jam and unshed tears nearly choking him.

> *My sin, oh the bliss of this glorious thought!*
> *My sin, not in part but the whole,*
> *Is nailed to His cross, and I bear it no more,*
> *Praise the Lord, praise the Lord, O my soul!*

"Mister Gilbert? You all right?" Marguerite stepped up beside him, concern etching deep lines in her dark face.

"Fine, fine." He set his unfinished plate of toast on the counter, seized his cane, and marched out the back door.

☙

"Mum! I can't find those apples I put up last year." Mary squinted in the dim light of the cellar and scanned the labels of dust-covered canning jars. "How am I going to make an apple pie without apples?"

Her mother peered down from the kitchen. "Look on the bottom shelf next to the snap beans."

"Ah, here they are!" Clutching two jars to her bosom, Mary scurried up the stairs. She brushed past her mother and set the jars on the counter next to the pie crusts she'd just rolled out.

"Honestly, child, you're making much too big a to-do out of Evelyn's visit." Mary's mother poured herself another cup of tea and carried it to the table. "Just be yourself. No need to put on airs. After all, it's Gilbert you'll be marrying one day, not his mother."

"Don't say such things, Mum." Mary resisted the impulse to cross herself. "I don't dare even hope for a marriage proposal, not while we still have things to sort out between us." She tapped her chin. "Now, where did I put the cinnamon?"

"Right under your nose, girl." Rising, Mum snatched the cinnamon tin from behind a jar of apples and thrust it into Mary's hand.

An embarrassed flush crept up Mary's neck. "I can't help being flustered. You know Gilbert's mother will be appraising every little thing I do. And I'll never in a million years earn her approval." She smothered a moan with her apron hem. "Oh, why—*why*—did I ever open my big mouth and announce she was coming to Sunday dinner?"

"Mary Elisabeth Assumpta McClarney." Her mother caught her wrists and forced her to lower her arms. With a flinty glare she backed Mary over to the table and forced her into a chair. "Now then, young lady, you'll listen to your mother, and you'll listen good. It wasn't from me you learned to care what others thought of you. Especially the likes of hoity-toity Evelyn Ballard and her society friends."

"But, Mum—"

"I mean it, Mary." She shook a finger in her daughter's face. "I won't have any more of this fussin' and cookin' and cleanin' like we were expecting King George himself. Evelyn may act the royal snob, but you can bet she dons her knickers one foot at a time just like the rest of us."

At the image of Gilbert's mother working her well-endowed rear into silk undergarments, Mary couldn't resist a chuckle. Then once she started, she couldn't stop. Doubling over, she hugged her abdomen and shook so hard with laughter the pins slipped from her topknot and sent a riot of red curls falling across her face.

By then, Mum was chortling as well. "See what a ninny you've been?" She drew Mary to her feet and wrapped her in a hug. Then with one hand she smoothed back Mary's hair and with the other tapped her on the end of her nose. "You've worked yourself into a state over nothing, haven't you? And now, if we don't hurry and get those pies into the oven, they won't be done before it's time to leave for Mass."

Collecting herself, Mary mopped up her tears of hilarity and returned to the counter. "You're right, Mum. I'm being utterly ridiculous. If Gilbert's mother cannot accept me for who I am, it's her problem, not mine."

Or so Mary desperately needed to believe. As she emptied a jar of apples into a pie crust and then sprinkled cinnamon over the top, she could only hope Gilbert possessed the inner strength she'd always sensed in him, the strength to leave his mother as Scripture directed and to cleave only to his wife.

A shiver raced up Mary's spine. Oh, how she longed to become Gilbert's wife, to stand beside him proud and complete, never again to question the depth of his love or his commitment to her.

With practiced hands she wove dough strips into a lattice top, dotted the crust with butter and more cinnamon, then put the second pie together and slid them both into the oven. After making sure the roasting chickens were ready to go into the oven as soon as they returned from worship, she doffed her apron and hurried to bathe and dress.

An hour later, with the enticing aroma of apples and cinnamon filling the house, Mary checked the pies. Satisfied they were done, she set them on the windowsill to cool. Shortly afterward, she and her mother popped over to Genevieve Lawson's house, climbed into her car, and left with her for Mass.

As always, Mary visited the confessional before worship began. Through the filigreed screen she glimpsed Father Francis's silhouette. "Bless me, Father, for I have sinned. It has been one week since my last confession."

The old priest chuckled softly. Of course he recognized her voice, and, as always, began by chiding her for thinking herself such a hopeless sinner that she felt compelled to confess so often. "Child, child, if I wouldn't be considered a heretic, I'd assign you the penance of studying the life of Martin Luther. Take a lesson from the great reformer and live in faith, not guilt. God doesn't withdraw His forgiveness, nor His love, each time we fall short."

"I know, Father. But when I know I've sinned, I want to confess and receive absolution."

"All right, all right." Father Francis heaved an indulgent sigh. "Tell me, my child, what grievous sin have you committed since last Sunday?"

"Well, I . . ." Where to begin? Envy? Coveting? Pride? Vanity? What all these sins boiled down to was one thing: "I have allowed the opinions of others to blind me to the truth that I am created in God's own image and likeness." She sat a little straighter as she spoke. "I have let myself forget I've been made perfect in Christ Jesus and accepted as God's very beloved child."

Father Francis remained silent for several long moments. Finally, he nodded. "To forget how much God loves you is indeed a terrible thing. Mary McClarney, I absolve you of all your sins in the name of the Father, and of the Son, and of the Holy Ghost. Now go in peace and live in the truth you have just spoken. This is the only penance I impose."

Buoyed by his words and sensing the Lord's touch upon her spirit more tangibly than ever, Mary murmured a thank-you and joined her mother in the sanctuary to wait for Mass to begin. With hands folded and head bowed, she prayed, *Lord, grant me the faith to trust You in every area of my life, but today most of all with my deep and growing affection for Gilbert. Let our love be strong and pure and pleasing in Your sight.*

She glanced up at the statue of Mary gracing one corner of the chancel and added a petition for Jesus to impart a measure of His earthly mother's grace upon Evelyn Ballard. *For if You don't, dear Lord, You'll have to increase my faith a hundredfold— not to mention my patience—if I'm to endure her judgment.*

Gilbert encountered only a handful of hospital staff going to and fro as he made his way through the administration building. A receptionist at the front desk had told him Samuel should be in his office at this time on a Sunday morning. She'd even offered to telephone upstairs to announce Gilbert's visit, but he'd asked her not to. No point risking Sam's refusing to see him.

Not that he would. Samuel Vickary wasn't that kind of man.

Gilbert hoped *he* was no longer "that kind of man" either. Only time would tell.

The corridor echoed with the *click-click* of Gilbert's cane tip, the syncopated footfall of his artificial leg. Sam would hear him coming a mile away. He might already be planning a polite but hasty escape.

Outside Sam's partially closed door, Gilbert paused and inhaled a steadying breath. Through the crack he glimpsed Sam tilted back in a wooden swivel chair, one ankle crossed over the opposite knee, a sheaf of papers in his lap. His mouth moved silently, his brow creased in concentration.

Perhaps Gilbert shouldn't interrupt. He started to back away, when Samuel glanced up and their gazes met.

Samuel set both feet on the floor, the pages slipping from his lap. "Gil."

"Hello, Sam." He nudged the door with his cane. "If this is a bad time . . ."

"Not at all!" Samuel stood so quickly his chair careened into the bookshelves behind him. "Come in, please."

Gilbert took a hesitant step into the room. "Are you sure? You look busy."

"Just going over my message for this morning's chapel service." Samuel fumbled to retrieve the papers he'd dropped. He looked as ill at ease as Gilbert felt. "It's good to see you, Gil. You look well."

"You too, Sam." Gilbert squared his jaw and wedged sincerity into his tone. "Married life clearly agrees with you. I hope you and Annemarie are very, very happy."

"We are. Thank you." An uncertain smile tugged at Samuel's lips. "Do you want to sit down? Care for some coffee?"

Gilbert took the nearest chair but waved away the offer of coffee. Twisting the handle of his cane, he waited for Sam to settle into his chair while he framed his thoughts. But then everything he'd intended to say—all the excuses and apologies and assurances he'd changed—came out in four whispered words: "I miss you, Sam."

Samuel froze for a moment, hands gripping the chair arms. He breathed out slowly, his tense features relaxing. "I've missed you, too."

"I'm so sorry—sorry for everything—"

"Stop. It's all forgiven." Samuel rose again and moved around to Gilbert's side of the desk. He eased onto the chair beside Gilbert's, leaning close, hands clasped between his knees. "You've always had my forgiveness, Gil. Even when you didn't want it."

Gilbert tipped forward, tangling his fingers in his hair. He stared at the toes of his shoes through a sheen of wetness. "You have every right to hate me. So does Annemarie."

"Do you remember the story of Joseph from the book of Genesis?"

"My Bible knowledge is kind of rusty," Gilbert answered with a weak laugh.

"Well, Joseph was a very spoiled boy who was sold into slavery by his jealous brothers. Things were tough for quite a while, but, to make a long story short, he earned a position of authority under the Egyptian pharaoh and ended up saving thousands of lives, including his brothers'. And when they came to him pleading for forgiveness, here's what he said: 'As for you, you meant evil against me; but God meant it for good.' "

Gilbert shot Samuel a disbelieving glance. "You're saying God had a hand in what I did to you?"

"I'm saying despite every wrong we fallible humans inflict upon each other, God is able to turn it all to His sovereign purposes."

Images flashed through Gilbert's thoughts. Bullets flying, bombs exploding, bodies broken and bleeding. He shuddered. "Even war?"

Samuel didn't answer right away. Eyes clouding, he seemed lost in his own memories of the terrible time. "I don't presume to understand God's ways," he said at last, "but I believe with every fiber of my being His sovereign hand never left us, even in our darkest hours. I believe He carried us when we had neither the strength nor the faith to continue. And I believe God is yet working out His highest good in our lives."

Gilbert shook his head. "I don't know, Sam. There seems so much *bad* in my life—in *me*"—he thumped his chest—"I have trouble seeing what's good."

"Then trust the people who love you. Try looking at yourself through their eyes."

"Are you sure they're not just seeing what they want to see?" Gilbert pictured Mary in all her innocence, the way she could look at him sometimes and make him believe he could be or do anything. Then, just as quickly, he recalled the pain in her eyes every time he unintentionally hurt her. He groaned and looked away. "What if I'm hopeless? What if I'm too far gone even for God?"

Only the whispers of Samuel's slow, steady breaths filled the silence. Then, almost as quietly, he murmured, "I wasn't."

Gilbert glanced toward Samuel to find his gaze fixed on some invisible point beyond the office wall. A memory, or perhaps a distant hope or dream. Whatever Sam saw in his mind's eye, his rapt expression suggested it must be something beautiful. A desperate longing made Gilbert want to turn and see this vision for himself, but he knew the moment he looked, it would vanish.

Samuel seemed to shake himself back into the moment. He lowered his head briefly then lifted his eyes to Gilbert's. "I wish I knew how to convince you God hasn't given up on you and never will." With a quick glance at his watch, he stood, his features twisting into an apologetic frown. "I have to get to the chapel service. Can we talk more afterward, or . . ." He shot Gilbert a hopeful smile. "Maybe you could come to the service."

Gripping the handle of his cane, Gilbert took only a moment to decide. Or maybe he didn't decide at all but listened to his heart for a change. "Yeah. I think I'd like to."

15

*D*onald wasn't sure why he'd accepted Nell's invitation for Sunday dinner with the Ballard family. He couldn't think of anything more distasteful than sitting across the table from the man who'd almost ruined Sam Vickary's life.

Even worse—if anything could be worse—was enduring Evelyn Ballard's condescension, no matter how hard she tried to disguise it as polite conversation.

He had to admire both Mary and her mother, though. No putting on airs for them. Nell continued to amaze and enthrall him with her outspoken Irish wit. All the qualities in Mary that had first attracted him, making him wish he were twenty years younger, he'd found even more appealing in Nell. Finding himself in love at his age? Sometimes he still felt the need to pinch himself to make sure he wasn't dreaming.

"More pie, Donald?" The woman who held his heart reached for his empty dessert plate. Her eyes sparkled invitingly.

"I shouldn't, but . . ." He patted his belt buckle and sighed. "Maybe just a sliver?"

Nell rose and started around the table. "Anyone else? Evelyn? Gilbert? How about you, Thomas?"

Gilbert's brother pushed back his chair. "I'd love some, Mrs. McClarney. Let me help."

The Ballard family boasted one gentleman, at least. Donald decided to tag along. Slicing pie and refilling coffee cups had to be less stressful than avoiding eye contact with Gilbert.

While Nell dished up more pie at the kitchen counter, Donald served the coffee. After Mrs. Ballard refused, he topped off Mary's cup, then paused at Gilbert's place.

Gilbert looked up with a start. His mouth twitched with a nervous smile. "Uh, no, thanks."

Interesting. Maybe Donald had been too busy trying *not* to converse with Gilbert to notice the man wasn't talking much at all. He refilled his own cup before returning the pot to the stove. While Thomas carried pie plates to the table, Donald edged up beside Nell. "Dinner went better than I expected," he said under his breath.

"I must agree." She winked at him as she laid a clean white napkin over the leftover pie. Then, slanting a look toward the table, she whispered, "Can't help worrying about my girl, though. She and Gilbert both seem preoccupied about something."

"Any idea what?"

Nell drew her lower lip between her teeth. "It's just they seem so serious, like maybe it's time for a heart-to-heart."

She started for the table, but Donald caught her arm. His pulse throbbed beneath his collar. "Nell . . . I was hoping later . . ."

She looked up at him expectantly. "Yes, Donald?"

He swallowed. "Do you think later we might have our own heart-to-heart?"

Mary couldn't have been more relieved for dinner to end. Though everyone had remained civil, the atmosphere at the table had crackled with tension. She could sense it in Mrs. Ballard's stiff politeness, in Thomas's attempts to lighten the mood, and most of all in Gilbert's silence.

She'd known the moment he arrived something had changed, but with his mother hovering, he said little more than he'd spent the morning with Chaplain Vickary. Mary could only pray the visit had gone well.

Now, seated with Gilbert in the shade of an elm tree, Mary nudged the backyard glider into motion. "I love a quiet Sunday afternoon."

"It's nice, isn't it?" Gilbert tilted his head to gaze up into the branches, and Mary grew fascinated by the way the breeze toyed with his ebony curls.

She shifted slightly, her hand creeping into his. "Won't you tell me about your talk with Chaplain Vickary?"

"Not much to tell. I asked forgiveness, he gave it." He looked away briefly, his jaw firm. Then he squeezed her hand and smiled. "I don't mean to be curt. I need some time to sort out my thoughts."

"Then . . . things are better between you?"

"I hope so." He pushed up from the glider and locked his artificial knee. One hand in his pocket, the other resting lightly on his cane, he struck a casual pose as he swiveled to face Mary. Mischief lit his eyes. "A more interesting topic, if you ask me, is what's going on between your mother and Dr. Russ."

The statement made Mary suck in her breath. Concerning this subject, Mary desperately needed to sort out her own thoughts. The more she saw Mum and Dr. Russ together, the more she realized how close they'd grown. After the dinner dishes were done, the two of them had excused themselves for a Sunday drive, and the look in Dr. Russ's eyes suggested he had more on his mind than seeing the sights.

Arms locked at her waist, Mary kicked the glider into high gear, the chains groaning and creaking with every push. She looked up to see Gilbert laughing at her. "'Tisn't funny. See how you'd feel if it was your mother with a new man in her life."

Her remark only made him laugh harder. "Maybe a man in her life is exactly what my mother needs! Then she wouldn't have so much time to interfere in her sons' lives."

Mary rolled her eyes. "Heaven knows I could do with a little less of your mother's interference."

"So who could we introduce her to? Any other unattached doctors at the hospital?" He wiggled his brows. "Or maybe the orderly who's been giving you trouble. Bet they'd get along famously."

It was Mary's turn to laugh. "I can see the two of them now, your mum in furs and jewels, Ernest in his stained scrubs and puffing away on his cheap, smelly cigarettes."

"You're right. Forget the orderly. Let's focus on finding her a rich doctor." Gilbert shook his head and sighed as he returned to the glider. "Probably a waste of time, though. My mother's too self-absorbed. No single man in his right mind would dare risk such a liaison."

Seeing Gilbert in such a teasing mood, even at his mother's expense, cheered Mary like nothing else. And to know he'd begun to make peace with the chaplain—all the better! It gave her hope they'd get past the dark times and someday find the happiness together she'd prayed for.

They chatted awhile longer in the shade of the elm tree, Mary hanging on every word as Gilbert described the progress on the farm. Then his whole face brightened as he told her about the horse he'd found virtually abandoned at the racetrack and described his dream of buying a couple of quality broodmares. "With Mac's lineage, he could sire a whole herd of championship thoroughbreds."

Mary pulled away slightly, her stomach tensing. An unwelcome memory surfaced—flashing hooves and a little girl's terrified scream. Clenching her fists, she forced the images from her mind and tried to breathe.

"Prohibition can't last forever," Gilbert was saying, clearly oblivious to her distress. "Red-blooded Americans simply won't stand for it. Oaklawn will open again someday, just wait and see."

His words gave Mary something solid to latch onto. She twisted to face him. "All this talk of breeding horses—you mean to *race* them? So people can *bet* on them?"

"That's what people do with thoroughbreds. They're born to run." Gilbert's lips flattened. "Are you implying you don't approve of my plans?"

"I—I simply can't believe you'd intentionally involve yourself in an undertaking to promote such vice!" Mary wrung her hands, a troubling malaise curdling her stomach. "Have you learned nothing from the past few months?"

Gilbert glanced away, his forehead furrowed. "Of course I have, Mary. How can you ask such a thing?"

"Because apparently you've forgotten how you squandered insane amounts of money at the racetrack last spring. How you gambled not only on horses but cards and anything else you could bet on to pay for your morphine addiction."

"You bring it up *now*?" Gilbert stumbled to his feet and strode across the lawn. "Obviously I'll never be good enough to meet your holier-than-thou expectations. Why do I even try?"

"Gilbert, wait!" She rushed after him, barely snagging his shirtsleeve. "I only meant to remind you—"

"That I'm a hopeless failure?" He shook her off, pain and disappointment darkening his gaze. "The bottom line is you don't trust me. I have no right to blame you, but it still hurts." Giving a shudder, he turned away and marched through the side gate.

"Gilbert—" Her voice broke on a muffled sob. She followed him as far as the front lawn and watched with one hand over her mouth as he climbed into his roadster and drove away.

What have I done? Dear Lord, what have I done?

⚘

A brisk southerly breeze clawed at Nell's hair, until she finally gave up the battle, tugged the pins from her chignon, and let the wind have its way with her curls. Today she didn't feel forty-two. No, in fact, she felt sixteen again, the same age when she'd fallen wildly in love with the devilishly handsome Charles McClarney.

She'd loved Charles, yes, and dearly, faithfully. But something told her the man who now claimed her heart would never disappoint her the way Charles had. Would never risk hurting her—or her daughter—by seeking respite in intemperate pursuits.

If only she could trust Gilbert Ballard had the same regard for Mary. A sensitive soul, to be sure, but so troubled. And Mary, bleeding heart that she was, could never turn away from someone in pain, no matter how deeply she herself might be hurt.

Donald, sitting beside Nell on the grassy slope halfway up West Mountain, caught up a handful of her tresses and drew them against his cheek. "I love your hair loose like this. And the color—shiny as a copper penny."

Nell tossed aside her troubled thoughts. "With a bit of silver thrown in for good measure," she said with a laugh.

"Which only makes you all the more beautiful." He scooted closer, his arm reaching around her waist, and released a long, noisy sigh. "I wish I could make this afternoon last forever."

"Why?" she murmured, leaning into him.

"Just . . . because." He rested his head on hers for a moment, then pressed a kiss to her temple.

Mercy, but it felt nice to have a man beside her again, a good man like Donald Russ who made her feel more womanly than she had in years. She nestled deeper beneath his embrace.

He sighed again. "I lied."

"What?" Nell sat straighter, searching his face for some deceit, but saw only a teasing smirk.

"I lied, because I know exactly why I wish today would never end." Shifting his weight, Donald cupped her cheek. He tilted his head, angling his lips over hers. The kiss both shocked and thrilled her, and she wrapped her arms around his neck, drinking in the warmth.

Finally, he drew away, his blue-gray eyes smoldering. "Nell, am I crazy? Is there a ghost of a chance you could ever love a crusty old army doctor like me?"

"Oh, Donald, Donald . . ." Gentle laughter burbled in her throat. "I already do love you, you crazy old fool."

He gazed at her for a moment as if he didn't quite believe her. Then his mouth spread into a smile as wide as the verdant valley below them, and he kissed her again, this time with quick urgency. "I realize we haven't known each other long, but if the war taught me anything, it's that time is precious. I'm not getting any younger, and I don't want another second to pass without you in my life."

Her heart stammered. "Wh-what are you saying, Donald?"

"Marry me, Nell." Easing onto one knee in front of her, he clasped both her hands in his. "Say you'll be my wife, and we can spend the rest of our lives learning everything there is to know about each other."

"Oh, my. Oh, my!" Nell gulped air. "You *are* a crazy old fool, Donald Russ. And I suppose it makes two of us, because, yes, I'll marry you!"

⁂

At the farm Monday morning, Gilbert stood with Mrs. Frederick in the newly repainted entry hall, where sunlight beamed through the transom and tinged the eggshell-white walls with gold. He cocked a hip and let his gaze travel the long, narrow space. "Well? What do you think?"

With an appreciative sigh, Mrs. Frederick pressed a hand to her chest. "I cannot believe you have accomplished so much in only a week's time!"

Gilbert smiled to himself, grateful his wealth made it possible to employ so many out-of-work soldiers to speed progress along. "There's still much more to do, but once the work is finished, we'll have electricity in every room and a state-of-the-art kitchen, plus hot and cold running water upstairs and down."

Mrs. Frederick looked at him askance. "Running water upstairs? But how?"

"The front bedroom was so large I've decided to section off one end and turn it into a bathroom. The pipes have already been installed, and we'll be shoring up the floor to handle the extra weight of a bathtub." Gilbert motioned her down the rear hallway. "I'll take the rooms upstairs. You'll have this section of the downstairs for your private living quarters, complete with your own bath."

They stepped into a small room, with the furnishings pushed out from the walls and covered with drop cloths. Two of the walls now gleamed with a fresh coat of pale green paint.

Mrs. Frederick gave a delighted sigh. "My favorite color—how did you know?"

"I took a cue from the pretty green throw pillows I found on your sofa. Someone did nice embroidery work on those."

Tears glistened in the woman's eyes. "I made them many years ago, before John and I were wed."

"Then we'll move the sofa in here, and this can be your sitting room." Gilbert showed her into an adjoining room, where two corner windows let in light and fresh air. "I thought this could be your bedroom. Would you like the same shade of green? Or maybe a cheery yellow?"

She touched a handkerchief to the corner of each eye. "Yellow would be lovely. I will awaken to sunshine every morning and be reminded of your kindness."

Jaw clenched, Gilbert glanced away. Mary certainly didn't think him so kind after the way he'd walked out on her yesterday.

Again.

This was becoming a painfully bad habit, and he needed to get control of himself before he lost her for good—if he hadn't already. On the other hand, if she couldn't forget the man he used to be and have faith he'd changed, what chance did they have?

After showing Mrs. Frederick the rest of the work underway at the farm and introducing her to Obadiah, Gilbert conferred with the contractor and then drove Mrs. Frederick back to town. A headache had begun behind his eyes, leaving him in no mood to subject himself to the racket of hammers and saws. Taking the baths at the Fordyce seemed like the ideal way to pass the afternoon.

If nothing else, maybe he could sweat out the deep-rooted irascibility that always managed to spoil things with Mary.

A challenging workout in the Fordyce's third-floor gymnasium soon had him drenched in perspiration. Not always easy modifying exercise routines for an amputee, but he prided himself his mangled left arm grew continually stronger. From the gym, he went to the men's bath hall and luxuriated in a long, hot soak in the mineral waters Hot Springs had grown famous for. A needle shower, followed by a nap in the cooling room, then a deep-tissue massage, and Gilbert felt almost human again.

Returning to the third floor, he found an empty chair in the gentlemen's parlor and settled in with a cool drink. Cigar and pipe smoke formed a hazy cloud above his head, the aroma pleasantly soothing. Through half-lidded eyes, he gazed through the wide doorway toward the lavishly furnished assembly room, which ran across the entire front of the building. Panels of art glass decorated the ceiling, and tall, arched windows along the front gave the room an airy, open feel. At the south end of the long room, someone plied the keys of a grand piano, while a delicate female voice lifted in song.

Mellow from the baths and lulled by the sweet music, Gilbert drifted in and out of awareness until someone called his name, and he startled awake.

Arthur Spence, Gilbert's former schoolmate, nudged a cushioned wicker chair over and plopped down. "I was hoping we'd run into each other again. A little hot for the baths today, but relaxing nonetheless."

"Yes, very." Gilbert hauled himself higher in the chair and tried to shake off his lethargy. He took another sip of ice water. "How've you been, Art? Enjoying your time at home?"

"Actually, I'm bored silly." Arthur glanced over his shoulder before leaning closer to Gilbert. He lowered his voice. "Rumor has it you know where to find a good poker game and maybe a little bathtub gin."

Stiffening, Gilbert rubbed his jaw. "Where'd you hear that?"

"Oh, around." Arthur lit a cigarette and blew smoke toward the ceiling. "So clue me in, pal. You always were the best at knowing where to find a good time."

"You must be thinking of someone else." The songstress now crooned the familiar tune "When Irish Eyes Are Smiling," and Gilbert had no doubt Mary's eyes would surely *not* be smiling if she were privy to this conversation.

Arthur stretched out one leg and smiled toward the assembly room. "Okay, okay. I wouldn't want to get you into any trouble. I just thought, for old time's sake, you might be up for a little fun."

They sat without speaking for a few minutes, while Gilbert wrestled with his conscience over temptations he'd hoped he'd overcome. The plain fact was he'd *never* be good enough for Mary and not because her expectations were too high. She was light where he was darkness. She lived in perpetual hope, while he'd become an incorrigible cynic.

Where did I go wrong, God? What's happened to me?

He knew very well what had happened to him: the war. Thanks to the cursed Great War, he'd lost his leg, lost Annemarie, lost his self-respect.

With an inward groan he sat forward, gripping the hilt of his cane. Making a show of checking his watch, he stood. "Didn't realize I'd been sitting here so long. Sorry to rush off, Art, but I'm late for an appointment."

If he hurried, he might make it to the hospital in time to escort Mary home from work.

And maybe—just maybe—she'd find it in her heart to forgive him one more time.

16

$\mathcal{M}$r. Deeds." Mary laced her fingers and leveled an icy glare at her nemesis. "You were supposed to deliver these blood samples to the lab an hour ago. Dr. Cadwallader can't begin correct treatment for this patient until he gets the results."

"Don't get your knickers in a wad." With a roll of his eyes, the orderly snatched up the tray.

"And don't use that tone with me. I'll not abide your disrespect."

"Or what—you'll have me fired?" Ernest Deeds snorted a laugh. "Then who'd empty those nasty bedpans and mop puke off the floor?"

Seething, Mary gritted her teeth and silently prayed for strength. As calmly as her roiling stomach would allow, she extended her hand. "I'll take the samples, please."

Deeds hesitated. He glanced at the tray and then back at Mary. "I'm on my way right now, okay?"

"No, Mr. Deeds, it isn't okay." Mary stepped closer and firmly removed the blood sample tray from his grip. "You have abused my authority for the last time. Please leave word with the personnel department as to where your final check should be mailed."

The man's eyes narrowed to mere slits. His chest rose and fell with several angry breaths before he spun around and marched off the ward.

Mary set the tray on the counter before it fell from her trembling fingers. She needed a few deep breaths of her own to quiet her jangled nerves.

Lois appeared on the other side of the counter, her mouth agape. "Did you just fire that creep?"

"I did." Mary frowned in the direction Ernest Deeds had gone. "And good riddance."

"I'll say. I knew it was a mistake, their hiring a civilian to work at a military hospital. Lazy, good-for-nothing freeloader never learned to follow orders." Sorting through some folders, Lois handed one to Mary. "Here are the reports you've been waiting on. And don't forget, Mrs. Daley wants supply requests on her desk first thing tomorrow morning."

Mary massaged her forehead. "I haven't had a spare moment to take inventory." She glanced at her watch pin—past four-thirty already—and she still had those blood samples to deliver to the lab.

"The evening charge nurse should be coming on duty soon. Ask her to fill out the requisition."

"She has her own responsibilities. I'll just be a bit later getting home tonight." Shoulders sagging, Mary gathered up the blood samples.

"Want me to take those for you? The lab's on my way."

"I'd be so grateful!" Mary breathed out a sigh of relief as she passed the tray to Lois.

With one less task on her ever-growing to-do list, Mary set to work inventorying the supply room. Dressings, hypodermics, tongue depressors, catheters. Sheets, blankets, washcloths, towels. Mary estimated upcoming needs and noted quantities on the requisition form.

Moving to the medicine cabinet, Mary tugged the key from inside her smock. As she counted vials and pill bottles, her thoughts carried her back to last spring and the discovery someone had been stealing from the hospital's morphine supply. The news had compelled her to confront Gilbert about his addiction, setting in motion a series of events that could easily have ruined two lives if not more.

Praise God, Chaplain Vickary had survived the anguish of being forced to confront long buried memories of war.

And praise God, Gilbert had escaped his addictions and truly sought to atone for his cruelty.

If only she could believe he really had turned a corner. Had she overreacted yesterday? Breeding thoroughbreds didn't automatically mean Gilbert would succumb to gambling again, and she'd been wrong to insinuate as much.

He was right—she *didn't* fully trust him. How many times would he have to prove himself before they could both let go of the past?

It's more than just Gilbert's past you must let go of, Mary McClarney.

A wave of uneasiness swept through her, but before she could analyze the source, one of the floor nurses tapped on the doorframe. "Miss McClarney, you have a telephone call."

"Thank you, Christine. I'll be right there." Would she ever grow accustomed to being called *Miss McClarney* by the staff she now supervised?

Gathering her wandering thoughts, she realized she'd completely lost track in her inventory count. She glanced at the pill bottle in her hand and started again.

And stopped.

No, it *couldn't* be correct. She kept meticulous records regarding every milligram of medication dispensed. Yet, clearly, a sizable number of morphine tablets remained unaccounted for.

Her stomach plummeted. *Please, Lord, not again. Not now!*

"Miss McClarney, your caller's waiting." Christine smiled from the doorway. "Shall I take a message?"

"I'm coming." Flustered, confused, Mary locked the cabinet, tucked the key into her bodice, and jammed the inventory list into the folder. Clutching the folder, she darted around the corner to her office and snatched up the telephone. Breathlessly she answered. "H-hello?"

"Mary? Is everything all right?" Gilbert. He sounded worried.

No more so than she. Darting a glance toward the supply room, Mary sank into her chair. "I was in the middle of something." A sour taste rose in her throat. She swallowed. "Where are you?"

"I'm calling from the reception desk. It's after five. I hoped I could take you home and we could . . . talk."

"Oh, Gilbert." Mary pressed stiff fingertips beneath her brows. "I can't leave yet. There's a . . . a situation I must deal with."

A pause. "How much longer will you be?"

She hated the desperate plea in his voice. Hated even worse the suspicions arising in her thoughts. "I can't say. It could be awhile."

"I can wait. As long as it takes." He lowered his voice. "I need to see you, Mary."

Running her thumb across the mottled brown folder, Mary mentally recounted the drugs she'd been inventorying—as if doing so would change what she already knew to be true. She'd know if Gilbert were still abusing morphine, wouldn't she? A nurse should be able to tell. And he'd tried so hard to overcome his dependence.

Honestly! How utterly ridiculous to even suspect the missing drugs involved Gilbert. The abuser could be anyone connected with the hospital—anyone from the entire population of Hot Springs.

The evening charge nurse peeked into the office. Seeing Mary on the telephone, she nodded politely and signaled she'd wait at the nurses' station.

"All right, Gilbert, but only for a few minutes," Mary said, hating herself for suspicions even logic couldn't drive from her thoughts. She tucked the inventory folder into the bottom desk drawer under some other papers. "I'll be down shortly. Meet me behind the administration building."

After explaining to the evening charge nurse she still had work to finish and would return soon, Mary exited the ward and marched across the lawn. Reaching Gilbert, she stood before him, arms locked across her ribcage. "I don't have long, but I wanted to—"

Wanted to what? Search his eyes, examine his demeanor for any sign of addiction? Any sign he'd broken his promise and fallen into old habits again?

You don't trust him.

Hitching a breath, she pressed a hand to her forehead and turned away.

Gilbert caught her arm. "Mary, what's wrong? Did I—" He thrust her away. "Well, of course I did something. I'm *always* doing something. Or *not* doing something. Or doing the *wrong* something."

"Stop." She faced him again, a torrent of emotions churning beneath her heart. "I love you with all my being, but when every day brings new questions or awakens old doubts—it's just too hard."

He dropped his cane and clamped down on her upper arms with ferocity, tugging her against him though she fought to pull away. His lips parted, and his mouth devoured hers until she feared she'd swoon. The kiss ended with a final searing jolt, his gasping breaths slicing the air between them, his gaze smoldering. "Doubt anything," he rasped, "but not this, not what we have between us."

Her fingers clawed his shirtsleeves. How could she think clearly when his kisses, his fiery passion, never failed to reduce her to a weak-kneed, love-starved fool? Avoiding those ravenous dark eyes, she buried her face against his chest and struggled to breathe.

"Mary . . . Mary." Gilbert's arms encircled her with gentleness. His lips brushed her temple. "I'm sorry for yesterday. I'm sorry I'm always hurting you. But don't give up on me. Promise you won't stop loving me."

"I will always love you, Gilbert Ballard." She inhaled slowly through her nostrils, the scent of starched cotton mingling with his cologne. Easing out of his embrace, she stood straighter and forced herself to meet his gaze. "But we're trapped in a never-ending cycle of wounding each other and then asking forgiveness. This isn't the way love is meant to be."

The helpless, hurting look in his eyes squeezed Mary's heart. When he opened his mouth to speak, she silenced him with an upraised hand. She stooped to retrieve his cane and held it out to him. "I must return to the ward now. And . . ." She looked away, her lower lip trembling. "And we should take some time apart."

"Mary, no!"

Ignoring his outstretched arm, the shock and pain in his voice, she steeled her spine and strode away.

After Mary's pronouncement last evening, Gilbert couldn't think of a single reason to rouse himself from bed.

Time apart? Exactly when he needed her most?

Groaning, he rolled away from the mocking sunlight pouring through his bedroom curtains. After a sleepless night, his head throbbed and his belly ached with a different kind of hunger, the oblivion one morphine tablet could bring. Did the human body ever forget such cravings?

A thorn in the flesh—just like Samuel had preached about last Sunday at the chapel service. His message had dealt with the various wounds, both physical and emotional, no soldier could completely escape after serving in battle. Then he'd reminded his listeners of the Lord's words to Paul: "My grace is sufficient for thee: for my power is made perfect in weakness."

Gilbert didn't like thinking of himself as weak; his pride wouldn't let him. And yet it was because of his weakness—not the strength he prided himself in—that he'd broken his engagement with Annemarie. Weakness made him believe she couldn't love a cripple. Weakness made him afraid to give her the chance.

And weakness had convinced him that lashing out at his best friend would send Annemarie rushing back into his arms.

He hammered the pillow, wetness seeping from the corners of his eyes. *You stupid, stupid man! Annemarie is lost to you, and now—thanks to your idiocy—you're in danger of losing Mary as well.*

Someone knocked on his door. He could feign sleep, and maybe they'd go away.

"Gilbert, are you awake?" His mother. "It's half past eight, dear. We missed you at breakfast."

That late already? Gilbert pushed himself upright and scooted against the headboard. "Come in, Mother."

She nudged open the door, worry lines furrowing her brow. "Darling, are you ill? Shall I send Marguerite up with a tray?"

"I'm fine, just overslept." He palmed his eye sockets.

"Are you sure? You weren't yourself at dinner last night either." His mother swept over to the bed and sat on the edge. She felt his forehead with the back of her hand. "No fever."

"I said I'm fine. Can't a guy sleep late once in a while?"

"Your eyes are red." She made a *tsk-tsk* sound. "I sincerely hope this isn't a hangover. Have you been dipping into the last of our sherry?"

"No, Mother." Though he wished he'd thought of it last night when he couldn't sleep. "Please stop hovering. Give me ten minutes and I'll be up and dressed."

She rose and immediately sat back down, hands folded in her lap. "This is about that girl, isn't it? A mother always knows when her boy's heart has been crushed."

Her words stabbed him like a bayonet. Before he could stop himself, he blurted, "I'm losing her, and I don't know how to stop it from happening."

"Oh, son." His mother sighed and patted his arm. Genuine concern shone in her eyes. "I hate seeing you hurt, but I can't say I'm surprised. Surely you've realized she wasn't at all suitable for you."

"'Suitable' or not, I'm in love with her. She makes me happy—happier than I've been in years."

His mother frowned. "Are you saying Annemarie didn't make you happy?"

"Of course she did, but it's different with Mary." Gilbert plucked at the sheet, his gaze drifting toward the open window where a light breeze ruffled the curtains. "I don't know if I can explain it. It's the difference between summer and springtime, a wildflower and a rose. Being with Annemarie was comfortable, uncomplicated, like coming home at the end of a journey."

He sensed a smile creeping across his face. "Mary makes me excited to pack my bags and set out on new adventures with her by my side."

"New adventures may not always be wise." Gilbert's mother flattened her mouth as her gaze slipped to the vacant space at the end of his thigh. "Sometimes adventure can bring troubles we never planned for."

Unexpected sympathy welled for his mother. Sometimes he forgot what war had cost her, the emotional price she paid in grief and worry. He drew her hand into his lap. "I came home alive, which is more than I can say for thousands of others. I couldn't admit it at the time, but I really am one of the lucky ones."

Pulling a handkerchief from her pocket, Gilbert's mother sniffled. "An answered prayer, most certainly."

Gilbert didn't care to think of all the prayers gone unanswered during the war. Maybe he'd take up the subject with Sam one of these days.

In the meantime, he had a farm to get up and running. Crying into his pillow wasn't getting the job done. If he could prove to Mary he could stand on his own two feet—figuratively, if not literally—leaning on nothing other than his cane and his wits, maybe she'd stop doubting him.

Dropping a kiss upon his mother's hand, he nudged her off the bed. "Go on, now, and let me get dressed. And have Marguerite warm me up some breakfast. I'll be down in two shakes of a lamb's tail."

More like three or four or twenty by the time he'd hobbled to the bathroom to shower and shave, then fastened his stump into the prosthesis and donned shirt, slacks, socks, and shoes. Standing before his dresser mirror, he ran a comb through his hair and inspected the scar that sliced across his left temple and over his ear. Tinnitus still plagued him, though he'd learned to tune out the incessant ringing. If only he could be rid of these infernal headaches!

Downstairs, he took his seat in the dining room just as Marguerite brought in a plate of scrambled eggs, bacon, and buttered toast. The aromas made him forget all about his pounding head.

"Miz Frederick was wantin' to know if you're going out to the farm this mornin'," Marguerite said as she filled his coffee cup.

"Later, probably. I have some business in town first." Gilbert peppered his eggs then spread blackberry jam across his toast.

"Be sure you let her know. She said somethin' about talkin' to your new man about those bees." Marguerite shivered. "Oooh, I don't like bees. They give me the willies!"

Gilbert chuckled. "I prefer to stay away from them, myself. But Obadiah and Mrs. Frederick seem to know what they're doing."

While Marguerite fussed with linens and tableware, Gilbert polished off his breakfast. Last week, at his mother's dinner party, he'd talked at length with an acquaintance who had horse breeding connections. Today would be a good day to follow up.

And Mary was wrong. Just because Gilbert wanted to breed race horses didn't mean he'd relapse into old habits. This was an investment, nothing more.

✍♥

Mary felt as if she could crawl right out of her skin.

She also felt she could count every day, hour, minute, and second since she last saw Gilbert.

She'd forgone the confessional before Sunday Mass earlier, unwilling to bare her aggrieved soul to Father Francis yet again only to be told her feelings were perfectly normal. How could a priest, a man who had never experienced the throes of romantic love, ever understand how she suffered?

And now, to sit here at the dinner table with Mum and Dr. Russ while attempting, for their sakes, to project an aura of good humor—the effort required every last measure of fortitude she possessed.

While her mother and the doctor laughed over yet another shared joke, Mary pushed away from the table. "We've berries and cream for dessert. Who wants coffee?"

"Sit down, lass," her mother said, rising. "You're the one who's worked all week." Frowning at Dr. Russ, she patted Mary on the shoulder. "This poor girl's been especially tired these days. Not even the energy for an evening out with her beau."

The doctor turned toward Mary with a concerned frown. "Your mother told me you'd worked late a couple of days this week. I hope the charge nurse position isn't proving too taxing for you."

"I enjoy the challenge. It's just . . ." Mary pressed her lips together. She hadn't yet confided in her mother about the missing drugs, nor about how the discovery had reignited her latent concerns about Gilbert.

She wanted to trust him, truly she did. But every day brought fresh reminders of everything standing between them.

Her mother returned to the table with bowls of blackberries dolloped with sweetened whipping cream. "Coffee should be ready soon. Let's have our dessert now, and we can take coffee out on the porch where it's breezier." Taking her seat, she fanned herself with a napkin. "We're in the hottest part of the summer, I fear."

Dr. Russ spooned up some fruit. "You were saying, Mary? What's troubling you about the work?"

"Well, I . . . I had to request termination of our civilian orderly this week." Perhaps that would satisfy their curiosity.

Mum sucked in a breath. "What a shame. But if you found it necessary, then I'm sure he deserved it."

"I suppose he did." Mary pushed her berries around the bowl, the purple juices staining the pristine white cream just as surely as suspicion had tainted her heart. Perhaps she should have gone to confession after all.

"Personnel problems are always distressing." Empathy filled Dr. Russ's tone. "I heard about what happened. You did the right thing, Mary."

His words brought little comfort. Oh, she had no qualms about ridding herself of Ernest Deeds. But the day would be forever linked in her mind with walking away from Gilbert.

Conversation ceased as they finished their dessert. Mary helped her mother clear the table while Dr. Russ poured coffee. As they each collected a cup and saucer to carry out to the front porch, Mum cast Mary a secretive smile. "Perhaps Donald and I can cheer you up a bit. There's something we've been waiting all week to tell you."

A sharp twinge in Mary's abdomen signaled a warning. If she hadn't been so preoccupied with her own troubles, she might have taken more notice of the telling looks passing between her mother and Dr. Russ.

She followed the couple out to the porch. Mum and the doctor sat hip to hip on the wooden swing while Mary chose the old wicker rocker across from them. Gingerly she sat down, careful not to spill coffee. She took a sip of the steaming brew and then donned a smile she didn't feel. "All right, you two. Don't keep me in suspense a moment longer. What's this news Mum just hinted at?"

Glancing shyly at the doctor, her mother whispered, "Do you want to tell her, or shall I?"

"If I may . . ." Dr. Russ set his cup and saucer on the porch rail and cleared his throat. "Mary, I've asked your mother to be my wife, and we'd very much like your blessing."

She shouldn't have been surprised. Even so, she couldn't suppress a stunned gasp. "This is . . . so sudden."

"I know, darlin'," her mother said, coming to kneel beside Mary's chair. She looked up beseechingly. "But Donald's right. Neither of us is getting any younger, and we don't want to waste a moment more. Please say you're happy for us."

"I am, of course!" Mary set her coffee aside and drew her mother into her arms. "Your happiness means everything to me. Yes, yes, I give you my blessing!"

17

Thomas never made a trip to Kendall Pottery without remembering all those years Annemarie had covered the front desk. But ever since Annemarie had opened her ceramics shop on Central Avenue, a former doughboy by the name of Jack Trapp had taken over office duties at the factory. Jack had clerked for a colonel while stationed in France during the war, so he'd learned the ins and outs of managing the pottery factory office in no time.

"Mixing bowls, canisters, pitchers—most of these items are already in production and can be delivered a week from Tuesday." Jack shoved a hank of blond hair off his forehead as he looked up from the purchase order. "Anything else you need before I figure your total?"

"That should do it. Bill the hotel as usual." Thomas roved the area between the desk and the front door, his gaze sweeping framed sepia photographs depicting the pottery-making process. Nothing nearly so fancy as the artistic pieces Annemarie created. He hoped her shop venture continued to be profitable.

Although he might never forgive his brother for making certain Annemarie would never be a part of the Ballard family.

Thomas had always been fond of the beautiful dark-haired girl, even harbored a secret crush on her most of his life. But she'd always belonged to Gilbert, and a little brother didn't encroach on his older brother's territory.

Speaking of Annemarie, the front door flew open and the blushing bride herself breezed in. Eyes sparkling, a smile bright enough to light downtown Hot Springs on the darkest night of the year, she looked the picture of wedded bliss.

"Thomas, what a nice surprise!" She clutched his hand and tugged him close for a quick kiss on the cheek.

"You look radiant. Guess I don't have to ask how you're enjoying married life." Making a pretense of admiring her wedding ring, Thomas inspected her hand. "Ah, just as I thought. You've been slaving away at the pottery wheel again. I see the evidence under your fingernails."

Light laughter bubbled from her throat as she jerked her hand away. "Guilty as charged. In fact, the reason I'm here is to ask my father if he can spare a few supplies. My workroom at the shop is in dire need of restocking."

Jack rose from the desk. "Your dad's already put some things aside for you. I was planning to deliver them when I take my lunch break."

"My car's out front," Thomas offered. "I'd be happy to do the honors."

Annemarie looked up with a shy smile. "Are you sure it's no imposition?"

When Thomas persuaded her it wasn't, Annemarie excused herself to look over the supplies her father had gathered and disappeared through the door behind Jack's desk.

"Thanks," Jack said, returning to his seat. "I've got a couple of other stops to make and would have been pressed for time. Let me just get you your copy of the Arlington purchase order."

As Jack gathered up the paperwork, an envelope slid to the floor. Thomas recognized the foreign postmark; he'd seen enough of them when Gilbert had written home from France. He stooped to retrieve the letter and handed it to Jack. "Is this from your sister? How's Joanna doing?"

Jack tapped the envelope against his palm, his expression sobering. "I don't know why she won't come home. She was released from the Signal Corps after the peace treaty was signed."

Thomas had heard about the "Hello Girls," civilian women who had served as telephone operators for the American Expeditionary Forces in France. Women whose bravery and duty to country must rival that of the soldiers who fought at the front. "Your sister's certainly to be admired, Jack. I know your family's proud."

A look of uncertainty momentarily darkened Jack's gaze. "No more than yours for Gilbert's service. I sometimes feel guilty I had it so easy over there, sitting in offices or bunkers through most of the war."

"At least you served. Thanks to my bum heart, the Army wouldn't have me." Thomas tucked the purchase order copy into the pocket of his suit coat. "But I suppose, as the saying goes, 'They also serve who only stand and wait.'"

"John Milton. I often pondered those words while my buddies were getting slaughtered on the battlefield. It was the only way to convince myself my clerical work over there made a difference."

"You and Joanna both performed very necessary duties. Don't doubt it for a moment."

The rear door opened, and Annemarie waltzed into the office followed by her father hefting a large crate. Jack popped up to grab one side.

"Thanks, Jack." Mr. Kendall bellowed a laugh. "My only daughter deserts me to open her own shop and still mooches clay and glazes off her old man."

"Now, Papa, I told you to bill me. It's just the factory gets a much steeper discount than suppliers will grant me." Annemarie heaved a rueful sigh. "Business at the shop is good, but not so good I don't need to watch expenses where I can."

Thomas held the front door while Jack and Mr. Kendall carried the crate out to his latest splurge, a butter-yellow Jeffery Touring Car. Once the crate was securely loaded in the back, he helped Annemarie into the passenger seat.

As they turned onto Whittington Avenue toward downtown, Annemarie quietly cleared her throat. "I'm glad I found you at the factory today. Sam told me Gilbert came to see him at the hospital and they had a good talk."

"Really? I didn't know."

"Sam won't say much more—he'd never break a confidence—but I can't help wondering how Gilbert has been."

"He's . . . well." Thomas was still digesting the news that Gil had made an effort to patch things up with Sam. It had to be a good sign. "You heard he'd purchased the Frederick farm."

"My parents and I were shocked to learn about Mrs. Frederick's sad state of affairs—we had no idea! I'm so glad Gilbert has been able to help."

"He spends most days out there overseeing the restoration. The work seems to agree with him."

Annemarie rested her arm on the open window and gazed at the passing scenery. Her voice barely a whisper, she asked, "But is he happy?"

Thomas made the turn onto Central Avenue, slowing behind a trolley. "Quite honestly, no." At Annemarie's sharp look, he added quickly, "It isn't because of you. I've had the sense for a while now he's accepted your marriage to Sam. He's trying very hard to be happy for you both."

A mixture of relief and concern clouded Annemarie's dark eyes. "The nurse, Mary—is he still seeing her?"

"He was, but I get the feeling they've broken up." Taking a side street, Thomas steered the car up a short hill and around the corner to the street behind Annemarie's building. When he reached the back door of her shop, he shut off the engine and leaned back wearily. "I've seen Gil despondent over his war wounds. I've seen him in both deep despair and blinding rage over losing you to Sam. But this past week he seems . . . dead inside, like he's just going through the motions."

Going through the motions.

As Friday drew another work week to a close, Mary could say little more about how she'd passed the time. The business with the missing drugs had consumed most of her mental energy. At least Mrs. Daley's understanding had mitigated her worries. Such things happened, the chief nurse stated, and the best they could do was to keep the cabinets securely locked and a sharp eye peeled should the perpetrator return.

Mary had formed her own suspicions, considering the drugs had been discovered missing at almost the same time she'd released Ernest Deeds. The fact no new shortages had come to light since last week only reinforced this belief. Unfortunately, Mary had no evidence with which to accuse the man, so chances were he'd get away with the crime.

If only she could silence her doubts about Gilbert!

What's wrong with me, Jesus, that I can't trust his heart?

By the time her shift ended, a summer thundershower had let loose on downtown Hot Springs. Best to wait it out in the shelter of the administration building. In the lobby, she plopped down on a bench near an open window as a cooling mist filtered through the screen while raindrops pelted the veranda.

"Hello, Mary." Chaplain Vickary motioned toward the vacant spot next to her. "Not a good day for walking home, is it? May I join you?"

"Of course." She doubted her feeble smile spoke much of a welcome, but it was the best she could do.

The chaplain lowered himself onto the bench. "Dr. Russ shared his good news with me. I hope he and your mother will enjoy many years of happiness together."

"Mum's sacrificed so much. She deserves to be happy." Mary sighed and glanced away.

"And you, Mary, you deserve to be happy as well, but . . . I see very little evidence of happiness in you these days." Chaplain Vickary shifted slightly and tilted his head. "Has something changed between you and Gil?"

She gazed at the curtain of rain and breathed in the moisture-laden air. "We can't seem to stop hurting each other. I've told him I can't be with him for now."

"Love sometimes hurts, it's true. A relationship is a continual give-and-take, a never-ending learning experience." The chaplain uttered a soft chuckle and shook his head. "Listen to me, married scarcely over a month and handing out romantic advice as if I knew what I was talking about. I'm sorry, Mary. There are no easy answers, especially considering all you and Gilbert have been through. But please don't give up on him. Don't give up on the hope of a future together."

"I don't want to. But I don't see how it can ever work between us."

"I thought the same of Annemarie and me. But God had different ideas."

At the mention of Annemarie's name, Mary couldn't suppress a shiver of resentment. She closed her fists around the clasp of her handbag. "I've grown to seriously doubt God's ideas for my future include Gilbert. Look at all we'd have to overcome. The damage the war's done is bad enough, and then there's his guilt over what he did to you and Annemarie." A harsh laugh burst from her throat. "Not to mention his mother's low opinion of my social standing."

"Those sound like excuses, and poor ones at that. Yes, the war changed Gilbert. It changed us all. But he's changing for the better, mark my words. As for his mother, Gilbert is in love with you, which makes her opinion irrelevant." Chaplain Vickary thrust out his jaw. "Be honest, Mary, with yourself, if not with me. What's really keeping you and Gilbert apart?"

Before she could defend her arguments, a tall figure loomed over them, the tip of a cane appearing near Mary's feet. "I'd like the answer, myself."

She looked up with a start. *Gilbert.* Nerves dancing, she stumbled for a reply. "I thought we'd agreed . . ."

"We didn't *agree* on anything. You simply shut me out of your life." He dipped his head toward the chaplain. "Hello, Sam."

Chaplain Vickary rose. "I should let the two of you talk."

"No need. We've nothing more to say." Mary also stood, keeping her eyes averted.

"I think there's plenty," Gilbert insisted. "Anyway, it's raining. The least you can do is accept a ride home."

"The rain appears to have let up. I'd rather walk."

"Mary, please." Gilbert's hand brushed her arm, but she shook off his touch.

"Mum will be holding supper. Good day, Chaplain," she added with forced brightness. "Nice visiting with you."

Rushing out the exit, she nearly collided with a trio of nurses striding across the hospital grounds, Lois among them.

Lois stopped and furled her umbrella, droplets spattering Mary's shoes. "I was hoping to catch you before you left for the day. My friends and I have the weekend off, and we're taking the train into Little Rock for some fun. Why don't you come with us?"

Still flustered after her encounter with Gilbert, Mary drew a breath and glanced toward Lois's companions, two young nurses from the ward across the way. Mary had crossed paths with them often enough to peg them as flighty and flirtatious. A weekend with these women in the bustling city of Little Rock was sure to be fraught with impropriety.

She pulled her shoulders erect with all the indifference she could muster. "Thank you, but I have . . . other plans." *Laundry. Ironing. Cleaning. Errands.* Plans, nonetheless.

"Well, if you change your mind, we're meeting at the depot tomorrow morning at nine sharp." With a cheery toodle-oo, Lois caught up with her friends, all of them giggling like school-girls as they skipped up the hill toward the nurses' quarters.

Mary tried hard to resent their carefree enthusiasm, but truth be told, she envied them. Some days, especially of late, she wondered if she'd forgotten how to laugh.

A tingle at her nape made her glance up at the building, where she glimpsed Gilbert watching her from the veranda. A confused frown marred his handsome features, and he looked ready to charge down the steps after her. But then, Chaplain Vickary stepped into the doorway. Resting his hand on Gilbert's arm, he shook his head gently, and murmured something Mary couldn't hear. A moment later, both men returned inside, and the door closed behind them.

Thank you, Chaplain. He must have sensed Mary couldn't bear a scene just now, especially not here, where Mrs. Daley, along with every staff member on duty, might witness their exchange.

With leaden steps, she set her feet toward home and felt it only her just deserts when halfway there the sky opened up and drenched her to the skin. She arrived home a sodden mess, shoes soaked from trudging through puddles and hanks of hair clinging to her neck and face.

"Oh, lass!" Mary's mother ran for towels. "Why ever did you walk home in the rain?"

"When I started out, I thought it was over and done." Dripping onto a rug in the foyer, Mary plucked off her rain-soaked nurse's cap and tugged the rest of the pins from her bun. Though the day was warm, she'd begun to shiver and could think of nothing more comforting than filling the tub with hot water and climbing in for a good long soak.

Then she looked up to see Dr. Russ standing in the archway to the parlor, and only then did it register she'd walked right past his roadster parked in front of their house. Dressed in civilian clothes, the doctor cast her an apologetic grimace. "I'm so sorry, Mary. When the rain started, I thought of coming to fetch you, but your mother and I were talking and the time got away from us."

Mum wrapped a towel around Mary's shoulders. "Hurry along and change into dry clothes, because we've something important to tell you."

Cold and dazed, Mary could do little more than comply as her mother urged her toward the stairs. They'd already told her they planned to marry. What other "important" news could there be?

Once she'd changed into a housedress and combed the tangles out of her wet hair, she slipped her arms into an old wool sweater in hopes of staving off the shivers long enough to find out what her mother and Dr. Russ had to say. Hugging herself, she scurried downstairs to the parlor.

The sight of Mum and the doctor holding hands on the settee never failed to take her aback. Not to mention their nervous glances and tentative smiles did little to alleviate her growing concern. She sank onto the edge of a chair across from them. "All right, what's this news you can't wait to share?"

"Mary, darlin', I don't quite know how to say this." Her mother sucked in a quick breath and squeezed the doctor's hand. "Donald's being transferred back to Walter Reed. He's to report for duty there a week from Monday."

"Oh, Mum, how awful for—" The words died in Mary's throat as meaning sank in. A physical pain shot through her abdomen. She gave a soft cry, and her next words came out in a moan. "You're going with him."

⚜

"I don't understand, Sam. I told her I love her. I'd marry her tomorrow if she'd have me." Gilbert's chin sank lower as he and Sam followed the puddled gravel path around the hospital buildings. The clouds had thinned and the western sky brightened to a pale orange-gold, but after more than an hour of hashing things out with Sam, Gilbert felt no closer to finding a way to win Mary back.

Reaching the upper gates, Samuel paused to gaze out across the bathhouse rooftops. "Maybe a period apart for self-examination is the best thing for both of you. Marriage is a step I doubt either of you is ready to take."

Gilbert snorted. "You and Annemarie sure didn't waste any time."

Samuel flinched, and Gilbert instantly regretted both his words and his tone. Groaning, he drew a hand across his forehead. "I know, I know. It's unfair to compare our situations.

Maybe it's hindsight, but I can admit now you and Annemarie were meant to be together."

Relaxing slightly, Sam offered a sad smile. "I believe you and Mary are meant to be together as well. It's just going to take a little longer for each of you to get past the barriers in your way."

"What if we can't?" Gilbert ground his teeth together. "I overheard part of what Mary told you earlier—she fears my mother's disapproval."

"It's true, your mother can be quite intimidating. I'll never forget the way she swept in to claim you at the train station the day we arrived. Poor Annemarie never had a chance . . ." Sam pressed his lips together and glanced away.

"Don't feel you can't mention Annemarie's name around me. I mean it, Sam. I'm over her."

"Are you?" Sam's eyes darkened.

"Of course, I am!" A growl tore from Gilbert's throat. "I couldn't honestly say so until recently, but I'm more certain than ever it's Mary I love, Mary I want to spend the rest of my life with. What Annemarie and I had . . ." Swiveling away, he stared at the hospital gates, the central design shaped into iron-work outlines of cannons, rifles, bayonets, and crossed swords. Rage spewed through his gut. "Blast the war. Blast it to hell!"

Sam edged up beside him, and for a long moment they stood in silence. Judging from the subtle lift of his friend's chin, Gilbert surmised Sam's thoughts carried him back to bleaker times as well.

Finally Sam sighed. "I've given up trying to understand why God allows war, why He permitted the suffering and death we witnessed over there. All I'm left with is the assurance, no matter how distant God seemed, He never abandoned a single one of us. I find some comfort in recalling the Psalmist's words: 'Precious in the sight of Jehovah is the death of his saints.'"

Bitterness rose in the back of Gilbert's throat. "Maybe that's my problem. I'm not dead, and I'm definitely not a saint."

"Don't talk like that, Gil." Sam stepped in front of him, his gaze steely. "I don't know why some of us came back alive and others didn't. I don't know why you lost a leg or why I—" He swallowed, the pain of remembrance etching deep furrows around his eyes and mouth, and his voice dropped to a raspy whisper. "Why my crisis of faith resulted in taking the life of one of our own."

"Stop, Sam. It wasn't your fault." Ravaged anew by guilt over exposing his friend's most desperate moment, Gilbert tightened his grip on his cane. "I know what you're trying to tell me. There are no answers this side of heaven. We just have to keep the faith, keep trusting God's in control. Well, it isn't as easy—"

A stabbing pain skewered Gilbert's temple. He clamped his eyes shut, his mouth contorting in agony. Feeling his way to the gray brick stanchion beside the double gates, he collapsed against it.

"Gil?" He sensed Sam's presence next to him. "What can I do?"

Gilbert gave his head a quick shake, which only intensified the pain. He breathed in and out with deliberate slowness while stifling the scream begging for release. Behind his eyelids mortar fire flashed. His ears echoed with the roar of cannons and the stutter of machine guns. He groped for Sam's arm. "Get . . . Mary."

18

Somehow—Gilbert wasn't certain how—Sam got him back inside the administration building and upstairs to Sam's office. While Gilbert sat hunched over in a chair and cradled his throbbing head in sweaty palms, Sam telephoned Mary's house. Gilbert also wasn't sure where he found the presence of mind to inform his friend the McClarneys now had a telephone. He only knew how desperate he was for the healing touch of the woman he loved.

"Hello, Mrs. McClarney, it's Chaplain Vickary calling from the hospital. Could you put Mary on, please?" A pause. "I see. No, of course, I wouldn't want to disturb her."

Gilbert tried to lift his head, ignoring the fiery darts ripping through his eyeballs. "What—"

Samuel held up one hand. "Yes, ma'am, but Gilbert is here with me, and I thought she'd want to know—" Another long stretch of silence. Eyes closing briefly, Sam inhaled slowly through his nostrils. "I understand. I'm sorry to have troubled you. Please tell Mary I hope she feels better soon."

As Samuel replaced the receiver, Gilbert forced himself upright and willed his blurry eyes to focus. "She's ill? What's wrong?"

"Her mother only said she'd arrived home cold and wet and had gone upstairs to lie down." Sam massaged the back of his neck as he came around the desk.

"She should have let me drive her home." Gilbert worked his jaw back and forth a few times, feeling the stretch in his temples.

Reaching for the water pitcher on the corner of the desk, Samuel poured a glass and handed it to Gilbert. "Would an aspirin help?"

Gilbert clutched the water glass in both fists. Aspirin was better than nothing. Certainly safer and more respectable than the alternative his body craved. He nodded, and Sam retrieved an aspirin bottle from his desk drawer. After downing two tablets, Gilbert set the glass on the desk. "I hope Mary didn't catch her death of cold walking home in the downpour."

"Her mother did sound worried. Do you want me to go over and check on her?"

"Would you?" Gilbert glanced up hopefully. "You could take my car. It'd be faster than walking."

"And be recognized immediately. No, I think I'd better walk. Are you able to drive yourself home, or should I call for Zachary?"

Gilbert rose slowly, testing for any signs of lightheadedness. "I think the worst has passed." He found his cane and started for the door. "You'll let me know as soon as you learn anything?"

"You know I will."

Together they walked out to where Gilbert had parked his roadster. From behind the wheel he watched as Sam started up Reserve Avenue toward the McClarneys' neighborhood. Emptiness and longing carved a hollow in his belly, and he fought the impulse to drive straight over to Mary's himself and put an end to the torture of their separation.

Wait. . . . Wait and trust.

He would. He'd try, anyway. Maybe Sam was right—God did care and somehow through all this was already working things out for the best.

ℒ♥

Weak sunlight filtered through Mary's bedroom shades. The rain had moved on, but the fresh, clean scent still lingered. Any other time, the sweet fragrance of a rain-washed day would have filled Mary with hope and anticipation. This evening, however, she felt only dread.

How can You do this, Lord? Mum's all I have, and You're taking her a thousand miles away!

She'd tried with all her might to nod and smile and congratulate the happy couple. Tried to convince herself Mum's happiness was all that mattered. Even when her mother shyly asked Mary to stand up with her next weekend when Father Francis united them in marriage in a private ceremony, Mary had held her chin high. When a tear slipped down her cheek, she'd flicked it away with a tinkling laugh. "Oh, I'm just so happy for you both!"

She'd sat primly awhile longer as Mum and Dr. Russ eagerly shared their plans, but as soon as she could graciously take her leave, she'd claimed fatigue and a chill and excused herself to go upstairs. Now, her tear-soaked pillow mocked her best intentions.

Through the open window came the sounds of footsteps on the front walk. Mary hoped it meant Dr. Russ had left— she didn't think she could bear up under further scrutiny if he stayed for supper tonight—but then the door chime sounded.

Seconds later a man's voice drifted upward from the front porch. "I'm sorry to intrude, Mrs. McClarney, but I was concerned about Mary and just wanted to make sure she's well."

Chaplain Vickary—what brought him by? She wouldn't mind the chance to confide all her fears about her mother's leaving. The chaplain had a gentle way about him, easy to talk to, easy to trust, the spirit of the Lord always evident. Though the Great War had nearly broken him, he'd come back stronger in his faith than ever.

If only the Lord would do half as much in Gilbert's life.

And why do you insist it's Gilbert who's most in need of the Lord's healing touch? Look to yourself, Mary McClarney.

Yes, yes, of course, she had faults of her own—no denying it. Lack of trust her greatest weakness. *Father in heaven, increase my faith!*

But it wasn't happening tonight, not with the weight of her sorrows so heavy on her shoulders. With a tired sigh, she roused herself. She pinned her still damp hair into a loose bun at her nape, patted her blotchy face with a cool cloth, and slipped on her shoes.

By the time she reached the foot of the stairs, she heard Dr. Russ breaking the news to the chaplain about his transfer to Walter Reed. She paused to listen just out of sight.

"Truth is," Dr. Russ explained, "my skills will be put to better use at Walter Reed than here. I've loved my time in Hot Springs—finding Nell most of all—but I guess it's for the best."

"I'll hate to see you go," the chaplain replied, "but I'm sure you're needed."

"I was planning to come by your place tonight to tell you all about it, but since you're here . . ." Dr. Russ cleared his throat. "Nell and I have decided to get married sooner than later—a week from tomorrow, in fact. Nell's parish priest will perform the ceremony, but I'd be honored if you'd be my best man."

Chaplain Vickary gave a surprised laugh. "My honor entirely!"

Mary peeked around the doorway in time to see the two men embrace, giving each other hearty backslaps.

Mary's mother caught sight of her and hurried over. "Darlin', are you feeling better?"

Not trusting her voice, Mary could only reply with a weak nod.

"The nice chaplain telephoned earlier asking for you. Apparently I worried him when I said you came home drenched." Tilting Mary's head with a fingertip under her chin, she studied her daughter's face. "Oh, child, you've been crying, haven't you?" She drew Mary close for a quick hug. "I feared our plans would hit you hard."

"You've every right to follow your heart, wherever it leads." Mary kissed her mother's cheek, willing confidence into her tone. "I'm a grown woman now. I'll be fine."

The look in her mother's eyes said she didn't quite believe Mary's words. "We'll visit often, and you will, too. Or—" Mum uttered an eager gasp and stretched her hand toward Dr. Russ. "Donald, couldn't you pull some strings and find a position for Mary at Walter Reed?"

"Well, I suppose—"

"Mum, no." And yet, the idea of leaving Hot Springs behind, putting distance between herself and the man she couldn't seem to purge from her heart . . . what if this was God's way of telling her she should accept once and for all a future with Gilbert simply wasn't meant to be?

Chaplain Vickary's glance shifted between Mary, her mother, and Dr. Russ. "Clearly, this is an exciting and challenging time for all of you." Then, as if reading the indecision in Mary's eyes, he looked directly at her. "But may I advise caution about making too many plans too quickly?"

"There's plenty of time, of course." Mary's mother nodded firmly. "Donald and I should get settled first, and you'll need to submit your transfer request and train your replacement." She fixed Mary with a sad but knowing smile, her voice softening. "You'll see, darlin'. A fresh start in Washington, where you'll meet new folks and things will be so much brighter."

Mary didn't dare meet the chaplain's gaze. Fighting to keep her lower lip from trembling, she clasped her mother's hand. "It all sounds wonderful! But I—I need some time to think about it."

The chaplain edged toward the foyer. "You all have a great deal to talk about. I should go."

"Let's get together this weekend, Sam." The doctor walked him to the door. "Since you're an old pro now, I need to pick your brain about this wedding business."

Alone in the parlor with her mother, Mary dredged up a smile. "We should shop for your wedding dress tomorrow. And a trousseau. You'll be hobnobbing with those Washington folks, so you'll need something more stylish than housedresses and sensible shoes."

Mum laid her hand upon Mary's arm. "No need to pretend with me. I can see where your thoughts are taking you."

"I told you, I'll be fine. I'll miss you, of course, but seeing you so healthy and happy—it's all I could ever hope for!" Mary touched her mother's cheek. "Now why don't you spend a few more minutes with your groom. After I've taken another swipe at these red eyes of mine, I'll help you get supper on the table."

Nell knew as only a mother could, Mary wasn't being fully honest—not with her, nor with herself. As Mary scurried off to the bathroom, Nell gave her head a worried shake and waited at the front door while Donald saw the chaplain off.

"I'll be over later this evening, and we can talk more," Donald said with a wave as Chaplain Vickary started down the street. Returning to the porch, he wrapped Nell in a firm but tender embrace. "Is Mary all right?"

"I don't see how she can be." Nell nestled deeper against his chest, drinking in the manly scents. Along with the pleasantly musky aroma of aftershave, a faint antiseptic smell still clung to him after his long day at the hospital, but the combination was one she'd quickly grown to love.

"This idea about getting Mary transferred to Walter Reed . . . do you think she'd seriously consider leaving Hot Springs?" Donald kissed the top of Nell's head. "I mean, how certain are you it's really over between her and Gilbert?"

"Oh, not at all certain. She's still in love with him, it's plain for all to see. But how many times can one man break a girl's heart before she decides enough is enough?"

"You never told me why they broke up. Was it something he did?"

"Why else? Mary won't say much, but she's too in love to cast him aside without good reason." Nell grasped Donald's hand and led him toward the kitchen. "Tell me, how handy are a surgeon's skills for mashing potatoes?"

"I've mashed a potato or two in my time."

"Then while you're mashing, we can talk more about getting Mary to Walter Reed."

Donald held back. "Let's not get ahead of ourselves. I don't think it's wise to push Mary into a move she isn't emotionally ready to make."

"Who's pushing? I only want to protect my daughter from more hurt." Nell forked the potatoes she'd put on to boil. Satisfied they were done, she drained off the water and set the pot back on the stove. She thrust a potato masher into Donald's hands. "Don't leave any lumps, please. And don't pretend you have any great liking for Gilbert Ballard."

Donald attacked the potatoes with a two-fisted grip on the masher. "I don't, of course. But I know from talking with Sam, Gilbert is working hard to turn his life around. If he and Mary really are in love—"

"Believe me, I've done my best to give the rascal the benefit of the doubt. But some men . . ." Nell clamped her lips together as she reached around Donald to lift a pan of baked pork chops from the oven. She set it on the stovetop with a clatter. "Some men will break your heart every time."

Laying aside the potato masher, Donald clasped Nell's wrists to still her fluttering hands. "Who broke *your* heart, Nell? Was it Charles?"

She looked up at him in surprise, her heart suddenly thundering in her chest. "Why ever would you say such a thing? I loved my husband. He was a decent, hardworking man."

"Who was trampled by a horse, suffered a massive brain injury, and required constant care and attention the rest of his too-short life." Donald released one of her hands and brushed a lock of hair from her cheek. "But there's more to the story, isn't there? What are you holding inside, Nell?"

"Nothing. Nothing!" She tore free of his grasp and went to the cupboard for plates, while her mind's eye filled with images of her late husband.

"Just a pint or two with the mates, Nelly-girl. Ain't no sin in drinkin' in moderation."

"Moderation, I can tolerate. But comin' home drunk near every night? Charles, have a care for your wife and child!"

"I work hard. I provide for you the best I can. If that ain't havin' a care, tell me what is!"

Squeezing her eyes shut, Nell lowered a stack of plates to the counter and then pressed a fist against her chest. When a sob escaped her lips, she found herself wrapped in Donald's tender embrace.

"It's all right, dearest. When you're ready, you'll tell me." He tightened his hold. "Just know, as far as it is within my power, I will never break your heart."

"I know. . . . I know." Nell melted against him, drinking in the comfort of his love. "But I still have to protect my Mary."

Samuel's report to Gilbert after checking on Mary was far from encouraging. Though he didn't offer details, he implied Mary seemed intent on moving on without Gilbert. Sam also said Mary's mother and Dr. Russ had moved up their marriage plans, *and* the good doctor had received orders to report to Walter Reed on August 4.

Well, good riddance. Donald Russ had never liked Gilbert anyway and had certainly done everything possible to discourage Mary's affection. Gilbert had no right to blame the man, all things considered. Even so—*blast it all!*—what gave men like Russ the audacity to judge others, much less interfere in their lives?

By Sunday morning, Gilbert had had enough. Enough of trying to prove himself to everyone. Enough of wondering when or if Mary would change her mind and take him back. Enough of pretending to manage his own life while everyone around him forced their personal agendas down his throat.

He had a farm to run, for crying out loud. Mrs. Frederick depended on him for her livelihood and a roof over her head, and now so did Obadiah Squires. Let the world think what they chose. Gilbert no longer had the time or the inclination to concern himself with the opinions of others.

Except there was one Other he couldn't escape. Someone whose opinion mattered, and mattered greatly. Someone who, he'd only recently realized, had been quietly calling his name for a long time now.

Help me, Lord. Help me find my way back to You.

He'd start by going to church. Not the compulsory attendance of the past, more a matter of social appearances than faith, but with a heart intent on worship, on seeking God, on granting his heavenly Father access to the darkest corners of his soul.

But not at Ouachita Fellowship, where he'd only subject himself and his motives to further scrutiny. No, this morning he'd worship at the Army and Navy Hospital chapel and hear the Word of God preached by the one man Gilbert knew he could trust to tell him the truth, no matter how hard to hear.

Two hours later, sitting in the back pew of the chapel while patients and hospital staff filed out after the service, Gilbert felt both chastised and challenged. Samuel had preached on the text from Matthew about the rich young man who asked Jesus how to obtain eternal life. Explaining how the man simply didn't understand what was required to truly follow Jesus, Sam had tied the Scripture to 1 Corinthians, where the Apostle Paul wrote about how God chose the foolish, the weak, the lowly and despised, to shame those who thought themselves wiser and stronger and more worthy, "that no flesh should glory before God."

You can do nothing in your own strength, God seemed to be saying, and Gilbert had never felt so convicted of the futility of trying.

As the chapel emptied, Sam slipped into the pew and sat down next to Gilbert. "I'm glad to see you here again."

Gilbert folded his arms. "How is it you always know how to hit me where it hurts?"

"You mean the sermon topic?" Sam chuckled softly. "I just preach on what the Holy Spirit puts on my heart. If the message hit home, then I can only assume the Lord knew to expect you this morning."

"Tell me how to do it, Sam. How do I stop striving and turn everything over to God?"

"For starters, it isn't something you *do*. It's more about *not* doing. About letting go of the reins and trusting God's lead." Samuel tugged a hymnal from the rack and flipped through the pages, turning once again to the hymn they'd sung at the start of the service. He laid the book in Gilbert's lap. "Here, this says it better than I can."

Gilbert had been too self-conscious at first to pay much attention to the words of the opening hymn. Now he let his eyes graze the page.

> *Take my life and let it be*
> *consecrated, Lord, to thee.*
> *Take my moments and my days;*
> *let them flow in endless praise,*
> *let them flow in endless praise.*

> *Take my hands . . . my feet . . . my voice . . .*
> *Take my silver and my gold . . .*
> *Take my will . . . my love . . . my heart . . . myself . . .*

"I get it, okay? God wants all of me." Gilbert snapped the hymnal closed and clutched it in both hands. "So I'm supposed to give up my wealth, my status, my aspirations—everything that makes me who I am?"

"Not give them up. Just give them to God. Give Him the chance to turn everything about your life into something so much better than you could ever imagine for yourself."

Gilbert stared at the cross embossed on the hymnal cover, afraid to give over to God the one thing in his life he was loath to lose. "But what if God's idea of 'better' doesn't include Mary?"

"Perhaps the question you're most afraid to ask is, What if it *does?*" Sam's hand locked around Gilbert's forearm, and he gave it a small shake. "If you love her, Gil, then she's worth risking everything for. Trust God. Let Him show you how to win back Mary's heart."

19

$\mathcal{T}$he last day of July—surely the hottest part of the summer. Mary dreaded the long walk home along blistering pavement, the late-afternoon sun hammering her skull and sending rivers of perspiration down her sides. What she wouldn't give for a return of last week's cooling rain shower!

She'd just passed through the hospital gates along Reserve Avenue when an automobile horn blared. She turned to see Dr. Russ's roadster creeping up behind her.

He leaned out the window. "Hop in, Mary, and I'll drive you home."

"Now there's an offer I won't refuse." Sighing with relief, she slid into the passenger seat. "I'm glad you and Mum decided on a morning wedding ceremony. The chancel gets hotter than blazes by afternoon."

"Equally glad our train leaves early Sunday morning. With any luck, we'll make it farther north before the heat of the day sets in."

Mary's stomach churned. While at work, she could forget for a while her mother would be leaving in only a few days. At

Dr. Russ's unwelcome reminder, she bit her lip and stared out the window.

His tone laced with understanding, the doctor said, "I told you, Mary, if you really have your heart set on leaving Hot Springs, I'll do whatever I can to get you on staff at Walter Reed."

"I know, and I'm grateful. I know it's what Mum wants, too. It's just I've lived in Hot Springs most all my life. I need to be certain before making such a drastic change."

"Certain about how you'd fare in new surroundings . . . or certain there's nothing left between you and Gilbert?"

Mary stiffened. "Of course there's nothing left between us. The question was answered days ago."

"Um-hmm." Glancing his way, Mary saw his right eyebrow shoot up, while his mouth flattened into a doubtful smirk.

She cocked her head. "You don't believe me?"

"I don't think *you* believe you." Dr. Russ eased the roadster around the next corner. "Look, Mary, I've made no secret of the fact I think you're worth far more than the likes of Gil Ballard. But if you really love him, then you owe it to yourself to find out if it could work."

"Why, when I'm already absolutely convinced it *can't* work and never would?"

Parking the car at the end of Mary's front walk, the doctor gave his head a small, quick shake but said nothing. Was everyone conspiring against her? First Chaplain Vickary urging her not to make a hasty decision about leaving, and now Dr. Russ suggesting she didn't know her own mind where Gilbert was concerned.

And she wasn't fully convinced her mother was on her side. Despite Mum's enthusiasm about having Mary join them in D.C., this week she'd begun dropping subtle remarks suggesting the wisdom of tying up loose ends.

Before the car interior grew any warmer, Mary shoved open her door and stepped to the curb. Straightening her skirt, she leaned through the window to thank Dr. Russ for driving her home and then strode to the porch—only to realize he'd followed her up the walk.

He cast her an apologetic smile as he held the front door for her. "Your mother invited me to supper again. We have a few last-minute details to discuss."

"Naturally."

As she'd done all week, Mary tamped down her self-pity and tried her best to offer cheerful support as her mother and the doctor ironed out their wedding and travel plans over a supper of baked chicken, snap peas, and buttery yeast rolls.

The doctor. Who would soon become family. Mary's stepfather, to be exact. Away from the hospital, at least, "Dr. Russ" would seem too formal. Perhaps eventually she could try "Donald," but she doubted she'd ever be completely comfortable with the idea. He was her superior, after all. Besides, "Da" belonged to Mary's own father, and no one would ever take his place in her heart.

Leaving the couple to their list-making, Mary excused herself to put away leftovers and wash up the dishes. By the time she finished, damp ringlets clung to her forehead and cheeks, and she longed to plop down in front of the electric fan and kick off her shoes. Glancing out the kitchen window, she noticed Mum and the doctor had taken their conversation outside to the backyard glider, where they could enjoy the evening breeze.

Loneliness and longing stabbed Mary's heart. Only days ago she'd sat in the same spot, Gilbert's arm around her shoulder as he'd shared all his plans for the farm. Then she'd had to ruin it all by bringing up his addictions. If only she'd kept silent, if only she'd once clamped down on her untrusting and judgmental nature.

But didn't she have the right to expect better of him? He'd made so many promises about leaving his old ways behind. To associate in any way with questionable pursuits only risked trouble. Could he not see that? Or didn't he love her enough to try?

"Mary, darlin', I'll just be goin' across the street for a bit. You wait here for me in the five-and-dime, ya hear?"

Her father's words, long forgotten, filled her mind as if he'd only just spoken them. She'd thought of Da so often of late as bits and pieces of her childhood filtered back. And each time an unwelcome sense of foreboding grew stronger. What else could she attribute it to but her mother's impending marriage?

Shaking off the troubling thoughts, she set the last of the dinner plates into the cupboard. Moments later the telephone rang. She tossed the dishtowel over a hook and hurried to the foyer, shivers of anticipation rushing through her—*Gilbert!*

Then immediately chastised her fickle heart and prayed the caller was anyone in the world but Gilbert.

Her fingers trembled as she lifted the earpiece. "Hello?"

"Mary, it's Lois. You busy?"

Mary drew a deep breath through her nose and let it out slowly. "Just finishing the supper dishes."

"Listen, my friends and I had such a grand time in Little Rock last weekend, we've decided we need to do something fun more often. After our shift tomorrow, we thought we'd splurge on outrageous desserts at the Eastman Hotel restaurant. Why don't you come along?"

"Thanks for asking, but I really can't, not with Mum getting married the next morning."

"Rats, how insensitive can a gal be?" Lois gasped. "I meant me, not your mother! With all you've had on your mind this week, I should have offered to help. Can I style your hair, bring something for the reception, anything at all?"

"The wedding's just a small affair—immediate family, closest friends. I believe everything's under control." Everything except Mary's heartache over saying goodbye when her mother left with her new husband Sunday morning.

"Well, let me know if you think of anything. I should get back to work. Got the late shift tonight, and I'm already yawning."

Mary thanked Lois again for both the invitation and the offer of help. After ending the call, she went upstairs to her room and pulled out the summer frock she planned to wear for the ceremony. It was the same yellow dress she'd worn the evening Gilbert's mother hosted the dinner party, but taking it off, she'd caught her heel in the hem and needed to stitch it up.

As she snipped a length of thread and held it to the eye of the needle, moisture blurred her vision. She'd choose another dress if she had anything suitable—why torture herself with unpleasant reminders? When she'd shopped with her mother last weekend, Mum had encouraged her to buy something new for herself, but she'd demurred. With their limited funds, her mother's wardrobe needs were much more urgent than her own.

So the yellow dress it would be, and Mary would hold her chin high and smile through her tears. Closing her mind to everything but running the needle through the fabric, she finished her mending and then prepared for bed without so much as a trip downstairs to bid her mother and Dr. Russ good night. Exhaustion overwhelmed her, the emotional toll more grueling by far, but sleep was long in coming.

By morning, however, she'd made up her mind. She would speak to Mrs. Daley first thing about her desire to transfer to Walter Reed—or if not there, then any other military hospital in the country where she might serve.

Because staying in Hot Springs had become untenable. With every passing day, she grew more certain being near Gilbert, subjecting herself to the draw he held on her heart, would be the worst kind of torture. If only she could turn back time, go back to the first encounter with Gilbert in the hospital day room after he'd returned from the war . . .

Except what would she change? Could she have kept herself from being attracted to him? Would she have seen the danger coming and asked for assignment to a different ward?

Dear God above, how could You let me fall in love with a man I can never have?

"That's good, stop right there!" Gilbert signaled the driver parking a horse trailer next to the refurbished barn.

Obadiah strode over to the trailer, unlatched the rear door, and lowered the ramp. "Easy now, ladies. We'll do this one at a time." Edging alongside the calmer of the two mares, he snapped a lead rope onto her halter, released the trailer tie, then carefully backed her down the ramp.

"She's a beauty!" Gilbert stroked the horse's sleek brown neck. "Look at the muscling, the power in her haunches."

"Yes, indeedy, a racehorse mama for sure." Obadiah handed Gilbert the lead rope. "First stall on the left is all set up for her. I'll fetch our other gal and be right behind you."

A few minutes later, with both the new additions settled into their stalls, Gilbert paid the driver then returned to the barn to admire his mares. From the paddock behind the house came Mac's anxious whinny.

Obadiah pushed back his tweed cap and laughed. "Sounds like he be ready to get busy on buildin' that herd."

"We'll let them get acquainted one at a time, don't you think? No sense giving either of the ladies cause to be jealous."

"Good plan. Soon as they's rested from the ride over, I'll take Miss Glory out first. I can tell already she's gonna be his favorite."

The other mare, a chestnut thoroughbred nicknamed Cricket, pranced nervously in her stall. Gilbert spoke soothing words and offered a sugar cube. Her nostrils twitched as she took a tentative step closer. Her velvety muzzle tickled Gilbert's palm, but after a quick sniff, she snorted and sidestepped away.

"Come on, girl. Nothing to be afraid of. You're safe here." Gilbert stretched his arm farther across the stall gate.

She nickered and edged nearer, this time snatching the sugar from Gilbert's hand. Her mouth worked as she crunched, and seconds later she nudged Gilbert's arm in search of more. Finding another lump of sugar in his pocket, he held it out to her then rubbed behind her jaw while she munched. The horse's eyelids drooped as she gave a contented sigh.

Obadiah chuckled. "Thought you done told me you don't know much about horses."

"I know you can't treat them like machines." Images of horses stumbling and dying in the mire of war-torn France brought an ache to Gilbert's chest. "They need tenderness, patience, and care. They need to know they can trust you."

"Yep, jes' like most any woman I ever met."

The man's words elicited a different kind of ache, this one twisting through Gilbert's heart. He'd failed miserably to inspire trust in Mary. Just the opposite, more often than not. If he could only make a go of this farm, prove to her he was free of the past. If he could only convince her how much he loved her, how desperate he was to make a life with her.

He could call her later, invite her out to see the progress he'd made. Once she saw the house and barn in good order, the fields seeded for grazing or cleared for planting, she'd grasp the seriousness of his intentions. She'd *have* to give him another chance.

She had to, or this was all for nothing.

Buoyed with determination, Gilbert left the horses in Obadiah's care and went to check on the work crew finishing things at the house. The power company had finally connected electricity yesterday, and contractors were now installing an electric pump for the well and completing installation of the kitchen appliances. All that remained now was to get a telephone line out this way, which wouldn't happen for at least another week or two.

Still, Gilbert had been pleased last night to inform Mrs. Frederick the house would be ready for occupancy this weekend. In fact, he'd already begun packing his personal possessions. The day he finally got out from under his mother's roof couldn't come too soon.

By midafternoon Gilbert felt comfortable leaving Obadiah to supervise the last of the workmen still finishing up. If he didn't dally, he might have time to stop at home for a quick bath and change of clothes before meeting Mary as she left the hospital. *Just a few minutes with her, Lord. Help me persuade her not to give up on me.*

At ten of five, freshly shaven and wearing his favorite blue pinstriped shirt tucked into gray slacks, Gilbert drove up beside the Eastman Hotel and parked his roadster along Reserve Avenue. From here he could see both the hospital's main gate and the long flight of steps between the hospital grounds and the Imperial Bathhouse. Stepping from the car, he propped his hips against the fender to wait for Mary.

Only a few minutes later the chatter of female voices drew his attention. He looked toward the steps to see five young women starting down. With all of them dressed in street clothes, Gilbert didn't immediately identify them as nurses, until he recognized one in particular.

Lois Underwood's laughter rose above the rest. "Now, girls, we're just going for dessert. No flirting with the waiters."

"Waiters? Are you kidding?" A blonde wearing a red polka-dot blouse flicked her hand at Lois. "Personally, I'm holding out for a rich doctor."

"Or lawyer," another chimed in. "Someone like—" She stopped at the bottom of the steps, her mouth dropping open as she caught sight of Gilbert. Then she snapped it shut and pasted on an alluring smile. Nudging her friends, she giggled and said, "Someone just like him!"

Lois looked up, her eyes widening in recognition. Hips swaying, she marched across the street. "Hi, Lieutenant! Waiting for anyone in particular, as if I had to ask?"

"Hello, Miss Underwood." Gilbert straightened, instinctively on guard. He remembered all too well how the nurse had flirted with him the day she'd so artfully finagled a ride in his automobile.

The girl in the red polka dots linked her arm through Lois's while batting her eyes at Gilbert. "You know this handsome guy? Come on, Lois, introduce us."

"Ladies, this is First Lieutenant Gilbert Ballard, a regular war hero."

"You were in France?" one of the other girls asked. "I've heard it was awful over there."

Lois nodded gravely. "The lieutenant was wounded, lost a leg."

A chorus of sympathetic moans surrounded Gilbert. His jaw muscles bunched. "If you don't mind, ladies . . ."

"Oh, of course." Lois stepped closer while shooing the other girls on down the street. "Listen, if you're waiting for Mary, it could be awhile. Last I saw her, she was going into a meeting with Mrs. Daley."

Now Gilbert tensed for another reason. The last thing Mary needed was more trouble with the chief nurse. "Any idea what it's about?"

"Not for sure, but there's been some gossip floating around this afternoon." Lois pinched her lips together before lowering her voice. "You heard Dr. Russ is getting sent back to Walter Reed?"

"No, I hadn't heard. When?"

"He's leaving this weekend. Right after he marries Mary's mother."

One of Lois's friends called to her. "Hurry up, Lo. I hear a chocolate éclair calling my name!"

She frowned in apology. "Guess I should go."

Gilbert gave a half-hearted wave, his mind already assessing the import of this latest development. If Donald Russ and Mrs. McClarney had moved up their wedding date, it must mean they'd be leaving Hot Springs together.

Which meant Mary faced the loneliness of remaining behind.

All the more reason he needed to be with her, to comfort her, to assure her he'd never leave. To make her believe with unwavering certainty his heart was hers alone.

Forget standing at the curb like a day laborer or a cabbie waiting for a fare. He'd go straight up to Mrs. Daley's floor and park himself in the corridor outside the woman's office until Mary appeared. Then Mary would have no choice but to talk to him—more importantly, to *listen* to him—and this time he'd make sure she heard everything he had to say.

"There's nothing more to say." Releasing a sigh, Mary clasped her hands in her lap. "If you won't approve my transfer, I've no choice but to resign from the Army Nurse Corps."

Mrs. Daley pulled off her glasses and pinched the bridge of her nose. "Mary, Mary, it isn't like you to be so rash."

"As I told you, though my request seems sudden, I have given it a great deal of thought. While you may not understand or accept my reasons, they are *my* reasons nonetheless, and I won't be dissuaded."

"Very well." Exhaling through pursed lips, Mrs. Daley slipped on her glasses, extracted a form from her desk drawer, and filled in some blanks. Then she scrawled her signature across the bottom. "There. Transfer request approved. But under protest."

Rising, Mary gave the chief nurse a deferential nod. "Thank you. Until the transfer comes through, I shall do everything necessary to train my replacement."

"Indeed you shall. Good day, Miss McClarney." Stone-faced, Mrs. Daley snatched up a file folder and continued her work as if Mary had never entered the room.

So much for the rapport the two women had fostered in recent weeks. Clearly, Mrs. Daley's good opinion of Mary had vanished.

Sick with remorse, Mary slipped from the room. She'd anticipated Mrs. Daley's disapproval, but hadn't been prepared for how strongly she would feel the woman's disappointment.

It's only a job, she kept telling herself. A job she could do just as well at Walter Reed or at any other military or civilian hospital. So why did the thought of leaving *this* hospital tear her heart to shreds?

Then, as she squared her shoulders and lifted her head, the answer stared her in the face.

Gilbert.

Pulse racing, she hoped he didn't notice the quaver in her voice. "Why do you keep showing up here like this? I've told you, Gilbert. I don't want to see you anymore."

"But I had to see you." Gilbert reached out to her, but when she shrank back, he lowered his arm, fist clenched. "I heard about your mother and Dr. Russ. I was worried about you."

"No need." She managed a weak smile. "I'll be joining them soon in D.C."

He recoiled as if she'd slapped him. "Mary, you can't!"

Standing taller, she squared her shoulders. "You've nothing to say about it."

His tone dropped to barely a whisper. "Not even to say I love you?"

"Don't, Gilbert." His damp hair curled in dark ringlets, and he stood near enough for her to catch the enticing scent of bay rum aftershave. She squeezed her eyes shut. One more word from him and she'd lose her resolve. "Why can't you understand? There's no hope for us. Goodbye."

Fleeing down the corridor, she took the stairs to the lobby and barged out the front doors, her only thought to get away before the tears flowed. She dodged an elderly couple coming up the steps and then skidded around the corner of the building. A copse of trees stood nearby, offering a refuge where she could give vent to her anguish. She crouched down amid the trunks and crumpled her skirt against her mouth to stifle the sobs.

Slowly and with effort, control returned. She was a skilled nurse, after all, not a silly schoolgirl. She would master her emotions, do the wise and sensible thing exactly as she'd decided. She'd—

The sound of whistling cut through her thoughts. She stood erect and listened, praying whoever it was would walk on by without noticing her. When a shadow fell across the path, she stepped deeper into the copse, only to snap a twig beneath her foot.

The shadow froze. "Who's there?"

Mary clamped a hand over her mouth. She'd recognize the voice anywhere—*Ernest Deeds!*

He stooped beneath the foliage, his gaze locking with Mary's. "Well, hello there, Nurse McClarney. Fancy meeting you here."

She lifted her chin, fighting for bravado she didn't have. "I could say the same of you. What are you doing on hospital property? Surely you've already collected your severance pay."

"Collected and spent." His scowl hardened into a sneer. "Actually, I've been hoping to run into you again. People don't mess with Ernest Deeds and get away with it."

Mary's breaths grew shallow. She pressed a hand against her abdomen. "That sounds very much like a threat. I could report you."

"You do and—"

Suddenly someone jerked Deeds backwards and shoved him to the ground. Mary gasped to see Gilbert standing over him, jabbing him in the chest with his cane. "You filthy piece of garbage!"

Flat on his back, Deeds raised both hands, a snide laugh grating between his lips. "Gil Ballard, right? Figured out who you were the day you brought your gal those pretty roses. Been meaning to look you up ever since."

"I can't imagine why." Gilbert glanced Mary's way. "Did he hurt you?"

She shook her head and muttered a quick "No."

"Guess you ain't heard we have a mutual friend," Deeds went on, a hideous grin aimed toward Gilbert. "Our pal told me you might be needin' something I got."

Need something—from Ernest Deeds? Choking on a sob, Mary thrust her fist against her mouth as all her suspicions found substance.

Deeds slithered from beneath Gilbert's cane tip and scrambled to his feet. Keeping a wary eye on Gilbert, he brushed the dust off his clothes and then patted his shirt pocket. "I got what you want right here, Gil. The price has gone up a bit, though. You can thank Nurse McClarney for that."

Beads of sweat popped out on Gilbert's forehead. He drew a hand across his mouth. Mary could see in his eyes how badly he craved what Deeds had offered. Then he looked at Mary, his face crumpling. He dropped his chin to his chest and in a raspy voice said, "Get out of here, Deeds, before I beat you to a bloody pulp."

Deeds edged around Gilbert, then turned with a gloating laugh. "Gimme a holler when you're ready to deal." Moments later he jogged out of sight.

Heart thudding, Mary crept from beneath the trees. Without so much as a glance at Gilbert, she marched toward the hospital gates.

"Mary, wait! Please!"

She walked faster.

"It isn't what you think!"

No, it never was, was it? Always an excuse, an explanation. *Just like Da.*

The sudden thought jabbed her like a scalpel. *No!* It was Gilbert who couldn't be trusted, not her sainted father. Breaking into a run, Mary swung out onto Reserve Avenue. She couldn't escape Hot Springs soon enough.

20

"Oh, Mum, I'll miss you so much!" Tears flowing, Mary clung to her mother while the conductor called final boarding.

"I know, luv. I hate leaving you like this." Releasing a soft sob, Mary's mother kissed her on both cheeks. "Don't forget, Ginny said you could stay with her, so you won't be alone."

Dr. Russ came up beside them. "Darling, we have to go."

Mary's mother gave a shaky nod as she pulled away. "And Donald promised he'd set to work right away on recommending your transfer to Walter Reed. It won't be long, dearest, you'll see."

Heart tearing in two, Mary waved as her mother and the doctor boarded the train. "Take care! I love you!"

She watched for her mother to appear in one of the passenger car windows, waving frantically when she spotted her. Then the plaintive moan of the train whistle sliced the morning air. Steam burst forth and the engine groaned, wheels screeching as the locomotive pulled out of the station.

The emptiness left in its wake nearly brought Mary to her knees. Clutching her handbag against her abdomen, she struggled not to make a spectacle of herself amid the others who'd come to see passengers off.

"Mary, dear." Genevieve Lawson, who'd driven them all to the station, drew her aside. "Let's go home, shall we? Or better yet, let me take you to breakfast at the Arlington."

"I couldn't. I'm a mess." Even so, the thought of returning to her empty house held no appeal. Mary found a handkerchief in her handbag and mopped her eyes. "I thought I might go to the hospital and try to catch up on some paperwork."

"On your day off? Nonsense. It'll save until tomorrow." Mrs. Lawson linked arms with Mary as they started toward the car. "Today you must do something fun and different, something to cheer you up."

"I'm afraid it's a lost cause." Mary hiccupped and wiped more tears.

"You poor dear. You've barely held it together this past week."

"For Mum's sake I tried, but . . ." Sniffling, Mary climbed into the passenger seat of Mrs. Lawson's car.

As they pulled away from the depot, the silver-haired woman reached over to pat Mary's knee. "Honey, don't think your mother was fooled for a second. She knows your heart is breaking over your young man."

The memory of Gilbert's hungry expression two days ago when confronted by Ernest Deeds brought a fresh wave of nausea. Turning away, Mary pressed the handkerchief to her mouth.

"There, there, sweetie. If Gilbert Ballard hurt you so badly, he doesn't deserve your tears."

With a final shudder, Mary wadded the handkerchief in her lap. "You're right, he doesn't. I was a fool for entrusting my heart to him in the first place. I should have known he couldn't keep his promises."

Two more turns and they arrived at Mrs. Lawson's house. She swung the car into her driveway and shut off the engine. "Don't go home to your empty house just yet. I'll whip us up some breakfast and then we can go to Mass. And afterward—I won't take no for an answer—we'll choose a nice restaurant for lunch and then spend the afternoon playing tourist at Happy Hollow."

Riding burros, shopping for kitschy souvenirs, and getting silly photographs taken might be just the distraction Mary needed. She heaved a weary sigh as she followed Mrs. Lawson into her cheery yellow kitchen. In many ways she felt relieved to have someone else take charge for a while, for she hadn't the energy to think for herself. It would require all her focus just to get through the day, and the next, and the next, until she could join her mother in D.C.

Please, dear Jesus, let Dr. Russ arrange a position for me soon!

$\mathscr{L}$♥

Thomas didn't particularly care to spend his Sunday afternoon engaged in hard labor, but Gilbert needed help moving out to the farm, and Thomas wasn't of a mind to refuse. Besides, he'd grown concerned about his brother's mental state ever since Mary had broken things off.

Which Thomas still couldn't understand. What had gotten into the girl, anyway, shattering his brother's heart? He'd like to shake some sense into her, give her what-for.

"A little help here?" Jack Trapp, whose help Thomas had also enlisted for moving day, struggled to heft a large wooden crate out of the truck bed.

"Sorry, just taking a breather." Thomas swept a kerchief across his perspiring face before grabbing one end of the crate. Together they muscled it up the porch steps and into the parlor.

The box hit the floor with a thud, and Jack groaned as he massaged his lower back. "What's Gilbert got in there—gold ingots?"

"More likely his book collection. He's been amassing quite a library on farming and horse breeding." Thomas headed for the kitchen. "I need some water. How about you?"

"Good idea. I saw the horses out back. Is it true the stallion is out of Bonnie Scotland?"

"So Gil tells me." Thomas filled two water glasses and handed one to Jack. "Though why he wants to breed racehorses when Oaklawn's been shut down is beyond me."

Gilbert entered through the screen door off the back porch, his face streaked with mud—or at least Thomas hoped it was mud. "I'm looking to the future, if you must know. There'll always be a demand for horses of quality, even if racing never makes a comeback." He took another glass from the cupboard, filled it at the sink, and downed it in one gulp. "Is the truck unloaded yet?"

"Still have a few more boxes. Also the bureau for your bedroom. You want to show us where to put it?"

"Anywhere's fine. Suit yourself." Gilbert polished off another glass of water and then marched back outside.

Thomas shared a look with Jack. "His attitude's about to convince me I *never* want to get serious about a girl."

"Woman trouble, eh? Explains a lot." Jack led the way out to the truck.

"You got a girlfriend, Jack?"

"No one special." Reaching the truck, Jack hefted another crate and balanced it on one shoulder. "What about you? Bet you run into lots of rich and glamorous hotel guests over at the Arlington."

Thomas slid another box from the truck bed, grunting as he braced it against his torso. Not many opportunities to build muscle sitting behind a desk. "Unfortunately, most of the female guests at the Arlington are old and arthritic. They come to town for the baths, not romance."

"Well, then, I'll have to be sure and set you up with my sister when she gets home." Jack heaved several noisy breaths as he started up the porch steps. "I should say, *if* she comes home. Not sure Joanna ever plans to leave France."

"Just as well. Like I said, with Gil's example, I'm not sure any woman's worth the risk."

Mucking stalls. Hard on the back but excellent therapy for the soul. Exactly what Gilbert needed to get his mind off Mary.

Except it wasn't working. He kept picturing the look on her face the moment she'd connected Ernest Deeds with Gilbert's former morphine supplier. Deeds must be one of the "insiders" the supplier had positioned at a couple of the hospitals in town. How the lowlife had gotten himself hired as an orderly was incomprehensible.

If he'd hurt Mary . . .

Gilbert's hands tightened around the pitchfork. With a fierce growl, he rammed the tines into the nearest wall.

"Hey, now, Mistah Ballard." Obadiah gave a low whistle. "Remind me not to git on yo' bad side."

Breathing hard, Gilbert yanked the pitchfork free. "Maybe you should take over before I bring the whole barn down on top of us."

"Good idea." Obadiah stepped into the stall and claimed the pitchfork. Nudging Gilbert aside, he shoveled up a forkful of soiled shavings and tossed them into a wheelbarrow. "You want somethin' to do, you could mosey out to the pasture and fill up the mares' water trough."

Taking orders from his hired man—is this what Gilbert had stooped to? On the other hand, taking orders came very naturally to him. Sure was easier than making decisions on his own.

If someone would only tell him what to do to win Mary back . . . or else learn to live without her.

At the crunch of tires on gravel, Obadiah stopped forking manure and glanced toward the barn door. "Sounds like we got company. You 'spectin' anyone else out this way, Mistah Ballard?"

"I'll see who it is." Gilbert found his cane where he'd left it propped against a horse stall. Exiting the barn, he spied a Hot Springs Police car parked near the house. He waved as two uniformed officers stepped from the vehicle.

One of them turned his way. "Mr. Ballard? We're here to ask you a few more questions about Ernest Deeds."

Good, they'd wasted no time in following up. After his encounter Friday evening, Gilbert realized he had no choice but to report what he knew about Deeds's drug-dealing connections, even if it meant implicating himself. He'd risk whatever it cost to ensure Mary's safety.

Inviting the officers to take seats on the front porch, Gilbert responded honestly as they asked when and how he'd initially met his supplier, if he'd ever dealt directly with Deeds, and what he knew of Deeds's other contacts within the hospital system.

"Arrest me as well if you have to," Gilbert stated. "Just get those men off the streets."

The lead officer waved a hand. "We'll take care of Deeds and his friends, but we've no interest in prosecuting a war hero."

His partner nodded grimly. "My cousin served with Major Whittlesey in the Argonne Forest. He was one of the few to make it out alive, but he was burned so badly he'll be on pain pills the rest of his life."

Once the officers were satisfied they'd gleaned as much information as Gilbert could provide, they thanked him and left. Heaving a tired breath, Gilbert leaned against a post and watched them drive away.

The screen door opened behind him, and Thomas stepped onto the porch. "I couldn't help overhearing. You okay?"

"Just another chapter of my life I'm ready to close the book on." Gilbert scrubbed a hand down his face. "It sickens me to admit how easy it would have been to take what Deeds offered the other day." A tremor ripped through his belly. "I wanted it. Badly."

"But you said no. You stayed strong." Easing up beside him, Thomas clapped a hand on his shoulder. "I'm proud of you, Gil. In so many ways."

Gilbert slid his gaze toward his brother, and a tiny portion of his self-loathing fell away. His voice came out in a raspy whisper. "You have no idea how much those words mean to me."

Brows knitted, Thomas looked deep into Gilbert's eyes. "Don't you know, big brother? I've always been proud of you. So you went through a rough time. What matters is how you come out on the other side."

"I'm not sure I'm there yet." Staring into the distance, Gilbert gave a cynical laugh. "Not sure I ever will be."

21

*H*ow Mary had survived nearly a week on her own, she could only attribute to leaning on the Lord's strength. By Thursday evening, as she trekked home from the hospital, she was too exhausted to care if she hadn't shopped for groceries all week. Supper would be another cold roast beef sandwich. As her mother's good health returned, Mary had quickly grown spoiled by coming home to hot meals on the table and lightness in her mother's heart.

Now, the idea of coming home at all left Mary feeling utterly bereft.

Bypassing the empty parlor, she headed straight upstairs to change from her starched nurse's uniform into a cool cotton housedress. As she peeled off her white stockings to wiggle toes too long cramped inside stiff leather shoes, the ringing telephone startled her. Probably Mrs. Lawson. The neighbor had invited Mary over for supper twice this week already—truly a lifesaver, but Mary had grown weary of even pretending she was coping with her mother's departure.

Barefoot, she plodded downstairs and snatched the earpiece from the hook. "Hello?"

"Mary, darlin'!" Her mother sounded tinny and faraway.

"Mum!" A bubble of happiness swelled Mary's chest. "How are you? How's Washington? Is the weather nice? Are you happy there?"

Her mother's laughter rippled through the telephone line. "What are we playing, 'Twenty Questions'? Oh, dearest, it's good to hear your sweet voice! If Alexander Graham Bell were standing here right now, I'd give him a great big kiss."

"Not in front of your husband, I hope!" Mary sank onto the stool next to the telephone table and pictured her mother's smiling face. "Tell me truly, Mum, are you well and happy?"

"Indeed I am. D.C. is an exciting city—what I've seen of it, anyway; we've been so busy settling in—and Donald treats me like a princess." Mum sighed. "My only complaint is missing my girl."

"No more than I miss my mum." Mary tightened her grip on the earpiece. "Has Dr.—I mean, Donald—has he had a chance to look into my transfer?"

"It's the very important reason I called." Mum's pitch ramped up a notch. "What with so many wounded soldiers still recovering here, the need for well-trained nurses is ongoing. The chief nurse told Donald she'd gladly put you on the roster as soon as you can get here. She's already mailed the paperwork to Mrs. Daley."

Mary sucked in a breath, her head reeling. So much to think about, so much to do! First thing tomorrow, she must ask Mrs. Daley to name a charge nurse replacement immediately. Though the chief nurse had signed off on Mary's transfer request, without confirmation of a new position, there had been no urgency.

Now, as her mother rambled on about the train trip to D.C., the furnished brownstone apartment they'd rented, and the adventure of shopping for linens, dishes, and other household goods, Mary could hardly marshal her thoughts. All she could think was within the month she could be living and working in Washington, D.C., an idea that both thrilled and terrified her.

When her mother finally ended the call, Mary wandered to the kitchen and filled a glass with water. Sipping slowly, she stared out the window over the sink. Her gaze fell upon the backyard glider, and thoughts of Gilbert brought a catch in her throat. On Monday she'd learned Gilbert had turned Ernest Deeds in to the police, for two officers had come to the hospital to question her. She had nothing concrete to offer, only her suppositions, but they assured her they'd already collected enough evidence to haul him in. Deeds wouldn't be bothering her again.

She was relieved, certainly, but held out no hope the orderly's arrest could change things between her and Gilbert. The plain truth was she'd destroyed whatever chances they had with her continual distrust and doubt. The best thing for both of them would be to try to heal and move on.

Releasing a resigned sigh, Mary strode to the icebox and brought out the plate of leftover pot roast. A quick sandwich, a long soak in the tub, then early to bed. She slept fitfully, dreaming of a locomotive engine that became a galloping horse with smoke and fire pouring from its nostrils. The horse reared, its hooves flashing like molten steel. A little girl screamed, a man fell—*Da!*

Alarm bells clanged, startling Mary awake. She sat bolt upright, only to find her bedside clock jangling mercilessly. Drenched in sweat, gasping for breath, she slapped her palm on the button to silence the ringing. Five a.m. had come far too early.

Within the hour, she was on her way to the hospital and thanking the Lord she had the weekend to look forward to—

partly to catch up on much needed rest, but also to begin preparations for moving to D.C. Besides the packing, she must decide what to do about the house. Mum owned it free and clear. Would she want it sold? Rented out? And what of all their furniture and housewares? Residing in the nurses' quarters at Walter Reed, Mary would have no need of such things.

Her head was spinning by the time she clocked in and reported to her office on the ward. She'd just begun to glance over the night charge nurse's report when Mrs. Daley appeared in the doorway.

"Well, it's official," the frowning woman stated. "The principal chief nurse at Walter Reed telephoned first thing this morning. Apparently, the need there is great. She asks for me to expedite your transfer and have you on a train to Washington no later than next Tuesday."

Knees shaking, Mary stood. "So quickly? But what about—"

"As for your replacement, I've decided to promote Miss Underwood." Mrs. Daley quirked her lips. "She certainly has a long way to go to fill your shoes, but there is presently no one else more suitable. I'll expect you both to work through the weekend so you can familiarize her with your duties."

Mary dipped her chin, grateful for the backhanded compliment, yet struggling to hide her agitation. If she wasn't to have her weekend off, where in heaven's name would she find the time to do everything necessary before leaving on Tuesday?

With a curt nod, Mrs. Daley marched off the ward, and Mary collapsed into her chair, head in her hands. She could almost hear her mother's firm reminder: *No matter how busy you are, there's always time to pray.*

If ever prayer was needed, it was now. Finding one of the floor nurses, Mary instructed her to keep an eye on things for the next fifteen minutes or so. Then she hurried across the hospital campus and slipped down the aisle of the empty chapel.

Kneeling at the altar rail, she crossed herself and folded her hands.

"Dearest Jesus, I hardly know where to begin! Nothing's turned out the way I'd hoped. Mum is married and starting a new life, I'm about to make the biggest change yet in my nursing career, and worst of all, the man I love—the man I thought I'd—" Her words broke off on a sob.

A gentle hand rested upon her shoulder, and she glanced up to see Chaplain Vickary standing at her side. He smiled a sad smile. "Would you like to talk?"

She nodded and allowed the chaplain to help her to her feet. He led her to the front pew, where they sat side by side. Haltingly, she explained about the transfer to Walter Reed. "It's the right thing for me, I'm certain. But it's all happening so fast, and I'm suddenly terrified!"

"I know you miss your mother, but . . ." Chaplain Vickary pressed his lips together, momentarily glancing away. "How can you leave before you've fully resolved things between you and Gilbert? He still loves you, Mary."

"Sometimes . . . sometimes love isn't enough." With a shaky sniff, Mary shoved to her feet. "Thank you for listening, Chaplain. But there's nothing you can say—nothing anyone can say—to make me change my mind about leaving Hot Springs."

❦

By Monday afternoon, Mary had given Lois all the guidance she could for taking over the charge nurse position—and had a gigantic headache to show for it.

Seated at Mary's desk, Lois looked up with a grimace. "I don't know, Mary. I just don't know if I can handle this."

"You can, and you will." Mary rose and patted Lois on the shoulder. "Mrs. Daley has confidence in you, or she'd never have given you the promotion. You'll rise to the occasion and show her ten times over what a fine nurse you are."

"Oh, Mary, I'm sure gonna miss you!" Lois shoved up from her chair and wrapped Mary in a bear hug. "Promise you'll write, okay?"

"Of course." Though she suspected she never would. The less contact she had with her old life in Hot Springs, the easier the transition would be. She retrieved her purse from the bottom desk drawer. "Now, I really must be on my way. I still have last-minute packing to do."

Slipping out of the hospital unnoticed proved a challenge, but Mary hadn't the heart for lengthy goodbyes. Earlier, she'd filed a final report for Mrs. Daley and settled things with the personnel office. Escaping with only a few perfunctory fare-wells, she made her way to a back stairwell, then skirted the administration building along a seldom-used path. A long trek up Reserve and soon she arrived at home.

Except this wouldn't be her home much longer. Four days of frenzied preparations, and now . . . the finality of it all clawed at Mary's chest until she couldn't breathe. *Dear God, am I doing the right thing?*

But she had to go—no turning back now. The sooner she put Hot Springs behind her, the sooner she'd purge Gilbert Ballard from her heart.

She'd barely had time to change out of her uniform before Mrs. Lawson came over with a pot of savory beef stew. After they'd eaten, the white-haired neighbor stood in the center of the parlor and glanced around at the sheet-covered furniture. "Oh, Mary, it's so sad-looking. Are you sure you wouldn't rather sleep at my house tonight?"

"I'll be fine." Mary wedged a smile into her tone. "Anyway, busy as these last few days have been, I won't be long for bed."

"All right, then, I'll be ready at seven in the morning to take you to the depot."

Mary clutched Mrs. Lawson's hand. "Thanks for supper, and for . . . everything." She held back tears as her neighbor drew her close before scurrying out the front door.

Left alone in the silent house, Mary took a deep breath and shoved her emotions down deep, the only way she'd get through her last night in the house where she'd grown up. With forced detachment she finished her packing, then took a long, relaxing soak in the tub before crawling into bed. She fell asleep quickly and slept soundly—no doubt a combination of fatigue and sheer force of will.

But the next day, trapped on the train and with nowhere to run from her skittering thoughts, she wished she'd stayed up all night cleaning house or doing laundry or sorting through Mum's cupboards. As the journey carried her farther and farther from home—from the man she still loved with all her being—she longed for the blessed escape of dreamless sleep.

He'd been married less than two weeks, but already Donald had trouble remembering what it was like returning to an empty apartment after a long rotation at the hospital. To walk through that door and see Nell's beaming face, to wrap himself in her welcoming embrace while inhaling the sweet scent of her perfume—could there be a more perfect ending to the day?

"Ah, luv, you look exhausted." Nell guided him to an overstuffed chair and ottoman, one of their first furniture purchases for the townhouse—and one he'd be eternally grateful his thoughtful wife had chosen. "I've a fresh pitcher of lemonade in the kitchen. And cookies, too."

"You spoil me, Nell." With a blissful sigh, Donald worked his backside deeper into the upholstery. He tugged one foot and then the other across his knees to loosen his shoelaces. Then, kicking off his shoes, he splayed his legs across the ottoman, leaned his head back, and closed his eyes.

Moments later, he sensed Nell's presence and looked up as she set a plate of cookies on the side table. She handed him a frosty glass of lemonade. "Supper won't be for another hour. I was late getting the lamb roast in the oven."

"Out shopping again, were you?" Donald shot her a teasing grin and drew her onto the arm of the chair. "What did you bring home today to brighten our humble abode?"

"Nothin' for us this time. I bought a new frock for Mary. I thought it might cheer her up." With a quiet sigh, Nell pressed closer and kissed the top of Donald's head. "Did you keep an eye on her at the hospital as I asked?"

"I tried, but being her first day, they kept her pretty busy with orientation." He squared his jaw and swirled the lemonade in his glass. "I hope she's up to this. Walter Reed is quite a change from Hot Springs."

For that matter, Donald hoped *he* was strong enough to cope with the return to treating wounded soldiers. Hot Springs had been a welcome respite from the carnage he'd witnessed in France. Now, once again, the majority of his patients remained hospitalized for amputations, burns, festering gunshot wounds, and all manner of battlefield atrocities.

Thank God for his beautiful wife, his peaceful haven at the close of a trying day.

Nell handed him a cookie. "Mary's smart and spunky as they come. She'll settle in fine, you wait and see."

As Donald savored a bite of the warm, chewy oatmeal cookie, he wondered if Nell was as certain as she pretended to be. From his vantage point, Mary had seemed harried and exhausted when they'd met her at the train station yesterday. This morning, when he'd escorted her to the hospital and introduced her to the chief nurse, she'd donned an air of confidence. Even so, she couldn't disguise the dark circles beneath her eyes, nor the slight hesitation in her step.

The front door clicked open, and Nell scurried to the entryway. "Mary, come in, child, and take a rest before supper." Arm around her daughter's shoulder, she prodded her toward the sofa. "You'd no trouble finding the right trolley connections?"

"No trouble." The corners of Mary's mouth turned up ever so briefly. She stared at the sofa as if she couldn't decide whether to sit down or fall down.

Donald sat up straighter, concern tightening his chest. "I'd have waited to see you home, but I didn't know how long they'd keep you on your first day."

"It's fine. I ended the day with a tour of the nurses' quarters." Mary unpinned her cap. Clutching it at her waist, she ran trembling fingertips along the crest. "Everyone was very nice. They'll have a room for me by the weekend."

"That's lovely, dear." Nell gave her daughter another nudge toward the sofa. "Would you like a glass of lemonade? How about an oatmeal cookie?"

Mary gave her head a small shake. "If it's all the same, I'll just lie down for a bit."

Nell pressed her hand to her mouth as she watched her daughter trudge to the guest room. Then, facing Donald, she released a gentle sigh. "Did we do the right thing bringing her here?"

"It was her choice, darling." Setting aside his glass, Donald pushed up from the chair. He drew his wife into his arms and stroked her silky red hair. "Mary's resilient, just as you said. Give her a few days to get her bearings and catch up on her rest, and I'm sure she'll be fine."

He only wished he believed his own words.

Chapel worship had already begun when Gilbert slipped into the back pew the following Sunday morning. He'd come to crave Samuel's preaching—even more, his friendship—like the drugs he vowed never to fall victim to again.

Afterward, as Samuel greeted the departing patients and staff, Gilbert held back until only he and Samuel remained.

Samuel turned toward him with a knowing smile. "Saw you sneaking in during the opening hymn. Next time, why don't you actually sing with us instead of pretending to find the right page?"

"Too obvious, eh?" Gilbert chuckled. "You haven't heard me sing, or you wouldn't even suggest such a thing."

"You're right, I haven't. Not in all the time I've known you." Samuel motioned Gilbert through the chapel doors. "Which is sad, isn't it? Don't you know singing is good for the soul?"

"I doubt my off-key caterwauling qualifies. As for my soul?" Gilbert's voice thickened. "It'll take a lot more than a church hymn to cure what ails me."

Sam gave Gilbert's shoulder an understanding pat. "Got any plans for Sunday dinner?"

Gilbert shrugged. "I have a standing invitation at Mother's, which I prefer to ignore."

"Then come home with me. Annemarie will have something delicious on the stove, I'm sure."

Gilbert's heart gave a slow, deep thud. He drew to one side of the corridor. "Thanks, but . . . I don't think it's such a good idea."

Halting a few steps away, Sam glanced over his shoulder, brows meeting in a disbelieving scowl. "It's a perfectly fine idea. And I won't take no for an answer." His mouth softened, turning up at the corners. "Neither will Annemarie."

"Are you sure?"

"Positive." Backtracking, Sam grabbed Gilbert's arm and steered him toward the exit. "You're driving, naturally. It's too hot to walk, the trolleys can be crowded, and I still refuse to buy an automobile."

Gilbert couldn't help but laugh. "What I like about you, Sam, is you never change."

It was the truth. Even with all they'd been through, all that had once stood between them, Gilbert always knew he could count on Samuel's unwavering friendship and loyalty. Although he wasn't so certain about Sam's sanity just now. Did the man honestly believe the three of them—Gilbert, Sam, and Annemarie—could sit down together for Sunday dinner as if the last several months had never happened?

By the time Gilbert parked his roadster in the driveway of Sam and Annemarie's house, perspiration soaked his undershirt, and only partly because of the noontime August heat. He shut off the engine and then scraped damp palms along his pants legs. "I haven't seen Annemarie since before . . ."

Sam caught his wrist. "It's all right, Gil. Trust me."

Together they walked to the front door, Gilbert's stomach churning more violently with every step. Reaching the porch, he held back. "You should go in first, make sure she's okay with my being here. No sense blindsiding her with a surprise dinner guest."

Lips pursed, Samuel pulled open the screen door and stepped inside. "Annie? I'm home, and I brought company."

"Oh, good," came Annemarie's cheery reply, "because I fried up much more chicken than the two of us could eat in a week! Who is it, sweetheart?"

"An old friend." Sam glanced through the screen at Gilbert. "Come and see for yourself."

Seconds later, Annemarie appeared from the back of the house, a crisp gingham apron tied at her waist. Gilbert held his breath as she met Samuel in the foyer and they shared a kiss. Then, peering over Sam's shoulder, she gave a quick gasp, and her huge brown eyes widened even more. A happy smile lighting her face, she brushed past Sam and pushed open the screen door.

"Gilbert . . . Gilbert!" His name upon her lips brought an ache to his chest. She cradled his cheeks in her palms, her gaze filling with both welcome and forgiveness. "I'm so glad you've come. I've missed you terribly."

Gilbert couldn't trust his own voice to reply. He closed his eyes briefly, too overcome to do more than stand there and savor this blessed moment of reconciliation. Then gently, ever so gently, he probed his emotions, searching, testing, examining each fleeting response. With sweet relief, he found only the deepest friendship in his heart for Annemarie. No jealousy, no resentment, no desire to reclaim what once was his . . . what once he'd so callously tossed aside.

"Well, come in, come in!" Looping her arm through his, Annemarie virtually dragged him into the house. "Sam, pour some iced tea, and both of you get down to your shirtsleeves. Dinner will be on the table in five minutes."

Stunned, Gilbert allowed Sam to help him out of his suit coat. While Sam went to the bedroom to change out of his uniform, Gilbert wandered into the cozy parlor, where the breeze from an electric fan played with the gauze curtains. Spying Sam and Annemarie's wedding portrait over the fireplace, Gilbert moved in for a closer look.

His breath hitched. He'd never seen Annemarie looking more beautiful . . . or more in love.

And now he *was* jealous. Very jealous indeed. And not because he begrudged Annemarie and Samuel their happiness, but because he desperately wanted to taste such happiness for himself.

With Mary.

He turned away, pain arcing through his chest. Would he ever see her again? Would he ever have the chance to prove he could be the man she needed him to be?

Later, seated at the Vickarys' dining room table, Gilbert strove to be a polite guest, but though both Samuel and Annemarie did everything possible to make him feel welcome and accepted, he couldn't relax. When at the end of the meal Annemarie rose to gather their dinner plates, she paused at Gilbert's place and cast him a worried frown.

"Was it my cooking?" she asked, inspecting a half-eaten chicken breast lying amid the lima beans he'd done little more than push around with his fork. "Mama's been giving me lessons. I thought I'd improved."

"No, not at all. I mean, you have. I mean—" Groaning, Gilbert crumpled his napkin beside his iced tea glass. "It was delicious. I guess I wasn't very hungry."

Annemarie's hand drifted across his shoulder in a comforting gesture before she carried a stack of plates to the kitchen.

Pushing back his chair, Samuel laid his napkin aside and crossed his legs. "You don't have to pretend with me, Gil. I can see how badly you're missing Mary, and I'm sorry if inviting you over today has only made it worse."

"Actually, in a strange way I think it's helping. Spending time with you and Annemarie has been . . . healing. Yes, I want what you have, but even if happiness with Mary is never to be mine, I know somehow I've got to pull myself together and find a way to go on without her."

"You've heard nothing from her? Nothing at all since she left for D.C.?"

Gilbert slowly shook his head. "And I don't expect to." Clenching his fist, he quietly pounded the table. "What's wrong with me, Sam? Why do I keep ruining things with the women I love?"

Sam didn't answer right away while he thoughtfully rubbed his chin. "Don't put all the blame on yourself, Gil. I have the sense Mary's leaving had less to do with *your* failings than with her own."

"That's crazy." Shifting, Gilbert shot Sam a dubious glare. "*I* caused this. I've abused her trust too many times to count."

"But she knows you've changed. She knows how hard you've worked to put the past behind you. No," Sam continued, leveling his gaze upon Gilbert, "something else is holding her back. The problem, I believe, is Mary is afraid to trust her own heart."

22

*O*ver the next few days, Gilbert couldn't get Samuel's words out of his mind. If it was true the problems between Gilbert and Mary weren't entirely his doing—if Mary just needed time to sort out her feelings—then maybe she'd yet come back to him.

Except how would he ever convince her while she lived and worked a thousand miles away?

"Are you paying attention?" Mrs. Frederick's sharp tone snapped Gilbert back to the present.

"Of course. We were talking about wheat." He scraped a hand across his eyes and tried to focus on the agricultural notes spread before him on the kitchen table. "So we're looking at an October planting date?"

"Correct. It also means we must begin preparing the fields now." Mrs. Frederick used her pencil to circle a large area on a roughly drawn map of the property. "John always liked to plant his wheat in this section here. It has the best drainage."

Gilbert nodded as if he understood, but this farming business made him nervous. Combine his lack of knowledge with all the variables—weather, equipment failure, market conditions—and it was a risky business indeed. "So . . . what do we do first?"

Mrs. Frederick narrowed her gaze, clearly annoyed by his ignorance. "I tell you what. You go play with your horses, and I will take charge of the farming. As long as you have money to pay, I know men we can hire to plow and plant, and later to harvest." Gathering up the papers strewn across the table, she rose and marched from the room.

Money. Yes, at least he had his money. But he'd give it all away if he thought it would bring Mary back.

All right, then, Mrs. Frederick was perfectly welcome to manage the planting while Gilbert wrote the checks. In the meantime, tending to his horses seemed as good a pastime as any, no matter if Mrs. Frederick deemed it a frivolous pursuit. Considering Mary shared an equally negative opinion, the woman was in good company.

Gathering up his cane and a battered felt fedora, Gilbert plodded out the back door and across the yard to the paddock where Mac grazed. When he braced his arms along the fence rail and whistled softly, Mac lifted his head with a nicker and ambled over. Always in search of the sugar cubes Gilbert spoiled him with, he nuzzled Gilbert's shirtfront, leaving behind a trail of grass-tinged saliva.

"All right, all right! Wrong pocket this time, fella." Laughing, Gilbert fished two lumps of sugar from his trouser pocket. While the contented horse munched, Gilbert used his handkerchief to blot the slimy wetness from his shirt.

Obadiah ambled out from the barn. "Mornin', Mistah Ballard. Got some good news."

"Great. I could use some." Gilbert tipped back his hat.

"Miss Glory's showin' signs of comin' in season. I think she'll be ready for ol' Mac any day now." Obadiah shot him a wide, white grin. "This time next year we could have us a fine little colt or filly."

Gilbert reached across the fence to scratch Mac behind the ear. "Whaddya say, boy? You ready to be a papa?"

What he kept to himself was the crushing dread the horses might be the only "children" Gilbert would ever claim.

✍

"Please, Mary, you can't spend another Friday night holed up in the nurses' quarters." Aggie Hinkhouse, the petite blonde Mary roomed with, adjusted a colorful scarf at her throat. "We won't go anywhere expensive, just a nice dinner out somewhere."

"It isn't the expense that concerns me," Mary said as she slipped on a comfy pair of slippers. "It's my aching feet. The charge nurse on my floor had me running all over the hospital today."

"Well, you *are* the new girl." Aggie plopped onto the bed next to Mary and gave her head a disbelieving shake. "Everyone thinks you're crazy, you know, trading your cushy position at a tame little Arkansas hospital for this." Her sweeping gesture implied everything from the long hours to the grueling, often gruesome duties of caring for the recovering war wounded.

Mary tightened the sash of her bathrobe. "It's a change I welcomed, I assure you."

"Humph. Must be a man involved." Scooting farther onto the bed so she could lean against the wall, Aggie folded her hands and tapped her index fingers together. "Let's hear it, Mary. Every word."

"You think you're so smart, do you?" The tiny dorm room suddenly seemed even smaller. Mary strode to the dresser and snatched up her hairbrush.

"Here, let me." Joining her at the dresser, Aggie took the brush and began stroking it through Mary's thick curls. "And, yeah, I consider myself *very* smart, at least when it comes to recognizing a broken heart when I see it."

Mary didn't dare meet her own reflection in the mirror. Instead, she whirled past Aggie and went straight to the closet they shared. "I just remembered I haven't had a chance to wear this frilly new dress my mum bought for me last week. Dinner out would be the perfect occasion."

And why shouldn't she get out and enjoy herself? Aggie was right—she'd moped around in this drab little room too many nights already. Twenty minutes later the two of them met another pair of nurses out front, and shortly afterward, a taxi collected them. Following Aggie's instructions, the driver wound through town toward a restaurant one of the corpsmen in Aggie's unit had recommended.

The quaint Italian bistro claimed the best meatballs in D.C., and after one bite, Mary was convinced. The delicious food, her new friends' laughter, and the continual buzz of activity past their round corner booth soon swept her cares away—perhaps only temporarily, but she determined to enjoy the respite for as long as it lasted. She decided she'd been a fool for never taking Lois up on her invitations to go out with the girls after work. If she'd only had the courage to expand her horizons beyond the hospital, her mother, and pining over Gilbert, who knew where life might have taken her?

One of the nurses had just begun an off-color joke when the waiter interrupted to clear their plates. "Would anyone care for a dessert menu?"

"Oh, definitely!" Aggie nudged Mary. "You'll have something, won't you?"

"I shouldn't." Shaking her head, Mary rested a palm against her full stomach, already straining the waistline of her new dress.

At the table across from their booth, the host had just seated two young men in natty slacks and blazers. One of the men leaned toward Mary and wiggled his brows. "If you say no, you'll regret it. They serve the best cannoli in town."

"The best meatballs, the best cannoli." Mary knew she must be blushing beneath the man's flirtatious grin. "Is there anything they serve here that isn't the best in town?"

"Well, obviously, they serve the prettiest girls here, too."

Heart fluttering, Mary glanced away.

"Hey, boys," one of her companions called, "we've got room in our booth. Why don't you join us?" She motioned for Mary and the others to scoot in toward the center.

The two men shared a look and then wasted no time in changing tables. Sitting on the outside edge, Mary suddenly found herself squeezed between Aggie and the young man who'd spoken to her. She couldn't suppress a shiver.

"Cold?" He glanced her way, his eyes reflecting the flickering candlelight. "I could lend you my jacket."

"Thank you, but I'm fine."

"My name's Vince. What's yours?"

"Mary."

"Nice to meet you, Mary." Vince rested his arm on the seat back behind her. When his hand brushed her shoulder, she sat up straighter and pretended to adjust her napkin. Vince cast her a puzzled glance and then quietly drew his hand into his lap. He looked almost apologetic before clearing his throat and asking, "So, what do you do?"

"My friends and I are all nurses at Walter Reed." Mary shot him a nervous smile. "And you?"

"I'm a congressional aide. Exciting stuff going on in D.C. these days."

"I'm sure."

The waiter, returning with dessert menus, gave a knowing roll of his eyes to discover the new seating arrangements. He signaled a busboy to bring place settings for the gentlemen and then took orders for their dinner and the ladies' desserts.

"And put those desserts on my tab," Vince said as the waiter turned to go.

"That's quite unnecessary." Mary's stomach grew more unsettled by the moment. She began to wish she'd forgone the cannoli.

"Now, Mary," Aggie chided, patting her arm, "it's rude to turn down such a charming offer."

Across the booth, Vince's friend and the other two nurses appeared to be making hasty progress getting acquainted. Mary prayed the men's dinner would arrive quickly so Vince would spend more time eating than flirting.

And then she thought, *Why?* What, really, was keeping her from enjoying the attention of a handsome man? And what better way to get over the man she could never have?

❧

"What did you think of *Daddy-Long-Legs?*" Vince asked as he parked his automobile in front of the nurses' quarters.

Mary pinched her handbag between her fingers. It was her fourth date with Vince, and she felt no less nervous than when she first met him two weeks ago. "I enjoyed the film very much. Mary Pickford is so beautiful and expressive."

"No more so than another Mary I know." Vince pried her fingers loose and seared the back of her hand with a tender kiss.

She swallowed and tried not to pull away.

Even in the darkened car, she could make out his bemused half-smile. "What is it about you, Mary? We've been seeing each other for a couple of weeks now, and yet I still feel I hardly know you. I've decided you're either incredibly shy or getting over a broken heart."

When she didn't answer, he placed his index finger beneath her chin and gently turned her head until he could gaze into her eyes. "Aha," he said with all the authority of a physician diagnosing a patient, "it's both. Who was it, Mary? Who broke your fragile heart?"

Shrugging off his touch, she glanced out the side window. "No one you'd know. He's in the past now and best forgotten."

"Except you can't forget him, can you? It's written all over your face." Vince slid his arm around her, and when he nestled her against his chest, she didn't resist. "If he was fool enough to hurt you—even worse, let a girl as sweet as you get away—" Caressing her hair, he released a noisy sigh. "If I could person-ally pound some sense into his thick skull for you, I'd gladly do it."

In spite of the tears never far from the surface these days, Mary chuckled softly, the sound muted by the nubby fabric of Vince's blazer. His comforting touch and gentle words made her feel safe, protected, cared for. Little by little, she relaxed against him. "You're a kind man, Vince. I'm sorry I've been so reserved."

"Don't apologize. It's amazingly refreshing to meet a girl who isn't throwing herself at every available guy she meets—and believe me, there are plenty in this town who do."

Mary sat up, one hand resting upon Vince's chest. She offered a shy smile. "And you're every bit the gentleman, for which I'm grateful." She moved to reach for the door handle. "I should go in. It's late."

"Wait." Vince caught her hand. "One kiss, Mary, is all I ask. I've been dreaming about kissing you since I first laid eyes on you in the restaurant."

Her stomach somersaulted. She stared straight ahead. "I don't know if . . ."

"If you're ready? I understand. But you don't have to be afraid." Vince slid toward her, reaching up to cup her cheek. "I would never hurt you, Mary, I promise."

When his lips brushed hers, her heart stopped. Short, panicky breaths struggled past her frozen throat muscles, while heat suffused her limbs. *Gilbert . . . Gilbert.*

With a shudder, she pulled away. "I'm sorry . . . I can't."

Vince's dark eyes grew flinty, even as he gently thumbed away the tear sliding down her cheek. "I could kill the guy who did this to you."

"Don't judge him. You don't know what he's been through." Mary shoved open the car door.

In a flash, Vince had rounded the automobile and helped Mary to her feet. "Okay, okay. Whatever happened, I can tell how much you cared for him. But like you said, he's in the past. Say you'll let me be part of your future. Please."

She gripped his forearms and heaved an exhausted groan. "I like you, Vince. Very much. But I'm making no decisions about my future beyond getting what sleep I can in the next few hours before my shift begins." Then, regretting her snappish tone, she pressed her lips together in an apologetic smile. "Thank you again for the lovely evening. Now I really must say good night."

&

"Good night, Gilbert." Mrs. Frederick nodded from the foyer. "I will have breakfast ready at seven as usual."

Yawning, Gilbert looked up from the dime novel he'd been reading. He was fairly certain he'd dozed through the last few paragraphs. "I'm headed up soon, myself."

Mrs. Frederick turned to go, then paused and faced him again, lips pursed. "Perhaps it is not my place to say anything, but as I am old enough to be your mother, I will take this liberty."

Gilbert laid his novel on the arm of the chair as curiosity nudged aside his lethargy. "Don't ever hesitate to speak your mind with me." He gave a short laugh. "Besides, I hold your opinions in much higher regard than those of my own mother."

Her stern glare spoke her disapproval of such a disrespectful remark. Hands folded at her waist, she stepped into the parlor. "What I have to say is . . . of a personal nature. You never go into town anymore except to purchase supplies. I worry because you spend so much time alone here at the farm."

"I'm not alone. I have you and Obadiah and the horses. And I've been attending chapel services at the hospital every Sunday." He reached for his cane and pushed up from the chair. "If anyone needs to be chided for choosing to be alone, it's you. When was the last time you took me up on one of my numerous offers to drive you into the city?"

Mrs. Frederick sniffed and glanced away. "I am old. I have no need for other people. I am happy here."

"I don't think so." Gilbert stepped closer. His voice softened. "I think you're as lonely as I am."

The woman answered with a pinch-faced frown, her tone harsh with rancor. "I am German, remember. Loneliness is the price I pay."

Her words twisted Gilbert's insides. Almost a year after the Armistice and the war continued to wrap its ugly tentacles around the people Gilbert cared about. He gathered Mrs. Frederick's hands into his own and held them firmly. Her palms were rough with calluses, while the backs bore dark spots from the sun and purple veins stood out like twisted ropes beneath the skin. Strong hands and yet so fragile, like the woman they belonged to.

"I know it sounds trite," he murmured, "but time does heal. People will come to remember the Frederick family as the good citizens of Hot Springs—of America—the way you've always been. But only if you give them reason to."

Doubt filled her eyes as she slowly shook her head. "How do I do that?"

"By standing tall and showing you're not afraid. By simply being yourself and trusting the ones who matter will stand with you, and the ones who don't . . . well, they aren't worth worrying about."

"Yes . . . yes." Mrs. Frederick firmed her mouth. "I know in my heart what you say is right. To honor the memory of my husband and son, I will try." She peered up at him with a hesitant smile. "You will ask me again next time you go into town?"

Gilbert nodded as he gave her hands a final press. "I will ask again."

Watching her disappear down the hall toward her rooms, he wondered if it was his imagination, or if she held herself slightly more erect.

Fatigue washed over him. He sank into the nearest chair and massaged his temples. Did he believe what he'd told her? Because if he did, it would mean letting go of Mary once and for all.

23

$\mathcal{A}$s the prelude began Sunday morning, Thomas felt a hand on his shoulder and looked up to see Gilbert signaling him to make room in the Ballards' usual pew. Thomas narrowed one eye. "This is a surprise. I thought you'd given up on church."

"I've been attending elsewhere, believe it or not. May we sit with you?"

"*We?*" Thomas looked past Gilbert to see Katrina Frederick waiting in the aisle.

Smiling nervously, the gray-haired woman waved two fingers. "Good morning, Tommy."

Thomas's mother, who had been engrossed reading the Sunday bulletin, leaned forward with a grating whisper. "What, pray tell, is so important—" Her eyes lit up. "Gilbert! Oh, do join us." She scooted farther along the pew, only to look askance at Thomas when he nudged her farther still.

"Gilbert brought Mrs. Frederick," Thomas explained. "And close your mouth. You look like a dying fish."

It was probably a good thing Mother had both Thomas and Gilbert to serve as buffers between her and Mrs. Frederick. Not to mention the worship hour gave her time to adjust her attitude. By the time they exited Ouachita Fellowship into the September sunshine, Evelyn Ballard was all smiles for her first-born son and his companion.

Though no doubt she'd much have preferred to see a young, rich debutante on Gilbert's arm.

"You *must* accompany us for Sunday dinner," Mother gushed, gripping Gilbert's wrist. "Thomas and I are meeting the O'Neals and their two lovely daughters at the Arlington."

"Thanks, but Mrs. Frederick and I have other plans." Gilbert freed his arm and then tucked Mrs. Frederick's hand in the crook of his elbow. "We've packed a picnic for Gulpha Gorge, and then we're going to take a leisurely drive around town before heading back to the farm."

A picnic sounded much more appealing to Thomas than a stuffy meal in the Arlington restaurant, even with the effervescent O'Neal twins present. Mother surely had matchmaking on her mind when she orchestrated this dinner engagement, but neither twin seemed quite Thomas's type—he'd dated each of them in high school. Unfortunately, Gilbert didn't look as if he'd welcome a tagalong.

In fact, there was something about Gilbert's demeanor that made Thomas slightly envious. He wished he could put his finger on what was different, but all he came up with was a sense of calm acceptance. Had Gilbert finally resigned himself to Mary's leaving, or was it something more?

Even Mrs. Frederick seemed changed from when Thomas had last seen her over a month ago when he and Jack Trapp had helped Gilbert move his things out to the farm. She'd kept to herself then with as much determination as when she'd stayed with the Ballards while Gilbert renovated the farmhouse. After having made no secret of her resentment toward Pastor Yarborough and the church members she claimed had tried to take advantage of her, the fact she'd accompanied Gilbert to worship suggested she'd turned a corner not only in her circumstances but emotionally and spiritually.

Saying goodbye to Gilbert and Mrs. Frederick, Thomas experienced a fresh surge of admiration for his brother. No doubt about it, Gilbert was getting his life back on track.

"He seems happy, don't you think?" Mother's tenderhearted tone caught Thomas off guard. A sigh raked through her. "I was wrong to discourage his purchase of the farm. Anyone can see how his work there has benefited him."

"I don't think it's just the work, Mother." Thomas offered his arm as they walked across the church grounds toward the car. "Equally important is his unselfish response to another person's great need. Because of Gilbert, Mrs. Frederick is getting her life back, too."

"Yes, poor woman." Thomas's mother paused as they reached the Peerless. With a thoughtful frown, she met his gaze. "You think me rather frivolous, don't you?"

Thomas weighed his reply, but in the end could only be honest. "I think you're much more concerned about keeping up appearances than with displaying genuine human kindness."

Her chin lifted ever so slightly. Slowly she turned and allowed Zachary to help her into the car. Sliding in beside her, Thomas wondered what thoughts raced beneath the feathered cloche she wore. Was there any hope his mother would ever step down from her ivory tower and let God work a miracle of loving-kindness in her soul?

Mary turned one way and then another, checking in the mirror for any loose strands from her chignon. "Aggie, be a dear and let me borrow your lovely new scarf."

"I don't know why I should." Sitting on her bed, Aggie stooped to tie the laces of her sturdy nursing shoes. "It isn't fair you have a midweek day off to go gallivanting through the Virginia countryside while I have to work a double shift. I won't see my pillow again until the wee hours of Thursday morning."

"I've done my share of double shifts lately. Besides, when you're finally heading off to dreamland at three a.m., I'll just be starting my shift, so no sympathy from me."

"Yes, but you'll get back from your outing with Vince all windblown and sun-kissed—and thoroughly *Vince*-kissed as well, I'm guessing—with a full day of romantic memories to carry you through." Aggie stomped over to the dresser and riffled through the top drawer. Whisking out a long, gauzy crimson scarf, she bunched it up and flung it at Mary. "There. Enjoy."

Mary rolled her eyes and drew Aggie close for a quick hug. "I don't know about all the *kissing* business, but I do enjoy Vince's company. Immensely."

"Yes, and here's another thing. You're in town not even a month and already you have a steady beau. What am I doing wrong?"

Releasing her friend, Mary offered a pensive smile. "Truth be told, I don't know what I'm doing *right*." She returned to the mirror and tied the scarf around her hair, leaving a few tendrils to spiral at her temples. "I certainly didn't go looking for someone new, and I'm still not sure I'm ready for this. But Vince is so kind, so understanding, so . . . comfortable."

"Comfortable?" Aggie peered over Mary's shoulder at her reflection. "What about romance, passion, fire?"

Mary's breath stuttered. She closed her eyes briefly. "I've had all that, and look where it got me. For now, *comfortable* suits me just fine."

"If I weren't late for my shift already, I'd sit you down and insist you tell me every last thing about the guy you left back in Arkansas."

"Well, you are late, and there's nothing more I'll tell you anyway, so best you're on your way." Mary shooed her roommate out the door then closed it with a sigh of relief. She'd spoken very little of her relationship with Gilbert, partly because it was no one else's business, but mainly because remembering hurt too much.

As for Vince, being with him soothed her spirit in a way she couldn't define. Perhaps she would let him kiss her again today. Maybe it would feel different from his attempt the other night. More romantic. Less . . . brotherly.

Dear Vince. If he knew his kiss had affected her that way, he'd be devastated.

Oh, Jesus, I want to return his affection, but how can I when my heart is still so torn? Even after all this time, the taste of Gilbert's kisses lingered upon her lips. Yes, even now, she craved his touch, his embrace, with a physical yearning that shamed her.

She couldn't think about Gilbert, not a second longer. Snatching up her handbag, she bolted into the hallway and dashed out the front door. Vince would find her waiting on the front lawn in the morning sunshine, and she'd smile and wave as he drove up. She'd climb into his automobile, and off they'd go to enjoy their day together in the countryside. Yes, she would relish every moment of it and never give Gilbert a second thought.

Then Vince arrived, and her resolve lasted only until they'd left the hospital campus and started out of the city.

"I've got something really special planned for us." Stopping at an intersection, Vince reached across the front seat to squeeze Mary's hand. "The congressman I work for owns a horse farm on the Virginia side of the Potomac. It's beautiful out there—white fences, green meadows, the river flowing past."

"A horse farm?" Mary's stomach shifted.

"You'll love it, I promise. We might even take a couple of horses out for a ride."

Bile rose in her throat. "Vince, I don't . . . I can't ride."

"If you're worried about your dress, they'll have something more suitable you can borrow, I'm sure." Vince cast her such a disarming grin, she hated to disappoint him.

But she must. She had to. "You don't understand, Vince." She swallowed, then tried to put more force behind her words. "I mean it, I don't ride."

"You don't know how?" He tore his eyes from the road long enough to sear her with a disbelieving stare. "Wow. I thought sure an Arkansas girl would have practically grown up on horseback."

Ire heated her cheeks. "So you assume we're all country bumpkins back in Arkansas? I'll have you know Hot Springs is a thriving cosmopolitan city. It's been many a year since I've had need of any form of transportation other than the trolley, a motorcar, or my own two feet."

Vince's jaw firmed. He took several slow breaths while maneuvering the car to the side of the road. Shutting off the motor, he rested one arm over the steering wheel and twisted to face Mary, his expression filled with concern. "I've clearly upset you, Mary. What did I say to make you so angry?"

"I'm not angry!" But even to her own ears, her sharp denial stung.

"Then maybe you could to tell me what's *really* going on here, because suddenly I'm very confused."

She looked away, and somewhere in the far reaches of her memory she heard her own little-girl screams. *"Da! Oh, please, someone help my da!"*

A sob caught in her throat. She pressed a fist to her mouth.

Vince touched her shoulder. "Mary, talk to me."

She twisted the tails of Aggie's lovely crimson scarf, but all she saw was the blood-soaked ground beneath her father's head. "A horse killed my father."

"Oh, Mary, I'm sorry. If I'd known—"

"He didn't die right away," Mary went on as if Vince hadn't spoken, "but he was never the same, never right in his head afterward. For years after, Mum and I did our best to take care of him, but it was never enough . . . never enough."

Gently, tenderly, Vince enfolded Mary in his arms. "There, it's all right." He slid the scarf from her hair and brushed a kiss across her forehead, his breath warm and moist. "I'm here for you, Mary. I'll always be here for you."

She nodded and burrowed deeper into the crisp cotton of his shirt. "Thank you."

"Can you tell me how it happened?" More kisses, soft as butterfly wings, traced her brow. "A shared burden isn't nearly so heavy, you know."

"I don't remember much, really. I was just a wee child then." Mary shuddered. Truth be told, she didn't *want* to remember. Yet she could still hear the horse's startled whinny, still see those slashing hooves, still smell the metallic odor of her father's blood seeping into the street.

"I'm guessing you remember more than you think you do, or you wouldn't still be so upset by the mere thought of being around horses."

"It isn't just the horses. It's the—" Abruptly Mary sat up as long-repressed memories assailed her. She drew a slow breath through her nostrils. "It's the *stench*."

"Of the horse?"

"No, not the horse." Mary's hand shot to her mouth as nausea threatened. She couldn't believe she'd ignored this memory for so long, and yet there it was where it had always been.

"What, Mary? What did you smell?"

With a moan, she replied, "The whiskey on my father's breath."

☙

"Hello, the horseman!"

Surprised by the shout, Gilbert set down the water pail in Miss Glory's stall, gave her a quick pat on the rump, and latched the gate. Now moving more easily without his cane, he strode out the barn door to see who'd come calling.

Arthur Spence, wouldn't you know it. Bad pennies always had a way of turning up. "I thought you'd have returned to Boston by now."

Thumbs hooked in his suspenders, Arthur pulled a wry grin and toed the ground. "Suffice it to say my uncle no longer has need of my services."

Gilbert snorted. "In other words, he fired you."

"Can I help it if the textile business doesn't suit me?"

"Does *any* line of work if it involves actually showing up?"

Arthur glared. "Low, Ballard. Really low."

"You forget how well I know you." Giving his head a quick shake, Gilbert turned toward the barn. "I have chores to finish. You're welcome to watch."

Ambling alongside him, Arthur tipped back his straw boater. "I heard you'd snagged a retired thoroughbred and a couple of brood mares. Gambling on racing making a comeback—either you're a very shrewd investor or the biggest sucker ever born."

"Guess we'll find out, won't we?" Gilbert crossed over to Mac's stall and fished a sugar cube from his pocket. Mac whinnied his gratitude and rewarded Gilbert with a not-so-gentle nuzzle against his chest.

"So this is your prize stallion?" Arthur rested an elbow on the rail. "Handsome fella, but I don't know about his limp."

"We all have our flaws. It's what you do with the rest of your life that matters."

"Oops, hit a nerve, did I?"

Wiping dirt and horse hair off his hands with a grimy handkerchief, Gilbert faced Arthur with an annoyed glare. "I'm sure you didn't drive all the way out here because of sheer boredom. Why don't you tell me what's really on your mind?"

"Not one to beat around the bush, are you?" Arthur narrowed his eyes, his glance darting around the barn. "Are we alone out here? This isn't for just anyone's ears."

Gilbert had a feeling he'd be sorry he didn't run Arthur off the property the moment he arrived, but now he was curious. "Mrs. Frederick's in the house, and my stable hand went into town to pick up some feed. It's just you, me, and the horses."

"Good, good. . . ." Another surreptitious glance toward the door. "See, I got to thinking, who'd make the perfect partner for this little . . . enterprise I'm undertaking?" Arthur plucked a piece of straw from one of the hay bales stacked against the wall. "And I thought, my ol' school chum Gilbert Ballard. Here you are miles from town, living out amongst hills, rocks, and trees. Plenty of places where a body could hide just about anything."

Suspicion curdled Gilbert's belly. "Hide what, exactly?"

Arthur's gaze swept the barn yet again, his obvious concern about being overheard heightening Gilbert's misgivings even more. Arthur dropped his voice to a rasping whisper. "Why, a still, of course." His mouth widened into a provocative grin. "Just think of the money we could make off moonshine. Plenty for you to subsidize your horse breeding venture, plenty for me so I don't have to go crawling to my uncle and beg him to put me back on the payroll."

Gilbert backed away, every nerve on edge. "You're asking me to break the law."

"A law nobody around these parts is interested in enforcing. In case you haven't noticed, there are stills all over Garland County, lots of them owned by relatives of local law enforcement." Arthur spread his hands. "Come on, Gil, look at the potential. I've already got a solid in with a successful operation. You've got the acreage to grow the corn we'll need. I'll handle everything else, including marketing our product."

"Our product. You mean illegal whiskey."

Arthur aimed his finger at Gilbert's chest. "You wait right there, my friend. Just so happens I've brought samples." With a chortling laugh, he jogged out the barn door.

Drawing a hand across his mouth, Gilbert swallowed hard. He could already taste the illicit brew, feel the bite of the alcohol as it slid down his throat. He should call out to Arthur, tell him to take his moonshine and get off the property at once, but he couldn't get the words past his thick tongue.

Moments later, Arthur returned with a brown paper sack tucked beneath his arm. He set it on the ground in front of Gilbert, peeled back the top, and plucked a cork from the neck of a jug. The unmistakable odor of distilled spirits assaulted Gilbert's nostrils as Arthur lifted the jug and held it out to him.

As if his hands belonged to someone else, Gilbert cautiously reached for the jug. The weight of it surprised him as he cradled it against his abdomen. He swallowed again then breathed in and out through clenched teeth, fighting the urge for just one taste.

But then one sip would lead to another, and another, and there'd be no turning back. It would be so very easy to succumb to the lure of alcohol and drink himself into a stupor of forgetfulness. What reason did he have to stay sober anyway? Mary wasn't around to hold him accountable.

Sure, prove her right. Be the weak-willed addict she thinks you are.

The sound of a truck bouncing up the lane jolted Gilbert with a much-needed dose of good sense. He thrust the jug into Arthur's arms. "My hired man is returning. He's honest as the day is long and will have no qualms about reporting you. If our local police won't do anything, I'm sure the federal authorities will gladly step in. So I suggest you take your illegal spirits *and* your ill-conceived schemes and get off my land."

Arthur cast a nervous glance toward the door. "You'll be sorry, Gil. When I'm making money hand over fist, you'll wish you'd taken me up on my offer."

"I don't think so." Gilbert stood a little straighter as he watched Arthur jog out to his automobile. Moving to the barn door, he waved to Obadiah.

The wiry stable hand parked the truck next to the barn and climbed out of the cab. He tugged off his tweed cap and waved away the dust raised by Arthur's speedy departure. Joining Gilbert in the barn door, he said, "Your visitor sure seemed in a hurry to leave."

"And good riddance. He was trespassing. If you see him on the property again, I want you to notify the sheriff."

"Yessuh, Mistah Ballard, if you say so."

Gilbert followed Obadiah to the truck, and as they unloaded supplies from the feed store, a mixture of satisfaction and relief rose in Gilbert's chest. He'd done it—stood his ground and resisted temptation. A year ago, even a month ago, he wasn't so sure he'd have succeeded.

Dear God, am I finally becoming the man You want me to be?

Too late for Mary, perhaps, but even if she never came back to him, he had to live with himself, didn't he? Besides, Mrs. Frederick and Obadiah depended on him. If he needed reasons to walk the straight and narrow, he had them. God help him, he'd make his life count for something. Something good. Something worthy.

24

I'd like to go back now." One hand on the door handle, Mary kept her gaze averted. She didn't want to talk anymore, didn't want to think or remember or be forced to examine feelings she could no longer justify.

Vince started the motor. "I'll take you home if you really want me to, but I won't leave you alone. Not like this."

Home. Certainly not the austere nurses' quarters at Walter Reed. The only real home she'd ever known was back in Hot Springs in the little cottage she'd shared with her mother.

Now, suddenly, Mary didn't feel as if she belonged anywhere.

She could never return to Gilbert, of course, not after having so irrationally transferred all her prejudice against drunkenness and irresponsibility from her father to him. Because clearly she had done so. Like it or not, eventually she'd have to come to grips with the truth about the man whose memory she'd distorted for so many years.

Vince swung the car in a wide U-turn, and soon they passed through the entrance to the Walter Reed Hospital complex. When Vince parked in front of the nurses' quarters, Mary turned to him with a sigh. "I'm so sorry for ruining your lovely plans for the day. Please forgive me."

"There's nothing to forgive. I just wish you'd let me keep you company awhile longer." Unspoken questions furrowing his brow, Vince fingered one of the curls at her temple. "We could take a walk, or . . . I could just sit here and hold you."

Mary's heart clenched at his pleading tone. She could see in his eyes how much he cared, and it only made her heart hurt all the worse. "You're too kind to me, Vince. I know you mean well, but I need to be alone. And I think—" Oh, this was so hard! Tilting her head, she touched her fingertips to the frown line at the side of his mouth. "I think I'd rather you didn't call me again."

He flinched. "Mary—"

"I'm not saying never," she hurried to add. "But I've already failed in one relationship, and I can't risk ruining another."

"You wouldn't. You couldn't. Please, Mary, give us a chance."

"Not until I've sorted a few things out." She pushed open the car door and set one foot on the gravelly drive. "Don't wait for me, though, because I can't make any promises about the future."

"I don't need promises. I just need hope."

Stepping from the car, she turned to cast him a regretful smile. "I'm afraid I can't even offer you that much. I've enjoyed the time we've spent together, Vince, but for now, this is goodbye."

Resolutely, she straightened, closed the door, and turned her back on the man whose heart she'd surely just ripped in two. Guilt weighed heavily upon her shoulders, but better to end things sooner rather than later. Where men were concerned, Mary could no longer trust her own judgment—if she ever could.

Had she really turned a blind eye all these years to her father's failings? She couldn't honestly say she hadn't known of his weakness for alcohol, but she'd needed to believe in his goodness. He was her da, after all, and a girl needed a father she could admire and depend upon. To admit the accident might have been his fault simply didn't bear thinking about.

Crossing the foyer, Mary paused as she passed the telephone. With a bracing breath, she lifted the earpiece and rang her mother's number. "Will you be at home awhile? I'd like to come over."

"You're always welcome, dear. But I thought you were goin' out with the nice young man today." Her mother gave an unladylike snort. "He didn't stand you up, now, did he?"

"No, no, nothing like that. I just . . . need to talk to you."

Within the hour, Mary had walked to the nearest streetcar stop and made her way to her mother's townhouse. Her mother welcomed her inside with a hug and led her to the kitchen.

"Sit down, luv. You look like you could stand a strong cup of tea." Mum set the kettle on the stove then took the kitchen chair across from Mary. "Now tell me what this is all about. Are you not likin' your work at the hospital here?"

"The work is fine." In fact, most days work was the only thing keeping Mary from losing her mind from pining over what she'd left behind in Hot Springs. She reached for her mother's hand and ran her thumb across the softly wrinkled knuckles. "Tell me about Da."

Her mother uttered a confused laugh. "What is it you want to know?"

"Tell me about the drinking."

The hand Mary held grew suddenly cold. Mum jerked away and strode to the counter, busying herself with the tea canister. "Oh, sure he drank some, like any working man."

"He was drinking the day of the accident, wasn't he?"

Her mother's fluttering hands stilled. "Yes, I suppose so. Your da often went to the pub for a pint after a hard day's work."

"But this was the middle of the morning, one of his rare days off. He'd taken me along on a trip to the market." Mary pressed her lips together as the memories coalesced. "You were baking bread and had run out of flour."

"That's right." Mum smiled over her shoulder as she retrieved two teaspoons from a drawer. "I've no cream today. Will sugar do?"

"When we left the market, Da saw some friends across the street outside the pub. He told me if I waited for him at the five-and-dime, he'd buy me a penny candy after he'd shared a pint with his mates. But he stayed so long I feared he'd forgotten me."

Mum stood at the stove, her back to Mary, arms crossed. "I don't know what's taking this water so long to boil."

"And when he did leave the pub, he was weaving and staggering." Mary closed her eyes, seeing it all as if it were only yesterday. An ache formed deep in her chest. "I waved and called to him, and he waved back, laughing so loud, and I remember wondering what was so funny. Then he stepped into the street right in front of the horse and dray—"

"Stop!" Mary's mother pressed a fist to her mouth. "It does no good to dredge up such horrible memories. Let your poor da rest in peace."

Mary rose and tucked her arm around her mother's waist. "I know it's hard, Mum, but maybe it's time we faced the truth about Da's drinking . . . together."

Choking on a sob, Mum turned and drew Mary into her arms. "I loved him. God help me, I loved that fool of a man. Oh, Mary, I wish you'd never had to remember that side of your da."

"No, it's better I did. My feelings about Da . . . my doubts about Gilbert . . . make so much more sense now." The kettle whistled, and Mary gave her mother a final squeeze before reaching for a folded towel to grab the handle. While she poured boiling water over the tea strainer in her mother's favorite blue china pot, Mum carried cups and spoons to the table. Several moments of silence passed as they waited for the tea to steep.

Dabbing at her eyes with the corner of a napkin, Mum sniffed and said, "Have your feelings changed, then? For Gilbert, I mean?"

"I love him as much as I ever did—more, if it's possible." Her own gaze grew watery as she watched her mother pour the tea. Slowly, deliberately, she stirred a lump of sugar into her cup.

Her mother pinned her with a worried frown. "You're not thinkin' of going back to him, are you?"

"There's nothing left for us." Mary drew a shaky breath. "What we had is damaged beyond repair, and I'm mostly to blame. I never really gave Gilbert the chance to prove he could change."

"He's still the man he was, and being sorry for judging him because of your da won't change it."

Mary cringed at the sharpness of her mother's tone. She searched her mother's gaze. "You haven't forgiven Da, have you?"

"Of course I have. I took care of him all those years, didn't I?" Mum stirred her tea with a vengeance. Amber droplets splashed over the rim into the saucer.

"Tending a sick man isn't the same as forgiving him." When her mother's spoon clattered to the floor, Mary stooped to retrieve it. Laying it to one side, she stilled her mother's trembling hand. "We spent so many years caring for Da, we neglected to take care of ourselves. You held your feelings inside—worry over Da's drinking, resentment about the accident forcing him out of work, anger for everything his disability stole from us, including your health."

Mum straightened and forced a smile. "But I'm fine now, almost good as new."

"I know, and it's all thanks to Donald, and I couldn't be happier." Mary squeezed her eyes shut briefly. "When I think of how hard I resisted accepting his presence in your life—and all because of my misguided loyalty to Da—"

"Oh, darlin', don't. You loved your da and he loved you, despite all his faults. And truly, I have forgiven him. It's only I don't want to see my own daughter hurt by a man who can't resist temptation, and I feared from the start it's exactly what Gilbert would do."

Mary sighed and looked toward the window, her heart a thousand miles away in Hot Springs, Arkansas. "But what if I hadn't been so self-righteous and critical? What if I'd given him one more chance?"

"One more chance, Mary, please!"

But she wouldn't even look at him. Her departing figure faded into a thick, devouring mist as white as her nurse's uniform, until all he could see was a faint tinge of red from the mass of curls cascading across her shoulders.

"You're hopeless, Gilbert Ballard." Her words drifted back to him through the fog and echoed in his brain. "You'll never change."

"I have. I will! Don't leave me, Mary. I need—"

Gilbert sat up with a start. Breathing hard, a catch in his throat, he ground his fists into his eye sockets. "I do need you, Mary. I need you, because I'm so desperately in love with you!"

Blast it all, why couldn't he stop dreaming about her? Even now, his mind filled with the sharp, decisive sound of her footsteps as she walked away.

Except the sounds kept getting louder. Gilbert shook his head. Was he still dreaming?

Someone rapped hard on his bedroom door—no dream. "Mistah Ballard. Wake up, Mistah Ballard!"

"Obadiah?" Gilbert thrust aside the sweat-soaked sheets, almost forgetting his missing leg as he tried to stand. He caught himself just in time. Grabbing his cane, he hopped to the door and yanked it open. "What's happened? Is it the horses?"

The whites of Obadiah's eyes gleamed bright as the nightshirt stuffed haphazardly into his trousers. "They done got out—or someone let 'em out, I s'pect. I caught Cricket an' got her back in her stall, but Miss Glory an' Mac is long gone."

Leaning hard on his cane, Gilbert ran his other hand along his scalp and tried to think. "We keep the main gate closed. They can't have gone far."

"I don't know, suh. I'm thinkin' I heard a automobile leavin' in a hurry."

"Are you sure?"

From behind Obadiah, Mrs. Frederick stepped forward, a thin chenille robe tied at her waist and her steel-gray braid hanging across one shoulder. "I heard something, too. And saw headlights from my window."

Shirtless and suddenly feeling exposed in nothing but his pajama bottoms, Gilbert pushed the door partway closed. "Give me a minute to dress. Then we'll find the horses and figure this out."

What time was it, anyway? Gilbert made his way over to the dresser and found his watch—barely half past four. Who would have been on the property at this unholy hour? And what kind of mischief were they up to?

By the time he'd attached his prosthesis and pulled on shirt, trousers, and boots, his mental fog had begun to lift. One name rose to the surface: Arthur Spence. Had the man been angry enough with Gilbert for turning down his bootlegging proposition that he'd sneak out here to take revenge?

He'd have to deal with *that* question later. In the meantime, Gilbert needed to find his horses and make sure they were safe.

He hobbled stiff-legged downstairs, where Mrs. Frederick had just returned to the entryway with two kerosene lanterns. "Obadiah is already out searching," she said, handing him one of the lanterns. "I will help."

Gilbert pushed open the screen door. "Thank you, but there's no need for all of us to go stumbling about in the dark. The horses could be frightened. You'll be safer inside."

"I can handle a frightened horse," she insisted, following him onto the porch. "I will—" She flinched. Waving both hands, she stumbled backwards.

"What—" A split second later, a buzzing noise and a sudden sharp sting on Gilbert's neck answered his question—*bees!*

Mrs. Frederick was already bounding down the porch steps, the hem of her robe flying. "Oh, no—the hives!"

"Don't go any closer! They're angry!" Waving away another swarm circling his head, Gilbert tore after her. When he stumbled on the steps, he grabbed the rail and cursed himself for leaving his cane behind.

"The hives have been tipped over," Mrs. Frederick shouted over her shoulder as she dashed toward the barn. "We need to get the smokers to calm the bees."

Heaven help them, what more could go wrong? Limping along at the quickest pace he could handle without landing flat on his face, Gilbert ignored two more stings. When he realized the bees were flying toward the lantern light, he doused it.

With a full moon sliding across the southwestern sky and his eyes beginning to adjust, he could see well enough.

"Mistah Ballard!" Obadiah's voice came from the other side of the house. "I found Mac in the field out yonder, but I ain't seen no sign of Miss Glory."

Gilbert swung around and slapped at another bee. "Keep him over there. The bees are swarming."

"Tarnation!" came Obadiah's shout. "I'll put him in the back pasture and come help."

Turning toward the barn again, Gilbert looked up to see a cloaked figure emerge—Mrs. Frederick in her netted hood, two bee smokers in hand. The smell of burning burlap bit at Gilbert's nostrils as she neared. "What can I do?" he asked, reaching for one of the smokers.

She held it fast and marched past him. "You cannot help without a hood. Go find your horse. I can take care of the bees."

She'd almost reached the overturned hives when Miss Glory's anxious whinny cut through the darkness. Gilbert snapped his head up to see the dark shape of a horse galloping across the lane. In another moment, the animal would land smack in the middle of the hives.

"Mrs. Frederick, look out!" Gilbert limped after her, the stiff artificial leg hindering his speed.

Just as he caught up, Miss Glory plowed through the hives, riling the bees even more. Screaming in terror and pain, the horse stumbled and pranced in search of escape. Eyes wide, nostrils flared, she leapt over a hive and barreled straight toward Gilbert and Mrs. Frederick.

With a shout, Gilbert shoved the woman out of the way. She fell sideways, one of the smokers flying from her hand. Hooves slashed the air as the startled horse skidded and reared. Gilbert raised his arm to shield his face, but Miss Glory's momentum brought her full weight bearing down upon him.

Pain—blinding pain—as her hoof impaled his thigh. Something cracked, someone screamed. The sky overhead shattered into a million stars, and then blackness.

⁂

Mary claimed precious little sleep before reporting for her shift at three a.m. Now, with dawn creeping over the horizon, she prayed for the energy to get through the next few hours. If the chief nurse burdened her with another double shift today, she didn't think she could survive.

"Nurse McClarney, give me a hand here." A doctor motioned her over to where he examined a victim of mustard gas inhalation. Even after months of intensive respiratory treatments, the soldier suffered from a weakened heart and repeated lung infections.

Mary stepped up beside the doctor. "What can I do, sir?"

"He's delirious with fever. I need you to secure his wrists so he doesn't thrash about so much."

Stomach heaving, Mary sucked in a tiny breath as images of Gilbert rushed to the surface. Barely home from France and out of his mind with pain and shell shock, he'd lashed out and struck Mary in the jaw when she'd tried to quiet him. Mrs. Daley had immediately ordered him strapped to his hospital bed. If the chief nurse had had her way, he'd have been shipped off to the nearest psychiatric facility.

"Nurse McClarney, if you please." The doctor's stern rebuke snapped her attention to the present.

"Yes, sir, just let me get a roll of gauze to tie his wrists." She hurried off to the supply cabinet behind the nurses' station.

Within minutes, she'd secured the soldier to the bed rails— and was none too happy to do so. His red-rimmed eyes followed her with a dazed look, and he kept whimpering, "Cara, is that you? Where's my Cara?"

"Is Cara his sweetheart?" Mary whispered to the doctor.

"His wife. Or used to be. Couldn't deal with the aftereffects of the war, so she left him." The doctor gave his head a disgusted shake as he listened to the soldier's lungs. "What ever happened to 'till death us do part'?"

Skewered with self-loathing, Mary longed to escape the ward and seek out a corner somewhere to give vent to her emotions. She wasn't committed to Gilbert by marriage, but hadn't she been equally cruel in the way she'd walked out of his life? Whether her suspicions proved true or not, Gilbert couldn't help what the war had done to him any more than the man lying before her—or any of the countless other suffering soldiers she cared for every day.

As soon as the doctor indicated he no longer needed her assistance, Mary excused herself. A patient in a wheelchair rolled in front of her. "Going my way?" he asked with a grin.

She smiled back and strove for a pleasant tone. "Depends on which way you're going."

"Outside for some fresh air. Sure would enjoy the company of a pretty nurse."

Fresh air sounded most inviting just now. Mary looked longingly toward the exit. "I shouldn't . . ."

"Aw, come on. Bet you could use ten minutes off your feet. As for me, it's gonna be for the rest of my life." The soldier straightened the robe covering his lap, and only then did Mary notice his legs stopped mid-calf.

Her heart flip-flopped. Though her work here at Walter Reed brought its own rewards, how was she to heal if everywhere she looked, she faced reminders of Gilbert? Perhaps she should have resigned from the Army Nurse Corps and gone into civilian nursing. Somewhere up north, or California, perhaps. Somewhere far away from the reminders of war and the toll it took on human lives.

"Sorry, didn't mean to shock you." The soldier looked up with a sheepish frown. "Joking about it keeps me from crying in my soup."

Squaring her shoulders, Mary gripped the handles of his wheelchair and started toward the door. "You may have the better end of the deal. There are days my feet hurt so badly after a fourteen-hour shift, I'm sorely tempted to cut them off."

The soldier guffawed. "See there? Always a silver lining if you look for it."

They hadn't gone ten feet when Donald burst onto the ward. "Mary, glad I found you." A mixture of relief and concern clouded his expression. "Can we go somewhere and talk?"

"Now?" She glanced down at the patient. "We were just—"

"The doc looks serious. You can catch up with me later, sweetheart." The man reached up to give her hand a friendly pat before gripping the wheel rims and propelling himself toward the door.

Mary laced her fingers together, a knot forming in her stomach. Donald's duties usually kept him in the surgical wing. If he'd come all this way to find her, his reasons must be urgent. "Please tell me it isn't Mum."

"She's fine. No, it's . . ." He flattened his lips as another nurse bustled past. Then he ushered Mary off the ward and into an unoccupied office. "Sit down, Mary. I'm afraid I have some bad news."

25

"Mother, please stop pacing. You're making me crazy." Thomas clenched his fists and glanced about the waiting room outside the surgical unit.

His mother continued as if she hadn't heard him. "Three hours. It's been *three hours*. When will they tell us something?"

"When Gil's out of surgery. So you might as well—"

A doctor entered the room and breathed an exhausted sigh. "Are you Lieutenant Ballard's family?"

Thomas's heart thudded. He rose and stepped forward, bracing his arm around his mother's waist for fear she'd faint if the news was bad. "What can you tell us? How is he?"

"He came through the surgery just fine, but . . ." The doctor's lips thinned. He lowered his gaze.

"But what?" Thomas's mother pressed a hand to her chest. "Please tell me he'll recover."

"Of course. But I'm afraid his amputated thigh has been crushed beyond repair. It's doubtful he'll be able to wear a prosthesis again."

Thomas's mother collapsed against him with a shudder. "My poor boy! My poor, poor boy!"

Thomas helped her to a chair and handed her the hand-kerchief she'd already soaked with endless tears. Chest aching, he turned to the doctor. "You're certain there's nothing to be done?"

"He'll likely be in a wheelchair the rest of his life. I'm very sorry."

Nodding slowly, Thomas massaged the back of his neck. "When can we see him?"

"It'll be awhile before he comes around from the anesthe-sia, and then he'll be quite sedated with pain medication." The doctor offered a sympathetic smile. "Take your mother home. A nurse will telephone you when Lieutenant Ballard is awake enough to have visitors." Turning, he trudged out the door.

"This can't be happening." Thomas's mother blew her nose as he helped her to her feet. "He was doing so well, and so happy at his little farm. Now what will he do?"

Thomas wished he had an answer. *Why, God? How much more must You take from my brother before You're satisfied?*

"We must make plans at once to bring him home." His mother gathered her handbag and allowed Thomas to guide her along the corridor. "You and your young friend Jack can bring his bedroom furnishings back from the farm, and we'll set everything up in the study. I'll commission a ramp to be built so he can roll his wheelchair straight into the house."

While she prated on, ever the practical planner, Thomas tried not to think about what this devastating setback would do to his brother's self-esteem. Did Gilbert have the inner strength to face permanent incapacitation? Or would the loss of mobility—more importantly, the independence he'd fought so hard to regain—drive him into despair so deep he'd never be able to claw his way out?

Mary hunched forward in the hard wooden chair. Barely comprehending what Donald had just told her, she clutched at the stabbing pain in her heart. "Saints above, are you sure?"

"I have the telegram from Chaplain Vickary right here." Donald pulled his chair closer and gently patted Mary's shoulder. "Are you all right? Would you like some water?"

Sitting up, she shook her head. "Please let me see it. I want to read it for myself."

He passed her the flimsy yellow slip of paper, the words WESTERN UNION emblazoned across the top:

GIL SERIOUSLY INJURED. IN SURGERY NOW. MARY SHOULD KNOW. MORE DETAILS TO COME. SAM.

The words blurred before her eyes. "That's all? You don't know what happened, or how?"

"We can try to call the hospital. By now, maybe they'll have some answers." Donald rose and moved to the other side of the desk. Lifting the telephone earpiece, he spoke to the operator. "Yes, can you connect me with the Army and Navy Hospital in Hot Springs, Arkansas?"

Seconds ticked by as Mary's anxiety increased. *Dear Jesus, let him be all right. I'll do anything if only You'll save his life.*

Finally, Donald looked across at her with a nod. "Hello, Naomi, it's Dr. Donald Russ, calling from Walter Reed. . . . Yes, yes, I'm fine. Nice to hear your voice, too. Sorry I don't have time to chat. May I speak with Chaplain Vickary, please? It's urgent."

More waiting. Mary thought she'd climb right out of her skin.

"Sam, it's Donald. Mary's with me. Any news about Gilbert?" His face hardened as he listened. "I see. . . . I see."

Mary popped up from her chair and braced her hands on the desk. "Tell me!"

Palm extended, Donald signaled her to wait while he concluded the call. With a tired groan, he replaced the earpiece and folded his arms along the edge of the desk. His avoidance of Mary's gaze sent shivers up her spine.

"It was an unfortunate accident," he said at last. "Gilbert's horses got out, and there was something about bees. One of the horses panicked, and Gilbert got in the way. He was trampled."

Mary's stomach plummeted. With a muted sob, she sank onto the chair and buried her face in her hands. "No . . . no . . ."

Donald's voice softened. "The good news is Gilbert will recover. He's out of surgery now and doing as well as can be expected."

Mary dared a hopeful glance. "They're certain he'll be all right?"

"Sam assured me the injuries weren't life-threatening. Gilbert's amputated leg took the force of the blow."

"His leg? How bad?"

Donald drew a hand across his mouth and once again kept his eyes averted. "It's why he was in surgery. The remaining thigh bone was shattered beyond repair."

"Dear Jesus, no . . ." Mary stood and then wished she hadn't. Bright yellow flashes danced at the edges of her vision. The room spun.

Strong arms caught her and eased her into the chair. "Head down, my girl. Deep breaths. I'll be right back with some water."

Alone in the small office, Mary released a flood of tears into her apron. How could God let this happen, after Gilbert had worked so hard to recover from his war wounds? All the surgeries and physical therapy, the effort he'd put forth to walk again with a prosthesis—to have it taken away from him so cruelly. *Jesus, Jesus, why?*

Donald returned with a glass of water. Mary inhaled a quick breath and dried her eyes before accepting the cool drink. "Thank you."

"Gilbert is in good hands there. And Sam said he'd keep us updated." Donald took the chair next to Mary's, his expression filled with concern. "This has been a shock, I know. Would you like me to send for your mother?"

Mary took another sip of water then set the glass on the desk. She raised her eyes to meet Donald's, desperation turning her tone ragged. "You must have performed surgery on far worse injuries than this. You could help him. I know you could!"

Donald sadly shook his head. "If what Sam said is true, there's nothing more to be done."

"But you haven't examined Gilbert. You're taking another surgeon's word. Won't you please return with me to Hot Springs and *try*?"

Seconds passed as misgivings paraded across Donald's face. Then, just when Mary felt certain he'd turn her down, he let out a pained sigh. "All right. I'll see what can be arranged."

She flung her arms around him. "Thank you. Thank you!"

"I can't make any promises."

"I know," she murmured into his lab coat, tears falling afresh.

Freeing himself, Donald grasped her shoulders and forced her to look at him. "I'm not even sure hospital administration will grant us leave to go."

"Then I'll resign." Mary sat taller. "With or without you, I'm going back to him. He'll need me now more than ever. And I need to be with him."

Pain. Pain like a raging inferno tore through Gilbert's left thigh. Scorched his hip. Lacerated his lower back. Somewhere in the black labyrinth of his mind, cannons fired and tracers lit the night sky like shooting stars.

My leg—oh, God, it's gone!

"Gil. Can you hear me?" A familiar hand wrapped around his, and he held on for dear life. "Wake up, Gil. You're safe."

With effort, Gilbert pried open stiff eyelids. His mouth tasted like sawdust. "Sam."

"I'm here." Sam held a straw to Gilbert's lips. "Just a sip. It'll help your throat."

Gilbert filled his mouth with refreshingly cool water and let it sit on his tongue for several moments before swallowing. "How long . . ."

"It's only been a day." Sam offered Gilbert another sip of water before setting the glass aside. "You've had surgery on your leg. It was damaged pretty badly, I'm afraid."

"Hurts like—" Gilbert sucked air between his teeth to silence an expletive.

"I can call for the nurse. She'll have orders for more pain medication."

"No."

"But, Gil—"

"I said no. I won't go through that again."

Sam glanced away with a frown. "You don't have to be a martyr."

"Don't worry, it's not my intention." Gilbert groaned, his left hand reaching downward toward his heavily bandaged thigh. He pinched his eyes shut and saw Miss Glory looming over him, rearing up in pain and fear. "Was anyone else hurt? Obadiah? Mrs. Frederick?"

"Both fine, except for a few bee stings."

"And the horses?"

"No harm."

"Thank God." Gilbert breathed a little easier and tried to shift to a more comfortable position. Only there was no comfort to be found, and he couldn't stifle a cry. "What did they do to me, anyway—cut off the rest of my leg?"

When Sam didn't answer right away, Gilbert fixed him with a glare. "It *wasn't* a rhetorical question. Tell me the truth, Sam. How bad is it?"

"Bad enough." Head down, hands folded between his knees, Sam inhaled deeply. "It's unlikely they can fit you for another prosthesis."

Gilbert rolled his head away as he let this news sink in. "Guess it's a good thing I didn't get rid of my wheelchair."

"Gil—"

"I'm tired. I'll try to sleep for a while."

"Of course." Sam silently left the room.

Sleep would have been a welcome respite, but between the unrelenting pain and the knowledge he'd likely be confined to a wheelchair the rest of his life, Gilbert could do nothing but lie there in agony. Only a year ago, recovering in a French field hospital after an artillery explosion severed his leg, mangled his arm, and left him temporarily deaf and blind, he'd have given anything for access to a pistol. One shot to the head would have ended his misery forever.

One shot could have saved him from a year of torment and struggle, of fighting back to some semblance of a meaningful life.

One shot would have prevented him from ever meeting Mary and exposing his heart to the anguish of losing her.

If someone handed him a gun right now . . .

He clenched his fists. *No!* He was neither a coward nor a quitter. He'd fought his way back before, and he would do it again.

With God's help, he would do it again.

Waking from a brief nap, Mary peered around her mother to see flat stretches of farmland flying past the window. "How much farther?"

"Not long, luv." Mum toed Donald's shin as he dozed in the facing seat. "Dearest, we'd best gather our things. We'll be in Little Rock soon."

"Already?" Donald yawned and stretched. "You ladies stay put. I'll make sure we have everything."

Stiff and exhausted from the long train ride from D.C., Mary didn't object. She only wished they'd been able to leave sooner, but Donald had surgeries on his docket he couldn't easily delegate to other doctors. The chief nurse was reluctant to grant Mary leave so soon after her transfer, so those arrangements took some finagling as well. At least Mary hadn't been required to tender her resignation from the Army Nurse Corps.

Now it was Monday, a full four days since Gilbert's accident, and Mary ached with the urgency to be with him. He might well push her away, considering how she'd mistrusted and then spurned him, but she'd gladly risk rejection if only he'd permit Donald to take his case.

At the Little Rock depot they disembarked for a short layover before boarding another train that would take them into Hot Springs. Donald found a vendor selling sandwiches and brought back enough for all of them, though Mary ate little of hers. Nerves turned her insides to jelly in anticipation of seeing Gilbert again.

Please, Lord, let him forgive me. Let him give me another chance.

It was late Monday afternoon when the final leg of their journey came to an end. Whistle wailing, the steam engine rumbled into the Hot Springs depot, and Mary was on her feet and in the aisle before the train came to a complete stop.

Her mother grabbed her arm to keep her from stumbling. "Darlin', have a care."

"We can go straight to the hospital, can't we, Donald?" Mary fetched her small travel case off the overhead rack.

"Of course." After helping Mary's mother gather her things, Donald led the way to the exit. They stepped off the train into the humid warmth of the September day.

Across the way, a familiar face welcomed them, and for the first time she could recall, Mary didn't flinch at the sight of Annemarie Kendall Vickary.

Annemarie marched toward them. "I brought my father's car. It should be roomy enough for all of us plus your luggage."

Donald greeted her with a quick hug and a kiss on the cheek. "Sam isn't with you?"

A sad smile flickered across Annemarie's face as she shook her head. "He spends as much time with Gilbert as he can." She reached for Mary and squeezed her hands. "I'm so glad you're here. You're just what Gilbert needs."

Mary's heart fluttered. "Did you tell him we were coming?"

"Sam thought it best not to until you actually arrived. Gilbert is . . ." Annemarie bit her lip. "He's coping, but not well. He continues to refuse pain medication."

"He *what*?" Agitation increasing, Mary pulled away. She clenched one hand on her throat. "This is my fault."

"Don't be silly." With a gentle, chiding laugh, Annemarie tucked Mary beneath her arm. "It's only Gilbert's stubborn male pride rearing its ugly head again."

"No, it's more than that. If I hadn't continually accused him, if I'd only trusted him, believed in him—"

"Mary, stop. You're here now. You can show him you *do* believe in him. You can help him believe in himself." Annemarie guided Mary across the platform. "Now, shall we get your luggage in the car so I can drive you to the hospital?"

Sniffling, Mary nodded. Then she stopped suddenly and turned to Annemarie. "First I must ask you—can you forgive me for harboring such resentment and jealousy against you all these months?"

"Oh, my dear friend, you never even had to ask." Annemarie drew Mary into a warm and sisterly hug. "And we *will* become dear friends if you stay in Hot Springs as I hope you will. I'm so very thankful Gilbert has you in his life."

Hope filling her, Mary pressed deeper into Annemarie's embrace. "Then pray for us. Pray he's willing to give me another chance."

26

*J*ust . . . push the chair over here." Gilbert gritted his teeth against the pain and shifted to the edge of the mattress.

Sam locked the wheels. "Are you sure about this? We could wait for an orderly." His tone held disapproval. "Better yet, your doctor's permission."

"The sooner I'm up and around—in a manner of speaking—the sooner I can get back to the farm and my horses." Bracing himself on the chair arms, Gilbert slid off the bed and thudded into the seat. He gave a yelp as his bandaged thigh took the brunt of his descent.

"I told you this was a bad idea." Sam stood in front of him, arms crossed.

"It wouldn't have been if you'd helped."

"I *did* help. I fetched the wheelchair, didn't I?"

Gilbert glared. "I meant you could have gotten behind me and helped lower me into the seat."

"Yes, but then you'd be angry I didn't let you do it yourself."

He had a point there. Grimacing, Gilbert shifted to straighten his pajamas and robe. Sweat broke out on his forehead as another shaft of pain sliced through him. He ignored the I-told-you-so look in Sam's eyes. "All right, Jeeves, once around the block, if you please."

"What, so now I'm your chauffeur?" Sam moved behind the chair and gripped the handles. "You realize the trouble we'll both be in when your doctor finds out about this."

"You're the chaplain. Simply inform him you report to a Higher Authority."

"This is the Army, Gil. I'm afraid—"

Someone knocked on the door. It eased open and Annemarie peeked inside. Her eyes widened. "Gilbert, you're out of bed!"

"And against my better judgment," Samuel stated. He cleared his throat. "Did you . . ."

Annemarie nodded, apparently understanding the unspoken question. "Will it be—"

"I think so."

Gilbert clapped his palm against the chair arm. "Do you two *ever* communicate in complete sentences?"

Tittering behind her gloved hand, Annemarie stepped farther into the room. "Gilbert, I've brought someone to see you."

He cast her a curious frown. His mother and brother had visited often in the past couple of days. Obadiah had brought Mrs. Frederick up this morning. Who else—

Annemarie motioned someone in from the corridor, and suddenly Gilbert's vision filled with the one face he'd longed to see more than anyone else in the world.

"Mary!"

"Hello, Gilbert." Timidly she crept closer, her eyes brightening with each step. "I've been so worried about you."

Barely noticing when Samuel escorted Annemarie from the room and eased the door shut, Gilbert could only stare. If he was dreaming, he hoped he didn't awaken. If this was real, he prayed the woman he loved was back to stay.

Mary's gaze fell to the empty pajama leg tucked beneath his robe, and sorrow filled her eyes.

"Don't, Mary. Don't feel sorry for me. I can bear anything but that."

She knelt at his side and pressed his hand against her moist cheek. "It isn't pity I'm feeling. It's regret."

"You have nothing to regret," he murmured. Feeling the brush of her tears on his hand, the feathery softness of skin he thought he'd never touch again, he could hardly breathe. "You've always stayed true to your convictions. I'm the one who's sorry—sorry for all the times I gave you reasons to doubt me."

"My *convictions*." She spat the word as if it were a curse. "I held you to such high standards there was no room for failure. No room for forgiveness."

"I understand, Mary. I had to earn your trust, and I didn't always—" His leg began to throb, and he clamped his teeth together. A growling moan escaped between his lips.

Mary searched his face. "Gilbert, there's no reason you have to suffer like this. You must take something for the pain."

He shook his head firmly. "I won't risk addiction again."

"It's a medical fact, Gilbert. Pain management is essential for healing." Mary stood and started for the door. "I'll find a nurse immediately, and I won't take no for an answer."

"Please, Mary, don't go." The aching eased slightly, and he managed a shaky breath. "The worst has passed. I can get through this."

"Stubborn as you ever were, aren't you? Well, it'll get you nowhere with me, Gilbert Ballard. *I'm* seein' to your care now, and you'll follow orders or else!" Scowling over her shoulder, Mary marched into the corridor.

Seconds later, Sam returned, a worried look creasing his brow. "Is everything all right?"

Still gritting his teeth against the pulsing pain in his thigh, Gilbert shot his friend a hopeful smile. "Not yet. But Mary's back, so I'm praying it will be soon."

⁂

"I'm sorry, miss, but you can't—oh, Mary, it's you!" A nurse Mary had seen often on the officers' floor came around the desk. "I thought you'd transferred out of Hot Springs."

"I did, but I'm back." She pointed to a line on the chart she held. "Lieutenant Ballard has orders for pain relief. He'll have his medication now, if you please."

"But he's adamantly refused to take morphine."

"He'll take it now, if I have to strap him to the bed and administer it myself." Mary shoved the chart into the nurse's hands and strode back down the corridor.

She found Donald introducing her mother to one of the doctors. Seeing Mary, he paused. "Here she is now. Mary, I'd like you to meet Dr. Bryan, Gilbert's surgeon."

"So you're the one responsible for telling him he'll never walk again?" Mary hiked her chin. "Clearly, you don't know Gilbert."

"Now, Miss McClarney, I simply believe in being honest with my patients."

"There's a fine line between doling out honesty and preserving hope. Dr. Russ will be consulting on Gilbert's case. Maybe he'll find some hope there you've overlooked."

Dr. Bryan harrumphed. "Lieutenant Ballard may certainly request a second opinion if he so desires. If you'll excuse me, I have other patients to see."

"Mary, darlin'," her mother said as the doctor stormed off, "I know you're concerned about Gilbert, but don't you think you were a wee bit rude just now?"

Fatigue catching up with her, Mary lowered her forehead into her palm. "I suppose I was. I promise I'll apologize later." She looked up at Donald. "But can you examine Gilbert now? I have to know for certain how bad the damage is."

The difficulty, of course, would be convincing Gilbert to permit Donald's examination. Though the two had never been on friendly terms, Mary prayed time and forgiveness would pave the way.

They arrived at Gilbert's room to find Chaplain Vickary and an orderly helping Gilbert from the wheelchair into bed. The nurse stood nearby with a small medicine tray. Seeing Mary, Gilbert cast her a pleading look. The lines etched deep around his eyes and mouth spoke volumes about the pain he endured.

"It'll be all right," she whispered, hurrying to his bedside. "We'll monitor the dosage—only what you need, no more. And as your healing progresses, we'll cautiously wean you off the morphine, so there'll be no concerns of addiction." Seeing the lingering doubt in his eyes, she leaned closer and stroked his cheek. "Trust me. I'll be with you every step of the way."

He nodded weakly, and Mary stepped aside so the nurse could administer the medication. When she finished, Mary asked for a moment alone with Gilbert and then waited while the others left the room.

"Mary." He reached for her hand. "Are you really back to stay? Because if you're not, I wish you'd leave right now while I still might find the willpower to let you go."

She gazed into his longing eyes and her heart stammered. She could barely find her voice as she asked, "Do you want me to stay?"

His chest rose and fell in quick breaths. His hand crept up her arm and cupped the back of her head. Slowly, tenderly, he drew her close until his lips met hers, searing them with flames of quiet urgency. Heat ravaged her limbs, until she thought she'd drown in the gladness and gratitude of knowing he still loved her . . . still wanted her . . . still needed her.

Only her lungs crying for a full breath finally drew them apart. With a sigh, Mary curled next to Gilbert on the bed and rested her head upon his chest. A shiver of delight ran through her as his fingertips grazed her arm.

"Did that kiss answer your question?" he asked hoarsely.

Reluctantly she sat up, swiveling to face him. "Can you ever forgive me for doubting you?"

"You never had to ask." He blinked several times, the lines around his eyes softening, and Mary surmised the morphine must be taking effect. Even so, the love in his gaze was unmistakable. He smiled lazily. "But you still haven't answered *my* question."

She skewed her lips. "What did you ask me?"

"Are you back to stay?"

Nell paced the corridor. "What do you suppose they're talking about in there?"

"I *suppose* it's none of our business." On her next pass, Donald caught her wrist. "And wearing a trench in the tile won't speed the process along. They have things to work out between them. Best we give them the time and space to do it."

Eyes narrowed, Nell frowned at her husband, but deferred to his wisdom and sank onto a nearby chair. "I can't help worrying about my girl. If he turns her away, she'll be crushed."

"That's why they need time to talk." Donald glanced at his watch and then at the closed door to Gilbert's room. "Even if Gilbert does agree to let me examine him, there's not much we can do yet tonight. It's late. I'll leave word for Mary we're going to get some dinner and will wait for her at the house."

A pang of homesickness caught Nell by surprise. Nothing had been done yet with the little cottage she and Mary had shared for so many years. Nell and Donald had planned to return to Hot Springs later in the fall to pack up what possessions remained and put the house up for sale. But perhaps sooner was better than later. Accepting her husband's arm, Nell rose with a tired sigh.

As Donald left a message for Mary at the nurses' station, Chaplain Vickary and his wife approached. "Any word yet?" the chaplain asked.

"Nothing. Mary's still with him." Nell pursed her lips. "Chaplain, do you think there's hope for them?"

He smiled a knowing smile and tucked his wife's hand beneath his arm. "When we put our trust in the Lord, there is always hope."

❦

Gilbert's insides vibrated with the stirrings of panic as he felt the morphine working through his system. The euphoria, the sense of floating above himself . . . sensations all too familiar, all too rife with temptation.

Of course, he might attribute part of his euphoria to the woman snuggled beside him. She'd drifted off to sleep moments ago, clearly exhausted from her long journey.

But not before confessing she'd never stopped loving him and promising she'd never leave again.

She'd told him other things as well—things she'd come to remember about her hard-drinking father and the alcoholism that became a constant, if well-disguised, source of friction between her parents. About how her father had gone to the tavern with friends the day of his accident, how in his inebriated state he'd stepped into the street and startled the horse.

And Mary had witnessed it all. No wonder she couldn't trust Gilbert's promises of sobriety. No wonder she doubted him at every implication of intemperance.

Lord, help her to trust me again. Help us both to trust in You.

A strange detachment crept over him, and it was as if he looked back on the past year from somewhere far away. He saw himself returning from the war utterly broken and dejected, the will to live ripped from him along with his missing limb. He saw himself pushing Annemarie away, so terrified of her pity, so afraid to trust her love. He saw his mother's anguish, his brother's loss of respect. He saw how jealousy, selfishness, and pride had turned him into a monster willing to destroy his best friend.

God help him, he'd never be that man again!

Mary stirred, nestling deeper beneath his arm, but her breathing remained slow and steady. Gilbert exhaled a contented sigh and brushed a kiss across her silky curls. No, pride would never again separate him from the woman he loved. Even if the doctor was right and Gilbert never stood on two legs again, he could face whatever the future held as long as he had Mary at his side.

A twinge in his thigh elicited a groan, and Mary lifted her head. Shifting to face him, she smoothed away the hair from his forehead. "Is the pain worsening?"

"It's bearable. Especially now you're here." He pressed a kiss into her palm then held her hand against his cheek. "Mary . . . if I don't walk again . . ."

She silenced him with a finger to his lips. "One day at a time. Gilbert, I've asked Donald to examine you. He has the experience—"

"Dr. Russ?" Stomach twisting with guilt he could repent of, but never forget, Gilbert looked away. "I can only imagine what he said."

"Can you, now?" Mary straightened and crossed her arms. "And will you always question others' opinions of you? God has forgiven you, and so has everyone who matters."

"I'm sorry. I know you're right." Casting her a hesitant frown, Gilbert murmured, "But if he does look at my leg and the news is bad, you have to accept it, Mary. We can't base the rest of our lives on false hope."

Her gaze turned curiously wistful. "The rest of our lives?"

"Emphasis on *our*." Gilbert found her left hand and caressed it between both of his. "I haven't exactly had opportunity to shop for a ring, and this certainly isn't how I envisioned proposing, but . . . Mary, don't cry. Oh, darling, don't cry!"

"I can't help it!" She sniffled long and loud then laughed through her tears. "You've no idea how long I've prayed to hear those words."

Now Gilbert laughed as he thumbed away the wetness from her cheeks. "But I haven't even said them yet."

"Well, then, you'd best get on with it." Mary grinned through another happy sniff and extended her left hand with mock formality. "You were saying . . ."

"Miss Mary McClarney, my heart's true love, would you do me the great honor of becoming my wife?"

Her sobs broke out afresh, and she fell into his arms. "Yes. Oh, yes, yes, yes!"

27

Two days later Mary hardly recognized the hospital chapel, now bedecked with bouquets of yellow snapdragons, deep blue delphiniums, and blush-pink roses. Their lush fragrance permeated the air.

And Gilbert—so dashingly handsome even after nearly a week in the hospital. Though wheelchair-bound, he had donned his uniform and looked as happy and hopeful as Mary had ever seen him.

Arranging yet another wedding on such short notice proved a challenge, but neither Mary nor Gilbert wanted to wait one day longer than necessary. Too much time had been lost already.

The ceremony went by in a blur. Father Francis presided, with Chaplain Vickary assisting and Mary's mother and Thomas standing up with them. Their families and a few close friends attended.

Mrs. Ballard shed a few noisy tears, and then surprised Mary afterward by crushing her into her voluptuous bosom. "You shall become the daughter I never had, my dear."

"That's very"—Mary gasped for breath—"kind of you."

"Mother, please don't smother my wife." Gilbert nudged his wheelchair between them.

Releasing her hold, Mrs. Ballard dug in her handbag for a handkerchief. "I'm just so terribly happy. For both of you."

"Thank you, Mrs. Ballard." Mary offered her most sincere smile. "And we're both very grateful for all you did to make today possible."

"A few flowers and candles, a cake and punch—" Mrs. Ballard waved her hanky. "It was the least I could do."

"Well, we appreciate it." Gilbert took Mary's hand, and she shivered at his touch, utterly amazed to know they were married. "And we hope you'll visit us often at the farm."

Only then did Mary realize she'd yet to see all Gilbert had done at the farm over the past few weeks. Anticipation quivered in her belly at the thought of going home with her new husband.

Her mother drew her aside and squeezed her hands. "My darling girl, I've never seen you more radiant. It breaks my heart Donald and I must return to D.C. in the morning, but then . . ." She smiled coyly. "I doubt you'll have a moment to miss me."

"Oh, Mum, of course I'll miss you." Mary's throat tightened. "But it isn't so long until Christmas. We must plan a visit then."

Slipping up on Mary's left, Annemarie quietly cleared her throat. "Everyone's moving down to the reception room. You and Gilbert need to pose for photographs and cut the cake."

"Yes, we'll be right there." Mary kissed her mother's cheek and shooed her off with Annemarie. Then she turned to look for Gilbert and found him alone at the end of the aisle, head bowed before the simple wooden cross over the altar.

He looked up when she touched his shoulder. "I just needed a moment to pray."

Smoothing the skirt of her white organza dress, Mary sat on the low step at the foot of his chair. She could see in his eyes he still fought the disappointment over Donald's agreement with Dr. Bryan's prognosis. "Oh, darling, he didn't say it was hopeless, only that it could take time."

"And several more surgeries." Gilbert reached for Mary's hand and pulled her to her knees, then cradled her against him. "But I can live with God's answer, whatever it is, because today, He's given me the best gift of all."

She tilted her head to look into his eyes, as wet with tears as her own. "I've never been more proud of you, never loved you more."

"Nor I you, my dear, sweet Mary." He flashed a smile bright enough to light the darkest corners of the room, a smile filled with confidence, joy, and irrepressible hope. His smile shattered the last remnants of doubt.

For now, Mary saw before her the good and godly man she'd always believed Gilbert could be, the man who owned her heart and always would.

Discussion Questions

1. As the story opens, Gilbert watches from a distance as the woman he was once engaged to marries someone else. How would you explain his reasons for needing to be there? Do you believe it helped or hurt in his efforts to move on from Annemarie? How do you feel about the term *closure*?

2. When Mary agrees to assist Dr. Russ with research while ignoring Gilbert's desperate summons to meet him under "their" tree, how do you interpret her motives? Did she do the right thing, or only cause more problems between them? What are your thoughts about Mary's ongoing loyalty to Gilbert, despite their troubled history? Would you call it foolishness or faith?

3. In the early twentieth century, nurses often didn't receive due respect for their contribution to patient care. How much do you think this has changed over the years? Are there any nurses in your family or circle of acquaintances? Discuss the evolving role of nurses in today's health care system.

4. Gilbert's mother, Evelyn Ballard, continues to meddle in her sons' romantic lives. Why do you think she shows such intolerance toward those outside her social class? Do you have any sympathy for her? Any hope she'll someday change? Have you had experience with anyone like her?

5. Is Nell McClarney, Mary's mother, any less meddlesome or biased? Why do you think she suppressed the truth about her late husband's drinking? How has it influenced her opinion of Gilbert? Can you recall a time when you unfairly judged someone because of something in your own past?

6. Mary is unnerved when she first realizes her mother and Dr. Russ are falling for each other. Identify several reasons why the relationship frightens her. What changes in your life have seemed worrisome at first but then turned into blessings?

7. What are your impressions of Gilbert's relationship with Katrina Frederick? Mrs. Frederick believes she has been ostracized because she is German. Name other ethnic groups in America who have been shunned, maligned, or mistreated as a result of wartime prejudice. Do you believe threats to our security ever justify such prejudice, especially against U.S. citizens?

8. What does the Fourth of July mean to you? Describe how you usually spend the Fourth. Now imagine the holiday through Gilbert's eyes. Can you understand why many combat veterans, especially those dealing with post-traumatic stress, choose to avoid the noise and crowds?

9. When in their relationship do you think Gilbert realized he'd fallen in love with Mary? Why do you think it took so long for him to confess his love aloud? Identify the key events in Gilbert's character growth. At what point did you come to believe he'd really changed?

10. Can you understand Mary's reasons for pushing Gilbert away? Given what she knew of him at the time, did she have grounds to be distrustful, or was she only giving in to fear? Recall a time when someone broke your trust. What did it take before you were able to forgive and risk trusting that person again . . . or are you still struggling with the issue?

11. Gilbert finally reaches the point where he is ready to turn control of his life over to God, even if it means giving Mary up. Have you ever let go of something or

someone in complete trust that God's plan was better? What was the result?

12. Gilbert's accident threatens to destroy his hope just when he'd gotten on his feet again, both figuratively and literally, and yet his injuries become the turning point that brings Mary back to him. In light of his disability, what do you think enables Gilbert to embrace marriage to Mary when he refused to do so with Annemarie when he came home from the war? How do you see the future unfolding for Gilbert and Mary?

Want to learn more about author
Myra Johnson and check out other great
fiction from Abingdon Press?

Sign up for our fiction newsletter at
www.AbingdonPress.com
to read interviews with your favorite authors, find tips
for starting a reading group, and stay posted on what
new titles are on the horizon. It's a place to connect
with other fiction readers or post a
comment about this book.

Be sure to visit Myra online!

www.myrajohnson.com
www.myra.typepad.com
www.seekerville.blogspot.com

We hope you enjoyed Myra Johnson's *Whisper Goodbye* and that you will continue to read Abingdon Press Fiction Books. Here's a sample from Myra Johnson's *Every Tear a Memory*.

ℒ♥

1

Saint-Étienne-à-Arnes, France
October 8, 1919

*J*ack's letter, still unopened, accused her from atop the dresser. Hard to ignore her name pressed deeply into the vellum in her brother's precise cursive, but Joanna Trapp wasn't in the mood for more depressing news from the home front. Not today.

After securing unruly straw-yellow curls off her face with tortoise-shell combs, she turned from the mirror and glanced at her friend Véronique, snuggled in a narrow bed beneath a faded quilt. No reason to wake the sleepyhead. Joanna had planned all along to face this day alone.

Pulling on a thick wool sweater, she slipped out of the tiny bedroom they'd rented at a local *pension* and crept down the narrow stairway. Aromas of baking bread, sizzling ham, and buttery eggs wafted from the kitchen, but Joanna had no taste for food. As she stepped through the front door, a brisk breeze whipped strands of hair across her cheeks. She tugged the sweater tighter around her and picked up her pace. Not for the first time she wondered if coming here had been a mistake.

She hadn't been out of the house five minutes before footsteps thumped the hard-packed dirt road behind her.

"You did not wait for me, *ma chère*."

Véronique's breathless reprimand halted Joanna's steps. She turned with a guilty smile. "You were sleeping so peacefully. I hated to wake you."

Catching up, Véronique linked her arm through Joanna's. "I told you I would be with you today. We go together, *oui?*"

"*Oui. Et merci.*" Utterly useless to argue with a friend as determined as Véronique. Drawing a bolstering breath, Joanna resumed her purposeful march.

The rolling expanse of the Champagne, pockmarked by grenades and artillery shells, stretched in all directions. Pale sprigs of sprouting winter grass barely concealed the scorched earth. The ruins of stone barns and farmhouses stood like tilting obelisks marking this place of death and devastation.

Joanna and Véronique kept to the road, avoiding the detritus of battle—shell casings, rusting mess kits, rotting boot leathers, sad reminders of the lives lost here. Ahead, the land sloped gently toward Blanc Mont Ridge, where a ragged copse of trees reached skyward. A dusting of autumn-hued leaves adorned skeletal branches but failed to disguise the blackened, disfigured trunks. How long would it take for time and nature to erase the ugliness of war?

Joanna's gaze followed the arcing tree line until she spied the remains of a trench. She stopped suddenly and pressed a hand to her stomach. With her other hand she gripped Véronique's. Three tiny words nearly choked her: "There it is."

Véronique pressed her temple to Joanna's and released a mournful sigh. Together they stood in the road, silence shrouding them, while Joanna envisioned the battle that had raged here one year ago—the cannon fire, machine guns, grenades, and flamethrowers. The screams of the wounded. The pain, the sacrifice, the unflinching patriotism in the face of certain death.

A former "Hello Girl" with the Army Signal Corps, Joanna had come to France seeking adventure. She never expected to fall in love with a soldier, much less envisioned standing only meters away from the spot where he'd died.

Véronique tucked Joanna beneath her arm. "Now you have seen it. We should go back."

"I can't. Not yet." Joanna edged away, the gaping wound of the trench beckoning her.

"You must not leave the road," Véronique warned. "There could still be explosives—"

"I don't care." A fatalistic sense of bravado heated Joanna's chest. Striding toward the trench, she pictured Walter vaulting over the lip in what would be his final charge at the enemy. Did he hear the whistle of the artillery shell rushing toward him? Did he know the moment of impact, count his last breaths, feel his lifeblood draining into the earth?

"Joanna. You must stop." Firm hands clamped her wrists, and Véronique's pleading gaze pinned her to the spot.

The effect was like a cold slap to the face, wrenching Joanna back to the present. She blinked several times and forced her paralyzed lungs to take in air. A tremor snaked down her limbs, but she refused to cry. Tears wouldn't bring Walter back.

Clarity returning, she straightened and attempted a reassuring smile. "I'm all right now. It's just . . . harder than I expected."

"And why?" Véronique's eyes held both sympathy and reproach. "Because your sweetheart was killed here. You have never allowed yourself to fully grieve."

"I had a job to do." Once again, Joanna's glance drifted toward the ridge. She stifled a moan. "We all did."

Gently but firmly, Véronique nudged Joanna toward the road. "Perhaps, but one day you will pay the price for holding your grief inside."

Their return to the village of Saint-Étienne seemed endless. By the time they reached the *pension*, Joanna's steps had grown leaden, her chin drooping ever closer to her chest.

"Ah, you have returned!" Speaking in French, Monsieur Leveque, their rotund innkeeper, met them at the door. "Rather early for long walks, is it not? You must be perishing from hunger. Madame has kept breakfast warm for you, though I daresay the eggs will be hard as stones."

Out of politeness, Joanna followed Véronique to their seats at the rustic trestle table in the dining room and allowed Madame Leveque to serve her an ample portion of eggs and ham. Monsieur had exaggerated, though, for the eggs melted in her mouth like rich cream. No doubt the couple had taken extra pains to treat their only guests well. Not only had the war decimated France's economy, but many villages near the front had been reduced to rubble and now struggled to rebuild. Damage to the Leveques' *pension* had been significant, evidenced by plaster patches in the ceilings and walls as well as the cracked, mismatched pottery on which Madame Leveque served her delicious meals. When Joanna paid her bill upon their departure, she intended to add a sizable gratuity.

Two cups of coffee later, and with her plate mopped clean with a thick slab of Madame Leveque's crusty bread, Joanna felt a measure of optimism return. She was a survivor, after all— an adventurer—the qualities Walter had admired most. Tears were a waste of time. To continue living life to the fullest would be the best way to honor his memory.

She patted her abdomen as she eased her chair away from the table. "*Merci beaucoup*, Madame. *C'était délicieux*—better than the best restaurants in Paris."

The gray-haired matron clapped her hands together. "You will tell your friends, *oui*? Send them to Saint-Étienne for a lovely stay in the countryside?"

"But of course!" Véronique crumpled her napkin and rose. "Your hospitality is unsurpassed."

On their way upstairs to freshen up, Joanna whispered, "You don't think all those compliments will go to their heads, do you?"

"What of it? We have spread a little joy into their lives." Arriving in their room, Véronique plopped onto the bed, her feet dangling over the side. Her mouth stretched open in a gaping yawn. "A long walk, a big breakfast, and I am ready to sleep again!"

Joanna chuckled as she shrugged out of her sweater. "Shall I wake you in time for lunch?"

"Please do." Véronique kicked off her shoes. "Pull the shades, will you?"

"My, but you're bossy." And the best friend Joanna had ever known. She couldn't help being thankful her dear French companion had insisted on coming along on this pilgrimage. Véronique's pragmatism provided the perfect balance of strength and good cheer, exactly what Joanna had needed to survive the past year.

Smiling over her shoulder, she went to the dresser to brush the tangles from her windblown hair—only to be drawn up short at the sight of her brother's letter. She should never have brought it along, and certainly wouldn't have if the postman had not arrived with the mail at the same moment she and Véronique walked out the door of their Paris flat two days ago. Joanna had stuffed the letter in her handbag, intending to read it once they'd settled into a room at the *pension*, but then she'd talked herself out of it.

More than once.

Now she'd run out of excuses. A glance at Véronique revealed she'd drifted off to dreamland. Honestly, the girl could sleep hanging from her toes in a rainstorm with a locomotive thundering past. Joanna wished she could nod off half so easily. Unfortunately, she'd been cursed with a brain that didn't know when to shut itself down at the end of a busy day.

And now she knew her mind wouldn't rest until she'd opened Jack's letter and filled herself in on the latest doings back in Hot Springs, Arkansas. Bracing herself for another onslaught of her brother's pleas for her to come home, she sank onto the bed by the window and tore open the envelope.

$\mathscr{L}$

Hot Springs, Arkansas

"Of course I'm happy for you, Clare." Thomas Ballard willed his mouth into what he hoped passed for a congratulatory smile and fought to ignore the twinge between his shoulder blades. "You and Elliott have been wanting to start a family ever since the war ended. It's just—"

"I know, sir." The Arlington Hotel's blushing switchboard operator leaned forward and rested one hand on Thomas's desk. "I hate leaving you in a bind just when the busy winter season begins, but I simply wouldn't feel right about continuing to work after I'm . . . you know . . ." If her plump cheeks turned any redder, she could pass them off as ripe tomatoes.

Thomas suspected his own face had taken on a crimson hue. All this talk of babies and delivery dates made him extremely uncomfortable.

Not to mention envious. Happily married couples surrounded Thomas these days—radiant sweethearts who would probably soon be starting families of their own.

He cleared his throat and forced his attention to the matter at hand. Consulting a calendar, he counted off weeks. "Would you be amenable to staying on through Thanksgiving? I don't see how I can find and train a replacement much before then."

Clare pursed her lips. "I'll be nearly five months along."

"Perhaps you could . . ." With flicking fingers, Thomas motioned vaguely toward her attire.

"Wear something loose?" An acquiescent sigh hissed between her clenched teeth. "I suppose, so long as morning sickness doesn't do me in first." As if to prove her point, she covered her mouth to suppress a tiny burp.

Thomas shoved the calendar aside, his own stomach feeling none too steady at the moment. "Let's see how it goes, shall we? I'll place an ad in the paper today, and we'll hope for a quick response."

Clare thanked him and stood. "I'd best get back to the switchboard before Austin gets too many lines crossed."

As she exited the office, Thomas's telephone rang. Grateful for anything to get his mind off this conversation, he snatched up the earpiece. "Thomas Ballard."

"Oops. Sorry, sir, I meant to ring housekeeping."

At the sound of the desk clerk's flustered tone, Thomas suppressed a chuckle. "It's all right, Austin. Clare's on her way."

"Thank goodness! By the way, your mother telephoned. I told her you were in a meeting."

"Good thinking." No time was a good time to take a call from Evelyn Ballard. "Did she leave a message?"

"She asked me to remind you of your dinner engagement this evening at your brother's."

"Thank you, Austin." Hanging up, Thomas checked his watch. Still another hour before quitting time, but he dare not be late getting home. This so-called dinner engagement was all his mother had talked about the past several days. With Gilbert's new bride, Mary, nursing him back to health after he'd been trampled by a horse, Mother had been sending meals out to the farm several times a week. This evening, however, they would deliver dinner in person, complete with Mother's best china, silver, and stemware—a belated wedding celebration since the couple had married in the hospital and had yet to enjoy a proper honeymoon.

The humor in all this was that Thomas's mother rarely set foot in her own kitchen other than to instruct their servant Marguerite concerning the daily menu requests. Still, Mother's display of goodwill toward Gilbert's new bride boded well. Evelyn Ballard had resisted Gilbert's relationship with army nurse Mary McClarney with every ounce of her society-minded, blue-blooded bias.

Nor had Mother been especially kind to Gilbert's German-born housekeeper. After rescuing the widowed and destitute Katrina Frederick from near-starvation, Gilbert had purchased her farm and then graciously provided the woman with permanent living quarters in exchange for both her farming expertise and household management skills. Mrs. Frederick, as Thomas well knew from boyhood days playing with the Frederick children, was an excellent cook and more than capable of tending to Gilbert and Mary's needs. Thus, Thomas could only hope his mother's recent benevolence was in truth an act of atonement.

Thomas's telephone jangled again. Startled out of his thoughts, he lifted the earpiece and muttered a gruff greeting.

"Sorry to bother you again, sir." Austin, the front desk clerk, said. "Jack Trapp is here delivering the order from Kendall Pottery, and he'd like a moment if you're free."

"Certainly. Send him in." Clicking off, Thomas shuffled papers around his desk until he found the Kendall Pottery purchase order. Jack surely wouldn't be expecting a check already. Usually Mr. Kendall billed the hotel at the end of the month.

The office door creaked open and Jack stepped in, smoothing an unruly blond curl off his forehead. "Hope this isn't a bad time."

"Not at all." Thomas stood and reached across the desk to shake Jack's hand. "We aren't late with a payment, are we?"

Puzzlement flickered in Jack's eyes. "No, it's just . . ." He released a slow sigh. "I know my grandmother sent a note right after the funeral, but I've been meaning to thank you in person for sending the flowers. Mama would have loved them."

"I wish I could have done more." Remorse formed a knot in Thomas's stomach. Here he'd been worried about staffing issues and invoices while Jack and his little sister grieved the loss of their mother. "How is Lily holding up?"

"Not so good, I'm afraid. Grandmother is at her wit's end." Collapsing into the nearest chair, Jack knotted his hands between his knees and drew a ragged breath. "We knew Mama was tired and despondent—even more so after Dad died last year—but I never thought her health would decline so rapidly." His voice broke, and he looked away with a sniff.

Thomas swallowed hard to see such agony in his friend's face. Coming around the desk, he took the chair next to Jack's and wordlessly patted his shoulder. How did you comfort someone over such a difficult and unanticipated loss? Mrs. Trapp's obituary had tactfully alluded to what her family and closest friends believed: *The grieving widow and beloved mother of three has at last escaped the bonds of this earth and found the peace she sought, joining her recently departed husband in the heavenly choir.*

Giving Jack a few moments to compose himself, Thomas filled one of the water glasses on the corner of his desk and pressed it into Jack's hands. "Any word from Joanna?"

"Nothing yet, but hard telling when my letter would have reached her."

Thomas furrowed his brow. "You didn't send a telegram right away?"

"I should have, I know, but how could I tell her in a few short words that our mother died of a broken heart?" Jack's mouth twisted into a grimace, and he blew out a noisy sigh. "Joanna would never have made it home in time for the funeral anyway, and writing it all out in a letter made it easier to break the news."

"But still . . . don't you think she'd have wanted to know?"

"You obviously don't know Joanna."

Thomas had to admit he didn't know her well. Joanna had been a year behind him in school, and not particularly sociable. He did remember she'd had a rebellious streak. "So Joanna and your mother didn't get along?"

"They were always at odds." Jack took a sip of water then set the glass on the desk. He rubbed his palms up and down his pant legs. "Mama never could understand why Joanna wanted to go away to college. Then to choose career over family—and this whole business of enlisting with the Signal Corps."

"It had to be hard on your mother, having both you and your sister over in France with the war raging."

"Equally hard on Lily, especially after Dad died. At least I made it home soon after. Lily was only fourteen then, not an age when a girl needs to be burdened with her mother's . . ."

The unspoken reference to Mrs. Trapp's emotional instability hung between them. Thomas sat straighter, nervous fingers gripping the chair arms while he tried to think of something helpful to say. People simply didn't speak of psychiatric disorders in polite society, although the term *shell shock* had certainly come into common usage as soldiers fighting in the Great War came face-to-face with battlefield carnage. Thomas had seen such mental anguish firsthand while his brother, Gilbert, recovered from war wounds. Gilbert's friend Samuel, an army chaplain, had barely survived his own emotional trauma.

But a young girl losing her mother to mental illness? And not just in death but one painful day at a time through worsening bouts of depression. No wonder Lily Trapp was so troubled. Rumors abounded among their congregants at Ouachita Fellowship—Lily caught smoking behind the school building, filching the latest issue of *Harper's Bazaar* off the Schneck's Drugstore magazine rack, locking lips with the star of the high school football team.

Jack rose abruptly, clearing his throat. "Look at the time, will you? Mr. Kendall will wonder if I got lost en route."

Following Jack to the door, Thomas halted him with a touch on the elbow. "If there's anything I can do . . ."

"Just pray Joanna comes to her senses and gets herself home where she belongs."

❧

"Three weeks. She's been dead three weeks and I didn't know!" The wind in Joanna's face whipped the words from her mouth even as she spoke them. Why in heaven's name hadn't Jack wired her immediately?

Véronique shrieked a French curse when the motorcycle bounced over a pothole and nearly tossed her out of the sidecar. "Slow down at once, or your mother will be greeting the two of us at Saint Peter's gates before this day ends!"

Reluctantly, Joanna eased back on the Indian's throttle. She'd been battling an unholy mix of anger and grief since reading Jack's letter yesterday. She could forgive him for wanting to explain everything in a lengthy letter, but how could their mother have simply given up like this—on her children, on *herself*? Such weakness, such utter self-absorption, made Joanna want to scream.

The bottom line is I can't raise Lily alone, Jack had written. *Please come home, Joanna. If not for me, then for your little sister. She needs you.*

Their grandmother had come to stay temporarily, but she was getting up in years, and Joanna couldn't imagine her coping with a difficult adolescent without risking her own health.

So now, going against every conviction she held, every plan she'd made for life on her terms, Joanna had no choice but to return to Paris, pack her things, and book passage on the next ship bound for the States.

Véronique tapped her arm, then pointed up ahead. "A village—let's stop for lunch. I'm starved."

Tasting grit between her teeth, Joanna realized her thirst. Why she was in such a hurry to begin the dreaded journey home, she had no idea—except she couldn't help worrying about Lily. Jack was a wonderful brother and a hard worker, but how could he know anything about the needs of a fifteen-year-old?

Shutting off the engine in front of a roadside café, Joanna climbed from the motorcycle seat. Her body still thrummed from road vibrations as she offered a hand to Véronique in the sidecar. She avoided her friend's annoyed glare as they both tugged off their goggles. "We should wash up before we eat. I'm sure I look as awful as you."

"I am certain you look much, much worse." Using the tail of her scarf, Véronique scrubbed at the road dust coating her cheeks and forehead. With a huff, she marched into the café. "I cannot wait to get home and take a long, hot bath."

By the time they'd freshened up in the *toilettes* and had eaten their fill of ratatouille and brown bread, tempers had eased. Seated at a small table on the veranda, Joanna waved away cigarette smoke drifting toward them from nearby diners.

She gazed up the narrow village street at buildings scarred by bullets and shellfire. Again she wondered if France would ever recover.

"So sad," Véronique said as if reading her thoughts. "You Americans are lucky. You can go home to things as they were. The French must live with war's reminders every day."

Joanna slid her eyes shut. An image of Walter vaulting out of the trench at Blanc Mont Ridge wavered behind her lids. "Over a hundred thousand Americans dead, twice as many wounded, and we're *lucky*?"

"Forgive me, I know full well what the Americans sacrificed for us. But remember, the French were fighting for almost three years before your President Wilson brought the United States into the war." Heaving a shaky breath, Véronique brushed wetness from her cheek. "France lost over a million of her sons, brothers, husbands, fathers."

"I know. . . . I know." Joanna reached for her friend's hand. "Let's not argue, okay?"

"*Mais non*—of course not. You are leaving soon, and it breaks my heart!"

Joanna's throat shifted as she swallowed unshed tears. "You could come with me."

Véronique shook her head. "I could never leave France. This is my home."

"Mine, too, now." Blinking rapidly, Joanna looked away.

"No, *ma chère*, your home is with your family. They need you far more than you are needed here."

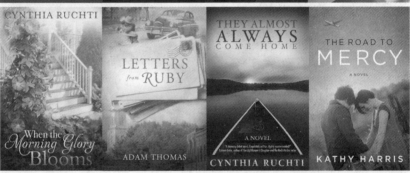